S.A. ALBA

King's Preparatory and the Book of Being

Cover designed by Miblart

First edition

ISBN: 979-8-9858360-1-1

This book was professionally typeset on Reedsy.
Find out more at reedsy.com

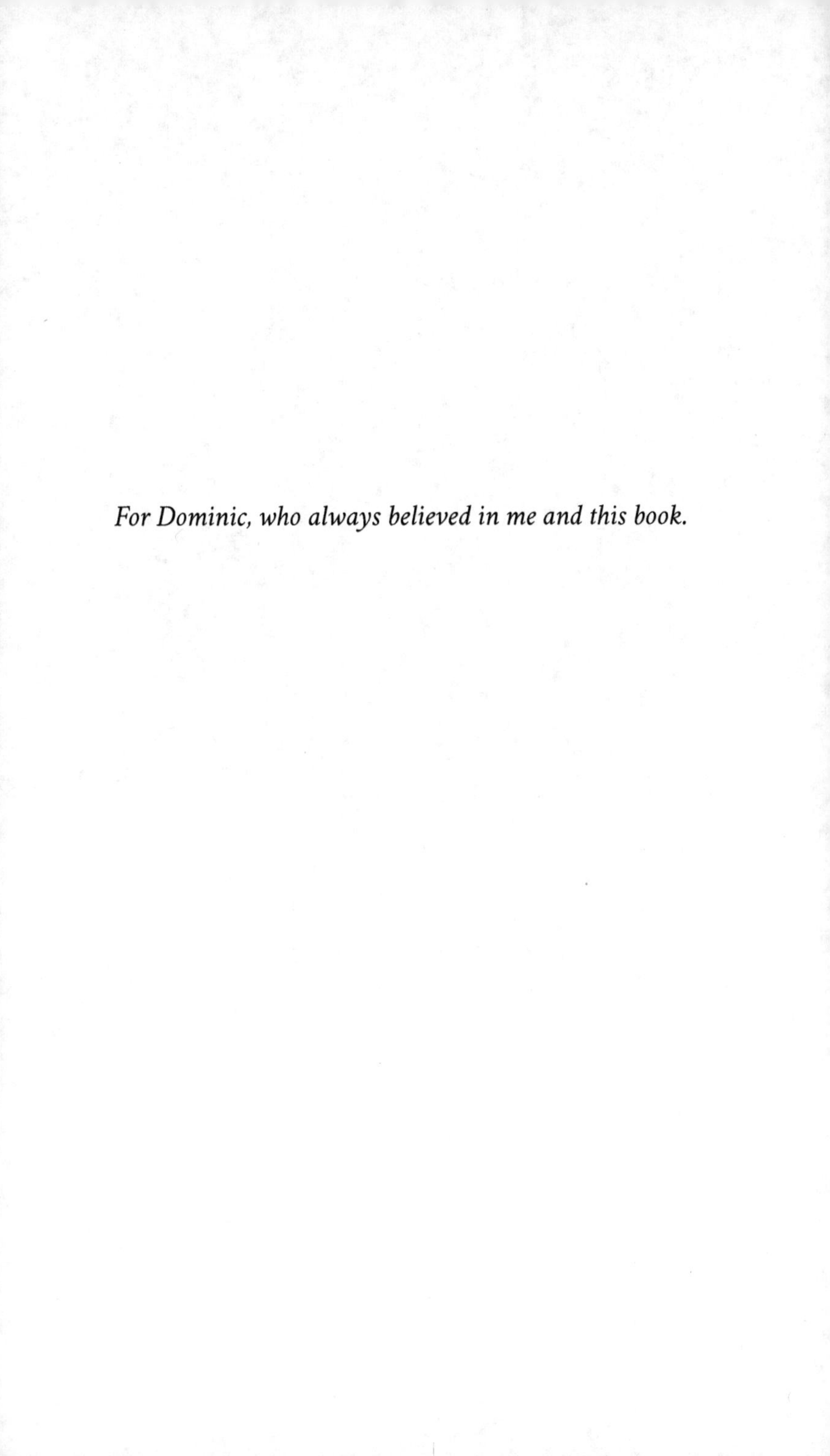

For Dominic, who always believed in me and this book.

Contents

Prologue

Professor Walker's smooth hands glided over each envelope with care and grace as she counted them again. She couldn't forget anyone.

"Are these all the invitations for the prospective students, Professor Walker?" Professor Shay asked with a forceful tone as she barged into Professor Walker's office.

"Yes," Professor Walker replied, dropping the envelopes and wrinkling one in a surprised panic. "Um, and might I add, we have a great selection of candidates this year."

"Sure, we do," Professor Shay said dismissively. "Make sure you send them by the end of day. Those families need more than ample time to respond, being the indecisive group they are. Hopefully, most fail the first test and we only have a small handful to interview. Keep me updated on the number of accepted candidates daily."

"Will do." Professor Walker stood and watched her superior strut from the office. Sitting back down, she glanced at the names on the envelopes. Doctor Witam and herself had spent months carefully analyzing each of the prospective students—exceptional outsiders who may be accepted into the school.

Professor Walker smiled as she struck a match, lit a candle

and placed it beneath a small, lifted cauldron on her desk. The mesmerizing black wax liquified, and she poured it over the opening of an envelope. Using the official school stamp, she sealed it shut.

When the wax had dried, she admired the emblem and flipped over the wrinkled invitation to see the recipient's name. "I hope you join us at King's Preparatory, Rose." She set down the invitation and moved to another.

When she finished, she left the school, hoping to catch the postman before the end of day. The hot air and beating sun caused her clothes to stick as she ran into town. Faces she recognized shot her smiles and hellos, but she had no intention of being distracted. Her course was dead set on the post office.

When the stack of invitations finally left her possession, relief flooded her body, and, as she sauntered to campus, Professor Walker dreamed of the candidates who would arrive on August fourteenth.

Chapter One

The piercing ring of the school bell echoed throughout the hallways and classrooms of Barrington Middle School. Students cheered and stuffed notebooks into backpacks, and Rosie realized it was over; summer school was finally over. There was an eruption of shuffling papers and clicking of pens as the students handed in their final exam packets. Rosie stood and made the pile of papers nice and neat before placing them in her bookbag for safe transport.

At only fourteen years old, Rosie was in charge of leading and teaching a class of her peers in Biology. The eighth-grade science teacher supervised her, of course, but Mr. Dumas was more concerned with his fantasy baseball team than the group of teenagers.

"Hey, Teach," one of her students and classmates called out as she walked down the hallway.

She needed to hand in the exams to the office administrator and leave for her next job, she thought, but still turned and waited for Josh to catch up to her.

"Do you think you'll be coming to the carnival downtown?" he asked, finally reaching her. "A bunch of us are, and we want to thank you for making sure we made it into high school."

"That's so sweet, Josh, but I actually have to work."

"What? More work? Are you teaching an advanced Math course or something?"

"No," Rosie said with a smirk. "I have a shift at the country club, but Riley might be there. I'm sure he would be more than happy to ride the Gravitator with you and tell me how much you two barfed later."

"Yeah, but maybe you're the one I want to barf with." And, with a wink, Josh strode away to meet a group of friends waiting for their leader.

They welcomed the boy with high fives and pats on the back.

Rosie's eyebrows lowered back into place, and she realized she was both amused and disgusted at Josh's idea of romance and couldn't help but laugh as she entered the administrative office.

"Done for the summer, Rosie dear?" Ms. Malby asked.

"Yeah, now onto more exciting adventures," Rosie replied with a hint of sarcasm. She returned to the hallway and glanced around, amazed this would be her last day in the school. Three years she had spent there. Though they weren't the best or most exciting, she did have a few good memories. Winning the debate club championship, getting the blue ribbon in the science fair, and, of course, speaking at her eighth-grade promotion, having her peers clap at the end of her speech and feeling appreciated and accepted by them.

She grazed her fingers along the lockers on the walls, and, as she came up to hers, she was consumed by darkness.

Hands covered her eyes, and a whisper crept into her ear. "No sudden movements."

"Get off," Rosie said, forcing back the body behind her and

whipping around. "What are you doing here?" Rosie asked, laughing. "Your mom is going to freak. You're supposed to be helping at the carnival."

Still on the floor from Rosie's countermove was her best friend and housemate, Riley.

Rosie Connors and Riley Zimmers had been best friends since first grade. The two had met on the playground during recess when a group of fourth-grade boys were bullying Riley. Rosie had punched the ringleader in the gut, and they had been inseparable ever since—even when Riley blossomed into a star athlete, grew six inches, and gained a new group of friends and a gawking flock of girls who constantly followed his cute, shaggy sandy-blond hair and crystal-blue eyes. And, while Riley was dominating every team sport the school offered, Rosie played individual sports, like golf, was president of the honor society, and made friends with her teachers and school staff. She was a pretty girl, with her round, bright green eyes, long eyelashes, smooth fair skin, full pink lips, and long auburn hair, but her classmates weren't set on befriending the weird girl who studied advanced calculus and Latin for fun. Thankfully, the popular crowd never teased her much, since she was Riley's best friend and apparently liked by Josh.

"You're finally done!" Riley shouted.

"Yes, now I can finally hang out and relax for one last weekend before school starts, and we are once again the small fish in a big pond."

"Rosie, high school won't be that bad. You'll only be there for half the day."

"Yeah, because the other half will be spent taking online college classes in the library. Do you think I won't stick out like a sore thumb? I'll be teased and called a teacher's pet or know-it-all." Rosie rolled her eyes. "Plus, none of the older students will want to come within five feet of me."

"Why only the older kids? You do sound like a weirdo." With a smile spread across his face, Riley stepped away, leaving a gap between them.

Rosie laughed and gave him a light punch in the arm and shoved open the door.

The Illinois humidity bogged down Rosie, and she chugged the rest of her water bottle. For the last three years, Rosie had walked the same path, and every day, she took in the beauty and essence of her surroundings. Tiger lilies, hydrangeas, roses, and succulents filled the yards of magnificent, charming homes. She always admired the greenery and the animals and dreamt of having her own garden filled with wonderful flowers and growing plants. *One day*, she told herself.

The two friends turned and walked the pathway to the Zimmers' household. Saying it was charming was an understatement; Riley's house happened to be the most impressive one on the block. It was a grand, stone-covered, two-story home filled with elegance, grace, and a basement full of vintage arcade games.

"Do you want to play Mortal Kombat? I deserve a rematch after you cheated last night." Riley playfully pushed her.

"I did not cheat," Rosie said, appalled at the accusation. "It isn't my fault I am a better fighter. Anyway, I can't right now. I have to go to the club today, and don't you have to help your mom at the carnival?"

The two entered the house and removed their shoes by the door.

"Ugh, yeah, but I have a few minutes before I have to go.

Plus, it's the last few days of summer, and my parents are taking me to football camp tomorrow morning super early. Four in the morning early. Can't you play hooky once and hang out with me before I go?"

"I'll see you Sunday night. We can be away from each other for a few days, and I can't risk running into Josh."

"Why? Josh is awesome. We're hanging out at the carnival tonight."

"I know. You're his date since I can't be."

"Wait, what?"

"He asked me to the carnival." Rosie stifled a giggle and waited for Riley to laugh at the thought of her being Josh's date, but he didn't have the reaction she had expected.

"Are you serious?" Riley's face shifted from an olive tan to a bright red.

Why isn't he reveling at such a humorous situation that I've been put in? Why does he look angry and concerned?

"Um, yeah," Rosie replied, still confused at Riley's tone. "But I said you could be his date and barf with him on the Gravitator."

"Oh, uh, okay. Good."

"Good that you're his date or good that you two can barf together?" Rosie asked as she awkwardly pushed a strand of hair out of her face and behind her ear. Her eyes shifted forward and she awaited Riley's response. Riley had never acted this way with her before; yet again, she had never been asked out before.

"Uh, good that I'm riding the Gravitator and you aren't." He chuckled, trying to lighten the conversation, forcing it to change. "Remember when you got so sick my mom had to take you home? Anyway, that's a no to playing hooky and hanging out with me?" His voice had returned to normal—playful and carefree.

"Riley, I can't." Rosie faced him. "I already feel bad mooching off your parents. The least I can do is chip in for groceries."

"But you're like the daughter they never had. You don't have to chip in. My parents love you. Plus, they never take your money."

"What? Of course, they do. I leave it in a nice envelope on the counter every time I get paid, and it's always gone when I check on it."

"Yeah, they take it, but not for themselves. They've been depositing it in a savings account for you. Did you honestly expect them to take money from a fourteen-year-old?" Rosie had a small feeling her unofficial guardians did something of the sort, but actually hearing it warmed her heart.

Dan and Glenda Zimmers were the parents Rosie had dreamed of having. The two had taken Rosie in as one of their own when Rosie's own mother didn't show an interest in taking care of her anymore. They had ensured Rosie's mother had been okay with the decision, and, to no surprise, she was. Occasionally, Rosie would overhear Glenda giving her mother updates, but these efforts were pointless. Her mother no longer cared what Rosie did like she once had. Now, she only worried about herself and ensured she had enough money for at least one bottle to soothe the pain Rosie didn't believe she had.

She knew if she had the desire to, she could live with her mother, but she enjoyed the stability and love she gained from the Zimmers', and she loved the feeling of being a part of a family, even if it wasn't hers.

Rosie closed the door to her room and changed into her dark green Medal Country Club polo, khaki pants, and white visor that laid on her bed. Glenda had washed and pressed them before she left for her glamorous job as an interior decorator, and, as she breathed in the fresh linen scent, Rosie wondered what would be in store for her today. She grabbed the protein bar and apple set out for her on the kitchen counter and left the house, not seeing Riley before doing so, and headed out of the wealthy neighborhood.

After twenty minutes of strolling, consuming her lunch and admiring her surroundings, Rosie stopped at mile marker twenty-five and made sure no one was watching her. She carefully stepped off the path and onto the moist soil, listening to the crunch of small plants and fallen branches as she traipsed away from the road.

Through the thick, overgrown trees, she waded through mud patches and jumped over marshes until she was face to face with a little shed easily camouflaged in the woods. She entered it and looked around, ensuring nothing was missing. On one side of the shed were typical greenskeeper tools and country club supplies—shovels, hoes, toolboxes, a lawnmower, extra couch cushions, and housekeeping items— and on the other side were the majority of her belongings— boxes filled with hundreds of books, stories she clung to, written worlds that allowed her to escape her reality. They were her treasures, and she had no intention of relinquishing her prized collection.

Moving and sifting through her hoard, she searched for the book she had thought about while teaching her classmates about storm patterns, *The Odyssey*. She had read it a few years prior and wanted to dive into the great journey of

Odysseus again and reread Homer's tale of a great man overcoming great obstacles and returning home, but, as she opened another box to search through, her stomach sank.

Rosie stared at the collection of keepsakes she didn't need or want but also couldn't discard. She grazed the soft, fragile baby blanket, scanning it, and finally lifting it out of the dust. The handsewn quilt was barely tattered, and Rosie gently followed the pictures depicted. She remembered her mother telling her the blanket had been in the family for over a hundred years and that it needed special care and a lot of love.

She brushed over the fabric mountains, and her fingers traced the threaded bolts of purple lightning raining down. Rosie, impressed, studied the blanket's vibrant colors, which had not faded, and the strong seams gripping pieces of fabric together. She thought someone must have put the blanket together with a strong sense of purpose for it not to rip or tear after such a long time. She set the blanket aside and removed a small pocketbook from the box.

After opening it, she read the names of her ancestors who had been in possession of the items before her, starting with Annabelle and then to the first Rose Connors. Her gaze drifted down, reading the list, descending all the way to her. The numbers beside each name always confused her, because, while she was Rose Connors the Eighth, only six other Rose Connors were listed before her. She always thought another Rose Connors wasn't listed in the book—a grandparent or aunt who had started the tradition. As she flipped through the pages to find if her theory rang true, she heard a flitter of paper, and her eyes caught a picture as it fell to the floor.

The small baby in it looked fragile and innocent as her

glowing and bright-eyed mother caressed her. Rosie recalled the time when her mother had lit up her world rather than darken it. How they used to play and laugh together. She remembered how she rode on her mother's back, reenacting cowboy scenes. Or how the sweet sound of her mother's voice would sing to her each night before bed and their tradition of saying, "*Goodnight. Sweet dreams. I love you,*" together before Rosie fell asleep.

With her heart softening, she returned the keepsakes to the box, remembering the good times the two once had together. She stood, stowed the box of delicate belongings and decided she would go see her mother after work, to check on her at least. She read the time on her watch and closed the shed door, locked it and ventured through the woods and marshes to the main clubhouse.

As she walked, she thought about her mother and the last raw memory she really had of her. One day during second grade, she had gotten off the school bus, and her mother hadn't been there to greet her. She had managed to find her way home, and when she had gotten there, she had found her mother laid passed out, lips blue, and barely breathing. She remembered using the phone to call Riley's house and watching Dan Zimmers speed off to the hospital while Glenda had taken her and Riley for ice cream to distract Rosie and help her forget the traumatic situation she had seen. She would never forget though, and she hoped she wouldn't find a similar situation when she went that evening.

As Rosie's mind played different scenarios regarding her visit to her mother, she didn't notice the wet goo she had stepped in at the daycare entrance. Brought back to reality, Rosie entered the playroom where she was in charge of watching the young camp kids during the afternoon and listened to the shrieks and yelling of small children. She took note of the chaos happening. All the kids who normally were there daily had left the room in complete disarray.

Her coworker, a narcissistic high school girl named Lucy who cared more about her looks than caring for children, stood idly by, scrolling on her phone.

Rosie surveyed the unfolding damage.

Kids ran around the room, screaming, throwing toys, beating each other up with foam bats, coloring the walls with markers, and shoving and smearing food all over each other and the room.

Rosie calmly walked behind the desk, placed her bag under it and pulled a whistle out of a drawer. She gave a good blow, and every child halted to face her.

Lucy, who was wrapped up in taking selfies and texting her boyfriend, dropped her phone. "Dammit, Rosie! If you broke my screen, you're going to pay for a new one!"

Not at all worried about Lucy's threat, Rosie clapped her hands in a rhythmic pattern at the children.

The kids copied and repeated the clapping, still quiet and attentive.

"Alright, everyone, I am going to count to ten, and once I hit it, all the toys will be put away, the snacks will be cleaned up, and you will be sitting crisscross applesauce on the storytime rug. Go!"

The children quickly clamored around the room, cleaning, organizing and making the room spick and span. As Rosie reached number ten, every little body was plopping onto the rug in the back corner.

The rest of the afternoon went on without a hitch. She

animated and acted out stories, played games and gave out prizes, and taught the kids fun facts about the world. Parents picked up their kids, and she cleaned the room then headed to the club kitchen for some dinner and then the locker room to shower. It wasn't until nine o'clock when she decided to finally leave and stop avoiding the trip to her mother's. The plan she had made earlier in the day seemed sound, but now she was filled with fear at the scene she would find.

With her backpack swung over her shoulder, her phone in one hand, and a flashlight in the other, she traipsed through the woods. A twig snapped behind her, and she whipped around to fill the space with light, but she only saw crowded trees and muddy ground. Shaking off her nerves, she hustled the rest of the way and finally found the end of the woods and the beginning of a parking lot connected to a dumpy pay-as-you-stay motel.

Her footsteps slowed as she grew closer to the worn building, and she stared at the neon red sign that lit the door her mother was behind. As she climbed the steps, she overheard arguments and televisions in the rooms she passed then silence as she stood in front of the door for room 13.

She stared idly at the chipped paint and splintered wood. *Why am I here? I should just leave.* But her body was telling her something different, because, as she was deciding to go, she heard her wrapped knuckles knocking.

A groan rose behind the door and dragged footsteps came closer.

Rosie held her breath as the door barely opened, and a single eye peered out. Without a word, Rosie's mother closed the door, and the faint sound of the chain unlatching and footsteps walking away let Rosie know she could enter.

It had been a few months since Rosie had seen her mother. The last time was while grocery shopping with Glenda. Rosie's mother was at the checkout, the cashier had just handed her a brown bag, and Rosie remembered turning her head and looking right at her. Her mother snatched the bag and quickly left the store.

Rosie pushed open the door and maneuvered through the cluttered room.

Her mother went into the small kitchenette and pulled a bottle from the fridge.

"Hey, Mom," Rosie said, evaluating the living quarters. The bed was unmade, clothes were scattered, and dirty dishes filled the sink.

"What are you doing here? Did that family finally give you up?" she said in a raspy, tired, and annoyed voice.

"Um, no. I wanted to check in on you. See how you were. I missed you, I guess."

Rose the Seventh grunted and paused before speaking.

Rosie thought she saw a glimmer of appreciation flicker across her face, but her mother replied, "Well, I'm fine. Thanks. I don't have anything to eat, but there's a pop in the fridge if you want."

"No, it's okay. Thank you." Rosie watched her mother shamble to a chair and turn on the television. Rosie moved to the counter and began clearing it and wiping it down. "Hey, Mom, do you want any of this mail, or is it all junk?"

"Toss it. Nothing good in there."

Rosie sorted through the envelopes, ensuring she wasn't getting rid of anything important. She passed over two bills, a coupon book, and a magazine. She opened the bills first and removing money from her wallet, which she kept on hand in case of an emergency, into the enclosed envelope included with the bill, she told her mom she would mail them out. Another grunt came in return.

Bored, she flipped through the magazine and coupon book, and decided to keep them for herself. Rosie bent down to open her bag to put them in, and noticed another envelope had fallen off the counter and drifted under the couch.

Getting on the ground and stretching her arm to grasp the envelope, a rush of goosebumps surged through her, sending a random shiver down her spine as she made contact with the piece of mail. Squirming from the sensation, she stood and examined the heaviness of paper and read the beautiful, curly calligraphy on the front under the dust, dirt, and mites that clung to it. *Rose Connors VIII*, it read. It was addressed to her. She flipped it over and carefully broke the black wax seal stamped with an ornate *K*.

"How peculiar," she said and gently removed a single piece of card stock.

Congratulations, Rose Connors VIII,

We are pleased to inform you that you have been selected to participate in a series of examinations and interviews at King's Preparatory private school located in sunny Arizona.

King's Preparatory has provided talented individuals, such as yourself, with a diverse curriculum and top-tier professors and staff at a beautiful mountain-view school for over 150 years. Our renowned boarding school houses unique students who come from extraordinary backgrounds, and our wonderful staff challenges these students to become the best.

Our distinguished alumni have gone on to be world leaders, top executives, and captains of industry. If you decide to accept this invitation, please be prepared to show us your best self.

Admission to our school is very competitive, and we scrutinize each applicant carefully. If you gain entry, you will be welcomed into one of the most prestigious schools in the world and receive not only a full scholarship, including room and board but also a monthly stipend. If you are interested in pursuing this unbelievable opportunity, please visit our website and click on the Potential Student tab. You will be directed to fill out a formal application, and we will be in contact shortly. If you fail to complete this step by 11:59 p.m. MST on August 13, you forfeit the chance to take the examinations. We look forward to hearing from you.

Rosie turned over the invitation and in small print near the bottom was the warning:

Disclosing any of the above information, except to your legal guardian(s), will result in immediate disqualification of your candidacy.

Rosie reread the invitation five more times before unlocking her phone and searching the website. Forgetting she was with her mother, she launched the homepage, and Rosie was awestruck. The homepage featured a picture of the campus. It had great Roman columns and looked over a massive lake. She clicked the About tab and read the same information from the invitation with a few more details.

James Kingsley, an ambitious educator looking to brighten the minds of youths, had opened the school in 1865. She perused the site and found the links for the athletics page and an arts page, but her thumb pressed Academics. A list of courses appeared, and Rosie's heart jumped. Anthropology,

Biological Sciences, Linguistics, Sociology, and many more interesting subjects covered her screen. Rosie read the small note at the top of the page.

High school students in advanced graduate-level courses welcome. Like the invitation said, *what an unbelievable offer*, she thought.

Then, her skepticism rose. *Is King's Preparatory an actual school?* She grabbed the envelope and found no return address. Surely a school wouldn't have mailed such an important invitation and only gave the recipient a few days to decide. She checked the post date next to the saguaro stamp. The invitation had been sent in early July, and today was the last day to accept the offer.

Her gaze peeled off the envelope, and she stared at her mother, attempting to suppress her anger. "Mom, why didn't you tell me you had mail of mine?"

"I didn't notice."

"Do you even know what this is?" Rosie raised her voice and the invitation. "This is an opportunity for me to get a real education. It's a chance to attend one of the world's most elite schools. Do you even care about my future?" Rosie glared at her mother, waiting for an answer, but all Rose the Seventh did was watch the dull screen and take a swig of her drink.

"Guess you won't mind if I go then?" Rosie muttered, leaving the paid bills on the counter.

Another grunt came from behind the bottle.

Rosie snatched her backpack and, holding the invitation, left the motel room. Her body filled with more hate than it had before. Of course, her mother didn't care about her, Rosie thought. Her thinking she did was silly, stupid, and juvenile. Rosie huffed and pushed through the thick branches, finally reaching the greenskeeper shed again. Inside, she reread the invitation and contemplated the opportunity.

She scrolled through the website and marveled at the idea of receiving an elite boarding school education where she would have a challenging curriculum and receive the attention she needed to be accepted into a competitive college. The website was insightful and secure. She went to the Potential Student page and clicked on the link to an online application.

Her fingers soared across the phone's keypad, and she finished the application in minutes. Reviewing the completed form, she ensured she hadn't included any personal information in case, by some chance, this was a scam. No social security number, no credit card number, and no personal information other than her cellphone number, email address, and personal accomplishments were listed. She double-checked the site's security, and with the little lock in the address box, she let her thumb lightly press down. She read the confirmation on the submission page and began to click the menu to read the website again, but before she could return to the homepage, her phone buzzed and the caller listed was unknown. Raising the phone to her ear, Rosie hesitated at answering. "H-Hello?" Rosie said into the static.

"Hello, Rose Connors the Eighth," a recorded woman's voice stated. "Thank you for responding to King's Preparatory before the deadline. If you are receiving this call before five p.m., press Three to have any questions you or your legal guardian may have answered. If it is after five, please try reaching us again tomorrow between our normal hours of nine a.m. to five p.m. Please press One to confirm you will be attending King's Preparatory for further testing and potential admittance. Press Two if you have decided not to attend after application submission."

Rosie's thumb hovered over the keypad. The message repeated three times before she firmly pressed the one button and put the phone to her ear.

"Thank you for accepting our invitation, Rose Connors the Eighth. Your first examination will take place at noon sharp on August fourteenth, and, if you are late, you will not be able to take the examination. Please use the link we have sent to your email to schedule your flight and further accommodations. Once completed, we will call you back with further instructions." The voice stopped speaking, and the call ended.

Rosie was amazed at their proficient automated system. A distinct chime came from her phone, indicating she had received an email. She opened the link, and it forwarded her to a landing page to book her flight and make reservations for a driver to pick her up and drop her off at O'Hare International Airport and Phoenix Sky Harbor Airport. Confidential credit card information had already been added, so everything she reserved was free to her. When she confirmed her reservation, her phone buzzed again, and when she answered, the same voice spoke.

"Thank you for placing your reservation to attend King's Preparatory for further testing and interviewing. Please press One to confirm your plane ticket has been booked and held for you at O'Hare International Airport for the eight-a.m. flight to Phoenix Sky Harbor International Airport. Please press Two if this is incorrect."

Rosie pressed One.

"Thank you for confirming. Please press One to confirm your car service reservation. A vehicle will receive you at five-thirty a.m. at the address you provided and transport you to O'Hare International Airport."

Rosie pressed One again.

"Thank you. Upon your arrival, a vehicle will receive you on the north side of baggage claim at Phoenix Sky Harbor International Airport. If you have any difficulties, please call us when you arrive, and we will ensure you have proper transportation. Please press One if you understand the directions given."

Again, Rosie pressed One and waited for the voice to speak.

"Thank you for confirming. Please note, if you do achieve acceptance, you will be placed into housing immediately, so please pack accordingly. If you aren't accepted, you will be placed on a plane back home the same day. Good luck, and we look forward to seeing you on August fourteenth." A beep indicated the call had ended.

Rosie's head swirled, and she was in disbelief at how fast this was happening. Thoughts bombarded her, worry crowded her mind, and her thoughts shifted. "I have to get on a plane tomorrow morning. I have to pack whatever belongings I have in case I'm accepted. I have to prepare for the examination, which I don't even know what I'll be tested on." And finally, her heart sunk at her next thought. "I could never see Riley again."

She started to dial his number but stopped when she remembered the invitation's daunting threat of being disqualified from candidacy. She had to hurry back to Riley's house, but how could she explain her whereabouts to them without spilling the truth? Her phone vibrated.

As if he had been reading her mind, a text from Riley illuminated her screen, wondering where she was.

She quickly replied that she had gone to her mother's and asked him to tell his parents.

His reply came fast, and somehow Rosie read disappointment in his words. *Oh, okay. Well, come home soon, and wake me up when you do. I need to tell you something.*

She turned over her phone and began plotting. She needed to pack her things at the Zimmers' house but couldn't let them know she was flying across country to test at a strange school, or they would never let her leave. Plus, they legally weren't her guardians, and she couldn't risk being disqualified. She checked the time on her phone—10:30. Dan and Glenda should be asleep by now, and Riley was bound to go to bed soon, even if he did want to talk to her. There was no way he would show up to football camp unprepared.

She scanned the small room, and her next thought made her laugh. *What books should I bring?* Her treasures and hidden worlds couldn't be forgotten, but she couldn't bring them all. She took her backpack and an old country club duffle bag that was wedged in the corner and filled them with her favorites, the ones she couldn't live without. Then she returned to the box full of her keepsakes.

Her anger grew within, and she kicked the box, making a hole, and from it, the picture of her mother holding her appeared. She picked it up, feeling the intense urge to tear it up, but logic stopped her. She might want the picture one day; she might want all those keepsakes one day in original form and not ash.

Rosie flung the backpack and duffle bag over her shoulders, hoisted the box and took it from storage to bring on this new journey as a reminder—a reminder to do better and to be better.

Chapter Two

When Rosie had arrived at the Zimmers' house, she quietly and quickly packed the rest of the few belongings she had and laid in bed. It was already 11:30, and she needed some sleep to prepare her mind for the test, but her brain was still running a hundred miles a minute. The door to her room clicked open. Someone was with her; Glenda checking on her maybe, she wondered. She closed her eyes, pretending to be in a deep sleep.

"Rosie," Riley whispered, but she didn't answer.

If she "woke," she wouldn't be able to keep her secret about leaving him. She figured he would leave after she didn't respond, but instead, she sensed his feet travel across the room. Hearing his light footsteps stop by the edge of her bed, she wondered what on earth he was doing.

His soft hands grazed the hair out of her face. He spoke again, his warm, sweet breath hitting her. "If I don't see you for a while, I hope you know I love you." And, with his smooth lips hitting her cheek, Rosie's heart sped.

She heard him leave and reviewed what had happened—surprised at his words, and how good they sounded coming from him. Smiling and burying her red cheeks into her pillow,

Rosie thought about Riley until her subconscious finally took over.

* * *

On the sandy lakeshore in the hot desert, Rosie spotted a faceless woman in a long white gown dancing in the rain. Rosie admired the woman's carefree attitude as she laughed and swayed and stumbled up the side of the mountain. "Wait!" Rosie called, not wanting to become lost in the new surroundings.

Rosie jogged over, but it was as if the woman was absorbed into the rocky wall. Scared and alone, Rosie ran up the mountainside, determined to find someone, determined to find the missing woman. As she searched, clouds billowed overhead, and rain hurtled down, causing the boulders she was holding onto to become slick and the dirt she stood upon to become mud. Sinking, as if being swallowed, she used all her strength to take one giant step, forcing her leg from the knee-deep sludge. She climbed a boulder, stood and stepped forward. Suddenly, as if her legs could no longer support her body, her footing gave way, and she slipped. Her body tumbled, and vision swirled as she bounded down the mountainside to her death.

Rosie's eyes shot open, and she burst upright in bed. *It was a dream, just a silly dream,* she told herself. She leaned over to check her phone—4:23. Her alarm was set to go off in seven minutes. With her heart still pounding and eyes afraid to close in the dark room, she stood to get ready for the exciting day.

She peeked out of her room and saw a note attached to the

door from Glenda stating they had left to drop off Riley at camp and would be back for dinner. Guilt filled Rosie for leaving without telling Glenda, but she reasoned if she wasn't accepted into the school, she would be home by the end of the day, and, if she was accepted, well, she would deal with it then.

Butterflies fluttered in her stomach, causing her hands to shake as she did her makeup and hair. She looked at the clock—5:25—and smoothed out her black wide-leg trousers and white button-up tank and draped her matching black blazer over her duffle bag before flinging it and her backpack on her shoulder. Descending the stairs and taking one last look at her temporary home, at the pictures she was included in, as if one of the family, she smiled and closed the door, thinking about Riley and hoping he would find the note she had left on his bed. She hoped he would reply fast and understand this amazing new future she was drawn to.

* * *

The screech of the plane's tires touching down on the hot asphalt pulled Rosie from her reading trance. She raised her head from the Arizona information guide she was lucky to find in the airport, and, as soon as the airplane door opened, heat and moisture filled the cabin. Rosie heard someone say, "I thought Arizona was supposed to be dry?"

Rosie packed her book into her bag and started talking without realizing. "Well, it's currently monsoon season here, which starts in June and continues through September. Arizona lies within the Intertropical Convergence Zone, and with the uptick in rain comes an uptick in humidity."

"Oh, uh thanks?" the passenger said surprised, not expecting an answer, especially one from a stranger.

Rosie finally got off the plane and followed the signs directing her to baggage claim. She was taking the long escalator to the lower level when she spotted a man in a suit holding a sign with her name.

She secured her bag and approached him with an air of confidence. Her mentality and reasoning being, if you act confident, you'd feel confident; when, in reality, her stomach was churning, her hands were shaking, and she was sweating profusely.

"Hi, I'm Rose Connors," she said to the driver.

"Hi, Ms. Connors. My name is Gerald, and I'll be escorting you to your destination today." Gerald led Rosie to a black town car equipped with an automatic start, so when she entered the vehicle, it was as if she was in a deep freezer. A cooler with her name rested on the seat next to her. "You can eat lunch if you are hungry, Ms. Connors."

"Oh, thank you." She opened the cooler, and under an ice pack was a loaded sandwich, a sliced apple, a bag of chips, and a bottle of water. After getting comfortable in the back seat and eating the delicious, filling lunch, she stared out the window at what her new home could be. The long desert mountain ranges, the tall cacti, and the southwest designs intrigued her, and she thought the scenery was magnificent.

Hypnotized by the valleys and peaks, she was surprised an hour had passed. Still driving, Rosie noted they were moving farther from civilization. There were fewer houses and more open desert. Her excitement turned into fear and nerves, and, like her stress, the car climbed in elevation.

Rosie remembered the invitation and website had said the

school was in Arizona, but she never read the exact town. They were now miles away from the crowded city, and her heart raced as she devised an exit strategy in case this became something it was not. The car turned off the paved road and drove onto a dirt one up a mountainside. A lump formed in her throat. She couldn't jump from the car without tumbling down the mountainside, like in her dream.

"U-Um, are you sure you're going the right way?" Rosie asked Gerald.

"Yes, ma'am. I was given clear instructions on where to go."

Rosie viewed her environment out the front windshield and noticed the road was going to end.

Gerald put the car in Park and turned toward her.

She was ready to fight if she needed to.

"Okay, Ms. Connors, I have been instructed to tell you to hike up the rest of the way."

Taken aback and surprised she was not about to be hooded and thrown into another vehicle, she asked, "Is there a path of some sort to follow?" She knew the school was on a mountain, but she assumed she would be driven to it. *Could there not be a direct access road?*

"All I was told was to drop you off here and tell you to follow the lightning, and where it strikes, you will find where you need to be." Gerald turned around and exited the car.

Very confused, she followed him out and took her bags and thanked him for the ride.

Gerald turned the car around and headed down the mountain, leaving Rosie in a trail of dust.

Rosie surveyed her surroundings, trying to find the school. *This must be part of the test.* "Follow the lightning?" she repeated to herself. She looked skyward and saw billowing dark blue clouds rolling toward her. A bright spark of electricity struck down on the other side of the second peak in the mountain range. Rosie estimated it was about two miles away. She checked the time on her phone. It was already 11:20. She had forty minutes to arrive at the school or she would be disqualified from the exam.

Determined not to miss her chance at a successful future, she opened her duffle bag, put on her gym shoes, repositioned her belongings so they were more secure and headed toward the lightning strike.

There wasn't a clear path. Rosie had to climb colossal boulders, step over bunches of cacti and ensure she didn't lose her footing and fall down the dangerous mountainside. She was sweaty, and her hair stuck to the nape of her neck, but she pressed on, determined now more than ever to prove herself.

Another bolt of lightning hit in the same spot as the previous strike. The electricity coursed through the air and forced the hair on her arms to stand up. *This is dangerous.* She could tell she was only a mile from the strike, but she wanted to ensure she had an exit route in case she got hurt or wanted to withdraw from the examination. She turned to ensure she could see the road, but it was nowhere in sight. The only things on the mountainside were tall saguaros, rocks stacked on top of each other, and other desert plants littering the entirety of the mountain.

"What?" she exclaimed at a tall stack of rocks and boulders and climbed them for a better vantage point. *Maybe the road is just out of sight.* Once on top of the boulders, she turned back, but still couldn't find the road. Confused and panicked, Rosie sat on the rock to take a breath.

"I don't understand." She checked her phone again. Eleven thirty and no cell service available. Only thirty more minutes. With no sight of the road and her stomach in knots about getting into this reckless situation, she decided she needed to call Riley. She needed his advice.

As she climbed off the rocks and turned to head toward the main road, a loud crack thundered overhead. Turning to see another lightning strike plummet from the clouds, Rosie noted this one was brighter and bigger than the previous. Beholding the awe of the lightning, her heart slowed, and a smile spread across her face.

"I have to go on. I'll regret it if I don't." She faced the lightning and ran, weaving around boulders, cacti, trees, and bushes. Nothing could stop her from her destiny. Another strike. She was only a hundred yards away. Fifteen minutes left. *I can do this. I'm so close.* But, the sound of a rattle stopped her in her tracks.

She scanned the ground, and ten feet in front of her sat a diamondback rattlesnake posed to strike. *No sudden movements. The rattle is just a warning not to come closer.* She decided to go around the snake, but, as she moved to the right, the snake followed. She went left, and it followed her that way too.

"What are you doing?" she asked the snake. Rosie realized the snake was tracking her. *Only ten minutes left.*

The snake hissed as Rosie searched, then she finally spotted what she needed to reach the lightning strike—a rock the size of her hand near her foot. Rosie grabbed it and threw it to the left of the snake, and, as it lunged, Rosie hurried by on the right.

"Yes!" She laughed and smiled at her accomplishment and

finally reached the top of the peak where the lightning had been striking. As she raised her head from surveying the scorched earth, her mouth dropped. A massive lake sat on the other side of the peak, and directly across from her on the other side of the calm water were tall Roman columns and grand wooden doors built into the side of the rocky earth. And encrusted above the doors in golden letters was, KING'S PREPARATORY.

Chapter Three

Rosie ran to the bank of the lake and sprinted to the doors. Only a few minutes were left before noon. The sand in the bank was hard to run through, and rain fell from the dark clouds blocking the sky and sun. She moved faster, but her foot dug into the sand and got stuck. She flew forward and tumbled. Wet sand clung to her, and she had to force her way up the stairs to the doors, trying not to slip down them. Then it finally happened. She was there, and she triumphantly pulled open the heavy doors.

The room she entered in no way resembled the chaos she had endured outside. The grand foyer had tall ceilings and beautiful artwork, and fresh flowers on a table centered in the room. With a sigh of relief, she strolled to the table. A small card lay upon it, and, in the same font as her invitation, it read:

Rose Connors VIII,

Please enter through the next set of doors and check in at the front desk with Francie. Please leave your phone on the table and your bags underneath it. They will be placed in a secure room.

Rosie's heart beat faster as she set her bags under the table and put on her blazer. She placed her hand on the door handle to enter the lobby, but, before pushing open the door, she caught a glimpse of herself in a hanging mirror. She was covered in dirt, her hair was tangled and depressed from the rain, and her cheap, clumpy mascara had stained her cheeks. She groaned as she approached the mirror. "Okay. No big deal. I can wipe off the mud and fix my hair and makeup quick. Don't panic." She turned to grab a towel from her bag and her heels to change back into, but her bags were gone.

"What?" She rushed to where she had placed them and bent under the table but couldn't see anything except the Persian rug. Feeling her heart rate rise, she attempted to control herself. She remembered that when she had entered the foyer, she had spotted a small camera hidden in a ceiling tile. Not wanting to show fear in case someone was watching her, she grabbed the vase with the flowers from the table and returned to the mirror. She poured out some of the water into her hands and wiped her streaking cheeks and made her face fresh and clean. Thankfully, the wet sand she had fallen into had already solidified, and she brushed it off in clumps. She collected the clumps and discarded them in the small wastebin in a corner. Then, using a hair tie she always kept on her wrist, she tied her hair, hiding the tangles and dampness. She glanced at herself in the mirror again. She was fairly happy with the result, as she didn't have a lot of resources. She only wished she had changed her shoes, but, in the mirror's reflection, her heels sat on the table.

She turned back, and sure enough, they were there. Confusion flashed over her. "I must've taken them out of my bag before I set it under the table," she reasoned as she slipped on the heels and set her dirty gym shoes under the table.

Rosie was finally ready and confidently turned the door handle and opened the foyer doors. As she gained visibility into the next area, the doors emitted a loud groan, and when they closed, a boom rang across the room. Rosie turned to see dozens of faces watching her. With her cheeks and ears rapidly reddening, she sauntered down a long pathway with a nervous smile to the front desk where a snooty-looking woman sat. The long and wide lobby had tall ceilings like the foyer, but it was made of glass. The rain hit it hard, and bright streaks of lightning flew across.

As she walked, she admired the beautiful paintings that covered the walls and Victorian furniture the students sat on. Like her, they were dirty and disheveled, which made Rosie less self-conscious about her appearance. Hanging above the front desk, she noticed a portrait at least ten feet high with a gold nameplate underneath of a handsome, twentysomething man with fair skin, strawberry-blond hair, and straight white teeth set in a glorious smile. After finally making it across the long room, with low whispers and eyes bouncing off her, she held her hands politely in front and, with difficulty, dropped her gaze from the man in the painting to the receptionist. "Hi, you must be Francie. I'm Rose Connors the Eighth." She proffered her hand.

Francie didn't look up as she typed on her computer.

Rosie, feeling awkward, lowered her hand, but maintained her eye contact.

Francie stopped typing and glanced at a paper next to her, and, in the most uninterested voice, said, "Rose Connors the Eighth, you've been checked in. Please take a seat where you can find one and wait for your name to be called."

"Okay, thank you," Rosie replied and she began to turn to find a seat, but before doing so she read the gold nametag under the portrait.

JAMES KINGSLEY
FOUNDER
1865

Rosie turned from the portrait of the young founder and scanned the room for an empty chair, but it wasn't hard to find one. Sitting in the middle of the room on a plush sofa and waving his arms, whisper-yelling, "Rosie! Rosie! Over here!" was Riley with a huge, goofy yet handsome-looking grin.

Shock and excitement engulfed her as she ran to him. "What are you doing here?" she asked.

"I assume the same thing you are! I got a letter inviting me to come test for admittance. I called the number, and my parents spoke to a school representative, and they were super impressed, so they sent me here early this morning."

"I can't believe it! So, no football camp?"

"No football camp." His bright smile shone at his convincingly fake story.

"I must have been on the flight right after you."

"This is so crazy, Rosie. Wouldn't it be so cool if we both got accepted? Wait, do my parents know you're here?"

"Um, not exactly. I'll call them after the interviews."

"Jeez, they are going to freak."

The same guilt she had before, when she first left the house that morning, overcame her. "I promise to call them as soon as the tests are over."

"Okay good. Also, I can't believe you didn't tell me you were coming to do this."

"You didn't tell me! Plus, I only found out about the test yesterday when I was at my mom's. She had the invitation and didn't even tell me about it."

"Really? That sucks."

"Yeah, looks like she'll miss out on the Best Mother Award again this year."

"Well, you're here now. Do you have any ideas of what we'll be doing? You're the smartest person here, and I can only assume you have an idea."

"Well, I expect we will be tested and interviewed, but beyond that, I don't know."

Desperately wanting to change the subject to not further worry about her abnormal lack of preparedness, Rosie asked if Riley had to hike to the school as she had and if he had to go around any obstacles.

"Yeah! I got dropped off at the base of the mountain—"

"Wait, at the base? Oh my gosh, I at least got driven halfway up!"

"Seriously? Well, I guess it's because they recognize my superior athletic ability." He chuckled, and Rosie playfully pushed him over.

"Okay, so you hiked up the entire mountain, what happened? Did your driver tell you anything? Mine said he got instructed to tell me to follow the lightning."

"Follow lightning? Mine told me to enter the dust. I was so confused, but, as I reached the second mountaintop, a huge wall of dust formed."

"A haboob," Rosie interjected.

"Excuse me? I am not a boob. I swear there was a huge wall

of dust."

Rosie laughed. "No, not you're a boob, I said haboob. It's a giant, intense dust storm. I read it in a book."

"Oh, I like that! Haboob. Ha-boob. *Haaaboooob*," Riley repeated with a giggle.

"You are such a boy."

"Anyway, I entered the haboob and immediately had to force myself forward. The wind was crazy strong, and it was so hard to see. I had to rip part of my shirt to make a bandana to cover my nose and mouth, and thankfully, I had sunglasses to shield my eyes from some of the dust whirling by. I continued forward, trying to find an exit, when something ran right through my legs and knocked me over. I got back up, but, as soon as I steadied my feet, I got knocked down again. On my knees, I looked around, and circling me was a huge coyote."

"What did you do?"

"I had to fight past the coyote somehow, so I stood, and it leapt toward me. While it was in midair, I dove to the side, dodging it, and ran as fast as I could, and then I was out of the dust and in a lake. The coyote howled over the whirling dust, but it never emerged. It was like it couldn't leave the haboob. Ha, *haboooob*. I got out of the lake, washed my face, brushed off as much dust as I could, and now I'm here."

"Wow, a coyote?" Rosie was in shock at her best friend escaping a coyote attack, but this day was all-around strange.

"Yeah, what about you?"

Rosie told him about the lightning strikes and the rattlesnake.

Both were appalled at the perilous lengths they endured to reach the school, and they surveyed the other students.

"I wonder if more people were invited but got lost or returned to the road and decided they wouldn't make it in time to take the examination," Rosie wondered.

"Mm, I hadn't thought about it, but yeah, I bet some—"

A door loudly opened, and they jerked their heads toward the front as a tall, muscular man with a mean-looking face exited from the door to the left of Francie's desk.

Rosie thought he had to be at least six foot eight and three hundred pounds of pure muscle. Veins popped out of his skin, and the vein on his forehead was especially noticeable, since he had a buzz cut. He wore a tight black shirt, black cargo pants, and black combat boots and held a clipboard.

As he approached the desk, he gave a slight nod to Francie and squared his body so he was facing all the potential students. With the clipboard in front of him and commanding the attention of everyone in the room, he spoke in a deep, thunderous voice. "If I call your name, please exit the building and enter one of the cars waiting outside. They will take you to the airport or your home. You have not been selected to attend King's Preparatory and will not proceed to further examinations."

Fear swept across the already anxious students in scattered whispers.

"Michelle Arnet. Raymona Bruns. Clay Clark. Dan Donovan ..." And the names kept sounding off.

Disgruntled candidates shambled outside.

Rosie and Riley were so nervous they weren't even mad they had to hike to the school, now knowing cars could access the building.

"How many names are they calling? How many people are already getting sent home?" Riley asked.

"I'm not sure, but I think I'm safe. He is reading the list in alphabetical order by last name, and he is already at *P*." Rosie gripped his hand as encouragement, hoping the curator wouldn't call Riley's name.

"Reyes Pein. Charles Riley …"

Riley squeezed Rosie's hand.

"Riley, it's okay. It was a last name, not your name." Rosie felt his grip loosen.

"Sue Winters. Valerie Zack. And, Lucas Zim."

Riley sighed in relief and smiled. "We aren't leaving, Rosie!" He went in for a hug, but Rosie quickly retracted.

Of course, she was happy, but she didn't want to seem like a showoff in front of the rejected candidates, but it was already too late.

"Oh yeah, don't mind us. Keep celebrating," Charles Riley yelled and turned toward the man who was dismissing the now angry and sullen candidates. "This is ridiculous! I killed a bobcat to be here! Do you know who I am? Who my family is?"

"I don't care." The large man pointed to the door and said with even more authority, "Get out now."

Charles turned, and, as he left, he ensured to be as disruptive as possible—knocking over lamps, kicking furniture—and when he walked out the door, he slammed it closed to make an even louder boom than normal.

Once the commotion had quieted, all gazes were focused on the big announcer.

"I am going to read another list of names. Now, if your name is on this list, enter the room to the left behind me and wait for further instructions."

Rosie scanned the room and estimated that twenty-five

kids had already been sent home. *What will the rest of the day look like?* she thought.

He read more names, and Rosie realized the man was already nearing the end of the list.

"My name wasn't called, Riley." She shot him a worried look, and, as he was opening his mouth to respond, the curator called the final name.

"Riley Zimmers."

Rosie looked at him, but she made sure she wore a smile filled with encouragement and gave his hand a light squeeze.

Riley approached the man, turning his head to give her one last look before entering the room.

The man followed Riley and closed the door.

The room went still again, and Rosie took another head-count. Twenty-two students left, including herself. While rescanning the crowd she caught a pair of eyes staring at her. A boy's eyes. A cute boy's eyes. She blushed, and he gave her a grin and a little wave. She waved back, and he stood and started toward her. She smoothed her clothes and hair and awaited his arrival.

The boy walked with an air of confidence. He wore a sly, intriguing grin, and his piercing hazel eyes focused on her. He brushed his hand through his thick, dark brown hair, then extended it in front of him. "Hi, I'm Justin Fent."

"H-Hi, I'm Rosie, Connors. Rosie Connors." She shook Justin's hand, and her cheeks blushed a bit more.

"Well, Rosie, pretty weird situation here, huh? I mean, who makes their candidates hike up a mountain with bizarre instructions and have them potentially encounter dangerous animals, like a pack of javelinas?" He chuckled and studied Rosie.

"Javelinas, huh? I got a rattlesnake, so I think I won," Rosie teased.

"Just one rattlesnake? Have you seen a pack of javelinas protecting their young? They are vicious."

Rosie laughed and was pleased by how easy it was to converse with him. "You're right about one thing. It has been a pretty bizarre day. Actually, a bizarre few days, but luckily we are here and weren't sent home with the first group." Rosie glanced into his eyes and thought they really were a special kind of hazel—mostly green with a tad of brown seeping into the outer edge and gold flecks scattered about. Her trance was broken when Justin laughed and gave her a sideways smile. Embarrassed, she returned the smile and covered her face with her hands. "Oh my gosh, I'm so sorry! I just … You have very pretty eyes."

"Good. Every guy wants to hear they are *pretty*," he replied jokingly.

"That's not what I meant," Rosie said, again embarrassed. "I just mean they are very intriguing."

"I'm only joking with you, Rosie." He lightly touched her arm, and the hair on the back of her neck stood. "Anyway, I can say the same thing about you. You are very pretty." Both remained quiet as they looked at one another, then, interrupting that moment, a door opened and closed with a *boom*. Rosie and Justin turned to the front desk to see a young woman trying her best to look cold and stern.

She had exited a second door behind the front lobby desk located to the right of the door the muscle man had exited. She was short but wore five-inch heels that helped her stature. Her hair was pulled into a tight, high ponytail, and her red lips were pursed. She scanned the room, and her gaze fell on

Rosie and Justin. In a surprisingly strong voice, she projected and spoke to the remaining candidates. "I can tell everyone's a bit nervous. Good. Nerves can help focus a person. On the other hand, it can also lead to a total mental breakdown. Let's find out what category each of you will fall into. Please, follow me."

Rosie and Justin gave each other a confused yet interested look and walked toward the second door. They were the last to enter as the woman's heels clicked behind them, and the door closed.

Rosie evaluated the room—a smaller version of the lobby with doors on each wall. As Rosie and Justin sat on a comfortable two-cushioned brown leather couch, she noticed something strange. Another candidate walked over a rug, and it let out a distinctive creak, and a floorboard bounced. "Strange," she muttered.

Once everyone was sitting, the woman walked to the front of the group. "My name is Professor Walker. I will call your name one by one, and you will follow me to your written examination."

A few students squirmed.

Of course, there would be a written examination. How could these kids not expect that? She eyed Justin, and he gave her a subtle grin as if to say he thought the same thing.

"Wyonna Acker," Professor Walker announced.

A shaking, green-in-the-face girl stood and followed Professor Walker through the farthest door.

Both Rosie and Justin sat up straighter, trying to glimpse at what was behind it but had no luck. The door had closed, and the candidates were left alone again.

Justin turned to Rosie to continue their conversation. They

discussed their pasts, what they did for fun, what they thought the exam would entail, and so much more during the next twenty minutes. Rosie was fascinated to learn Justin was from Monterey, California. She had always wanted to see the Pacific Ocean and smell the salty air.

As Justin was about to tell her more about it, Professor Walker re-entered the room. The hushed whispers and conversations dissipated as Professor Walker called back another student.

Rosie was curious where the first student, Wyonna, had gone. Did she pass the test? Was she asked to leave? Where was she?

"What do you think happens to the students who go back there?" Rosie asked in a hushed tone.

"Maybe they take another exit?" Justin suggested.

"Or they move to a different test?"

After Professor Walker had taken two more students through the door, with neither returning, she entered the room again.

Rosie sensed she would be called next. Her last name was close to the beginning of the alphabet, and they had already called a boy with the last name Clearn. She clammed up and wiped her hands on her thighs.

Justin grabbed them and squeezed them in a sweet, reassuring manner. He made her feel strong and confident. She wasn't even embarrassed that her hands were cold and sweaty, because Justin showed he didn't care.

Professor Walker acknowledged the pair, and powerful eye contact met Rosie as she announced, "Rose Connors."

Chapter Four

Rosie stood, ensuring her back was straight, and her head was high. She crossed the room, and, as she did so, she swore the eyes of one of the paintings tracked her. She reached the door, and Professor Walker gestured to her to enter, but she faced the painting. It was now firmly pressed into the frame. Someone was behind that portrait, she thought and, grinning, she turned back around.

Professor Walker closed the door and passed Rosie. For a moment, the two stood in total darkness, and then, after hearing a switch flick, light filled the hallway.

Rosie couldn't believe what was behind the elusive door. Yes, it was a hallway but not an ordinary hallway. This hallway didn't seem to have an end. *It must be an optical illusion*, she thought as she studied the walls. Portraits and paintings balanced perfectly, and along the ceiling, beautiful chandeliers dangled, and an evenly spaced plethora of doors seemed to go on forever.

"Ahem," Professor Walker cleared her throat and indicated to Rosie to enter the first door on the right. Another door was on the opposite wall.

Was Riley in there? Did he already have his test? Were the

other candidates who had gone before her in other rooms along the hallway? Her mind swirled, but she tried to calm it and put Riley and the other candidates out of her thoughts as she entered the room.

Rosie was surprised at how cold and uncomfortable it was. Rather than the warm, cozy design of the previous rooms, this room reminded her of a hospital—white walls, white tile flooring, an analog clock, and a silver metal table and chair in the middle of the room. On the table lay two pieces of paper and a pencil.

Rosie hadn't even made her way to sit down when Professor Walker stated, "You have twenty minutes to complete the written examination. If you answer every question correctly, you will move on to part two. Please fully answer all questions. When you are done, please put your pencil on the table and look me in the eye. No talking and I will not answer any questions. The examination starts now."

Rosie was astonished. She rushed to the seat and saw fifteen questions. Rosie's hand flew across the page, writing down all the knowledge she had consumed from her constant reading and studying. With the first seven questions pertaining to complex theories, historical events, and advanced philoso-phies completed, Rosie checked the clock. Ten minutes left. She continued, hoping for questions on subjects she had already learned.

The next six questions, however, gave her pause. They asked her if she had any unexplainable events occur in her life, if she thought there was any truth behind superstitions, if blood type and DNA could tell you about someone's personality, if she believed her ancestors guided her, if she thought supernatural occurrences happened, and if she had ever met someone for the first time but felt she had met them before.

With her interest piqued and the reminder sitting in her head to answer truthfully, Rosie detailed how she dreamed of places, people, and events she had never seen or heard of before and what happened in her dreams occurred in reality. She wrote about superstitions she believed and how they surprisingly worked for her or against her. She discussed her family history and how she wasn't aware of what her family line was but sensed her ancestors were watching over her, and she wrote about the tingling feeling that rushed through her veins and the tears that filled her eyes when she thought about them or concentrated on something she wanted. She listed the connection she had with Justin, even though the first time she met him was only a couple of hours ago.

Finally, she got to the last two questions. Question fourteen asked who was in the portrait hanging in the lobby, and question fifteen asked how many doors were in the second waiting room. Knowing her observation skills had once again come in handy, Rosie scribbled the answers. The portrait was James Kingsley, the founder, and Rosie wrote only one word for the last question. Six.

She had finished the exam with one minute to spare. She placed the pencil on the table and regarded Professor Walker.

Professor Walker eyed her, skepticism covering her face. She took the examination off the table and reviewed Rosie's answers. She smiled, still reading, and then looked at Rosie. "Congratulations, Ms. Connors. You have answered each question correctly. You will be moving on to the next part of the exam."

Rosie's stomach did a somersault. She had passed. She was

curious how her life events and opinions could be considered *correct* answers, but she decided she would investigate that further if she got into the school. Rosie stood up with a smile she couldn't hide spread across her face.

Professor Walker's expression had returned to judgmental and serious, and she turned her back to Rosie. "Follow me."

Rosie hurried behind her into the hallway. They went through the next door in the hallway, but it wasn't a room. It was a staircase.

Professor Walker descended the stairs, her heels clicking on each step. She held the supporting rail and glided down with ease and grace. She resembled an elegant queen, going down to meet her supporters and loyal servants.

Rosie peered up and down the staircase, but once again, confusion flooded her. Looking down, she couldn't see an end to the stairs, much like the hallway, but what surprised her was when she looked up, she saw the same thing, even though they were close to the top of the mountain. *The ceiling must be painted with an illusion, so it would seem the stairs continue upward.* As Rosie was observing the height and depth of the staircase, she didn't notice Professor Walker stop in front of her.

"I'm so sorry, Professor Walker. I was in awe at how many levels there were," Rosie stammered, stepping backward from her potential future teacher.

Professor Walker, trying to still seem stern, let a small smile play at the corners of her mouth. "It's quite all right. I know it is a lot to take in."

The two stopped at a door behind Professor Walker, and Rosie read the placard next to it—GROUND LEVEL. Rosie could only assume the door led outside.

Professor Walker opened the door, and bright sunlight streamed in.

The storm had cleared, and once Rosie's eyes adjusted to being outside, she saw a grassy area at least the size of a football field. Rather than bleachers, grassy hills surrounded the field. It was more of a colosseum than a football stadium. It was beautiful. What a wonderful way to watch and compete in sports and activities. When she finally stopped beholding the awesome view, she focused again on Professor Walker, who had her arm outstretched to a path.

"Please, follow the path to the tent. You will find a change of clothes inside. Put them on and meet me back here."

Rosie started down the path. It turned from grass into a hiking trail like one Rosie had seen in her Arizona information book. The rocky path wasn't too steep and it was bearable to walk in her heels. She studied the landscape as she moved along. The wildflowers and various cacti were beautiful, and the odd rock formations seemed like something someone had constructed, not something nature had placed there.

Rosie reached the tent, but it wasn't the sort of tent she was expecting. She thought it would be something she and Riley had used to go on camping trips, but instead, she was led to tall white cloth draped over carved wooden poles. The tent was secured, but the top lightly flowed in the wind. Rosie noticed a small black triangle flag flowing on the top of the tent donning the same emblem on the envelope wax stamp—the King's Preparatory emblem. It waved in the wind like it was welcoming her.

Rosie entered the tent and was surprised at the setup. The tent resembled something from an interior design magazine Glenda read. The ground felt solid and smooth like a foundation had been laid, a gorgeous framed mirror was displayed in one corner, and a vintage trunk had been converted into a bench. She turned around but couldn't find any clothes in the room. Then she heard a latch snap. Rosie turned to the trunk and noticed the snaps had clicked open. Rosie opened the trunk and saw athletic attire she was supposed to change into.

She stared at herself in the mirror and groaned. The black shorts and the black and white baseball shirt was a little snug but fit, and the white knee-high socks with two black stripes on the top and shoes could barely fall into the category *athletic*. But she could work out in the attire if need be. Rosie spun in the mirror and made another mental note. If this was what girls at the school wore for their athletic uniforms and classes, she would have to talk with the administration, but only after she got accepted. She redid her ponytail so it was higher and more secured and left the tent.

Rosie walked the path with more confidence filling her with every step, but, as she approached Professor Walker, she noticed she wasn't alone. The big, muscular man from earlier in the lobby stood next to her. If he was with Professor Walker, where were the candidates he was handling, like Riley?

"Ready for part two of the exam," Rosie said as she reached the two.

The man scrutinized her then gave a demeaning smirk and chuckle. "Alright, let's see what she can do," he said to Professor Walker.

Professor Walker, not following in the man's condescending tone, turned to Rosie. "Rose, this is Professor Manger. He will be taking you to the next part of the examination. Good luck."

Rosie proffered her hand. "It was nice meeting you, Professor Walker. I hope I have the pleasure of being your student."

Professor Walker smiled at Rosie—not a sarcastic smirk but a genuine smile. She shook Rosie's hand, but, at the touch, she gasped and recoiled.

Rosie gave a look of confusion as did Professor Manger, but Professor Walker recovered. "Sorry, you shocked me. Ha. Must be all the static electricity from the storm. It was nice meeting you as well, Rose." And with that, Professor Walker left Rosie wondering, as she hadn't felt a shock at all.

Rosie had to hustle behind Professor Manger to keep up with his long strides, taking five steps to each of his. Since she had to ensure she didn't fall behind, it was difficult for her to revel in the beauty around her, but she tried her best. Boulders of all sizes were stacked on top of one another, various cacti flowers were in full bloom, and lizards ran about, finding shelter in brushes and under rocks.

Professor Manger and Rosie ventured off the path they were hiking and ascended the rough mountainside. At one point, Rosie tripped on a sizable rock and cut her knee and scratched her stomach, leaving a slash in her shirt with blood staining the white cotton.

Professor Manger didn't turn around once to check on her though.

Maybe it was part of the test, she thought, so she didn't say anything and continued behind him.

After hiking for another ten minutes, other people came into view, barely visible behind Professor Manger's bulky body, but people nonetheless. They were bounding in midair. No, not midair; they were working across ropes and boulders and diving into nets.

Rosie noticed three different ropes courses—an easy, an intermediate, and a hard course. The farthest two courses were where the students were climbing, leaping, and belaying. Rosie assumed they were students because they were in a similar athletic uniform as her, and she hadn't seen any of these individuals in the lobby earlier in the day.

At the sight of Professor Manger, the students stopped and focused on him and the newcomer.

"Whoo! Fresh meat!" one of the boys yelled. This sparked some howls and whistles.

Professor Manger turned toward the boys and gave a stern look, and that was enough.

The boys turned around immediately with fearful faces and resumed their drills with one eye on Rosie.

"Alright, Connors," Professor Manger said while reviewing his trusty clipboard and manhandling a stopwatch hanging around his neck, "you will have twenty minutes to complete the ropes course. As you can see, it's a square. You will start here." Professor Manger indicated to the nearest tree. "You will climb the rope net to the landing on the tree. You will walk across the tightrope. You can hold onto and use the assisting rope to help you move across to the connecting tree's landing. Then you'll swing across the monkey bars to the third tree's landing. Once you have completed that, jump off the third landing to the dangling rope and swing across and to the fourth landing. Finally, you'll jump off the fourth landing and land in the rope net where you started." He approached the first tree and retrieved a harness and helmet and explained where she needed to clip on and off the safety lines at each step.

With Rosie strapped in and ready to go, Professor Manger checked his stopwatch and smirked. "You better start soon. You only have ten minutes left."

Rosie, realizing he had started the stopwatch when he first handled it at the beginning of the task, shot him a look of shock, then her face showed determination. She ran to the rope net and climbed. With swift movement, she reached the landing in less than a minute. She wanted to prove to the smug professor that she could do this.

At the first landing, she reached to connect her harness to the safety line, but the carabiner was broken and wasn't latching. "Guess I'll be doing this freestyle," she mumbled to herself. She stepped onto the rope and, using the assisting supports aligned with her hands, shuffled across.

Her concentration and focus were impeccable, even when Professor Manger yelled up to her, "Seven minutes left!"

She reached the second landing and had no time to waste. She leapt off the landing and reached for the first bar suspended in midair. She grabbed it and swung and kept going until she finally reached the last bar and swung her legs back and forth, forcing herself to propel forward to the third landing. It wasn't graceful, but she also didn't fall twenty-five feet to the hard ground. The dangling rope was at least five feet away, and the fourth landing was lower than the previous. She had room to land on the final platform.

"Two minutes left," Professor Manger called.

She reached the far edge of the third landing and got in one running stride before she bounded off and grabbed the rope. Her momentum carried her the rest of the way to the fourth and final platform. She stood there and, with a smile, looked at Professor Manger and jumped.

Lying face-up on the net, Rosie laughed. She couldn't help it. She was so happy to prove herself to the bulky professor and the onlooking students. She bounced up and out of the net and approached Professor Manger, his face stuck in a look of astonishment and anger. On one hand, she could tell he couldn't believe she had completed the task, and on the other, he was mad she had. All he could utter and grunt to her was, "Follow me," and he led her back onto the hiking trail.

Rosie had changed into her own clothes, and Professor Manger escorted her to the never-ending hallway. During their short walk, neither said a word to the other. It was uncomfortable, to say the least, but that didn't stop her from feeling proud.

In the hallway, Rosie expected the professor to lead her to the waiting room, but he took her to the next door down the hallway. With a strong fist, Professor Manger rapped his big hand on the door, and a thirtysomething man opened it.

"Ah, you must be Rose Connors." The man extended his hand, and she shook it. "Please come in. Professor Manger, thank you for bringing her to me." He pressed himself against the door so she could enter.

Before she did, she faced Professor Manger. "Thank you, Professor Manger." She proffered her hand, but he didn't shake it.

Professor Manger gave Rosie one more look up and down and walked off, mumbling to himself in a state of confusion.

Shrugging off the rejection, Rosie proceeded into the room and was in awe that each room she had seen down the hallway could be so different from each other. The first room was cold and plain, the second door led to a staircase, and the third room, which was the man's office, was very comfortable and calm. It had a desk and chair like most offices do, but it also had two high-back chairs facing the desk for any visitors, a long, cushy leather brown sofa for more comfortable seating, beautiful woodworking on the walls and baseboards, cute, little succulents on the coffee table in front of the sofa, an entire wall lined with books, and the room was a relaxing shade of green.

"Well, Rose, please take a seat anywhere you like. Do you like being called Rose, or is there another name you go by?"

"Rosie."

"Great. Well, Rosie, I'm Doctor Witam, and I am King's Preparatory's staff psychologist. Before we jump in, I want to say congratulations on passing the intellectual and physical examinations."

"Thank you, Doctor Witam. I'm excited I have made it this far and am here."

"Good. I'm happy to hear that. By the way, would you like a glass of water?" He gestured to a beautiful glass pitcher twisted every which way but still somehow held liquid.

"Yes, please. That would be great."

Doctor Witam poured Rosie a glass and handed it to her.

Rosie took gulps of water and noticed Doctor Witam smiling. As a rush of embarrassment flooded her, Rosie set down the glass. "Sorry, I guess I didn't realize how thirsty I was."

"That's quite all right. The Arizona heat can do that to a person." He took the glass and refilled it.

Rosie took another sip and set it on the table.

Doctor Witam picked up a notebook. "Rosie, I want to mention that you should be very impressed with yourself for making it this far in the examination."

Rosie blushed and grinned. "I am."

"Good. Now for this part of the examination, I'll ask you a few questions to ensure that if accepted to King's Preparatory, you are not only in the correct mindset and mental and emotional state to be admitted but that you will also succeed and fit in. We will call it the emotional personality examination. Does that sound all right with you?"

"Of course. You can ask me anything."

"Great. The first thing I would most like to know is how you would describe yourself?"

Rosie cleared her throat. "W-Well, I am definitely determined and strong-willed." As she spoke, her voice became steadier, and she became more confident in her answer. "But I am also kind and caring. And loyal. Not only loyal to my friends but also to my schoolwork and regular work."

Doctor Witam smiled. "That's good to know. What would you say has happened in your life for you to possess these qualities?"

Though Rosie had gained some courage, she hesitated. She wasn't sure how much she wanted to reveal or what was appropriate for this setting, and she definitely didn't want Doctor Witam to think she was crazy.

"Rosie, anything you say to me today won't be disclosed to another human," Doctor Witam said encouragingly.

With this reassurance, Rosie opened up about how she had left her mother and how her mother had never supported her ambitions, how she had never met her father, how Riley was the best thing to ever happen to her, and about how she lived with his family and worked multiple jobs. Finally, she explained that even though her life hadn't been perfect and that even though she didn't have a normal family life, she had never let it keep her down, that she knew she wanted to be happy and live a fulfilling life.

Doctor Witam smiled broadly and took down a few notes, leaving her in silence.

She surveyed the room, waiting for him to gather his own thoughts. When she refocused on him, she noticed his hand moving still. When he was finally done, it stopped, but she could have sworn his pen continued to move.

"Now that I know a little bit more about your past and who you are, would it be okay to ask you a few more questions? I can't promise they won't be as deep or personal as the first, but, if at any time you are uncomfortable answering a question, say so, and we can move on."

Rosie grinned. "Go for it."

They discussed Rosie's dislikes and likes, what she hoped to accomplish in life and where she saw herself in ten years. Doctor Witam asked Rosie some behavioral and situational questions. He wanted to learn how she solved conflicts, what she thought was the best way to earn someone's respect, what was more important to her: what someone or herself said or how they said it, what her dream job was, if she preferred working alone or with others, if she could change the world, what would she change, if she had a life philosophy that she lived by, and if she had read any good books lately.

Rosie was so happy and proud she answered every question with strong conviction and a positive attitude, and after each answer she gave him, he would nonchalantly jot down his thoughts in his notebook, like it was a normal part of their conversation. At least Rosie hoped it was his thoughts and he wasn't bored of her talking and was doodling instead. But she thought those doubts were all in her head because he was listening intently to every word Rosie said and nodded along, encouraging her to continue to let go and open up to him, and she surprised herself that she did.

For some odd reason, she sensed she was safe in the room with him. She was unsure if it was the plants that gave off a clean, fresh smell or if it was Doctor Witam's soft, soothing voice, but she felt she belonged there and hoped she could have more conversations with him, especially since their conversation seemed to flow so well—well enough that Rosie and Doctor Witam were startled when a knock came on the door.

Doctor Witam checked his watch and was shocked at the time. "Wow, an hour has passed already. Well, Rosie, I think I have taken up enough of your time."

Both Doctor Witam and Rosie stood, and Rosie proffered her hand. He grabbed it and shook it but not hard—more of a gentle squeeze and as a thank you for the intriguing exchange.

"It was a pleasure talking with you, Doctor Witam."

"Well, Rosie, it was a pleasure to talk to you as well." He opened the door for Rosie, and outside waiting was Professor Walker.

For some reason, Rosie wasn't expecting to see Professor Walker again. She had been handed off to different staff members a few times already, so she assumed she would meet a different teacher or administrator this time. As it turned out, her assumption was right, just premeditated. Professor Walker had met Rosie, but she also said to follow her to the next door down the hallway.

They stopped at the closed door, and Professor Walker placed a hand on the handle. "When you enter this next room, it is imperative you do not make a sound. Don't speak, don't let your heels click, and don't greet the interviewer."

Rosie was confused but ready to obey the directions. She gave Professor Walker a nod of agreement and opened the door to another office similar to Doctor Witam's, but the walls were a dark navy blue, and the only furniture present was a long, black cherry wood desk resembling a conference room table. A laptop sat open and running on the desk next to an armchair for Rosie to sit. Another armchair, facing away, rested on the other side of the table with a high back so no one could be seen sitting in it. It was only when someone spoke that Rosie was sure someone was there.

"Hello, candidate," a young-sounding man's voice said smoothly. The chair remained turned away while he spoke. "I am an influential board member for King's Preparatory and will be conducting this next interview. I ask that you do not speak, since I want your identity to remain anonymous. I ask that you please type your answers in the open window on the laptop provided and push Send. Once you've sent the message, it will repeat in a computer-generated voice so I can listen to your response. Please refrain from using any pronouns that may reveal your identity, gender, and so on. Are you ready to begin?"

Rosie lifted her hands and placed them on the laptop keyboard and pushed Send. "Yes," a robotic voice came from two speakers on the other side of the room near the man.

"Excellent. My first question is, why do you deserve admittance to King's Preparatory? My second question is, what do you wish to gain by attending King's Preparatory? And my third question is, what do you plan to do with the knowledge you gain here?"

Rosie's fingers glided over the keypad. She wanted to give thoughtful answers but also didn't want to take forever and have him wait in silence for too long. After a few minutes of typing and a quick glance over her answers, she hit Send. The robotic voice boomed once again. "I am not sure if I do deserve this. I have an idea of what to expect from the school, but again, I don't have much experience with a school of this caliber, so to say I deserve this is a little ridiculous.

Rather, I am determined to prove that if admitted, I will be one of the most dedicated students this school has ever seen. I will work harder than any other student. I will assist faculty and my peers, and I firmly believe I will be a positive force here, and that deep down inside being here is right. I feel something to my very core that makes me believe I am destined to be here.

As for what I wish to gain by being a King's Preparatory student, I hope I can be challenged mentally, physically, and emotionally so I can become the best version of myself and thrive. And to answer your third question, I plan to use the knowledge and skills I've learned at the school in my work and everyday life and also share them with future students and help them succeed and grow." After hearing her answer out loud, she interpreted it could come off as a bit cocky instead of confident, but she was hoping he would think it was the latter.

"Very good answers. I have reviewed some notes from the staff you have already met with, and I have to say you do look like a promising candidate, and I do think you could do great things here, but I have to ask you a few more questions to ensure you truly do belong."

"I understand," she typed and sent.

"Do you have an easy time accepting new things?"

"I do. I welcome change with open arms, and, as I said before, I like being challenged and provoked."

"I am happy to hear that because, at King's Preparatory, you will be introduced to many new and challenging things. Now, my final question won't be as serious as the last ones, but mainly, I would like your take and interest on a particular subject. Please, tell me if you have read any books or articles on past supernatural occurrences and creatures and if you believe they happened or existed."

What is it with this supernatural topic? Are they seeing if it might be a new elective they want to introduce? Rosie didn't want her skepticism to be confused with her interest. She had always found the supernatural subject to be alluring and thought-provoking, so she didn't mention the subject being discussed previously, and she got her fingers to work on the keyboard.

"I have read and researched this topic thoroughly and deeply. I especially enjoyed learning about various witch trials, Greek mythology, solar and lunar animal activity, and reading about humans who have encountered and performed superhuman abilities when adrenaline pumps through their bodies. I also have read about various studies and projects with the goal to change the basic structure of DNA and manipulate it, so it displays characteristics of superhuman abilities, like incredible strength or speed. So I do have an interest in the subject, and I do believe it is possible for these creatures and events to have existed and to have occurred. And some still may, we just don't have proof or scientific data for it, which is what most people need in order to believe something."

Her answer ended, and the interviewer let out a deep chuckle. Rosie didn't know if that was a good thing or a bad thing. She didn't know if he thought she was some naïve, little girl or if he believed what she had written. She didn't gain any clarity, because his next words were, "Thank you for your time. Please exit the hallway and return to the waiting room."

Her heart sank. *Why did I have to say I believed in that stuff? Why couldn't I have said no, this stuff isn't real. It was all made up to scare children and each other.* She shambled down the hallway. She was the only one in the waiting room, and she took her original spot on the couch. With her hands sweating and her stomach turning in knots, she stared at the door, waiting for someone to tell her she was fine, that she had gotten in. But no one came. Another ten minutes passed, and Rosie thought she would have a full-blown meltdown, then finally, Doctor Witam opened the door, entered the waiting room and, in a calm voice, said, "Rosie, if you could please follow me."

This is it. They sent the kind doctor to let me down easy. They walked down the hallway but passed his office and finally stopped at the fifth door. Rosie expected him to dismiss her from campus, but rather he was showing her to another room. Just when she thought they would enter the fifth door on the right into another office for another test or interview, Doctor Witam, instead, led her into the door on the left. Her intrigue and interest rose again, and her nerves were calming, because the door opened into a room resembling a teacher's lounge or break room, but rather than couches, there were a few round tables that could seat five comfortably.

Doctor Witam smiled. "You must be hungry. We have been

testing and interviewing you all afternoon. I have arranged for you to have a snack and sit and talk with a few students. You are encouraged to ask questions and learn more about the school. Do you have any questions before I leave you to it?"

"Can I help bring in anything? I would hate to sit around while someone else brings my food."

"You have nothing to worry or be guilty about. Plus, the food should be here at any moment. Just relax and have fun. Ahh … there they are now!"

A group of four students entered, each holding a tray of food, except one student held two trays.

"Rosie, I would like to introduce you to Megan Ship, Garrett Parker, Chase Wilber, and Bianca Rader."

Rosie smiled at them. "Nice to meet you."

"What will you have?" Garrett asked with a side smile and a twinkle in his eye. He was the one holding the two trays, and one had a plate with three different types of hummus, marinated chicken, and a piece of pita bread, and the other tray had apple slices with dipping sauces of caramel, chocolate, peanut butter, and toppings of nuts, sprinkles, and crushed cookie.

"Wow. I'm lucky if my school had fresh lettuce in the salad bar and two different types of dressing other than mystery flavor."

Garrett, Megan, and Chase laughed while Bianca gave a look of horror.

Rosie assumed she thought every school had gourmet lunches and elaborate snacks like this.

"Well, if I were you, I'd go with the apple, because the caramel is to die for," Megan said.

"Alright."

Garrett set the tray in front of her seat.

Between bites, Rosie asked as many questions as possible. She had already gotten the perspective of the professors and staff, but she wanted to learn the students' actual opinions of the school. She asked if they enjoyed being in the boarding school environment, what the classes were like, how long they had been there, what she can expect as a student, if students lead successful lives after graduation, and what it was like living on campus.

Megan and Garrett answered most of her questions, and Chase chimed in here and there. Rosie could tell he was a bit shy and closed off, but the hardest one to talk to was Bianca. For some reason, she had come off a little bit conceited. This didn't stop Rosie from talking and pointing questions directly at her though, and, if anything, it motivated Rosie more to attempt to have her open up. If these students had any say on whether she would be accepted, she needed all to like her. Finally, after Rosie complimented her a few times, Bianca's icy exterior warmed up, and she was much more talkative.

They had been conversing for close to an hour, and Rosie had learned something interesting she hadn't been aware of. All four students were entering their sophomore year, and all had been attending the school since kindergarten. She thought it peculiar that a boarding school existed where parents shipped their five-year-old children, but she guessed if a parent wanted the best education for their child, this was the place to send them.

Doctor Witam entered the room as the five were laughing at a joke Garrett had told. "Alright, everyone, I hope you had fun, but I think you four have somewhere you're supposed to be."

The four students said their goodbyes to Rosie and wished her luck on admittance.

Once the room cleared of the students, Doctor Witam faced Rosie. "Have fun?"

"I had a blast. Thank you."

"Good. Do you think you are up for one last examination?"

"Definitely!" Rosie knew now she was ready for any test they would throw at her.

Doctor Witam escorted Rosie down the hallway to another room similar to the previous one, but a divider with a window split the room in the middle. Doctor Witam placed his hand on Rosie's shoulder and told her not to worry, sensing her confusion.

The door on the other side of the window opened, and Megan, Garrett, Chase, and Bianca lined up next to each other. *This is so weird. Are they testing me on their names or what I've learned about them?*

Doctor Witam studied all her facial expressions and body movements. "Now, Rosie, you are about to see some extraordinary things. Things you have been told weren't real or didn't exist. I implore you not to scream. However, if this is too much to handle, turn around and tell me to turn out the lights in the other room. Am I clear?"

"Yes," Rosie said, still not taking her stare off the students.

Doctor Witam pushed a button on the wall by the window, and his voice sounded clear on the other side where the students were. "Begin."

The students in the other room looked into the two-way glass then lowered their heads. Rosie watched the students swaying and tensed up. They lifted their heads, and Rosie gasped at their transformation.

Garrett's eyes were no longer dark brown but a bright yellow and seemed to glow. His upper and lower canine teeth had elongated, and his hair had thickened. Thick fur covered his arms, and the binding on his shoes broke as gigantic paws burst into view.

Bianca's hair also thickened and grew but only the hair on her head. The entirety of her eyes were now black. Her hands became webbed, and her nails grew into long, sharp points. Her legs started to form together, but not completely, and had scales running up and down them. Gills protruded from her neck, and she gasped for air.

Rosie's attention moved to Chase, whose eyes glowed blue as he muttered something under his breath, and his hands pressed together around an object. When he pulled apart his hands, the object still in one of them, he slowly rose from the floor and floated in midair.

Finally, Rosie spied Megan who pet a white rabbit in her arms. Her eyes had changed from light brown to scarlet, and when she opened her mouth, razor sharp teeth appeared. She pulled the rabbit to her mouth and sunk her teeth into it. The rabbit struggled for only a moment then relaxed. Megan pulled the rabbit back and set it on the ground. Rosie was worried Megan had killed it, but it hopped off like nothing had happened. The only evidence it had been hurt was a mouth-shaped bloodstain in the white fur.

Rosie's mouth dropped open in shock, but she closed her mouth and approached the window. She put her hand against the glass, completely fascinated. She was looking at what she presumed was an enormous werewolf, a deadly mermaid, a magical wizard, and a blood-thirsty vampire. She turned her head to Doctor Witam and smiled, laughing in astonishment.

He smiled at her and nodded. She turned her head back to the students but whipped around as soon as she heard, "Welcome to King's Preparatory."

Rosie recognized the voice. It was the voice from the interview with the prominent member of the school board, but rather than a stuffy, older man, leaning against the wall was none other than the school's founder, James Kingsley.

Chapter Five

In a span of three minutes, Rosie had been accepted into King's Preparatory, found out supernatural creatures exist, and had met a man who had to have been at least a hundred and seventy years old.

James Kingsley shook Rosie's hand and gave her a hearty congratulations. He apologized for having to leave, but he had an important meeting to attend. Before he left, however, he asked for her name. She told him, and he responded, "Nice to meet you, Rosie. It's funny. You remind me of someone, *mmm …*" and he started to examine her. "Congratulations again, and welcome to your new home." He exited the room, leaving Rosie still stunned at the very old man who looked like his portrait from 1865.

A calm, steady hand rested on her shoulder. "Rosie," Doctor Witam started, "what you witnessed can be a lot for someone to handle. Do you need to take a moment and talk?"

"Obviously, I need to talk, but not about my emotions! Sorry, I'm shouting. I don't mean to. I'm just amazed."

"I would be worried if you didn't have some sort of reaction to this."

"I mean, who knew? Oh my gosh, who else knows? Does

the government know about this? Do they use them in their defenses? How is there a vampire this young? Are there other creatures I haven't seen yet—"

"Rosie, calm down. You will learn more soon, I promise," Doctor Witam said in a lighthearted manner and took Rosie to the lobby. "Once the other accepted incoming students arrive, if there are any more, you will be escorted to meet the other enrolled students and faculty." He left Rosie transfixed on the portrait of James Kingsley.

In the room, looking at the handsome features of the founder, Rosie wondered if he was a vampire and if that could be why he didn't age. Do all vampires not age? I mean, that is the entire premise of them, right? That they are undead? And what about werewolves and mermaids? Did they have the same lifespan as normal humans?

"Stop it," Rosie muttered to herself. This new world had captivated her so much she had only now remembered Riley and Justin.

I hope they got in, she thought, and like the school had read her mind, she heard shuffling behind the door Riley had gone through, and the door opened. Rosie tried to find a good view of who was being led out, but Professor Manger's gigantic body blocked and hid everyone following. She counted five bodies following Professor Manger, and the one in the very back had a big goofy grin covering his face.

Riley ran toward her and took her into a tight hug. "I got in! I got in! I got in!"

Rosie laughed. "Me too!"

Both sat on the couch, and the other four people who tested with Riley took seats near them as well, since it was pointless to distance themselves now that they were all King's

Preparatory students.

"Rosie, this is Reid, Flynn, Gunner, and Eleanor."

"Nice to meet you." Rosie was particularly happy to learn another human girl had gotten in. She didn't know what she would have in common with her, but at least they had that, and even though the other four students broke off to talk to each other, Rosie had a feeling her and Eleanor would get along well.

"What were your tests like?" Riley asked. "After Professor Mean-ger took—"

"Riley! What did you just call him?"

"What? Mean-ger, Manger, same thing, right?"

"Stop it," Rosie said, chuckling. "He'll hear, and you barely got accepted. Please don't be thrown out already."

"Alright, alright." Riley raised his hands, acting innocent. "Anyway, Professor Manger led us through that room, remember? And behind it was a smaller version of this room."

"Yeah, I went through the opposite door, and it had the same thing. It was like a nicer version of a doctor's office waiting room."

"Exactly! So, we walked right through the room and into this hallway."

"A never-ending hallway?"

"Yes! Down this never-ending hallway, we were told to each pick a door at random, and once inside, we had twenty minutes to figure out how to exit the room without going through the door we had entered through.

My room had a bookshelf covering an entire wall and a painting on another wall, a rug on the ground, and another door. I did the most obvious thing and tried to open the other door, but it was locked. I checked under the rug for a key. I fumbled around the frame on the painting for one too but no luck. Finally, I turned toward the bookcase, because maybe there was a trapdoor. I pulled the books until I found in the middle row of the bookshelf, centered, was a book called *Knock*. I went to the door and knocked. There was a click, and it opened, and I stepped out of the room. I was in a different never-ending hallway, and Professor Manger was waiting at the end of it - the never-ending part, ha. I started toward him, but it was like I wasn't getting close. I quickened my speed, but still, it was like I was on a treadmill. I stopped, and Manger was laughing at me. I went into a room, back into the first hallway, and ran to the end. Thankfully, the never-ending hallway does actually have an end. I went through the last door, and the door that led to where Professor Manger was on the other side was unlocked. And let me tell you, his smile faded so fast."

"Riley, that was so smart, good job!"

"Hey, he wasn't the only one who figured it out," Reid said.

"Well, I was the first," Riley proudly announced.

"Yeah, because you got an easy room," Gunner said. "The first room I went into had nothing in it, nothing on the walls or floor."

"How did you get out?" Rosie asked.

"I kicked down the door." He and the other boys erupted in laughter.

"Did you damage the door at all?" Rosie asked.

"I don't know. I did what I had to do to pass."

Rosie's stomach churned. The idea of damaging school property didn't sit well with her.

Riley continued with his story, "After the test was over and time was up, about fifteen people had made it to Professor

Manger. He then took us to this crazy rope course."

"I did one too! What course were you on? I did the easiest course, and I completely shocked him when I finished it on time."

This made everyone laugh because they felt the same way about Professor Manger as she did. He was condescending and didn't want a human to be accepted.

"That's great," Riley said. "We ended up doing the last one."

Rosie let out a low whistle. The last course was much higher than hers and contained not only the obstacles she had faced but also a rock wall, zipline, and bungee jump. "I can't believe you all passed that."

Eleanor chimed in mischievously, "And guess who had the best time?"

Rosie chortled while the boys glanced down, hiding their red cheeks.

"Can I continue, please?" Riley asked, joking to his new classmates. "As I was saying, us and, like, what? Seven others?"

"Six," Reid said.

"Right. We made it to the next test, which was like a physical fitness test in gym class but way more intense. I'm talking about running a mile in under five minutes, doing a hundred pushups in two minutes, completing two hundred sit-ups in three and sprinting fifty yards in five seconds."

"Doesn't sound hard at all," Rosie joked.

"After that, ten of us remained. He brought us inside, and we each got twenty minutes to answer five questions. They were weird, but now it makes sense."

"Were they about supernatural occurrences and superstitions and weird stuff like that?" Rosie asked.

"Yeah! After the test, seven of us had individual interviews, and I guess after the interviews and the *big reveal*"—he imitated a vampire biting into something—"us five were left. But tell me what you had to do. I am so happy we both made it!"

Rosie started to tell Riley and the others about her examination, but before she got to the part about the first test, a door opened. All eyes turned to it, expecting a teacher to appear, but Justin walked out with a great smile.

"You got in!" Rosie ran and hugged him.

"So did you!"

After a few seconds, Riley cleared his throat.

"Oh, Justin, this is my best friend from home, Riley Zimmers. He also got in."

"Congrats, bud. I'm Justin Fent. Any friend of Rosie's is sure to be a friend of mine," Justin said proudly and proffered his hand toward Riley.

Riley shook it vigorously. "Uh, yeah. You too."

As Justin sat next to Rosie, a door creaked open, but it wasn't only one door. Both doors behind the front desk exposed Professor Manger on the left and Professor Walker on the right. The two gazed at the seven newly accepted students.

"Please follow us," Professor Walker said to the group.

The seven curious bodies hustled into the room where Rosie and Justin had waited for their first exam.

After all seven students filed into the waiting room, Professor Walker shut the door and turned to Rosie and Justin. "Rosie, Justin, would you like the honors of taking us downstairs?"

Rosie and Justin turned to each other and smiled, noticing the confusion from the other students. The two lifted the coffee table off the rug and pushed back the couch they had sat on earlier.

"When we first came into this room," Rosie started, "we noticed the floor under the rug had a spring to it and made a thudding sound and faint echo."

"We figured there must be a trapdoor, especially when my foot hit a small bump that lifted underneath the rug," Justin added as the two rolled up the ornate carpeting and revealed a trapdoor underneath it.

They lifted the latch, and the students packed around the opening. They stared into the hole to see stone stairs descending and disappearing into the darkness below.

Professor Walker rubbed her hands together, and the small amount of friction started a fire in her palms. She opened up her hands and blew the fire into the staircase, and torches along the wall ignited. The staircase seemed to be as long as the mountain was high. No, even longer, Rosie thought. Next to the torches on the walls hung paintings and portraits and artifacts, and on every other step, two suits of armor stood opposite of each other, tall and ready for action.

"Too cool," Riley whispered.

Despite looking narrow, the staircase was pretty wide, and the group could easily walk side by side down it. It also helped that the steps were three feet wide, so the stairs weren't as steep as they looked. Rosie thought some spell must have made it wider than it was supposed to be and wondered what other enchantments had been placed upon the school. With Professor Walker leading the group at a reasonable pace and students following with Professor Manger flanking the back, Rosie could survey the paintings on the walls and study the armor and artifacts. Swords, shields, stone plates with carvings, framed documents—Rosie wanted to study so many things.

The group continued going farther down the mountain. After descending what Rosie estimated was seven flights, Professor Walker stopped and turned toward a painting hanging behind a suit of armor.

"Why would they do that?" Rosie asked.

"What?" Riley replied.

Before Rosie could tell him there must be a secret door, Professor Walker leaned close to the suit of armor and whispered into the helmet.

Rosie watched wide-eyed as the armor creaked.

The metal arm moved upward, and the torso turned, and the legs and the suit of armor was alive. It marched out of the way and stopped, so it was next to the painting, giving Professor Walker access to it.

The painting was as wide as the stairs and went from the floor to the ceiling. The young boy in the picture was playing in a dark forest with tall trees. Again, Professor Walker leaned up and whispered to the painting. It seemed like the little boy in the painting understood what Professor Walker had told him because the painting moved over and down a step.

"What did you say?" Justin asked bewildered.

"I told the soldier I would bring him some oil so he can move easier, and I told Gregory I would bring him some candy," Professor Walker replied like it was the most normal sentence ever uttered.

Behind the painting was a door. A subtle whooshing sound was audible, and a gold knob emerged adorned with strange carvings that appeared to be a face. Professor Walker leaned down and sang a few notes into the doorknob. It became animated and repeated the tune to the group and clicked.

The door swung open.

Excitement bubbled, and Rosie tried to see what was on the other side. Like the staircase, portraits and paintings hung on the walls, suits of armor stood tall, and torches lit the way down the hallway. Rosie was getting antsy and desperately wanted to reach their destination, but she understood a school like this needed diversions, secret passageways, and passwords.

Professor Walker kept the same steady pace, and finally, thirty feet into the hallway, she stopped and sang another tune.

Rosie couldn't help but worry about all the melodies she would have to remember to enter different rooms and passageways.

"Here we go again," Eleanor muttered.

But, to all the students' surprise, after the door clicked, the professor didn't lead them into another hallway. Instead, they entered a grandiose room—a cafeteria, but it was too nice to be called that. It was a dining hall. Ten long, rectangular wooden tables sat in the middle of the room, and at least forty comfortable-looking high-back chairs surrounded each of them. The first and last two tables in the line were empty, but the others had students seated around them who turned to look at the newcomers.

The third table contained seven empty chairs. On her way to take a seat, Rosie surveyed the room and all its beauty, but Justin nudged her in the arm and indicated her to look above them.

Rosie was amazed at the outstretched window that covered the entire ceiling like the lobby, but instead of seeing the sky, she watched whooshing dark water. She admired the schools of fish that swam by and the underwater plants that floated and swayed. She was absorbed in its beauty until a shadow covering the entirety of the ceiling passed over, dimming the room and sending shivers down her spine.

"What was that?" Gunner whispered with a shaky voice.

The tenured students thought the newcomers' reaction was hilarious, and low whispers and giggles floated through the hall.

The seven humans reached their seats, and once situated, all heads turned toward the table sitting upon a platform at the front of the room where Professor Walker and Manger took their seats with the other teachers.

Rosie caught Doctor Witam's eyes at the head table, and he gave her a small nod as the woman sitting next to him stood.

She was tall and alluring, and her long strawberry-colored hair fell over her shoulders. Her cheeks were rosy on her fair complexion, and due to the Arizona sun, freckles speckled her nose. Like Professor Walker, she wore tall heels but wasn't dressed as professionally. She wore a tight candy-red pencil skirt and silky white button-up blouse. She glided across the platform and around the table to a podium on the opposite side of the landing.

She inspected the crowd of students, and her gaze landed on Rosie. She stared at her for a moment then parted her red lips and smiled at everyone. She tapped on her ring and held it up as if it were a microphone. "Welcome, welcome! Welcome to our new students and welcome back to those who are returning."

Rosie thought that while her too-sweet voice sounded kind, her eyes were hard and bitter. She got the impression that if you had tripped, the woman would walk past or even over you.

"For those of you who don't know me, I am Professor Shay, and I am the headmistress here at King's Preparatory. I anticipate seeing all of you succeed and flourish during this school year, both in and out of class. It, of course, won't hurt being under my leadership and supervision." She chuckled and made a hand gesture that showed how much she thought of herself. "Now a word from our great founder, James Kingsley, to our freshman class."

"I thought he left," Rosie whispered.

"Wait, you actually saw him? In person?" Justin asked, astounded.

"Yeah, he interviewed me, but I didn't realize who it was at the time. He kept himself hidden."

A ball of light formed in the middle front of the room and grew and manifested itself. James Kingsley, or at least a hologram of him, stood on the stage. "Hello, freshman students. You must be both nervous and excited about the tryouts and the crystal examination. These tasks are intended to help you find your support system, team, and closest friends."

"More tests?" Riley groaned to Rosie.

"It can't be too bad, since we already made it in, right?" Justin replied.

"Yeah, I guess," Riley retorted, unimpressed with his reassuring attitude.

The holographic James Kingsley continued, "The team you will be placed on is based on the highly regarded wizard and intellect, Aristotle. Of course, we recognize the Myers-Briggs type indicator developed by two astounding intellects, but sixteen teams for interschool competition was a bit much."

Professor Shay let out a playful laugh as if James Kingsley was actually in the room.

"Therefore, those sixteen personality types have been placed within the temperaments strategically, allowing you to be your best self among your peers."

Rosie remembered she had learned her Myer-Briggs type indicator when she had taken the test for fun the previous summer. She wondered if she would be placed on the according team if she told Professor Shay.

"The first team, Haply, is where the relaxed, easy-going, and caring play well with others. The second team, Valtic, is for the courageous risktakers. The third team, Astive, is where deep thinkers and analytical minds use logic to succeed. And finally, the fourth team, Surgent, is for the ambitious, natural-born leaders. After you witness each team's skills and personalities, you will select which team you wish to apply for and give the crystal ball your answer."

The freshman students scanned the room but couldn't find a crystal ball anywhere.

Professor Shay flicked her hand in a circle, and by magic, the ball appeared in her palm. She approached the center of the stage, and a stand with a base floated from the ground. She placed the ball on the base and returned to the podium.

"Professor Shay and the ball have already spoken with the teachers and students you have been in contact with during your time here, and they've gotten their impression of you. Now the ball will read you and listen to your answer on which team you wish to join. However, while your answer will be considered, the ball may still choose a different path for you. If a conflict in the decision arises, you will audition for both teams, and the crystal ball will solidify your placement. I am excited to see all that you do and become during this current year."

The hologram dissolved, and Professor Shay waited until the whispers that had broken out over the sea of students dissipated before speaking again. "Freshman students, please stay seated and observe each team with great care. Students," Professor Shay addressed the students already on teams, "come forward and demonstrate your skills. The first team to find and retrieve the King's Preparatory flag will be exempt from homework for the first week of school."

Students cheered, and the teams scurried together, forming plans.

Rosie noted where the flag was positioned—swaying on the ceiling. *No*, she thought. It was attached to the ceiling but on the other side, floating in the water.

The non-freshman students moved into four groups and Rosie found the students she had met with earlier. Garrett was on the Valtic team, Chase on Astive, Bianca on Surgent, and Megan on Haply. *Of course*, she thought, she had met a student from each team so not only could they learn more about her, but she could understand the different teams better. She took note of what each group was doing.

Astive students were in deep discussion, planning how to retrieve the flag in the most strategic way. Haply students were laughing and working together, building a supernatural pyramid to reach the tall ceiling. The Valtic students were having a blast, transforming and scaling the walls, laughing when a shifter or werewolf would fall to the ground. Finally, Rosie focused on the Surgent team. While a few members stood planning, the majority were observing the other teams.

Rosie checked who was closest to the flag. A vampire

from the Haply team was about to reach the ceiling when an Astive wizard flew up and, using the support and power from the other witches and wizards to propel him, touched the ceiling first. He chanted, and without any effort, his hand slid through the thick glass to grab the flag. With it in hand, cheering erupted from the Astive team but stopped abruptly when Garrett in partial wolf form sprung up the walls and snatched the flag from the Astive team member's hand. Valtic was next to shout and cheer but, like Astive, was stopped suddenly. A large bulky boy, half shifted into a mean grizzly bear, had met Garrett in the air, ripped the flag from the wolf's paw and landed in front of Professor Shay to present the flag to her.

Rosie was astounded. The Surgent students had been planning to steal the flag from whoever retrieved it so they didn't have to do as much work. *Smart*, Rosie thought.

Holding the flag, Professor Shay went behind the podium and gestured to the Surgent students. "Our winners!"

The group laughed and applauded themselves as everyone returned to their seats.

"Now that you have an idea of how each team works and solves problems, you will give your answer of what team you wish to be a part of to the crystal ball, and it will decide if you belong to that team or if you need further evaluation."

A low murmur blanketed the room as the freshmen quietly discussed what team they wanted to be on and whether the crystal ball would agree with them.

Professor Shay cleared her throat over the enthusiastic students. "As I call your name, please come up and place your hand on the orb. A color will cloud the inside and confirm which team you belong to, or multiple colors will form, indicating further trial." Professor Shay reviewed her list on the podium. "Martha Ash."

A beautiful, tall girl stood and glided to the landing. She lifted her perfect manicured hand onto the ball. She gasped and started to transform but was stuck in a sort of in-between state of looking human and looking like a vampire. Her eyes turned red, her teeth grew sharp, and even though they weren't completely out, she still managed to cut her lip on one of them. After thirty seconds of her in this trance, the orb turned gold, and Martha's hand shot off the ball. Her eyes resumed their icy-blue state, and her teeth retracted. She wiped her bloodied lip and flashed the people cheering for her a smile.

"Surgent!" Professor Shay announced, causing the Surgent students to rumble and roar. Martha and the orb both agreed on her team placement. As Martha started to return to her seat, Professor Shay grabbed her hand and pulled her toward the ball. "Not just yet, Ms. Ash."

The color cloud inside the ball remained gold, but the ball melted into a shimmering metallic liquid. The liquid surrounded the base where the crystal ball had rested, and on the base lay a gold necklace with a one-carat diamond set in a pendant. The diamond twinkled up to her, and her mouth spread into an even bigger grin.

Professor Shay lifted the necklace off the base and put it on Martha.

A glimmer engulfed Martha's entire body and surged into the diamond, making it shine and sparkle even more. The crystal ball reformed into a solid on its base.

After the reformation, Professor Shay put her hand on Martha's shoulder and gently pushed her forward, indicating it was now time to return to her seat.

"Cordelia Blackwater," Professor Shay announced.

A tan girl with long brown hair approached the podium. She put her hand on the orb, and she too was taken into a trance. Her hand on the crystal ball became webbed, and scales formed on her legs. Her eyes turned black as Bianca's had. The cloud inside the ball swirled and transformed from white to dark silver, almost like gunmetal.

"Astive!" Professor Shay said.

Cordelia removed her hand, and like before, a necklace appeared on the base, but this necklace was silver with a sapphire pendant. After clapping ceased and the necklace was dangling around her neck, Cordelia returned to her seat, and as soon as she sat, she took a water bottle from an older girl and chugged it.

Rosie assumed, after seeing both her and Bianca partially transform, a mermaid feels extreme dehydration due to the dryness.

Behind the podium, Professor Shay scanned the list and eyed the freshman table. "Rose Connors!"

Her hands shook, but suddenly both stopped as Justin grabbed one hand and Riley the other. They squeezed for good luck, but Riley squeezed slightly harder after seeing Justin holding her other hand.

"Ow," Rosie muttered and took both her hands back and smiled at them as she stood. Every eye in the room drilled a hole into her head, and her hands clammed up. She stepped onto the landing, and Professor Shay now stood by the crystal ball.

Rosie faced the room of students and placed her hand on the swirling orb. Her vision blurred and went black. Her ears clogged, and she was swept into total silence. She closed her eyes and opened them again, but she wasn't in the darkness or the dining room. She was in a vast opening surrounded by white fog. She turned in a circle and realized she was on a mountaintop, like the one she had hiked up earlier.

"Rose Connors," she heard a serene voice echo.

She searched for someone, but no one was there.

"Rose Connors," the voice called again.

"Hello?" Rosie said.

"Rose Connors, firstborn to Rose Marie Connors. A name that has descended through generations. You are the first of this name in over one hundred and fifty years to carry extraordinary gifts."

The fog thickened then thinned again. She wasn't on the mountaintop anymore but in a dark, rocky room—a cave.

"You are strong, brave, intelligent, and a leader. But you don't step on anyone. You are also kind, sociable, and friendly. You think you can make your own way and don't accept help, because you are afraid of taking others down with you if you fail. You are afraid of connecting to others and will hide behind your intellect. You fit on each team. What I have seen from those you have met and from seeing how you handled each test and obstacle today and, in your life, I know where you could do wonderful things and become an even more extraordinary person. Now tell me which team do you desire to be on?"

The fog around her swirled and whooshed by.

"I'm not completely sure. Every house had something I admire."

The fog accelerated, whipping her hair around and over her eyes. She felt a pressure on her hand, and her vision returned to normal. The entire dining hall was quiet, and Rosie looked at the crystal ball. Gold, gunmetal, silver, and copper mist danced and circled.

Confusion filled Rosie, and, as she was about to ask what it meant, Professor Shay said, "Further examination needed. Ms. Connors, you have the rare opportunity to try out for each team. You may return to your seat until called upon again."

Rosie stepped off the landing and sat down, all eyes still on her even as the professor called the next freshman.

"What was it like?" Riley asked her.

"It was strange. I was here, but at the same time, I wasn't. And it was like I was talking to the crystal ball, like it was a person and not a thing. What did I look like?"

"Well, you glowed."

"I what?"

"What Riley means is," Justin interjected, "you emanated a type of energy that made you look brighter, and your eyes glistened more than usual. They were still a green-blue, but the color popped more."

"Thanks, Justin." Rosie smiled but noticed Riley clench his hands. "I can't wait to see what team you guys are on or if you have to endure more tryouts like me."

A girl named Fiona Eber was next, and when she touched the crystal ball, feathered wings protruded from her back and moved so quickly they were almost a blur. Rosie realized Fiona could shapeshift into a hummingbird. Fiona was a part of Haply and got a platinum necklace with an emerald pendant.

There were also fairies, and when one of them grabbed the orb, butterfly-like wings popped out of their back, but they appeared more delicate and transparent. They glowed so bright it was hard to look at them until they grew smaller, but before the person could reach their intended fairy size, their team selection was solidified, and they removed their hand, reverting them to normal.

Most of the supernatural students had already known which teams they wanted to be a part of and where they would fit best. Only she so far had been chosen for further demonstration and tryouts.

When it was Justin's turn to go, Rosie understood what he meant when he told her about her glow and her eyes. With his hand on the crystal ball, Justin's eyes gleamed but didn't change color, and he radiated a strong energy, like his aura was visible. The crystal ball changed color. Swirling within were copper and dark silver.

"Further examination needed. Mr. Fent, you can try out for both Valtic and Astive. Please return to your seat until called upon again."

Rosie breathed a breath of relief that she wasn't the only one who needed to audition.

"I'm sure you wanted to find out your team, but I'm happy I won't be alone for tryouts," she exclaimed to him.

"I'm happy to be a comfort for you," and he grabbed her hand.

As the list continued, Rosie was amazed. Witches' and wizards' eyes glowed bright blue, and sparks flew off their fingertips. She saw shifters of all shapes, sizes, and predatory-prey levels, including a boy named Max who could turn into a bison. Werewolves would go into mid-shift, and before their entire bodies cracked and transformed into a wolf, they would resume human form.

Rosie kept a mental note of how many students were on each team, what species they were, and how many needed further tryouts. They were almost to Riley, because Rosie had seen they were on freshman number thirty-nine out of forty, and Riley had a *Zi* last name.

Conrad Zex, number thirty-nine, was a jaguar shifter and was placed on the Surgent team. Out of the thirty-nine students, six—three girl fairies, two girl gentle shifters, and one boy werewolf—were put on the Haply team. Eight students—one wizard, three witches, two mermaids, a girl Gila monster shifter, and Reid—were placed on Astive. Ten students—a boy and girl vampire, two wizards, one witch, one boy and one girl predatory shifters, one girl werewolf, and Gunner and Flynn—were on Surgent. And six students— one wizard, two boy shifters, a bison and a cardinal, one girl vampire bat shifter, a boy werewolf, and Eleanor—found themselves on Valtic. Nine students, including herself, had to try out further.

Professor Shay announced Riley's name, and Rosie grabbed his hand like he had hers and squeezed it.

He smiled at her and winked. "Rosie, don't look so worried. We will be on the same team together, and these are going to be the best years of our lives."

On the landing, Riley placed his hand with confidence on the crystal ball, and his mind was transported into the fog. The same thing that had happened to the other human students happened to Riley. He glowed, as did his eyes, and he muttered under his breath, but he was doing a lot more than anyone else. He was angry and conflicted, like his conversation with the orb wasn't going the way he wanted. His hand shot off the crystal ball, and the cloud in it changed color. The orb swirled with copper and gold fog.

Professor Shay put her hand on Riley's shoulder and addressed the group. "If you have not been placed on a team, please come forward."

Rosie stood alongside Justin and maneuvered to the front of the room, wondering what their test would be.

"The orb will now watch and make your final placement. When I give the go-ahead, you will all attempt to catch one of the four flying jewels without using any of your powers." With the flick of her wrist, four jewels appeared and floated above the freshmen's heads—a ruby, a sapphire, an emerald, and a diamond. "At the end of five minutes, the tryout will conclude, and the orb will have its decision whether the jewels are caught or not. You are aware of what teams you are auditioning for, so I suggest you display your true identities to match with the correct one." Professor Shay signaled to the small group. "Begin!"

The students watching hollered and cheered, and the few classmates standing with her fought and used each other to catch the jewels as they floated and averted capture.

Riley eyed the sapphire soaring above the students and, with a running start, jumped into the air.

Rosie saw his attempt and cheered him on but became quiet as his hand was about to clasp the sparkling jewel. Another boy had leapt into the air, his eyes glowing yellow, and seized the object before Riley could. Rosie put a hand on his slumped shoulder.

"He cheated," Riley said with a scowl.

"I know. But hey, there are still three jewels to retrieve. Come on." As she walked toward Justin, she eyed the boy approaching the other students, showing off his prize.

"Hey, I have a plan," Justin said as the two walked up.

"Oh, you do?" Riley snarked.

"Yeah. You and I will act as a base, and when one of the jewels heads toward us, Rosie, you will run and jump onto our arms. We'll launch you into the air, and you'll grab one of the jewels. We'll catch you and hopefully find out what team we are on."

"Okay, let's do it," Rosie said before Riley could object.

She stepped away from the group, and Justin and Riley interlocked their arms. The twinkle of the diamond floated over the group.

"Now!" Justin yelled.

She sprinted toward the human trampoline, lunged through the air and felt the weight of Riley and Justin's arms as she landed on them, and they lowered and tossed her up. It was as if time had stopped, and rather than freefalling, she floated down. She looked into Riley's eyes as he caught her. Cheers erupted across the room, and Rosie opened her hand to reveal the two-carat diamond.

"Stop," Professor Shay pronounced across the hall. The two remaining jewels flew to her, and she placed them in her pocket. "Congratulations on your prizes. Now that the ball has analyzed you further, we will make team selections again." Professor Shay gestured for the boy who had caught the sapphire to approach the orb.

After placing his hand and mid shifting into an alligator, the orb burst with a gold color.

"Surgent!" Professor Shay announced and placed the gold class ring inlaid with a diamond on the boy's middle finger. Professor Shay pointed to another student who came up and was placed on the Astive team.

It continued until only Justin, Riley, and Rosie remained.

"Mr. Fent," Professor Shay indicated, and Justin approached the orb. The mist whirled and finally changed to a sparkling copper. "Valtic!"

Justin took his pendant ring and smiled and winked at Rosie and Riley as he returned to his seat.

"Mr. Zimmers," Professor Shay said.

As Riley turned to walk to the podium, he stopped and looked at Rosie. "No matter what team I am put on, I will always be with you." He kissed her cheek.

A loving sensation filled her as she watched her best friend cross the landing and put his hand on the crystal ball. The nerves within her shuddered with anticipation.

Finally, with the orb's fog changing, Professor Shay announced, "Surgent!"

Cheers erupted from the other Surgent students. They were especially loud from Gunner and Flynn. Riley collected his ring and returned to his seat, greeting his new friends.

"Ms. Connors," Professor Shay called.

The room went silent as she approached the crystal ball. Everyone watched her, especially since it was she who could try out for each team. Placing her hand upon the ball, her mind was transported once again.

"Rose Connors," the orb spoke.

"Yes?"

"I have watched and observed and yet still cannot place you."

"Please! I must fit somewhere. Just put me on a team. Any one. I will be happy with the result."

"No!" the voice boomed. "You must choose!"

Rosie had never been one to be indecisive, but this decision was too difficult to make. She did not want to select a team and not be happy there. "No," she said, standing her ground.

The fog zoomed by, and a searing pain shot through her hand. After being forced back to the dining room, Rosie stared at the shattered crystal ball oozing black metallic liquid. She focused on the pain in her palm and saw glass pieces protruding from it. Murmurs and conversations erupted over the dining room, and Rosie eyed Professor Shay, who was wearing a concerned look.

"Ms. Connors, it appears the crystal ball has left this decision to you." She picked through the broken glass and ooze, retrieving four different pendants. "Select your team."

The tension in the room grew as her decision was meant to be made then and there. Cheers and calls from each team erupted, but she could only focus on one voice—Riley's.

"Rosie! Come on!"

She lifted her hand, her fingertips grazing the cold diamond pendant, but she paused. A flame had shown in her eyes—a deep, forceful ruby blaze. Heat came off the necklace that desired her, and she felt its warm, welcoming presence.

Cheers and yells of approval rumbled the dining hall, and Justin and Eleanor clapped loudly, and Garrett stood on his chair, howling. In her palm was the ruby and copper necklace, symbolizing Valtic.

Rosie laughed. Not only at the scene of wild, happy students but because it was over, and the team she had chosen also wanted her. It was the right team for her, even though she had doubts when speaking with the orb.

Professor Shay took the necklace and pushed Rosie's ponytail, so it fell over her shoulder.

With the necklace secured, she walked to her seat with a

wide smile. It faded, however, once she saw Riley's upset expression. "Riley, I'm sorry. I didn't even realize I had grabbed the Valtic pendant until after it happened."

Riley didn't reply, and, as she pleaded with him to be happy and cheer up, Professor Shay addressed the group again.

"Congratulations, everyone. Now that the team selections are finalized, please move to your respective tables. Haply members, please move to tables two and three, Astive to tables four and five, Valtic to tables six and seven, and Surgent to tables eight and nine."

"Shall we?" Justin proffered his bent arm to escort her.

"We shall," she said, determined to enjoy the moment even though Riley's face grimaced as they walked to their assigned tables.

Garrett's table erupted with cheers as Rosie, Justin, and Eleanor approached.

"I knew you would be on Valtic!" Garrett yelled as he embraced Rosie and Justin. "I'm so excited, guys. I can't believe we not only got seven humans this year, but three of them are on our team. I have so much to show you and teach you. This will be the best year! Hey, why so down, Rosie? You chose the best team to be a part of!"

"I know." Rosie tried to grin. "I just wish Riley was happy."

"Well, it's completely understandable that he was put on Surgent," Eleanor said.

"What do you mean?"

"Well, when you three were doing your tryouts and you were thrown into the air, he pushed Justin out of the way to catch you alone."

"He did what?" Rosie turned to Justin to see if it was true.

"Yeah, but I don't think he meant it. He was probably just

worried if I had the strength to catch you or not. Which I totally do. I would never drop you."

Rosie was in shock. "I can't believe he would do that," she muttered.

"Yeah, real personalities are revealed during tryouts. The supernatural environment heightens them and shows true intentions," Garrett said to the three human freshmen. "Man, there is so much to tell you three about. Just think of me as your one-stop supernatural shop!"

"Garrett, shush. You're talking so loud." Rosie looked around.

"Oh, don't worry. An enchantment shrouds each team, so you hear loud chatter, but no words are distinguishable from one team to the next. This way, team secrets and conversations can't be overheard. Try to listen to the Surgent conversation behind me."

Rosie, Justin, and Eleanor leaned over, but they couldn't distinguish any words, only rumbling noise.

"Cool," Justin said.

"Is the enchantment always present?" Rosie asked.

"Oh no, only at times like these and team meetings and that sort of thing."

"What other enchantments or spells or weird supernatural stuff go on?" Eleanor asked.

He ogled her for a few seconds, smiled and pushed his hand through his hair. "Well, a lot. Ha! I mean, like those necklaces and rings you all got."

"Are they enchanted?"

"Yes and no. They are unique to each individual student. If you are a witch and have one, they help you control your power. If you are a vampire, they help you walk about in the sunlight. For me, they help me control my change during a full moon and help me transform if I need to when there isn't one. Like today. Understand?"

"Yeah," Justin said, "but what about us, as humans? Do they do anything, I don't know, special?"

"Of course! They have protection spells attached, so if you are in trouble, it will call for help. They also can give you guidance in troubled times or make you calm and stress-free. They can do so much more, but you'll learn as you go and have it in possession."

"What do you mean we'll learn as we go?" Rosie chimed in.

"I mean if you are in a situation where you need help, the stone will help you. Plus, you will learn about it in one class or another this semester."

"Okay, what other classes will we take?" Rosie asked.

"Well, it all depends on grade level, supernatural abilities, non-supernatural abilities, and a few other things. Like Rosie and Justin, you'll be in advanced, most likely graduate school-level classes, while Eleanor and I will be in only somewhat advanced classes. But Eleanor will be training more heavily with the werewolves and shifters since she is a protector, and you two might be training with witches and wizards. There are classes just for supernatural students where we learn to control our change without the stones or ones that are just for wizards and witches where they learn spells and enchantments. So, there are a lot of different classes you can take or won't be allowed to take. It just depends."

"Wait, so that's what I'm called? A protector?"

"Yep! And Rosie and Justin are intellects."

"I hope we can audit a few classes in our free time," Rosie said. "I would love to sit in on a few supernatural classes and learn the mechanics and anatomy and brain work they use."

"Ha! Spoken like a true intellect. It has been a while since one was accepted, but yeah, I'm sure if you work something out with Professor Shay and Doctor Witam, that should be okay," Garrett laughed. "Doctor Witam oversees Valtic students, so when you talk to him this weekend to set up your schedule, tell him that, and he will make something work. He is such an awesome advisor."

"Hey, Garrett," Rosie mused, "what do they do with the students who aren't cut out for the school?"

"Oh, it's obvious, isn't it? We kill them."

A long, steady pause hung in the air.

"Oh my gosh, you guys think I'm serious?" Garrett yelled, laughing uncontrollably. "I can't believe you fell for that! No, no, no, we don't kill them. But, from your faces, you totally thought we did!"

The shock of his joke washed off the humans, and they all laughed. Eleanor even playfully pushed Garrett in the arm, causing him to blush.

"Okay, okay," Justin said, still stifling laughter, "you got us. Now what actually happens?"

"Well, from what I understand, if you are asked to leave or fail a test or anything, they take you aside and shift around your memories and rearrange them."

"Rearrange them how?" Rosie asked.

"Say someone didn't pass an exam, their memories are modified, so they remember not passing the test but none of the weird paranormal, supernatural stuff. And they don't remember how to come back here if they had been paying attention to the ride. They simply remember failing their tests and returning to their normal life. They also don't have an inkling to even discuss the school or tell anyone they took the test. Not even the parents mention it. It is taken care of very thoroughly."

"What if they have seen the transformation of you or any other supernatural being and didn't take the news well?" Eleanor asked.

"Well, that memory is completely wiped from their mind, and they remember failing one of their interviews."

Rosie opened her mouth to ask him another question, but Professor Shay had removed the noise enchantment. The sudden change in volume surprised the students, and everyone became quiet. They stared at Professor Shay, who stood behind the podium.

"Now that you all have gotten somewhat acquainted, I think it is time for some dinner." She waved her hands like a music conductor.

Heads turned to follow her gaze at the back of the room, and a cutout in the wall appeared. Behind the cutout, dinner plates, silverware, glasses, napkins, and table clothes soared out and neatly set themselves on each table. After each student had a plate in front of them, food flew across the hall and landed on each plate.

Rosie had never had a more delicious meal. There was a crisp, fresh salad, cheeseburgers with Angus meat, toppings, perfectly melted cheese, and brioche buns, regular French fries, sweet potato fries, tater tots, zucchini fries, and so many more options.

"Is every meal like this?" Rosie yelled over the food chaos and cheers from students.

"No, this is only for tonight," Garrett answered. "Professor Shay likes to put on a show for the new students."

After finishing the entree course, the dishes swept themselves into the air, and from the back wall, desserts flew out on miniature plates.

"Just grab a plate of something you want," Garrett told them as he snatched two plates with brownies from the air and put one in front of himself and one in front of Eleanor.

Justin reached and got himself a chocolate mousse and Rosie a crème brûlée. They devoured their desserts, and again, their dirty plates swept themselves up and whisked to the kitchen. With their stomachs full, excitement waning, and tiredness taking over, the new freshmen were ready to see their dorms and hopefully have a good night sleep.

Professor Shay approached the podium. "Alright, students. Now that you have eaten, it is time for you all to retire to bed."

Garrett whispered to Eleanor, "Now it's time for the real fun to begin."

"Team leaders, please escort your teams to their respective common areas and show them to their dorms. Have a good night, everyone, and sleep well. The next few days will be busy ones." Professor Shay walked off the landing and into the hallway that connected to the staircase.

Cheers erupted, conversations started, and students walked around. Rosie, Justin, and Eleanor stood but didn't move; they had no idea where they were supposed to go. Thankfully, Garrett told them to follow him.

When they were all near him, he clapped Rosie and Eleanor on the shoulder and lightly pushed them near a door in the front right corner of the dining hall.

Rosie quickly turned to find Riley, but his team leader was guiding him to a different door along with all the other

Surgent students. Rosie turned to see the Haply and Astive students pass through other doors on the other side.

"Come on, Connors. Stay in the moment," Justin told her with a sly smile.

She faced forward and put on a fake smile. She was the last Valtic member to pass the threshold. The door closed behind her, and suddenly, she found herself in total darkness.

Chapter Six

"Garrett? Where are we? I can't see anything," Rosie called out.

"Here," she heard Garrett say and felt a hand grab hers and join it with another. "I have Eleanor's hand, she has Justin's, and you have his." Justin gave her hand a small squeeze and grew closer to her.

"Don't worry, Rosie, I'll protect you," he said jokingly.

"Oh, my hero," she replied in a playful, sarcastic tone. After carefully walking a few more feet, Rosie paused. A door across the room they were navigating had opened to reveal lights. What was weird was the light from the room didn't spill into the darkness. As they grew closer to the door, Rosie realized it wasn't a door but another passageway behind a painting.

They reached the opening, and all Rosie could see was an indiscernible white room filled with a bright light on the other side. *What the heck,* Rosie thought.

Garrett entered the room first. His dark contrasted figure stood in the vast whiteness, smiling back at them. "Well, come on!"

All three freshmen stepped through the portrait hole to

experience the room change from plain to full of color and pulsating music. People filled every inch, dancing, talking, and having fun. Rosie spotted a boy in the corner juggling knives but using magic instead of his hands. She noticed a group of older girls sitting on the couch close together, gossiping.

"So, what do you think?" Garrett asked the three, all still surveying everything.

"Where are we?" Rosie yelled over the loud music to Garrett.

"This, my friend, is the Valtic living room. We can use the space to study, talk, hang out, have team meetings. Oh hey, you should meet and become acquainted with the other Valtic freshmen." Garrett ran around the room, grabbing the other freshmen, and brought them to Rosie, Justin, and Eleanor. "Alright, guys. This is Oliver Hughes and Alec Quay, werewolves; Max Lexington, Reese Yicks, and Ellie Reed, shifters; and Everett Overton, wizard. Now talk, I'll be right back."

"Hey, there. I'm Justin Fent."

"I'm Rosie Connors."

"Eleanor Wags."

"Nice to meet you guys," Alec told them.

"So, which one of you are intellects and which ones are protectors?" Reese piped in.

"Those two are the intellects," Eleanor said with a head nod.

"Ah, so you're the protector," Oliver said in a sly, smooth voice as he tried to move closer to her.

"That, I am."

The group talked and got to know one another on a surface-level basis.

"Alright, everyone, here ya go," Garrett said as he returned to the group and distributed cups to everyone. The pink liquid inside swirling around by itself.

"Garrett, what is this?" Rosie asked skeptically.

"Loose juice." Garrett sipped his drink.

"Uh, is there alcohol in this?" She would not break laws and rules her first night at an amazing school and be expelled.

"No, don't worry. There isn't any alcohol or anything like that. It is a sweet beverage made to help you relax and unwind without impairing you."

Rosie watched the self-stirring, enchanted drink then noticed everyone sipping casually. She thought they all looked elated and happier. She took a sip, and as the sweet liquid passed through her and sloshed into her stomach, Rosie thought the liquid had transformed into actual butterflies that fluttered within her. She laughed and sipped again.

"Enjoying your lotus water?" a beautiful brunette asked, approaching the group.

"This is Katherine," Garrett said, introducing the newcomer.

"Hey," Katherine said to Rosie.

"Hi, so I thought this was loose juice?" Rosie replied, confused.

"That's what we call it, but the proper name is lotus water. Like the fruit from—"

"*The Odyssey*! Of course." Rosie laughed and looked into her cup.

"Okay, you need to explain this," Eleanor said, now staring at the contents of her cup.

"The lotus fruit is from the book *The Odyssey*. It comes from an island where people called the lotus-eaters roam, and they give voyagers and lost seamen this fruit, and it acts like a narcotic, making them not care for what they really want and causing them to fall into a deep, peaceful slumber."

"Now I understand the elated feeling," Eleanor said.

The group laughed and continued sipping.

The relaxing feeling Rosie gained from the drink allowed her to open up more. "Can you explain to me how you exist?" Rosie asked then realized how rude and obtrusive the question was. "Wow, I'm sorry. I didn't mean for the question to come off like that."

Katherine giggled. "It's okay. I was born a vampire."

"I thought vampires were made, not born."

"Both hold true," Katherine replied. "Obviously, we need blood to survive. The majority comes from blood bags rather than feeding on people, but we are offered the option to feed from volunteer humans. Their memories are wiped if they come to campus. But, if we are desperate enough for a drink, we can bite a human without releasing the transforming venom that would turn a human. We dry bite them."

"You dry bite them?" Justin inquired further.

"Like, if a venomous snake bit you without envenomation. No venom was released into your body because the bite was either in defense, or the venom glands were empty, or the snake got an imperfect hold on you. Since it bit you without envenomation, you received a dry bite," answered Rosie.

"Exactly," Katherine continued, "It's very rare and illegal to turn a human without proper authorization and paperwork going through the Superiority. We also take measures, like draining our venom glands, so we don't have any accidental transformations."

"What's the Superiority?" Rosie asked.

"It is our government. Like how the president and congress run the normal world in the US, the Superiority runs the supernatural world. You'll learn all about it in history class."

"I actually can't wait," Rosie said, laughing. "Anyway, you were saying how vampires are born."

"Right," Katherine continued. "So that is how vampires are created—a bite injecting venom that will kill and turn a human. But vampires are also born. Again, it is rare when you compare the number of vampires with the number of who are born. When a vampire is born, we have the same body functions of normal humans until our brains stop developing around twenty-five, give or take a year or two. We still need to drink blood and steer clear of the sunlight—our pendants help us with that—but we also eat normal food and go through puberty. Since we go through puberty, we have normal female reproductive cycles. But once our significant other or ourselves has stopped developing physically, that window closes, and we can no longer become pregnant or reproduce. Vampires also have to worry about teen pregnancy." Katherine giggled.

"What if a teenager is bitten, not born? Will they also continue to grow?"

"No. Since the venom kills them and then turns them, they will forever be that age. But again, that rarely ever happens, because it is illegal, and, if you are caught turning someone without permission, you are responsible for any deaths that occur from it."

"Wow. What about James Kingsley? Vampires stop aging, and he hasn't aged for a while now. Is he a vampire?"

"Ha! No, he is the one and only immortal being."

"Okay, you lost me. You are also immortal, aren't you?"

"Again, it is a yes and no answer. Vampires can be killed. We can be stabbed through the heart, beheaded, and a few other ways of dying, but Premier Kingsley can't die. Not only does he not age, but I heard if you stab him or try to end his life, he will just continue to live. It is like his skin is impenetrable."

"Premier?"

"Premier is his title, like President."

"Okay, and he is the only one like that?"

"Yeah, crazy right?" Katherine left to refill her lotus water.

Rosie sat on a couch, her brain, like her drink, now swirling. She thought long and hard about how James Kingsley was completely immortal and about the other supernatural creatures. Do they have special abilities that make them a version of immortal?

"Are you Rosie?" a tall, older girl with long braids asked.

"Yes," Rosie said, standing up.

"Great! I'm Paige. I'll be your dorm advisor. I already scooped up Eleanor and Justin, and I'll take you to your dorm rooms."

Rosie had completely forgotten about the dorms. She followed Paige to Eleanor and Justin, who were waiting by a different portrait.

"Alright, we are going to the human dorms. Each supernatural being has its own dorms for safety reasons. No other type of being knows where the other dorms are, only their own. It is against the rules to bring another type of being into our dorm. Again, safety concerns. Do you all understand?"

Rosie, Justin, and Eleanor nodded.

"Okay, let's go." She pushed open the portrait, and after they had stepped through, they again were magically transported into a different place—the lobby of the human dorms.

Rosie noted doors led outside, but why ever use them if you could just use the portrait holes? She decided she would explore more once everything settled.

Scanning the lobby, Rosie noted four portraits were specific entryways for each team, and there were couches and lounge chairs so they could hang out with other humans at night and study with them.

The four other freshman human students sat on a long brown leather couch, and an older boy, the same age as Paige, leaned against a wall.

Rosie caught Riley's eye and waved and smiled, but he resumed laughing with Gunner and Flynn.

The newcomers sat as Paige approached the front to address the seven new human students. "Everyone, this is a pretty sparse dorm since there aren't nearly as many human students as supernatural ones, but that doesn't mean the rules don't apply here like they do everywhere else. First, the boy's dorms for students under eighteen years old is on N-five then the floor for boys eighteen and older is N-four. Guys, this is Randy. He is the boy's dorm advisor, so go to him with your problems. Ladies …" Paige looked at Rosie and Eleanor. "Floor N-two houses girls under eighteen years old, while N-three is for girls eighteen and older. Both Randy and I will be on our respective floors, but we will be doing daily and nightly room checks, and, if you ever are in trouble or need something, let us know."

"Well, fellas, only tell me if it is an emergency," Randy said with a smirk.

Paige shot him an icy look and continued, "Now, if you're thinking, *Cool! Coed dorm!* Stop. You won't be able to access the opposite sex's dorm levels. Don't even try. It won't work."

Gunner and Flynn whispered, laughing quietly.

Rosie suspected they were planning something along the lines of sneaking onto the girls' floor. She was annoyed they were already scheming ways to break the rules and most likely ruining things for everyone else.

"Obviously, this is the lobby, and N-one has a multitude of study rooms and lounge spaces for studying and relaxation. Now, it's pretty late, and tomorrow you will receive a tour and learn more about the school, so I will read off your room assignments, and you can go to bed."

"What about our stuff?" Flynn asked.

"Already in your rooms. Gunner and Riley, you'll be in room five-oh-one. Flynn and Reid, you'll be in room five-oh-three, and Justin, you will be in room five-oh-two. Rose and Eleanor, you're in room two-thirteen."

Paige and Randy led the group to a bookcase as tall as the ceiling and as long as a car. Paige carefully pulled out a book halfway, and the bookcase whirled around. It stopped abruptly, causing the new students to lose their balance. Once recovered, Rosie saw they were on a platform that connected to a spiral stone staircase.

Paige and Randy descended the stairs with the new students following quickly behind. The group passed an exit landing that was level N1—the study rooms and the lounge. They kept walking and arrived at level N2.

"Alright, ladies, here you are."

"How do we get into our room?" Eleanor asked. "Do we have keys?"

"They're dangling from your necks. I assume you can read, so I won't show you to your room. If you have any issues, I am in room three-oh-two, so come down and knock."

Before Eleanor could ask another question, Paige opened the door for the girls, and while the boys tried to peek their heads around to see what their floor looked like, the door was shut immediately behind them.

Rosie and Eleanor surveyed the quiet hallway. Gold-encrusted number plates hung next to each door with old signs on a few of them, indicating who had previously resided in the rooms along with their room style.

"Do you have any desire to decorate our door?" Rosie eyed Eleanor, hoping it was a no.

"Not really. I'm not that crafty," she said, indicating with her thumb at a door. Multiple strands of diamonds hung in front of the entry, and they parted in the middle. A quote by Atticus adorned the door in a gold foil cursive decal: *Some girls look good in diamonds. Some girls make diamonds look good.* In light blue were two girls' names: *Ashley & Tammi.* "Do you think they were in Surgent?" Eleanor asked sarcastically.

Rosie chuckled, slipped her necklace off her neck and held it against the doorknob. The doorknob molded around the jewel's precise cuts and clicked. Rosie secured the necklace around her neck and pushed open the door. But rather than be overcome in awe, she let out a, "Huh?"

They were in a tiny hallway with two doors. One was to the right of their entrance and another in front of them. Eleanor pushed open the door to the right. Light flowed into the dark hallway as marble tile floors and light gray walls shone. The two girls entered the bathroom and were in awe at how a bathroom like this existed at a school for minors.

A chandelier hung from the ceiling with crystal beads cascading from it, and not only was there a floor-to-ceiling marble walk-in shower but also a roomie silver clawfoot porcelain bathtub. On the vanity counter was not only a sink but glass jars filled with bath salts, incense, and other items intended for relaxation. Shampoo and conditioner bottles, toothbrushes and toothpaste, and other things the two girls would need for their personal hygiene needs were meticulously stowed. A separate door in the bathroom led to a toilet for more privacy in case both girls needed to use the bathroom at the same time.

"The country club I worked at didn't even have a bathroom this nice," Rosie exclaimed.

The two girls returned to the hallway, leaving the bathroom door open.

"This must be our bedroom," Rosie said, pushing the door. Her eyes opened wide.

The huge light gray and white bedroom was bright and beautifully designed. Facing the door were two white wood four-poster queen beds with white linen curtains for privacy and white plush comforters and pillows that could have been clouds. Between the beds were matching white wooden desks and cute, light gray mesh swivel chairs. Between the desks was a long dresser with four columns and three rows of drawers for the two girls to share, which also sat below a window as long as the dresser and as tall as the four-poster bed, with light gray curtains closed over it. At the foot of each bed was a gray trunk for extra storage and a wall cutout closer to the entrance for the girls to hang their clothes. Next to the cutouts were full-length mirrors so the girls could inspect themselves if desired. As for lighting, a grand crystal chandelier—similar to the one in the restroom but much bigger—hung in the middle of the room, and small stainless-steel lamps sat on each desk. On each side of the entry door were makeup vanities with attached mirrors, and finally, two gray couches with white, fluffy throw pillows and white coffee tables sat against the wall. It was like they had designed the room so the two girls wouldn't want to leave it.

"I can't believe this," Rosie said with eyes as big as saucers.

"What? Didn't you have a nice bedroom at home?"

"Sort of, but it wasn't really mine."

"What?" Eleanor asked, confused.

Rosie faced her, realizing how she had decided to live was far from normal than others. "Oh, yeah. Sorry, let me explain." Rosie detailed her past and working for the country club and living with Riley.

"Wow, so this whole independence thing isn't new to you?"

Rosie chuckled. "No. Will this be the first time being away from your parents?"

"Kind of. I've gone to summer camps, but this is the first time I won't be with them for a long, extended period of time." Eleanor opened the trunk and found her bag and a cellphone. "Ah-ha! Here you are. Wait, this isn't my cellphone."

"Here, there's a note in the trunk with our belongings. It says, *Please accept these King's Preparatory cellphones in place of your old ones. We've added phone numbers of every student for your convenience. You can make calls outside of campus and use normal social media sites, but the phones have been enchanted so any indication of supernatural tendencies will be distorted or altered, ensuring outside individuals won't learn our secret. If you are fearful of divulging our secret, we urge you to limit cellphone usage and use the phone in the lobby. Remember, our school only works if it is kept hidden.*" Rosie immediately thought about her mom. Did she know she was here? Did she care she had left the state? Will she tell the country club so they can use

106

her shed for actual greens-keeping supplies, or will she have to make a call to them tomorrow?

"Hm, interesting. Let's try it out." Eleanor raised her cellphone with a mischievous smile.

"Who are you texting?"

"My mom, to say I got into a super-secret school full of vampires, werewolves, and other supernatural creatures, and I will never reenter the real world again."

A distinct swooshing noise came from the phone, indicating the message was sent, then a chime from a message being received.

"Ha, want to see what she said?" Rosie took the phone and read the message and reply.

Eleanor's message had been completely altered. Rather than what she had written, the message now read, *Hi, mom. I got into King's Preparatory. It is full of interesting people, and I can't wait to be a part of this world.* And her mother's reply was, *I know, sweetie! Congratulations. The school called to inform us, and we are so proud of you. Have fun and talk to you soon!*

"Wow." Rosie handed the phone to Eleanor, who was now typing into the phone again. "Now who are you texting? Are you trying to fool the system?"

"Ha, no. I'm messaging Garrett. I want to see if the phone will distort texts to others on campus." After a dinging sound, her phone screen illuminated with a new message. "Seems to be okay to mention supernatural stuff if you are talking to others on campus." She clicked off her phone and set it down.

"I hope we have some time to explore more," Rosie said while unpacking.

"Definitely. I would love to look around campus without having a chaperone follow me everywhere."

"Are you sure you don't want to find a secret spot to lure Garrett into?" Rosie asked, laughing.

"Yeah, maybe. Or maybe I'm looking for a spot where you and Justin can escape to."

"What?"

"Don't act like you haven't seen Justin looking at you with goo-goo eyes."

"I mean, no, he doesn't like me like that. No way he does."

"He does, and I'm pretty sure Riley doesn't like it. How does it feel to have two boys willing to fight for you?"

"Okay, now you're totally crazy. Riley is my best friend. We just have a super strong friendship."

"Wow, Rosie, for being a so-called intellect, you are really dumb." With a chuckle, she left the room to shower.

Justin and Riley don't like me, Rosie thought, but the more she pondered it, the more her own feelings for the two came into question. Distracting herself from the crazy idea, Rosie texted Glenda to let her know she was at the school with Riley. Glenda responded, saying she already knew and was happy she could keep an eye on Riley and was proud of her.

When Eleanor returned from the bathroom, Rosie showered, where her thoughts swarmed. It wasn't until she got soap in her eyes when she snapped from her emotional confusion to worry about other things. What would tomorrow be like? When would she find out her class schedule? Could she hang out and talk to Riley even though they were on different teams?

When Rosie entered the dark room, she heard Eleanor already breathing deep and slow in her bed. As she ambled to the left side of the room and climbed into her own bed, Rosie thought about Justin and Riley again. *Ridiculous. They are my friends.* Before her thoughts could continue, her eyes were closed, and she was fast asleep.

Chapter Seven

Walking around the lake, Rosie dug her toes in the sand and enjoyed the warmth of the small grains on the soles of her feet. She watched the descending sun. She had never seen a sunset so beautiful and full of so many different colors.

"Rosie! Hey, come on, we are going to hike this way and see what's over the next peak!" Justin yelled down to her.

Rosie slipped on her gym shoes and jogged to Justin, Eleanor, and Riley. When she reached where Justin had yelled for her to come to, the three were already gone.

"Guys! Where are you?" she yelled, but the only response was the distant echoes of her own voice. She climbed the rocky path on the side of the mountain, hoping to catch up with them while avoiding different obstacles. Finally, at the top, a short distance away was a grouping of stacked boulders. *Maybe they are walking through the rocks.*

She hurried down the side of the mountain and to the valley of boulders. The sun had set, and only a small glow remained for her to use to navigate. Amazed at how the boulders were stacked, she realized she was now lost in the maze. The glow had faded, and the only light source she had now was the brightness of the moon. With the shadows playing tricks on her eyes, Rosie panicked, thinking she saw movement. She was halfway into the valley when her gaze landed on a particularly tall, odd-shaped boulder. *Is that a glow coming from behind it?* Her steps were soft as clouds moved to cover the moon. Blackness fell over the valley, but it allowed Rosie to view the clear glow.

Rain fell, and she had difficulty maneuvering the tight spaces and squeezes through rock formations. As Rosie lifted her foot to step through a particularly small hole in a boulder, she found herself caught. Her body fell forward, and she slammed into the ground. Rolling onto her back, Rosie looked up and saw the top boulder wobble. Her heart stopped, and she held her breath, but it was no use. The damage was done. The boulder wobbled one more time and finally tipped over. It was falling fast, right toward her face. Rosie instinctively threw up her hands in front of her and opened her mouth to scream, but her voice didn't come out. Instead, a horn noise sounded, and the boulder plummeted and hit her; it didn't hurt. Instead, it was as if the boulder had liquefied into water.

Rosie sprung upright in her bed, dazed and confused. The lights had been flicked on, and both Rosie and Eleanor sat in a puddle, covering their ears from the air horns and whistles sounding in their room.

"Let's go! Let's go! Let's go! Move it!" Paige yelled at the two still in bed. The girl raised the horn and pressed it so hard Rosie thought her eardrums would burst. "Up! You have fifteen minutes to get dressed and downstairs to the Valtic common room!" And, as quickly as she had woken them up, she was gone.

Rosie and Eleanor had no idea what was happening, but they threw on the first clothes they found and rushed to the lobby and through the portrait hole leading to the Valtic team living room. They immediately spotted the other Valtic freshman front and center. They navigated up, and Rosie found herself standing next to Justin.

"Pretty funny, right?" Justin said, leaning over.

"Yeah, if you think getting waterboarded is fun."

As the rest of the Valtic members entered, low whispers and conversations started.

"Why are we here?" Eleanor asked Rosie.

She shrugged, and as Rosie was about to reply, she realized Garrett had squeezed between the two.

"We are here, ladies, so you can try out for the prestigious honor of being on the Valtic Illumination team."

"The what?" Eleanor asked.

"Illumination team. The Illumination Games are tasks that involve academics, sports, and other intense, dangerous challenges that the Illumination team competes in."

"What kind of challenges?" Eleanor asked with an eagerness.

"Well, I was on the team last year, and one of the challenges was navigating the desert at night, and we had to make it back to the school."

"That doesn't sound too dangerous."

"You didn't let me finish. One by one, team members were picked off. I had no idea where they were going. I was freaked out. I thought a serial killer was plucking us off one at a time. I forced myself to completely transform and use my wolf skills to my advantage, and luckily, I made it back to the school without disappearing. Unfortunately, a Surgent team member made it there first, and we lost that round. That's why I'm pumped we have three humans this year!"

"Do you think we could make the team?"

"Definitely! It's important to have a diverse range of personalities and supernatural and natural beings on the team. We never know what tasks we'll have to complete, so it is a good thing to have people of every background and who have a lot of different experiences. Now that we have you guys, we can find the right groove and actually come out as the top team this year!"

"Wow, so do you think you could put in a good word for me?" Eleanor asked with a little flirtatious tone.

"Ha, I wish. I have to try out like everyone else. The team captain is the only one who doesn't have to, and they are in charge of choosing the rest of the team, at least that is how it is done in Valtic."

"Who's the team captain?" Rosie asked.

Before Garrett could respond, a tall, surly girl stepped onto one of the ottomans, front and center so everyone could see and hear her. "Listen up, newbies! My name is June, and I am the team captain for the Valtic Illumination team. I am aware we have three new humans who have never heard of the Illumination Games until today. This won't be like any other sport you've played before. These games will test your brains, brawn, powers, and anything else you've got. They are exhausting physically, mentally, and emotionally. Only the strongest will make the team. Got it?"

"Jeez, June, going a little overkill, aren't you?" Garrett said.

"Garrett! This isn't a joke. These three have never seen or endured the type of rigor the games hold." She shook her head and addressed the entire group again. "As most of you know, we haven't won the games in over ten years. This year that changes. Today, every single person in Valtic is trying out."

A few groans erupted.

"Quiet! Aren't you sick and tired of being the laughingstock here? Aren't you sick and tired of losing? Everyone is trying out, and everyone is giving their all, and I will know if you are slacking." As she said "slacking," her eyes shone bright yellow.

She was a werewolf and apparently could tell a person's personal effort, Rosie thought. *Maybe by smelling their fear and attitude?*

"Alright, I'm giving everyone thirty minutes to eat breakfast and move to the field. If you are late, there will be consequences. Dismissed!" June stepped down and left the room while the other students talked excitedly with a few whines here and there.

"So yeah, that's June," Garrett said, trying to stifle a laugh.

"She seems very determined," Justin replied with a smile. "Alright, shall we go for a bite before we have to undergo the wrath of June?"

"Definitely," Rosie said.

Garrett led them to the portrait hole where they had entered the party last night.

Rosie stepped through and was awestruck at the then-pitch-black room she had walked through the night before. Rosie now saw a grand, multilevel library with books covering every wall. Rosie spun to take in every inch. Bookcases lined the walls, and different sizes of tables for groups to study together or for individuals to spread out all their materials filled the room. She approached a bookcase and read the shelves. Books, old but sturdy, begged to be read. She could have sworn she had fallen into the library in *Beauty and the Beast*, only this library was better.

"Crazy, huh? Each team has their own library and study rooms, and every dorm has study rooms too. We also have an enormous library open to every student. It's like they want us to learn here," Garrett said.

"How is this even possible? The room is so big, but we are in a restrictive-sized mountain."

"An enchantment was placed on the room. Actually, a lot of the rooms. It is as large as it needs to be without restricting itself to the size of the mountain. Don't worry, you'll learn all of this soon, but for now, let's eat some grub." Garrett steered her to the dining hall.

Before her foot stepped through the portrait hole, she glanced once more at the room she would be exploring the most.

"Okay, you three, things are a little different today than last night. Today and for the majority of your time here, you will take a slip of paper hanging on the kitchen wall and fill out what you want to eat." Garrett grabbed the small slip of paper and wrote, *scrambled eggs and bacon*. "Then you'll put the paper against the wall." As he did, the wall absorbed the slip, and almost immediately, a plate with eggs and bacon materialized for Garrett to grab.

"Wow! We can order anything?" Eleanor asked.

"Anything your heart desires," Garrett told her with a wink.

The three grabbed their slips and wrote their requests and waited for their meals to appear. Rosie grabbed her omelet, Justin took his pancakes, and Eleanor almost dropped her protein shake.

"Eleanor, you can't be serious! You can't only be eating that," Garrett said with wide eyes.

"Of course not. I plan on having a piece of your bacon." She took a bite of one of his slices and smirked.

As the four were about to take their seats, Rosie spotted Riley sitting with Gunner and Flynn. "Hey, Garrett, we can sit anywhere, right? We don't have assigned tables like last night, do we?"

"They aren't assigned, but it is normal to sit with your team. I guess you could sit anywhere you like."

With that reassurance, Rosie started toward Riley, not caring if the others followed her. She needed to talk to her best friend. "Hey, can I join you?" Rosie regarded Riley with sincerity in her eyes.

"Yeah, definitely." He made room for her next to him, but the smile that spread across his face vanished as soon as Justin sat on her other side.

Once the newcomers were situated and had their food in front of them, Rosie turned to Riley. "Crazy night, huh? What did you guys do after dinner? I tried to grab your attention in the dorm, but you were deep in conversation."

"Yeah, sorry about that. I was talking with the guys about the Surgent common area."

"Riley, I hope you aren't about to divulge any Surgent secrets," the vampire girl, Martha Ash, said as she glided up and sat with the group.

"No, obviously not, Martha. Just sharing the basics of last night."

"Good," she said as she scrutinized Rosie and pursed her lips in disgust.

"Anyway," Riley went on, "we checked out our common area and met everyone in Surgent and started to plan for the Illumination Games. Do you guys have tryouts today?"

"Riley!" Flynn yelled as he punched him in the arm.

"What? Oh, shoot." He leaned in and whispered to Rosie, "I forgot I wasn't supposed to tell you that."

She smiled. "Don't worry. Your secret, like all of them, is safe with me."

"Yeah, don't worry about it. We have tryouts today too. I'm sure everyone does, so no need for it to be a secret," Justin chimed in, and Rosie noticed Riley gave Justin a death glare and stiffly got up.

"We have to go," Riley stated, and the Surgent students all left, leaving Rosie and Justin sitting alone at the table.

"You guys about ready?" Eleanor asked behind them.

With the loss of her appetite, Rosie pushed away her plate and stood. "Yeah, let's go."

The four of them, with Garrett leading the way through the different passages and tunnels, meandered to the field for tryouts.

The books Rosie had read on the plane were not lying. She was sweating from the beating sun, and the humidity from the outgoing and incoming monsoons reminded her of Illinois. June bossily divided the Valtic members on the field according to supernatural and plain, ordinary being. She ranked each member in each group based on overall skill level. Since June had no idea what Rosie, Justin, and Eleanor were capable of, she ranked them last, since they were only natural humans.

Rosie was excited to finally witness every supernatural group perform their powers and changes. It was apparent, Rosie noted, that June wanted to cover her bases when selecting a team. She wanted someone from each group with a plethora of skills. *I guess the Illumination Games are very erratic and peculiar,* Rosie thought.

Rosie was brought out of inner dialogue when her ears rang.

She looked around, and her gaze finally landed on June who had blown into a shiny whistle with all of her might.

"Who the hell gave her a whistle?" Garrett whispered.

"Alright, we'll start with the physical exam. To be perfectly honest, I will only be really paying attention to those gifted with enhanced abilities."

"Seriously?" a girl yelled, annoyed.

"Yes, seriously. It isn't a mystery that vampires, werewolves, and some shifters will perform better on land physical tasks. Don't worry, Blossom, you'll have a chance to shine. Tryouts will last all day."

Groans were audible from almost every Valtic student on the field.

"Yes, all day! So everyone will be good in at least one thing or another, but my job is to find the best people in each area. Got it?"

"Sir, yes, sir!" Garrett yelled back with a military salute.

* * *

June wasn't joking when she said tryouts would last all day. All morning, Rosie and the other Valtic members were subjected to rigorous physical tests, just as she had been the day before, but today it seemed pointless to her to be put through this testing again. It was clear the vampires, werewolves, and a lot of the shifters were much faster, stronger, and beat out everyone else in most of the physical tasks. The one thing they failed at was swimming. The few mermaids in Valtic completely obliterated everyone. They swam circles around those still freestyling across a small section of the lake and would pull down people for fun.

After lunch, everyone was blindfolded, taken into the desert and forced to find their way back to school. Almost every fairy returned first by communicating with the wild and plant life. June tested all the witches and wizards, giving them complex spells to perform. She even had them jump off the highest landing on the ropes course and attempt to produce a spell that kept them from landing in the net below at full speed. Only one person completed the task—Penelope, who Garrett said was one of the best witches in the school. Rosie could see why June was the team captain; she effectively challenged the others. Finally, after everyone reconvened in the Valtic study room after June allowed them to have a quick dinner, they began the intelligence portion of the tryout.

Rosie and Justin answered the most questions in general knowledge, normal subjects and topics, and random facts during the trivia battle. While they lacked basic knowledge of supernatural creatures and powers, they made up for it in their extensive knowledge of normal human affairs and current events, with the exception of Eleanor who won in the subject of pop culture.

Everyone returned to the Valtic living room at eight o'clock and threw themselves onto the couches, armchairs, and floor in total exhaustion.

"Okay, good effort, everyone!" June said as she stood on the ottoman to grab attention as well as view everyone. "I will have the team roster posted on the bulletin board by eight-thirty, so if you think you had a fighting chance, stay put and wait for it."

"Ugh, do you guys want some dessert? I can't move much, but I could go for a milkshake right now," Garrett said.

"Yeah, why not?" Rosie agreed, and a group of Valtic

members shambled into the dining room.

Rosie was happy she had decided to grab something sweet because right away she saw Riley. She started toward him, and, as she grew closer, she wanted to talk to him more than ever, even though he was upset and talking heatedly to Gunner and Flynn.

"Riley, what's wrong?" she asked as she put her hand on his shoulder.

"None of the protectors made the Illumination team in Surgent. They said the only thing we bring to the table is normal human knowledge, and they can study up on that if need be."

"I'm sorry, Riley. That sucks, but at least you can cheer with me on the sideline?"

"You didn't make your team either?"

"Well, we don't know yet, but I'm sure I didn't if you didn't make yours. You're the best athlete I know."

"Yeah, well, that was before I was competing against vampires and mer-people."

"True, but it is only a game, right? Don't worry about it and have some ice cream with us." She gestured to the other Valtics chowing down sweets, but the only person Riley saw was Justin.

"No thanks," he replied coldly and turned back to Gunner and Flynn.

"Riley, wait." She grabbed his hand.

He yanked it away with one swift jerk and turned back to her, his face red and nostrils flared. "Rosie. This isn't just some stupid game to me. Like always, you brush off my feelings if I'm mad. Just let me have my pity party and leave me alone." With the words still fresh in the air and all heads in the dining room turned to the two, Riley huffed away, leaving Rosie with tears building in her eyes.

Gunner smirked at her as he turned and followed Riley through the Surgent painting.

"Hey, are you okay?" Justin asked softly, placing a warm hand on her shoulder.

Rosie wiped her eyes before a tear could fall. "Yeah, I'm good. Hey, did you get me an ice cream?" she asked with a small grin.

He handed her a vanilla/chocolate dipped cone.

The others had already finished, so Rosie nibbled on hers as they headed to the Valtic living room to find out if any of them had made the Valtic Illumination team.

As they passed through the Valtic library to the common room, Rosie admired all the books again—one of the few things that brought her joy. She had seen more of the library during the trivia battle but couldn't actually explore. *Tomorrow. Tomorrow, I will find the perfect reading corner and have a stack of books to look through.*

When they stepped into the Valtic living room, they heard roars of laughter and cheers while others yelled in anger.

"I guess the list was posted," Garrett said, and he pushed through the crowd for a better look.

Justin and Eleanor followed, but Rosie was exhausted. She sunk herself into the squishiest couch available and waited for the others to join her.

"Yes!" Rosie heard Justin yell.

Good, she thought, *at least one human made an Illumination team.*

"Rosie! You have to come look!"

"You made the team. Good job!" she yelled from her

comfortable position.

"No, seriously! Come here!"

Rosie peeled herself off the leather couch and traipsed through the swarming and hovering students to the bulletin board, and her gaze landed on her name.

"Rosie, we both made the team!"

"What? How? Why?" She couldn't wrap her head around why they'd put two humans with no supernatural abilities on the team.

"Congrats, guys. I didn't make it, but I am actually very happy for you," Eleanor said.

"Shoot, Eleanor. I'm sorry," Rosie told her.

"It's okay. I'll help you behind the scenes. I can feed you all my useless information about the latest reality TV and which celebrity got a nose job."

Rosie chuckled. "I will definitely take you up on that."

"Don't worry about it, Eleanor," Garrett said. "At least now you can cheer me on."

Eleanor playfully glared at him and punched him in the arm. "Yeah, right. I'll only be cheering on my girl Rosie."

"Ooo, ouch!" Justin laughed.

"Alright, alright. Settle down, everyone," June announced from her ottoman. "The team has been posted, and it is final. Please do not come crying to me about injustice. Now, for you freshmen, I am posting a schedule of the mandatory activities you will participate in tomorrow. Good night, everyone. And for goodness sake, go shower! You all smell!"

Rosie approached the posted schedule and memorized every detail.

8:00 a.m. – Tour of school and campus grounds

10:00 a.m. – Meeting with assigned guidance counselor

11:30 a.m. – Lunch
12:00 p.m. – Trip to town for school supplies
3:00 p.m. – Head back to campus
3:30 p.m. – Club meetings and signups
4:00 p.m. – Dorm meeting
4:30 p.m. – Team meeting
5:00 p.m. – Illumination team meeting
5:30 p.m. – Rules and guidelines meeting
6:00 p.m. – Dinner

"Going to be another long day tomorrow, huh?" Justin swung his arm around her.

"Looks like it. But, hey, I bet we will make our schedules and actually see what classes we can take."

With the common room clearing, Rosie decided to head to her room to shower and go to bed. Her muscles ached, and she had to force herself to keep her eyes open. Her head hit her pillow, and she was ready for her dreams to take over her consciousness. She had drifted off and didn't even hear Eleanor enter the room and slip into her bed.

* * *

Rosie had ventured back, deep into the maze of boulders. The glow behind the large rock guided and enticed her. She was getting closer, closer than she had been before. She was going to uncover where the light was coming from. She inched forward, but, as she turned the corner, everything shook. Boulders spilled over, and the ground underneath Rosie cracked. She panicked as a boulder hurled down the side of the mountain. She turned and ran, but the rock was gaining speed. It was right on her heels, and she felt a throbbing pain shoot up her leg.

She sat upright in bed, her phone buzzing uncontrollably, but the pain in her leg from the boulder crushing it was still present. Throwing off her comforter, she squealed. An adult bark scorpion sat in her bed. Using her phone, she slapped it off, and, as it hit the ground, she smashed it with her gym shoe. She placed the shoe on top of the crushed body, too tired to dispose of the arachnid.

Her phone buzzed again, and the light from the screen pierced her eyes. Riley was calling her. "Hello?" she answered in a panicked voice, still coming off her adrenaline rush.

"Rosie, are you okay? Can you meet me? Please?"

"What? Uh, yeah."

"Okay, meet me in the lobby in five." Riley disconnected the call before Rosie could object.

She slipped on her shoes and quietly left the room, trying her hardest not to wake Eleanor. Wide awake and ascending the staircase, she wondered what Riley wanted. She opened the lobby door and saw him waiting on the couch.

He seemed small slumped over. He raised his head and ambled to her. He reached for her shoulders and looked deep into her eyes. "Rosie, I'm so sorry. I freaked out, and I shouldn't have. I am just so sorry. Please forgive me."

"Of course, Riley. We have been friends for years, and we've been through so much together. How could I not? You just needed someone to vent to and take your anger out on. I was the closest person for that." She paused, and he took the opportunity to pull her in. She hugged him back and, still while hugging him, said, "Anyway, now that we are good, I wanted to tell you I made the Valtic Illumination team."

He pulled away. "Really? You made it?"

"Um, yes, really I made it."

Riley looked disappointed.

"It's stupid, really. I mean, Justin and I are only there for the brain work."

"Wait, Justin made the team too?"

"Um, yes."

"Huh, for as smart as you are, you obviously are completely blind to how I feel. I don't think the Illumination Games are a joke, and clearly, you do, so you must think I'm a joke."

"No, Riley, not at all."

He was already walking to the bookcase entrance.

"Riley, wait! Please! I'm sorry!" Rosie's heart sank, but she still reached for him and grabbed his hand and spun him toward her. "Riley, stop it. I'm sorry if I made you feel bad. It wasn't on purpose. Please just don't leave like this."

He brought his gaze to meet hers and, without saying a word, pulled her in.

Rosie thought he was going to hug her again, but he lifted her chin so she could stare directly into his eyes then kissed her. Completely caught off guard, she pulled away, and before she could ask him what was going on, he was already walking down the staircase, leaving her in the dark lobby alone and confused.

Chapter Eight

The entire night, Rosie tossed and turned, unable to go back to sleep. She was still wide awake when her alarm went off in the morning, and she was the first one in the Valtic living room. She took the opportunity with most of the school still asleep to venture around.

Alone in the vast room, she wandered up the stairs, down the hallways, and into hidden corners, scanning the books she would delve into during her time at the school. As she ascended the stairs to the third level and squeezed between bookshelves, she spotted something unique on the far wall. She moved closer. She couldn't put her finger on it, but something seemed different about this case compared to all the others she had seen. The books were placed in the correct order, no books jutted out, and no leaning candlesticks or holders could be levers to open a door. When Rosie thought she had inspected the bookcase long enough; she turned to leave but clumsily stepped on one of her untied shoelaces. Sitting on the ground and rubbing her elbow that had caught her fall, she decided her fun was over and to go to breakfast. She placed her hands on the bookcase shelves to help her stand.

"Huh?" she said and lowered her head, so her cheek touched the floor. A lack of dust an inch away from the bottom of the case raised suspicion, and when she bent lower, she discovered the case sat a mere two centimeters higher than the others. Excitement engulfed her, and she sprang up. She skimmed the edges of the bookcase, trying to find an opening, and found a barely visible lifted bump. She pressed it, and the case creaked open inward. Her cheeks ached from smiling, and she entered the room. The bookcase swung shut behind her, locking her in total darkness.

She grazed the textured wall for some sort of switch. "Where are the lights—"

Candles ignited and illuminated the room.

She turned in a circle and beheld the cozy room filled with a soft sofa, plush pillows, a small desk and chair, and an extra table to hold all the books she wanted to read. *It's perfect,* she thought. She had the most perfect place to escape to.

"Rosie! Rosie!" she heard Eleanor and Justin yelling in the distance.

"Shoot! Lights," she said and exited the room while the candles whirled and dimmed. She closed the bookcase and climbed to the third-floor railing, looking at the two. "Coming down, guys!" She descended the stairs, hoping no one else would ever find the secret spot. "Hey, are you two ready for breakfast and a full day of fun!" she half said, and half screamed at them. Nervous and caught off guard, she felt out of place and weird for hiding the room, but something in her told her to keep it a secret.

"Uh, yeah. What were you doing up there?" Eleanor asked suspiciously.

"Oh, I got up early, so I decided to explore the space. I can't wait to come here and read."

"Same. We have to find a cool spot to claim as our own and make it our study-slash-hang-area," Justin said.

"Oh, uh, yeah, of course," Rosie replied.

As the three entered the dining hall, she noticed Riley. She had to talk to him after last night's kiss, but when she started toward him, he turned his back and sped away.

"Seriously?" she muttered. She returned to her friends—*my real friends*—placed her breakfast order and sat in a huff. She jammed her fork so hard into her eggs, the tines bent.

"Are you okay?" Eleanor asked.

"Yeah, fine. Riley and I had another disagreement."

"What about?" Justin asked, interested.

"It's nothing. Let's talk about something else. What do you think today will be like? I can't wait to check out the school and town, and I especially can't wait to make my schedule."

"Definitely. I bet we will be in all the same classes! Sorry, Eleanor."

"Don't be. I want to be in normal high school classes with an emphasis on protector training."

"I wonder if the other students—the supernatural ones— will also be doing the tour and whatnot with us," Rosie asked.

And like magic, Garrett arrived with the answer. "Yes, they will be joining you." He set his plate right next to Eleanor's. "Any student in eighth grade and below has restricted access to the campus and grounds. A lot of the younger students live at home, nearby, with a few actually staying on the grounds. But it looks like you are learning about that now." He pointed to the head table where Professor Shay, Walker, and Manger stood in front of the landing.

"All freshman students, please gather around," Professor

Shay announced to the dining hall.

"Have fun. I'll see you all later," Garrett told the group.

"But what will you do all day without us?" Eleanor asked.

"Well, I do have other friends." He smiled as he stood then sat at another table with a group of very attractive and very handsy Haply girls.

Rosie could hear Eleanor grit her teeth, and when she swung around to walk toward the other freshmen, her hair whipped Rosie in the face.

"Ah!" she gasped through the strands.

"Oh, shoot. Sorry, Rosie!"

The three chuckled and joined the others, and it was only by accident that Rosie ended up standing by Riley. She was so angry with him still. *Why would he treat me like this? Aren't we supposed to be best friends? Why did he kiss me and run? I mean, who does that?* Wanting to prove a point to him, she kept her head straight and refused to acknowledge him, but he slightly brushed one of his hands on hers. Was it intentional, she wondered?

"Okay, everyone," Professor Shay started. "Professor Walker and Professor Manger will be your guides for the day. You should have all seen the itinerary posted in your respective living rooms. We will divide the teams into two groups. Surgent and Haply, you will be touring with Professor Walker, and Valtic and Astive, you'll be with Professor Manger. I'll meet back here with you later today."

Professor Shay exited the room, and the students turned toward the two Professors.

"Okay, Surgent and Haply students, please follow me," Professor Walker said in her kind but strong voice.

The group separated, and Rosie caught Riley looking at her

hand then at her face from the corner of her eye. She refused to acknowledge him and instead drew both hands in front of her, clasping them.

Finally, Riley walked away.

Rosie sighed in relief. She didn't know what was going on with their friendship. They were only on day three at the new school, and already they were becoming more and more distant.

"Okay, everyone," Professor Manger said in a glum, uninterested voice. "Let's go." He turned his enormous body toward the door that led to the staircase that would lead them to the lobby.

Once Rosie entered the staircase though, Professor Manger was leading everyone downstairs, not up. "These are the different classrooms," Manger said, lifting his hand as a guide for the students. "Obviously, we are in a mountain, so the farther down the mountain, the wider the base, the more classrooms. Elementary students have class on the topmost classroom level, then middle school students, and the next level has specified classrooms for each type of creature. Most of you know this, seeing that you have had classes here." He glared at Rosie, Eleanor, Justin, and Reid—the other protector who had been placed in Astive—and with an annoyed sigh and eye roll, he turned and descended more steps. "You all, however, have not had permission thus far to enter here."

He reached the door, and rather than whisper some sort of password like Professor Walker had, he made a fist, and with the ring on his middle finger facing the knob, he moved it forward so the two touched. Then, like someone pulled him from the other side of the door, he disappeared behind it.

The students turned to one another, confused, and after ten

seconds of waiting for Professor Manger to reappear, they heard his voice calling from the other side of the door. "What are you waiting for? You saw what I did. Now hurry up."

One by one, the students held their stones to the doorknob and were pulled through.

Reid, being curious and trying to understand how the door worked, tried to twist open the doorknob rather than propel through it. The doorknob only jiggled, as if it was locked. He tried it again. "Ouch!" he bellowed and flew backward, shaking his now-smoking hand.

"What happened?" Eleanor asked, grabbing the injury.

Reid's cheeks instantly flushed. "Oh, uh, nothing. It burned me. I'm fine." He put his hurt hand behind his back and used the other, with his Astive ring on it, to move through the door.

Rosie and Eleanor followed, with only a few other students following them.

"Finally. Okay, let's keep moving." Professor Manger continued on down the hallway.

Rosie's head swiveled, trying to take in all the rooms and their beauty. This floor of the school was unlike any other. Rather than the dim hallways and stone walls, natural light filled the floor. And, instead of having to enter through doors to discover what was on the other side, the walls were made of glass so she could look into each room. Actually, all the walls were made of glass. Rosie could see into every classroom down the hallway.

The rooms on one side of the hallway faced into the desert and mountainside. It was bright and warm and had a wonderful view. The rooms on the other side were darker, a lot more ominous, and when Rosie leaned closer to that side of the hallway, goosebumps rose on her arms and legs, and a shiver went down her spine. Most of the rooms on that side had the mountain as a wall, but halfway down the hallway, glass replaced it in one room. And on the other side of the glass was an opening that dove deeper into the mountain. Rosie stopped and leaned closer to view the end of the opening but couldn't.

"I wonder what the tunnel leads to," Rosie whispered to Justin, Eleanor, and Reid.

"How do you know it's a tunnel?" Reid whispered back. "Couldn't it be a cave?"

"Yes, I suppose it could be, but where is the excitement and imagination in that?"

Professor Manger gave short, bland explanations that according to intelligence level, transformation factor, supernatural abilities, and personality, each student would be placed into different classrooms and subjects. He smiled when he told the group the smarter they are, the farther down the hallway they'd go.

The group had reached the end of the hallway, which was the only wall in the hallway that was neither glass nor mountain.

Professor Manger pushed open the painting hanging on the wall and held onto the painting's frame, and when he had stepped over the threshold, he disappeared downward.

"Woah," Eleanor said, and the group surrounded themselves around the open painting.

They saw a faint light below, and then total darkness consumed the opening again.

"There's a slide." Justin laughed, and he hopped through and down, and the faint light from a door below was visible again.

Everyone else followed Justin's cue, hitting the landing below and heading outside to await further instruction.

"Okay," Professor Manger said. "This is one of the many paths you will discover on campus. It branches and turns and loops, so you better learn what path leads where."

"Can we have or make a map of campus and the grounds?" Reid asked.

"A map? Are you sure you're in Astive because that is the stupidest question I've ever heard."

Reid faltered and dropped his gaze. "Oh, uh, I just thought that—"

"You just thought, what? That a map would be useful? Now tell me, Norm—"

The supernatural students let out low, quiet chuckles.

"What would happen if you lost this so-called map? Let's say someone who has no idea about our kind or about any supernatural beings finds it. Do they think it is a cool hiking trail or a map to buried treasure, like the tales of the Superstition Mountains? And they decide to use the map and come here, and we are exposed. We are later taken, tested, and dissected. Now, Norm, do you still think it is a good idea to have hundreds of maps distributed to clumsy, irresponsible students for safekeeping?"

Reid's face had completely reddened. He shook his head no but mustered the courage to talk again. "No, sir, but my name is Reid, not Norm."

The supernatural students chuckled again, and Professor Manger smiled and bent so he was face to face with Reid. "Yeah, sure, whatever you say, Norm." He turned and traversed the path with the other students following him.

"You okay?" Eleanor asked Reid.

"Yeah, I'm fine. It was a stupid question."

"No, it wasn't. I was hoping there was some sort of map myself. I guess you'll have to help me remember where everything is and where to go."

Reid smiled at her, his face resuming its normal shade. "Yes, I suppose I will."

The four natural students caught up with the rest of the group to catch what Professor Manger was showing them.

"Alright, so this path here would take you to the rope courses and other training sites and facilities. This middle path will lead you to the amphitheater, and, if you follow me down this path"—Professor Manger took a sharp turn right—"we will go to the training field next to the school."

During the tour, the group walked all over the mountain-side, learning about the different paths and how the largest part of the lake was in front of the school but it disseminated into rivers and streams and led to other sizable bodies of water. Rosie was a bit relieved. At no time during the tour did she run into a maze of boulders and rocks.

Professor Manger finally led them back to the school through the front entrance. "A lot of these rooms are teacher and administrative offices, conference rooms, and meeting rooms for any parents who want to visit their child." Professor Manger led the group down the hallway, and when they reached the last room, Rosie learned it was a doctor's office with a staff of three people. "This is Doctor Geller, Nurse Chaplin, and Nurse Howard. If at any time you are sick, hurt, or dying, suck it up. You shouldn't bother them unless it's serious."

The three laughed, and Doctor Geller stepped forward,

patting the professor's shoulder. "That's not necessary, Professor Manger. Students, I recognize some of you already, while I also see some new faces. Please come visit us if you need help. We are here to heal."

The doctor stepped backward, and Professor Manger rolled his eyes. "Okay, let's move out, everyone."

The group went down the secret ground staircase, and rather than return to the dining room, they went through a passage in a different direction. This new hallway was longer than the dining room one, and when they finally reached the end, it connected to a staircase leading up. They hiked up the steps, and the group finally reached the top, which held another door. This door was gigantic, and consumed almost the entire wall.

Professor Manger whispered into the doorknob, and it swung open. Behind it was an immaculate library and greenhouse, like the plants and books were living in synchrony. One side of the vast room contained mostly books and tables to read at with a few plants scattered here and there, and the other side was the opposite. Plants and vines intertwined over a few books, but the greenery extended outward into a glass room filled with sunlight. Right in the middle was the sweet spot. A lot of books and a lot of plants met simultaneously, and while the books had a rich, musky smell, the plants had a fresh, sweet one.

"Wow," Rosie muttered.

"This is the library," Professor Manager said. "You all have your own study halls, but, if you need further information, this is where you would come. If you exit out the greenhouse and take the path to the highest peak, you will find the observatory. Okay, let's go."

But Rosie didn't want to go. She wanted to explore the library and see what books were there and not in her own Valtic library. She had no say in the matter though, and the group headed back. She surveyed the glass-dome ceiling that covered the greenhouse side and inhaled one last breath of musty books and fresh greenery. *Best smell ever,* she thought.

The group reached the dining hall at 9:45 and sat at one of the tables. They had returned before Professor Walker and the other teams. Rosie was jealous of this. Professor Walker had definitely taken the Haply and Surgent students on a proper tour and had given them a thorough explanation of where everything was and what things were used for.

"I know what you're thinking," Justin whispered to her. "Don't worry. We will go explore the school and get a better look at everything later." He smiled and winked at her, and a warmness in her stomach grew.

"Okay, good. Want to see if Eleanor and Reid want to come? Maybe we can have Garrett be our guide?"

"I don't think Eleanor would like having two of her suitors in such close proximity."

Rosie smiled and suppressed a laugh.

Eleanor turned to the two talking so close and quiet. "Hey, what are you two going on about?"

"Oh nothing," Justin said. "Just discussing what social aspects the school has to offer."

The other group entered the room. Professor Walker took her spot next to Professor Manger in front of the head table, and the other two teams shuffled to their seats.

"Alright, everyone," Professor Walker said. "You will now meet with your assigned guidance counselor for approximately twenty minutes to review your schedule, ask any questions, or discuss any concerns. I will be distributing folders to each of you that contain your schedule, who your guidance counselor is, where to find them, your meeting time, your book and supplies list, and a map of the grounds."

Reid glowered at Professor Manger who was watching him with a huge devious grin.

"Are you kidding me?" Reid whispered. "He just wanted to make me look like an idiot in front of everyone for no reason?" Reid was fuming, his face burning red, but when Eleanor put her hand on his, it settled back to normal fast.

Professor Walker continued, "There is also a King's Preparatory handbook filled with rules and guidelines that you must adhere to, and a few other things that will provide you with useful information. Please try not to lose or damage these papers. However, if by some chance you do, the papers will register that they are no longer with their rightful owner and will turn into ordinary printer paper." Professor Walker's eyes illuminated blue, and the folders floated to each student and landed with grace on the table.

Butterflies swarmed in Rosie's stomach as she grabbed the black leather-bound portfolio and opened it. On the right-hand side of the folder were notepads and a pen sitting in a holder ready for her to take detailed notes and write everything she deemed important. On the left-hand side were three stacked folder flaps, each filled with the papers Professor Walker had discussed before. She flipped through them until she found her schedule, but before she could pull it out, Professor Walker spoke again.

"I suggest some of you stop looking at everything in your folder and instead hurry to meet your guidance counselor. Some of your meetings start"—she checked her watch—"well, now."

Rosie found the little note card indicating who her guidance counselor was and when she was supposed to meet them.

"We both have Doctor Witam, right?" Justin asked her.

"Yes, and shoot. My meeting is now. I'll catch up with you later." Rosie sprang up and hustled to the door that would lead her up the stone staircase, through the trap door, and down the never-ending hallway to Doctor Witam's office.

She knocked on the door, and the same warm, gentle voice she remembered from her testing day answered her. "Come in, Rosie."

Rosie entered and sat opposite Doctor Witam. "Sorry I'm late. I didn't realize my meeting started right now."

"That's all right. The professors like to keep the students on their toes and moving. It is part of the nature here. We always have to be wary and have our eyes open for any potential threat that could either hurt us or expose us."

"I completely understand."

"So, I assume you haven't had the opportunity to check your schedule yet?"

"Not yet." Rosie shuffled through her folder to retrieve it. She removed it, and a smile appeared on her face as she scanned the list.

"Happy with your classes?"

"Unbelievably happy. I have never been able to take these types of classes before, only read books about them or found free online lectures."

"Shall we review your schedule? Just so you are aware of the days and times and what is expected of you during these courses?"

"Absolutely."

"Alright." Doctor Witam read his own copy of her schedule. "Most of your classes will be with the college students, while few will be with your own classmates. And you will even have some classes that are just the teacher, you, and Justin. You will also be in a lot more classes than your peers. A lot more is expected of you, Rosie, do you understand?"

Rosie nodded.

"Your schedule will be set up like a student attending college, so you will have classes on alternating days, and you also have a lot of free periods to catch up on school work and study. It is imperative that you use any resources you can to ensure proper time management. Got it?"

"Yes." Rosie studied her schedule, taking in every detail she was given.

Time	Monday	Tuesday	Wednesday	Thursday	Friday
8	History Prof. Shav Rm. 512	Psychology/ Sociology Dr. Witam Rm. 521	History Prof. Shav Rm. 512	Psychology/ Sociology Dr. Witam Rm. 521	History Prof. Shav Rm. 512
9	Chemistry Prof. Aster Rm. 524	Greek/Latin Prof. Tassi Rm. 528	Chemistry Prof. Aster Rm. 524	Greek/Latin Prof. Tassi Rm. 528	Chemistry Prof. Aster Rm. 524
10			Chemistry Lab Prof. Aster Rm. 524		
11	Number Theory Prof. Walker Rm. 536		Number Theory Prof. Walker Rm. 536		Number Theory Prof. Walker Rm. 536
12	Lunch	Lunch	Lunch	Lunch	Counseling Dr. Witam Office 3
1	Cryptology Prof. Walker Rm. 536	Adv. Nature Prof. Riff 518	Cryptology Prof. Walker Rm. 536	Adv. Nature Prof. Riff 518	Cryptology Prof. Walker Rm. 536
2					
3					
4					
5	Combat Training Prof. Manger Practice Field	Combat Training Prof. Manger Practice Field	Combat Training Prof. Manger Practice Field	Combat Training Prof. Manger Practice Field	Combat Training Prof. Manger Practice Field
6	Dinner	Dinner	Dinner	Dinner	Dinner
6:30	Illumination Games Practice	Illumination Games Practice	Illumination Games Practice	Illumination Games Practice	Illumination Games Practice

Rosie finally looked up at a smiling Doctor Witam.

"It is a jam-packed schedule, but from my understanding, you have a photographic memory, correct?" he asked.

"I don't think of it as photographic. Yes, I can remember everything I have seen and read, but only because I have trained my mind. I use my eyes to scan and take in the information presented, and once I've processed and understood it, I store it in a file in a specified place. My brain is like a storage facility, so whenever I need to access information, I locate the storage room with the filing cabinet containing the file with the particular information I need."

"Very interesting. You can also speed read?"

"Yes, thankfully that will help with the amount of work I'll have," she said, laughing.

"Yes, it will indeed. And every Friday during lunch, you and I will meet here for a confidential counseling session. We want every student at King's Preparatory to feel welcomed and to be successful. Are you okay with that? Do you want to go over anything?"

"I completely understand that need, and I don't think so. Also, I don't want to take up any more of your time. I know each student only gets twenty minutes to go over their schedules."

"For the other students, yes, their sessions are only twenty minutes. But, for you and Justin, you have forty-five minutes. Plus, this year, you two are the only students I am mentoring, rather than the entire Valtic team, so please tell me whatever is on your mind and ask any questions you may have."

"Okay, well, first, the school is a kindergarten through year two of college establishment, but I haven't really seen anyone from the lower grades around."

"You want to know if people really send their five-year-old children to a boarding school?"

"Well, yes."

"A lot of families have moved to the surrounding area and drop off and pick up their kids every day, but a few students stay in the dorm, like the older students, but are on a floor with a lot of supervision, and they follow a strict routine to help them adjust to life away from home. Their parents normally video call in the evenings, and each student is assigned a tutor-slash-nanny until they are in sixth grade.

The students in grades kindergarten to fifth eat breakfast at nine, lunch at eleven, and dinner at five, so you will rarely cross paths with them. There will be opportunities if you like, however, to tutor and teach them, but your schedule is full as it is. Maybe next year. Actually, I hate to say it, but other than the Illumination Games, you won't be able to participate in a lot of extracurriculars. Still, if you mosey around the club fair and find something you want to do and think you can handle another thing on your plate, you can definitely join or give it a try. Sorry to sound pessimistic, but I am trying to give you all the information you need to be successful. What other questions do you have for me? And remember, it doesn't have to be school-related. We can talk about other things if you wish."

"Well, this is stupid to talk to you about, but ..." Rosie paused, unsure if she should continue.

"Rosie, nothing you say is stupid. I am here to help you navigate any obstacles keeping you from being your best self. Now tell me, what's on your mind?"

"I guess I'll spit it out. Ever since I've been put on Valtic and away from Riley—my best friend from home—I feel guilty for having a good time without him. Or when I do try to talk to him and include him in things, he gets mad or standoffish, and a few days ago, we were two peas in a pod, and now we couldn't be more distant."

"Ah, teenage hormones."

"What?"

"Rosie, you have one of the highest IQs I have ever seen. You are truly a brilliant and bright pupil, but you are also developing emotionally and physically as a fourteen-year-old girl, and Riley is a teenage boy. Your hormones and emotions are on a roller coaster ride right now, and until you're done with puberty, and you have some more life experiences under your belt, you will be dealing with uncomfortable, awkward situations. Thankfully, you will learn more about your mind and those of others and various behaviors in my class."

"Okay," Rosie said, embarrassed discussing her hormones with her school counselor. "I guess it doesn't help being in a heightened environment."

"That, it doesn't." He leaned closer. "What other concerns do you have?"

"My next question isn't related to the previous questions. I have been thinking about it since Friday though."

"Okay, shoot."

"How often does James Kingsley come around?"

"Interesting question but not that surprising. All natural humans want to learn more about James Kingsley as soon as they learn he is immortal. But, seeing that he is the premier, James typically comes around once a semester to check in. There have been a few years, however, where he has come to give a lecture to select students. We are normally never aware when he is coming unless it is for a lecture or meeting. He likes to pop in."

"Alright, so if I see him cruising down the hallway, give him a high five and some finger guns?" She made the gesture to Doctor Witam, who was very amused by this.

"Ha, I would love to see James's reaction to that."

Rosie's cheeks flushed, her gaze shifted downward, and a small embarrassed smile took over. "I have no idea why I just did that," she said, laughing into her hands, but she was still thinking about the elusive James Kingsley.

"It's quite all right. I am happy you are comfortable around me to let loose and talk freely. Is there anything else you want to discuss?"

Rosie took a second and finally spoke to Doctor Witam with a serious face and tone. "One more thing. Earlier, during our school tour, Professor Manger referred to Reid as Norm. Do you know what that means?"

Doctor Witam exhaled a long, deep sigh. "Yes, unfortunately. I do, and I'll have to talk to Professor Shay about it."

"Oh, no, I didn't mean to get anyone in trouble."

"No, Rosie. You did the right thing by bringing this up. Calling Reid *Norm* was very offensive, and the fact a professor called him that in front of your classmates is extremely unprofessional."

"What does it mean?"

"Norm is short for normal. Which I am sure to you doesn't sound like a bad thing, but here, it is basically calling someone boring, not special."

"I understand. We're at a school where supernatural humans reign, and for a mere normal human to be accepted is like a slap in the face to those who have been here for years. They think us natural students are lowering the prestige of the school?"

"Unfortunately, a few might think that, Rosie, but it isn't true. Professor Manger was very discriminatory to Reid and everyone else like him. I am deeply sorry you had to witness and hear such things being said to your classmate and, effectively, you."

"Well, I plan on showing Professor Manger how great I am. We will see if he has the same mindset by the end of the year."

"Excellent attitude. Now, is there anything else you want to ask?"

"No, I think that's all."

"Okay, now I definitely don't want to forget to give this to you." Doctor Witam removed an envelope from a desk drawer and handed it to Rosie. "This is your stipend for the month with some extra money to cover books, uniforms, supplies, and any other school costs."

Rosie peeked inside the envelope. "Doctor Witam, this is three thousand dollars. Is this a mistake?"

"What? Do you need more? Because I am sure we can arrange that with Professor Shay if you don't think it will be enough to cover your costs?"

"Oh no, it is more than okay. Thank you." She smiled and carefully put the envelope in the folder, securing it so it couldn't fall out.

"If you have no other questions, Rosie, you can head back to the dining room and send up Justin please."

"Of course. Thank you again, Doctor Witam." Rosie practically skipped to the dining room.

"How did it go?" Justin asked, pressing her for details.

"Go find out yourself. Doctor Witam wants you in his office."

"Oh, okay!" Justin excitedly stood, collected his folder and rushed from the dining hall.

Rosie searched but didn't see Eleanor or Reid. She sat to go through her folder, consumed by its contents. First, she grabbed her schedule and map of the school and highlighted the quickest routes to each class. It was especially helpful when the provided pen changed to a different color by whispering the desired color into the tip. With her color-coded map and schedule, she moved on to her shopping list.

Entailed on the list were all the books she was required to have for each class, what school uniform attire she was required to purchase and wear to class each day, her Valtic Illumination team uniform slip, supplies she would need for specific classes—such as a lab coat and goggles for her chemistry lab—and all the normal school supplies she would need as well. Now she knew why she was given so much money. All her required items would be at least $1,500. She would have to practice responsible money management as she had before, she thought.

She started to remove the school handbook when a hand landed on her shoulder. She didn't even need to look up to know who it was.

"Hey. Can we talk? Please," Riley pleaded.

Rosie remained silent, debating whether she wanted to speak to him.

"Hey, leave her alone!" Justin had entered the room and strode toward them.

Eleanor entered next and rushed over as well, seeing what was about to erupt.

Riley turned to Justin, face reddened and fists clenched. "This doesn't involve you, Justin."

"Actually, it does, seeing that she's my friend. Do you know what that word means, Riley? F-R-I-E-N-D."

"Back off, Justin!"

"Woah, woah, boys," Eleanor said, putting herself between them. "Everyone needs to calm down. Riley, just give Rosie some space. I'm sure when she is ready to talk to you, she will."

Riley's eyes pleaded with Rosie, but she remained silent.

His eyes filled with pain, and he walked away.

"Are you okay?" Justin sat next to Rosie and put an arm around her.

"Yeah, I'm okay. How did your meeting go?" Rosie asked, wanting to change the subject and lighten the mood.

"Great! Want to compare schedules?"

"Hey, I want in!" Eleanor chimed.

The three put their schedules side by side. Rosie and Justin had the exact same schedule, while Eleanor only shared three classes with them.

"At least we start off each day with each other and get to fight each other in combat training," Eleanor said while the other two laughed.

As students filed into the dining hall and sat for lunch, Rosie overheard what other students said about their schedules and what shops they were excited to visit once in town.

When the last plate zoomed through the wall and into the kitchen, Professor Shay held her position in the front of the room. "Alright, students. It is time to journey into town and purchase what you need for your classes. Please be smart about what you buy, and refer to page twenty-two in your school handbook for a complete list of prohibited items on school grounds. Okay, outside to the buses you go!"

"Buses, huh? I guess this isn't so different from regular school after all," Justin joked, but the buses were far from the normal yellow school bus.

These were the crème de la crème of transportation buses. Sleek black leather armchairs, two per side, lined the interior of the bus with enough legroom for even the tallest student—an athletic stallion shifter named Duke in Astive—to sit comfortably. Cherry wood trim surrounded the various features, like the above headlights and air vents, windows, and doors. Finally, there were sizable overhead storage areas so students would have more than enough room for all the purchases made in town.

"Not at all like the gum-riddled, feet-smelling, vomit-yellow school bus I had to ride back home," Eleanor said, nudging Justin in the arm and sitting next to Reid.

"Yep, I take back everything I said before," Justin told himself, looking in awe and sitting next to Rosie.

Justin, Eleanor, and Reid discussed their guidance counselor sessions while Rosie drifted away from the conversation and stared out the window. The buses had picked them up near the base of the mountain, where they had gotten to by using a portrait passageway in each team study room that led them out of a cactus or boulder, depending on what team they were on. The buses drove through a dirt road—yet somehow still staying pristine and clean—through the mountain dips and valleys, and finally merging onto a paved path.

Rosie took in every detail of the gorgeous desert landscape, but she didn't have a long time to admire it, because soon enough, the buses parked in front of a grand arch with a sign hanging in the middle that read KINGSTOWN.

"I guess James Kingsley has literally founded every single supernatural place," Rosie said jokingly.

"He really has." Justin leaned closer to her for a better look out the window. "He was the one who developed these safe havens for supernatural creatures and taught them to blend in if any natural humans found them."

"Where did you learn that?"

"Doctor Witam told me in our meeting this morning."

The students exited the bus and entered the small town,

which could be described as a modern western town. While there were paved roads, there were also dirt side roads where one could secure a horse while they shopped in the wooden storefronts. Signs above each store reminded her of the ones from old John Wayne movies, and she even saw a saloon with batwing doors.

"Where to first?" Justin asked.

"Let's hold off on getting the books until it is the last thing we need. I don't want to have to carry those bad boys from store to store," Eleanor said.

"Excellent idea. Well, how about uniforms?"

The group agreed and entered a shop with a hanging sign that read, TAILOR. They were the first students to enter the shop, but Rosie thought that only the natural students would have to be fitted for full uniforms. The other students already had theirs from the previous year or only needed to purchase a few new items.

"Hello?" Rosie called into the seemingly empty store. "Hello?"

"One second, one second," an old, croaky voice replied from behind the front counter, and a moment later, a small toadlike woman emerged. Her gray hair was pulled back into a tight bun, tugging her forehead so much it was the only place on her body where wrinkles weren't visible. Her eyes were magnified under her thick spectacles, and her lips were oily and greasy, probably from the extra-moisture lip balm. Brown spots and freckles from being in the sun in her youth covered her face and arms, and the way her skin sagged and rumpled left what hung from her neck to wobble whenever she moved or spoke. "Yes, yes, how can I help?"

"Yes, ma'am, we need some uniforms," Reid told her.

"Of course, of course. The new school year is already about to begin again. Oh, how time flies. I have been running this store for the last fifty years. Good ones at that." She paused, staring into nothingness, reminiscing.

"Ah-em," Reid coughed.

"Oh …" The small woman regarded the group. "Alright, boys first." She grabbed Justin's and Reid's hands. "This way. Here, try this on." She threw clothes on hangers to the boys. "Hm, too big. Hm, that'll be too small," the little woman muttered to herself. "Alright, let's try this. Stand up here." She pushed the two boys onto a platform and, like an Olympic ribbon dancer, waved her tape measure all over the two uncomfortable bodies. After a few minutes passed, the strange tailor announced, "Okay, boys, down. Ladies, your turn."

The two girls were laughing at the scene before them, but once it was their turn, they realized they shouldn't have been gawking and giggling, since they were about to endure the same embarrassment.

"Up you go, pretties. Alright, let's measure you now. Oh, you are both so lovely. Let me have a closer look." She snagged Rosie's and Eleanor's hands and pulled them down so she could view their faces. "Oh, yes, yes, yes. Quite lovely girls. Well, you two are lucky, because I have new material and fabric and styles for the uniforms this year, and somehow all the other students think they are either too good to use me or don't believe they need me. Well, you two will receive all my new stuff, and they will be sorry. Okay, all done! Now, you four come back in an hour, and I will have everything you need."

"Wait, Mrs. Uh …" Rosie started but realized she didn't

know the woman's name.

"Ms. Peiler, my dear. Yes, do you need anything else?"

"Yes, do you also make the Illumination team uniforms?"

"My dear, I haven't in a long time, but it would be an honor! I think I still have the pattern somewhere though. Oh! This will be oodles of fun! Tell me, my dear, what team do you belong to, and I will have it ready for you."

"Valtic. And Justin will need one as well. Also for Valtic," she said, pointing to him and handing her the Valtic Illumination team slip.

"Yes, yes, I will have these ready, and you both will look fabulous for the games! Okay, go now, let me work!"

The four left the tailor, and, as soon as they had walked far enough away from the store, they burst into laughter.

"She's awesome!" Justin chuckled.

"I'm happy we could make her day," Rosie said. "Where to next?"

"Kids are dropping off stuff at the bus and going back for more, so maybe we just find our books now?" Reid commented.

But before anyone could answer, Rosie recognized Cordelia Blackwater—a mermaid freshman also in Astive—approach Reid. "Hi, Reid."

"Oh, hey, Cordelia."

"Is it all right if we talk?"

"Uh yeah. Oh, Cordelia, I don't know if you have been properly introduced to my friends. This is Rosie, Justin, and Eleanor."

The three Valtic students waved and smiled at her.

"A pleasure to meet you all." Her gaze fell back to Reid. "Listen, I wanted to apologize for earlier when Professor

Manger was poking fun at you during the tour. You are a part of the Astive team, and natural or supernatural, we shouldn't have laughed. Can we make it up to you?" Cordelia gestured to a handful of Astive freshmen waving and smiling to the group.

"Yeah sure. I have to grab my books first, though."

"Don't worry about that. We already got them for you. Kind of like one big team apology."

"Wow, thanks. How did you know what classes I was in though?"

"Please, we are in Astive. We know all." She tapped her finger to her head and laughed. "Plus, we snuck a glance at your booklist. Anyway, want to join us for some milkshakes at the ice cream parlor in the general store? We want to pick your brain on natural human behavior and life."

"Yeah." Reid turned to Rosie, Justin, and Eleanor. "I'll catch up with you guys later?"

"Yeah, we'll find you later, bud," Justin said.

Reid turned, smiling at the other Astive students, who embraced him with back pats and handshakes.

"Shall we, ladies?" Justin asked the two girls, proffering his bent arms to escort them.

"We shall." Rosie giggled as she hooked her arm in his.

The three walked down the street filled with the other freshman students who had already bought their books.

"At least we will have the store to ourselves," Justin whispered to Rosie. "We won't have to fight through anyone to a genre or have a rough time getting the store owner's attention."

They found the bookstore at the end of the road and were transfixed when they entered. Books laid everywhere, not only in cases and on shelves but inlaid in the floor, in the walls, floating in the air—they literally were everywhere.

"Uh, hello?" Rosie called out, raising her voice a little to ensure someone would respond to her even if they were in the back of the store. "Hello?" she voiced again as she had done with Ms. Peiler.

Books falling sounded, and a flustered man, sweating and red-faced, emerged from a room behind the checkout desk. "Yes, yes, I hear you! More students, I presume?"

"Yes, sir." Justin stood straighter like he wanted to show his respect and that even though they were students and kids, they should be respected in return.

"What books do you need? Do you have your lists?"

The three handed them to him.

"Alright, you first, young lady." He pointed to Eleanor. "Follow me."

She did as he instructed, and they left Rosie and Justin alone to explore the shelves and displays.

"Rosie, come check this out!"

She found Justin near the front of the store eyeing a grandiose display of books plastered with James Kingsley's face.

"I hope he isn't as vain as he appears," Rosie muttered, grabbing one of James Kingsley's books titled, *The Best Life: A James Kingsley Autobiography*. She set down the book and noticed Justin wearing a confused look. "What?"

He shook his head and focused again on the various books, reading their descriptions.

Rosie wandered off again, this time heading to the back, more hidden corners of the store. She found what she didn't even realize she was looking for—a dusty, old, untouched bookshelf filled with thick pages and unread stories, some even having cobwebs sticking to them. The best books, Rosie thought, were those others had disregarded for her to care for and enjoy. She grabbed one of the books off the shelf and blew a light breath to remove the dust—*The Natural and Supernatural Being* by Emerson Stiles. If the title reflected what Rosie thought, she couldn't wait to read it, but, as she cracked open its spine, Justin popped his head around the corner.

"Hey, I got the owner to grab our books for us. Let's head to the general store for some school supplies."

"Yeah, definitely." Rosie slipped the book back on the shelf and, while moving through the maze of books toward the checkout counter, a gliding shadow caught her eye. She whipped herself around, and a bookcase moved to the right. She heard a click. *Of course, there are hidden doors here,* she thought.

"Rosie! Come on!" Justin yelled.

She knew she had to come back another time to see who the mysterious figure watching her was. She turned to walk to the checkout counter but startled backward.

The bookstore owner stood inches from her, looking down. He placed his hand on her shoulder—"This way"—and guided her to the checkout. The shop owner rushed through the checkout process and shoved their books in the cloth bags adorned with the store's name and logo. "Alright, alright, thank you for shopping. Come back again." He rushed the three out the door and slammed it closed.

"Was it me, or was he a bit inhospitable?" Rosie asked, peering through the shop window at the man who was rushing through the door behind the counter.

"Yeah, maybe he was swamped with backorders and opening boxes," Justin speculated, walking with Eleanor toward the bus to drop off their books.

Rosie caught up and decided Justin had to be right. There had to be a reasonable explanation for the man's attitude. The three walked back into town and entered the general store, which was bustling with students, old and new.

"Finally. I was wondering when you three would show up," Garrett said, leaning against a team apparel display at the entrance of the store.

The store intrigued Rosie, because, while the outside looked like an old western general store, the inside reminded her very much of a retail store. The interior kept to the same western-town design, but the size of the store was bigger than the outside, which Rosie presumed had a similar growth enchantment upon it, and the items that stocked the shelves were more modern.

The wooden shelves held products like notebooks and pens, but they weren't the typical things one would purchase at a back-to-school sale. Rosie, inspecting the notebooks, noticed they were leather-bound, filled with textured ivory homemade paper, and various designs and gemstones were sewn into the cover. They were stunning. Everything in the store was as such—homemade, beautiful, decorative, and expensive. Rosie was the most thankful for having her stipend so she could buy these wonderful things she would never have afforded before.

"Garrett, how many notebooks do you think I need?"

"Notebooks? Why not just use a laptop?" Justin said.

"No laptops allowed in classes or for any schoolwork. We must protect the secrecy of the school and supernatural life. What if you accidentally uploaded a school assignment? Everything they had built to keep us a secret would be compromised."

"Why not use an enchantment, like our cellphones?" Eleanor asked.

"Because while the administration has accepted a few modern ways, they still like to keep it old school. You have to use these notebooks, because, like the maps, they are enchanted, so if lost or stolen or seen by a natural human, they will be blank notebooks that will also appear damaged. They will most likely be discarded, and our campus kept a secret still," Garrett explained.

"I still don't see the big deal if we make an active effort to keep the school a secret," Justin said.

"Because of human error, natural or not. Plus, there are viruses and hackers who could infiltrate your computer and access confidential files when not on campus. There is no reason to risk it."

"Okay, I get it. My hand is going to fall off with all the writing we will be doing though."

"Suck it up, Fent. You can always go to the potion part of the store for a joint relief capsule so as you write, your hand will flow without any pain. Anyway, Rosie, you only need to buy a few notebooks."

"But Justin and I have so many classes. One notebook won't be enough pages."

"True, but all you have to do is buy extra pages. It's a lot cheaper than buying multiple leather-bound notebooks. You just lace in new pages once you are done taking notes on a subject. You can file the old pages or toss them properly if you want. I recommend getting one of the thicker three-inch notebooks that come with ribbon dividers. That way, you only have to buy one notebook that has various sections for each subject. But, looking at the number of books you and Justin were dragging back to the bus, I recommend you buy at least two."

Rosie considered it and searched through the gorgeous display of gems and weaved leather.

He smirked and turned to Eleanor. "Anything you need help finding?"

"I think I can manage." She turned her back toward him, ensuring her hair did a little flip and walked to where Reid was standing, examining two types of pens.

Garrett's face contorted, and he asked Rosie, "What's with her? And why is she all over that other protector?" But before Rosie could answer him, he joined them, clearly intruding by Eleanor's facial expression which got even tighter when Garrett and Reid lightly punched each other and laughed.

"I don't think that's going how Eleanor wanted it to," Justin said, leaning over and chuckling.

"No, not at all," Rosie replied, joining the laughter.

It took almost an hour to find everything Rosie needed for her classes and semester. She and Justin walked around and gathered their supplies with the help of a wooden, self-moving cart to carry their items.

Then Eleanor whisked Rosie away to look at the cute, little section of homemade jewelry, clothing, and bags, convincing her to buy few dresses, blouses, skirts, pants, and five new pairs of shoes to update her wardrobe and an adorable black leather enchanted backpack that could store all of her belongings for each class without being heavy or bulky. Eleanor also forced Rosie to the cosmetics counter where the beauty consultant personalized an entire set of makeup and skincare products for the two girls from scratch.

"Are you girls done yet? Can we please grab our uniforms so we have some time to get a quick ice cream before heading back to school?" Justin suggested

"Yeah, I'm in," Garrett said.

"Why?" Eleanor retorted. "You don't have a uniform you need to pick up." She was still mad about him not being jealous, at least that she could see, at her getting closer to Reid.

"Yeah, but then I can see how good you look in a King's Prep uniform." He winked at her, and she couldn't hide the smile growing across her face.

"I'm going to look around here a bit more," Reid told them, understanding Garrett's alpha attitude and desire for Eleanor.

"Okay. Do you want us to grab your uniform for you?" Eleanor asked, understanding his slight disappointment.

"No, don't worry about it. I want to try it on anyway, you know? Make sure it fits."

"Okay, we will meet you on the bus."

As the foursome was leaving the general store, Rosie stopped to look at a bulletin board posted by the exit relaying information regarding town meetings and events, but she caught something else. As a corner of a help-wanted flyer flipped up, Rosie saw a grainy black and white photo of a middle-aged woman. In bright red letters above the photo was the word, MISSING. Rosie read the description, curious as to what information the flyer gave, but she was interrupted by a familiar voice.

"Sad, huh?" Katherine said.

"Did you know her?" Rosie asked, noticing the tears

forming in Katherine's eyes.

"Yes. Massie was a regular blood donor. I liked being paired with her. She would tell me about her kids and husband and how she dreamed about owning her own bed and breakfast one day and open it up to the supernatural community. She was one of the very few donors who didn't have their memory wiped, but I'm sure that policy will be changed if they find her." Katherine broke her eye contact with the flyer and faced Rosie. "I think Professor Shay is nervous someone has captured her and is torturing her to reveal our whereabouts. She was supposed to check in with the school three weeks ago, but no one has seen or heard from her." Katherine gave Rosie a grim look and walked away.

Rosie looked back at the flyer. She had assumed having supernatural creatures protect her would create a safe environment, free from crimes like this, but maybe she had it wrong. Maybe being around these creatures heightened danger rather than eradicated it.

"You coming, Rosie?" Justin shouted from outside, and Rosie left the bulletin to rejoin her friends.

The four entered the seamstress's lair—as Justin liked to call it—and the small, round woman came bounding out to greet them.

"Oh, my lovelies! I have your uniforms, and I must say it is some of my best work yet! Wait here a second while I finish up with my other clients."

A few moments later, Riley, Flynn, and Gunner exited a few dressing rooms, holding garment bags.

Rosie froze and drew her attention to something on the other side of the room. She could sense Riley staring at the back of her head, but she refused to turn around until the bell on the door rang, indicating they had paid and exited.

"Okay, now come with me! Come with me!" Ms. Peiler shouted as she grabbed Rosie and Eleanor's hands and dragged them into separate changing rooms. When she reappeared in the lobby, she gave Garrett a long glance over. "I'm sorry, lad. Do you need to be fitted for a uniform as well?"

"No thank you, ma'am. I already have my uniforms for the year. Got them from Julius's Western Wear."

"Julius's! Ha! What a hack! Come, my dear, let me show you the other young gentleman's clothes, and surely you will want one from here."

Garrett began to protest, but for a smaller, older woman, she still had her strength and dragged him across the room to where Justin was changing.

"All set, my dear? Please, I need you to show your friend your superior uniform. Come on out, deary."

"Uh, yeah, okay. One second," Justin replied and finally stepped from the dressing room.

"Oh! Yes! Gorgeous! How do you like it?"

"Strangely, I love it. It looked like a stiff suit at first, but it feels comfortable." Justin admired his reflection in the mirror, marveling the black slacks, white button-up, black and white striped tie, and black blazer with the King's Preparatory emblem stitched on the breast.

"Dang, yeah, you look good. Okay, tailor lady. Measure me."

"She can also do your Illumination uniform!" Rosie called out from her dressing room.

"Young ladies, please let me examine you!" the seamstress yelled at them.

Rosie and Eleanor stepped out at the same time, and both

Justin and Garrett couldn't help but look at them from head to toe. Both girls wore black knee-high socks, black pleated skirts that hit just above the knees, white button-ups with the same tie Justin was wearing, and a form-fitting women's blazer also with the school's emblem on the left breast.

"These fit amazing. Thank you so much, Ms. Peiler," Eleanor said and gave the old woman a hug, catching her off guard.

"Oh, uh yes, dear. I am happy you like them," she replied, returning Eleanor's gratitude.

The group tried on the rest of their pieces while Ms. Peiler took Garrett's measurements and told him she would have his items delivered later that day to the school.

After writing their names on their overstuffed garment bags and hanging them in a closet on the bus, they went to enjoy the last thirty minutes of the trip. They strolled around the small town with ice cream cones in one hand and became involved discussing the town and school.

"Garrett, are there opportunities for us to leave campus on our own and come here if we need to?" Rosie asked, thinking about the bookstore.

"Oh yeah, they do weekend trips, or, if you need to come during the week, you can arrange for a driver or ask a classmate to take you."

While the others continued to talk, Rosie walked alongside them, deciding when she would return to find the best reading material. She was brought out of her thoughts when she felt a vibration on her chest. She touched it and realized it was her necklace causing the sensation.

Justin and Eleanor also grabbed their stones.

"They're calling you back to the bus," Garrett reassured

the three freshmen who worried their King's Preparatory jewelry was malfunctioning. "Come on, I'll walk you back and hopefully can hitch a ride. Mine left an hour ago."

Garrett had no trouble talking his way onto the freshman bus, and when they reached the campus, Rosie checked out the clubs available but decided she shouldn't join anything until she knew what her classes were like and if she would even have any free time after Illumination practice. Then her dorm meeting was the same. The only difference was all the human students were in attendance, not just the freshmen. With a few more people taking up the lobby of the dorm, it was easier for her to avoid Riley and his constant, desperate stares. She couldn't have been happier when that meeting disbursed, and she could join the other Valtic students for their team meeting and Illumination meeting. Finally, at 5:45, her stomach rumbled and ached with hunger.

Professor Shay was almost done reviewing the rules and guidelines for the year, but one thing she spoke of made Rosie perk up. "Also, students, please be aware of your surroundings and the restricted areas. For instance, the boulder maze is off limits unless used for a school-sanctioned event and has been properly inspected, as well as the mud grounds, since it has been infested with sand trout.

Also, no trespassing in the graveyard. We are not going to disrespect the dead by doing nonsense séances and black rituals. I don't want to have another visit from a loogaroo. Do not tempt the wildlife that dwells and roams freely on and around campus. This is as much their home as it is ours—especially the other humanoids. If school property is destroyed because a student is terrorizing the sasquatch community or calling on the dark watchers, you will be expelled faster than you can say chupacabra.

Finally, it is with a sad heart I announce that one of our faithful human volunteers was found dead in her home early this morning. Local police are investigating, and it looks like an isolated matter. Let us pause for a moment of silence for Massie Touble." After a few seconds, Professor Shay continued. "Now, please let us enjoy dinner and adjourn to your respective team rooms and dorms for a well-rested night before a very busy first day." Professor Shay waved her hands and, like the previous nights, plates and food glided through the air and landed in front of every student.

Rosie was too interested in Professor Shay's mentioning of the boulder maze to eat though. She turned to Garrett, who was stuffing his mouth with mashed potatoes. "Garrett, what is that boulder maze Professor Shay had mentioned?"

"That?" he muttered before swallowing a mouthful. "It's a decent distance from campus. There is this opening over a ridge filled with stacked boulders and rocks. From what I gather, it isn't safe because a boulder or rock stack could fall with the slightest vibration and crush or kill a person. Why? Wanna go? Because I have always wanted to go check it out."

"No, I was just curious. Thanks." She resumed picking around her food, only managing to eat a few bites and wondering whether she would have the same dream she had been having since hearing about the school. She pondered this all the way through dinner and while walking to her dorm room. She opted out of hanging around the Valtic team living room or her dorm lobby. She wanted to go to her dorm, organize her supplies for the first day of class and retire early.

With Eleanor not in the room to discuss her boy troubles, Rosie could accomplish what she wanted to be done quickly while her mind drifted. She packed her backpack with the required textbooks, notebooks, and supplies for her first day of classes. She went to her closet to unpack her uniforms that were still in their garment bags and lay out what she planned to wear on her first day, but, as she put her hand on the zipper to unload everything Ms. Peiler made, the door to her dorm room opened.

"Hey," Eleanor said, entering the room. "Did you get your stuff ready for tomorrow?"

"Almost. How was the hang out after dinner?"

"Eh, it was okay. June was hoarding Justin and trying to further explain the Illumination Games to him. Like, he wouldn't understand it? He is one of the smartest people in the school, alongside you. And Garrett, Katherine, and I hung out and talked more about supernatural stuff. Nothing crazy. I guess that Massie lady was a blood donor for the vampires. Katherine seemed pretty upset. After comforting her best I could, I thought about what you were doing and thought it would be smart to head back and prepare myself. Do you mind helping me organize my books, and do you want to fill out our planners together?"

"Yeah, but can you help me pick out what to wear tomorrow?"

"I already have that figured out! I am wearing my black and white plaid jumper dress with a white short-sleeve blouse, cross tie, and white Mary-Jane heels, and you will wear your black and white plaid skirt, white long-sleeve button-up and regular tie but loosened. You'll also wear your black knee highs with your black and white oxfords."

"Alrighty then," Rosie said, smiling that Eleanor cared enough to select her outfit for her. "Are you really going to wear heels all day though, Eleanor?"

"Of course, beauty is pain. Also, Katherine asked one of her friends to help put a spell on all my shoes so my feet won't hurt or be sore, no matter how long I wear them for."

The two burst out laughing, because, while they both originally thought that magic could only be used to cure cancer or end world hunger, it was instead being used for assisting women in the fashion world, specifically footwear. It wasn't long before both girls climbed into their beds and said their goodnights.

"Hey, Eleanor? Do you think tomorrow will be weird? Are we about to get into something way over our heads?"

"Definitely. But think about how fun and exciting it'll be." Eleanor ended her statement by turning over.

Rosie stared at the ceiling, both nervous and excited and wondering what tomorrow would be like, and before she could even realize it, her eyes were closed, and she had drifted off.

Chapter Nine

Standing on top of a boulder, Rosie surveyed her surroundings.

"Come on, Rosie! You said you would do it!" Garrett yelled at her from the other side of the boulder maze.

"Yeah, Rosie. Do it!" Justin and Eleanor chimed in.

She contemplated all the paths she could take—how she could jump from one rock to another and dismount next to the group—but, as she weighed her decision, a faint glow behind a strange rock caught her eye. She hopped and flew over the spacious gaps between boulders. She was on a mount right next to the one she desired to inspect, but, as she bounded into the air, the rocks moved farther apart, and she was falling. Falling into darkness.

Rosie's head laid hard on her pillow, and when her alarm went off at five a.m., she knew it was only a dream. She wasn't falling, and she was in her room. She turned off her alarm and swung her legs out of bed while hearing Eleanor grunt in disapproval of how early she was waking up.

Rosie tiptoed to the bathroom and flipped on the lights. Her eyes stung at the brightness, but, as soon as she turned on the water, and the room filled with steam, her body eased and relaxed under the hot water. She began to wash her hair but noticed something was different. As she ran her fingers across her head and through her hair, it felt thinner and shorter. Wiping water out of her eyes, she inspected her hands. Thick clumps of strands covered them, as well as the shower floor. Panic rushed through her veins. She wrapped a towel around her, rushed to the mirror and wiped off the built-up fog. Staring back at her was a girl with choppy, poorly cut shoulder-length hair.

"Oh my gosh," she muttered and grazed her hair again. She was in disbelief that her long, thick hair had somehow been taken away from her. Confused and hurt, tears filled her eyes, and through the mist, something else appeared in the mirror. Leaning closer, she saw another face had replaced hers—a girl named Olive, a witch in Surgent—and stared directly back at Rosie, wearing a devious grin. The reflection lifted two fingers and moved them together and apart, mimicking a pair of scissors. "Snip, snip," she said and cackled before fading in the mirror.

She was behind this? She was the reason why her hair was hacked off? Rosie was in disbelief that someone she had never had a real interaction with could do something so cruel to her and for no reason. At least she didn't think she had done anything … then it came to her. Riley. That had to be why, she thought. Had he told them she was difficult and angry with him? *Ugh, why did this have to happen?* She allowed herself to have two more minutes to cry and be mad over her new hairstyle, and then she did what she knew how to do—pick herself up and persevere. She got back in the shower and finished washing her hair and returned to the bedroom to get ready for the day.

The lights were on inside, and Eleanor was getting out of bed when she spied Rosie and let out a shocking gasp. "What happened to your hair?" She rushed over and grabbed it. "Did you try to cut it yourself? Rosie, you shouldn't have!"

"I didn't." She gestured to her pillow where more of her hair lay.

"What do you mean you didn't? Then what in the world happened?"

"It seems a few of the Surgent girls are upset about my disagreement with Riley, and they have taken it upon themselves to punish me."

"Punish you? Are you kidding? What girls?"

"Well, there's one in particular. Olive, the freshman witch in Surgent. From what I guess, she used some sort of spell to cut my hair while I slept. Oh well, what's done is done."

"What a bitch! When I see her in the dining hall, I am going to—"

"Eleanor, don't. It's only hair. It'll grow back. Leave it alone. The best revenge is to show her I don't care what she does to me. I am more worried that people can cast spells on us even when we aren't in the same vicinity as them. We need to talk to a Valtic witch or wizard about a protection spell of some sort."

"Well, I think I already know how this happened." Eleanor pointed to Rosie's necklace sitting on her desk. "You can't take it off. That's what'll protect you from small spells, I assume."

Rosie walked over and put on the necklace. "You're right. It was stupid to take it off in the first place."

The rest of the morning, Eleanor helped Rosie apply her makeup and curl her hair in an attempt to hide the uneven, choppy lengths. Finally, the two removed the outfits Eleanor had selected them to wear on their first day from their garment bags. When the two girls put on their outfits, they were shocked. Like Rosie's hair, both outfits—in fact, all of their garments—had been altered.

"What a stupid spell," Eleanor announced. "What? All she could manage and muster to do was cut our clothes? Well, and your hair?"

"Maybe her magic isn't strong enough yet? Or this could've happened on the bus? We did leave our stuff unattended."

"Well, jokes on them, because with my legs and your butt, we look hot."

"Agreed," Rosie said, chuckling, "but I'd rather not have a professor reprimand me on the first day of school for breaking the dress code."

"What dress code? All Professor Shay told us in the rules and guidelines meeting yesterday was we had to wear a school uniform during school hours and classes. Nowhere does it state a required length of our skirts or dresses or shirts or how we can make the uniforms we wear our own. If anything, I see an amazing opportunity to show this school who we really are."

The two grabbed their book bags and strutted from the room with smiles on their faces. With the confidence they had filling them up, they strode to the lobby and into the Valtic living room.

The room was sparse, seeing that it was only seven and classes didn't start for another hour, but Justin and a few others were in the room already. "Woah, what happened to your hair?" he asked Rosie, and after she explained, he responded, "I am going to kill that guy."

"No, don't. I'm okay. Like I told Eleanor, it's just hair."

"Uh, I might be able to help," an older Valtic team member interjected. "Hi, I'm Cami, and I can fix your hair with a simple growth spell if you want."

"Oh my gosh, Cami. That would be amazing," Eleanor said, giving the senior girl a hug.

"Sure, no problem. What was your original length?"

"Actually, can you make the choppy pieces grow to match the other length? That way they are all even?"

"Yeah, definitely." Cami lifted her right hand while clenching her Valtic necklace. As her eyes turned a bright blue, Rosie stopped her.

"Wait, can you do one more thing?" She leaned in close to Cami and whispered in her ear.

"I can definitely do that." She smirked and resumed her stance and murmuring.

The spell took hold of her hair, and she felt it grow and change color. Her brown hair was now rich and had a tinge of ruby red glistening in it.

"Woah," Justin said, eyes wide and in complete awe.

Everyone in the room watched as well.

"Dang, Rosie, I didn't think it was possible, but you got hotter," Eleanor chimed in.

When Cami came out of her trance, she broke into a smile. "Your friend is right. You look great." She led Rosie to a hanging mirror.

"Wow, thank you, Cami. I love it." Rosie fondled her new smooth strands.

"No problem. Were you guys about to go eat breakfast?"

"Yeah."

"Wait a little longer. Until the dining hall is full and can witness your grand entrance."

A smile spread across Rosie's face. She would have never thought about doing that, but Cami was right. What better way to get revenge than by owning her new look and flaunting it to Olive?

The Valtic living room filled with students, all in awe at Rosie.

At 7:45, when she knew the dining hall was almost at capacity, she gathered her backpack and straightened her outfit. "Ready to go?" Rosie asked her friends.

"Hey guys, what's happening—" Garrett had said entering the room. "Wow, Eleanor, you look great in that uniform!"

Eleanor blushed and quickly turned the conversation. "I know I do, but have you seen Rosie?"

"Woah! Nice hair. Definitely in the Valtic spirit."

"You can thank Riley for it," Justin said and told Garrett what had happened.

"What is with that guy? He is becoming an issue I would like to deal with."

"No, Garrett. Let's eat some food before class," Eleanor said and linked her arm with Rosie's and strolled from the living room, through their library, and into the dining hall.

The door to the dining hall didn't make a lot of noise when it opened, but Rosie was under the impression it had because when she looked up, every face was staring at her. Faces of admiration, shock, awe, and finally, disgust came from her tormentor. With a wink and a smirk, she glided past Olive to fill out her breakfast slip. "Wow, that felt good," Rosie whispered to Eleanor.

"It should! You look amazing, and Olive is already regretting that she messed with you."

Rosie glanced at Olive, who was stabbing her breakfast with such force that pieces flew off of her plate.

After the group of Valtic students ordered and got their food, they found an empty table, but Rosie's path was blocked.

"Rosie, please, you have to believe me. I had no idea they were going to do this. I'm so sorry," Riley pleaded with her.

"Stay away from me, Riley."

"I won't. Not until you listen and believe me. I swear I had nothing to do with this, and I yelled at Olive and the others who were involved, and please Rosie. I wouldn't do this."

Justin stepped in front to separate them. "Riley, back off."

"This has nothing to do with you, Justin."

"Actually, it has to do with all of us," Garrett said, coming forward. "Just go in peace, and maybe if Rosie ever forgives you, you'll hear from her."

"Move and let me talk to Rosie." Riley lunged forward, trying to push through, but Justin and Garrett held him back. Riley hit Garrett in the nose with his elbow, trying to be released from the struggle.

Garrett's eyes flashed yellow as they had during his transformation, and he growled. Suddenly, fists were being tossed, and Gunner and Flynn had run over to assist Riley.

Rosie was in shock. Had she caused this, she thought? Finally, words poured out of her. "Stop! Everyone, please, stop!" But it was no use. The boys looked like a giant pretzel, entangled, with body parts flying.

Finally, to Rosie's relief, everyone within a twenty-foot diameter of the fight became frozen. Unable to turn her head to catch who had come to assist with breaking up the fight, Rosie stared at Riley, and he stared back at her with blood running down his nose and one eye turning black and swelling.

"Everyone who can move, leave for your first class." Rosie heard Professor Shay addressing the crowd of onlookers. "I said, *move!*" Her voice boomed throughout the dining hall, and the students who were still seated, wanting to see what would happen next, quickly gathered their things and left, leaving Rosie, Riley, Justin, Eleanor, Garrett, Gunner, and Flynn frozen in their place. Once the last student had exited, Professor Shay exhaled an irritated sigh and unfroze the seven. To Rosie, it seemed like Professor Shay had grown a foot in height as she stared down at them with rage-filled eyes. "Unbelievable! Only a few days into the new school year and already causing trouble! I would have expected this from the new students—naturals, no less—but you, Garrett? Well, do any of you have anything to say for yourselves?"

All remained quiet with their heads bowed.

"No? No one wants to come forward and explain what happened? Well, alright. All of you have detention and are suspended from extracurriculars for a week. That means no clubs, no Illumination practice, nothing."

Everyone in the group let out a defeated sigh and a few groans.

"Don't start! You will go to meals, class, study hall, and required community service as punishment for your immature actions until Sunday evening. Any free periods will be done in the library under the supervision of Ms. Pamfet. You will report to her, and I will relay your punishments for your poor actions later today. Now let's move to class. I believe you all, with the exception of Garrett, are in my first-period history class, and I hate to be late, so march."

The group of students grabbed their backpacks and other

things and shuffled down the staircase with Professor Shay leading the way. Rosie, Justin, Eleanor, and Garrett were about ten steps ahead of Riley, Gunner, and Flynn. Not a single word was spoken during the entire descent, and when the group finally reached the hallway for all the high school and college classes, all heads in the classrooms turned to look through the glass walls. Losing the confidence she had when first walking to the dining room, Rosie shambled down the hallway and followed Professor Shay into the classroom. The only other person in the classroom was Reid.

"I guess this is a class only for human students," Eleanor whispered to Rosie.

The six took their seats, and Professor Shay approached the front of the class. "Alright, everyone, please take out a notebook, pen, and your textbook, *Supernatural History: Our Past, Present, and Future* by Legend Antiquitos."

As the students retrieved their supplies, Professor Shay continued. "This will be a half-semester class. Once it ends in October, you will join your other classmates in the normal history course. This will be very fast-paced, so pay attention, ask questions, and make sure you study because extra credit will not be offered."

* * *

Rosie's first morning at the school went by ridiculously fast. After learning about the origins of the school and the supernatural community that has now formed into today's society from Professor Shay, Rosie and Justin went to Chemistry where they were surrounded by students at least three years older than them.

Professor Aster tried to be cool, Rosie examined, but was actually a stickler for the rules and was a fan of quizzing random students about chemistry knowledge they hadn't even learned yet. Rosie and Justin impressed Professor Aster by volunteering to answer questions he posed and answered them right on their first try. Then there was Number Theory and Cryptology with Professor Walker. Rosie and Justin didn't even bother going to the lunchroom, since they had so much studying to do already. Remaining in Professor Walker's room, with her permission, they used the hour to review their homework and reading and actually finished a few assignments. When lunch ended, Professor Walker gave a lecture on secret codes and messages and their significance in history. It was near the end of the class when Rosie finally brought up her attention from her detailed notes.

"What other codes have you seen or learned about that we haven't mentioned yet?" Professor Walker posed to Rosie and Justin.

"The Enigma Code, where Germans used a machine to send secure secret messages," Justin stated.

"Yes, what else? Anything simpler yet unsolvable?"

Rosie looked up at Professor Walker, who was staring down at her. "The Zodiac Killer."

"Yes …" Professor Walker moved to the glass to write on it like a whiteboard. "There have been times where ciphers have been decoded, but when the code appears again, symbols and characters have been moved around and randomized." She stepped away from the glass and displayed a code on it. "If you solve this by the end of the semester, you will receive an automatic *A* in this class."

Rosie and Justin scribbled down the cipher.

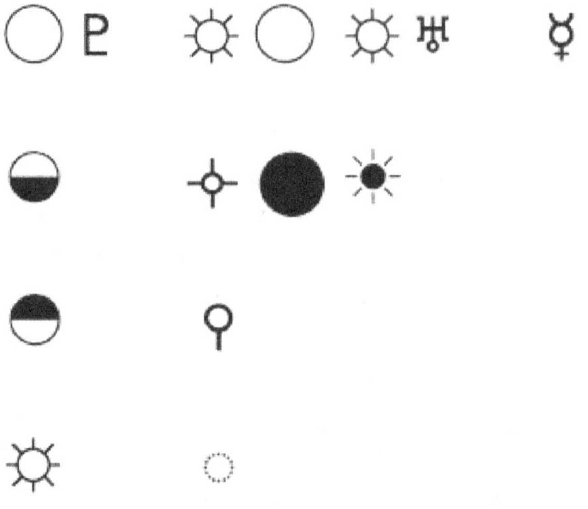

Rosie was studying the code when a chime rang through the school, indicating the end of the class.

"What do you think it says?" Justin asked.

She continued to marvel the characters as they enticed her mind, begging her to discover what they mean.

"Rosie?" Justin said, bringing her from her trance.

"Sorry." She smiled while packing her bag and looking at him. "Ready to go?"

Rosie was elated yet exhausted. Her hand ached from all the notes she had taken, and she couldn't wait to relax in a corner to continue reading and studying. Her excitement to eat and take a short break before she started her workload died, however, when two buzzing crackling pieces of paper folded like centipedes crawled in front of her and Justin.

"Yuck, creepy," Rosie said. Opening the notes, both faces grimaced and groaned. Professor Shay had sent the two a reminder to go straight to the library.

Glum and weary about meeting their doom—and on their first day no less—Rosie and Justin trudged to the library. Her attitude shifted though when she viewed again how beautiful a place it was. The light shining through the glass walls and the smell of books and fresh greenery eased her. As Rosie was once again beholding all the greatness while walking farther into the library, a small cough made her turn to her side.

"Oh, hi," she said, confused as she looked down at the mousy, old woman holding a plethora of books in her arms.

"Uh, yes, Rose Connors and Justin Fent? I'm Ms. Pamfet, the librarian. Professor Shay said you two would be my new library assistants."

"I'm sorry, what?" Justin asked.

"You two can set your bags behind the checkout desk and take these two carts and put the books back in their correct spot."

Now understanding this was their punishment, Rosie set down her bag and pushed one of the heavy carts to one of the many bookshelves and replaced the books as told. So, she thought with a smile, this was what she had to do for the rest of the week? Fantastic. She finished emptying her cart and sauntered to the front desk where Ms. Pamfet was sitting, reading a book.

"Alright, dear, you can make your way back here and take over the front desk. When someone wants to check something out, you take their stone and imprint it in this book. When you aren't busy, you can study and do your homework or read." As she finished explaining Rosie's job,

Justin approached with his empty cart. "You dear, follow me. I have a few more physical duties I need help with." Ms. Pamfet dragged Justin up the stairs and toward the greenhouse side of the room.

Rosie sat and worked on her schoolwork and occasionally helped a student find a book they needed or checked out something for them.

After an hour had passed, five students entered the library. Eleanor, Garrett, Riley, Gunner, and Flynn stomped in, unhappy they had to spend the first day of school in the library rather than exploring campus.

Rosie lifted her hand to wave hello, but a young student came up to her, asking for help. When Rosie was done with the student, Ms. Pamfet had already gotten to the group.

"Alright, Professor Shay has given me specific instructions for you five."

"Just us five? What about them?" Gunner pointed at Rosie behind the counter and Justin, who was descending the staircase.

"Don't you worry about them. Now follow me," Ms. Pamfet took them all throughout the library, dropping off each one at their own table to study. But only after thirty minutes of seclusion, Professor Shay arrived.

She walked stern and sharp, showing she was still upset at the events that had taken place that morning. She approached each student, who packed up their schoolwork and left the library looking disheveled and appalled. Finally, Professor Shay clopped down the steps after talking to Justin, who was also following her. But he didn't continue toward Rosie. He too left the library, giving her a small grimace on his way out.

"Alright, Miss. Connors. I am sure you have been sitting

here in suspense about what I am going to tell you your punishment is. Well, for the rest of the week, you will come here and work for Ms. Pamfet. You will do as she says, and when you aren't helping her, you will do your schoolwork and keep to yourself. If you finish your homework and Ms. Pamfet doesn't need help, you will read a book on supernatural history. Whether you read the book here or not, you will turn in a five-page report on what you have learned from said book to me. Now, I recommend you hustle upstairs and clean up the books the sparial plant is beginning to eat."

"Wait, sparial plant?"

"On level two, next to the genealogy section. Can't miss the ten-foot blue tentacles and excreting toxic red mist. Good luck."

Rosie couldn't believe it. That was her punishment, she thought. The faces of everyone else seemed like they had to scrub the dining hall floor with their toothbrushes and then continue to use them. Her wonder spun within, but after securing the book-hungry plant with a purple powder Ms. Pamfet had given her to use, her gaze landed on a book by its sharp mouth. Carefully lifting a heavy tentacle, Rosie retrieved the thick book with the same young, handsome face hanging in the main lobby and read the cover, *An Immortal Life: A James Kingsley Story* by Jones Parkie. Interesting, Rosie thought, and her curiosity for this lone immortal creature piqued her interest, and she knew what her report would be on.

Delving into the book and becoming completely immersed on the topic of immortality, Rosie jumped when Ms. Pamfet placed her hand on her shoulder to ask her for help replacing books.

"It's four forty-five already?" Rosie asked her, a lump rising in her throat. "Oh my gosh, it is! I'm sorry, Ms. Pamfet, I have class, but I'll be back later!" She grabbed her stuff and ran out of the library.

Rosie managed to find a bathroom to change into her training clothes. In a uniform like the one she had worn during her ropes test, she bounded up the stairs two at a time, attempting to sprint to the field as fast as she could. On the last step, though, her foot caught, and she crashed down, skidding her knee across the rough, stone floor. Pain shot up and down her leg, but she was more worried about the pain Professor Manger would cause her if she arrived any later than she needed to be. Leaving the building and running to the combat field, Rosie approached Professor Manger with a sorrowful look.

The entire freshman class was on the field in lines, following four leaders at the head of each line in stretches.

With blood covering her leg and bruises forming on her knee, Rosie expected Professor Manger to seem somewhat surprised by her appearance, but all he did was slightly turn his head and refocus on the other students.

"Professor, I'm so sorry for my tardiness. I promise it won't happen again."

Low snickers sounded, and she was sure they were warranted, as Professor Manger was sure to reprimand and embarrass her. But both her and the snickering students were shocked at her oversized teacher's reply.

"Hustle to a spot and follow your leader."

Confused but grateful that he only said that, she hustled to an opening in one of the lines and joined her classmates.

Rosie's eyes met Justin's, who was in the next line over.

Concerned, he mouthed to her, *Are you okay?*

She nodded, and both refocused on their line leader. Rosie scanned who was in her line. Martha Ash was leading, followed by Ryan Decker, a wizard in Surgent, Natasha Hampton and Dylan Xi, shifters in Surgent, Wendy Oxford, a shifter in Astive, Marina Manning, a mermaid in Astive, Stella Simmons, a werewolf in Surgent, Liam Webber, a vampire also in Surgent, and finally, right ahead of Rosie was Flynn.

Rosie scanned the other lines. They were comprised of all four houses. So why was hers more heavily Surgent based, she wondered? But then, it happened.

After performing rigorous physical tests in her same group, the tasks coming much easier to the supernatural beings, Professor Manger addressed the class. "We will now demonstrate to our new classmates the importance of combat and how we use what is around us to win a fight. Let's have ..." He checked his clipboard. "Natasha Hampton and Rose Connors demonstrate." As he said Rosie's name, a menacing smile slid over his face, and his eyes bore into her.

The class walked off the field and convened next to Professor Manger as the two girls stood in the middle. Her heartbeat rose, and her hands shook, which only worsened when Rosie remembered what Natasha shifted into—a mountain lion. Evading a rattlesnake was one thing, but attempting to outmaneuver a mountain lion with the brain and skills of a trained warrior was much different.

"Begin!" Professor Manger called out, and all the students with the exception of Riley, Justin, and Eleanor hollered and cheered.

Natasha, who had already started to charge at her, was

transformed and bared sharp teeth and strong paws, ready to swipe.

Rosie searched for something to help her. A grouping of trees. She ran toward them, but pain seared Rosie's skin as the quick swipe of Natasha's nails scraped her back. She fell to the ground and turned, so she was facing upward.

Natasha pounced, now completely shifted.

Adrenaline raced through Rosie, and, as Natasha was about to land on top of her, Rosie instinctively raised her knees and kicked Natasha in the stomach.

The lioness's form rolled next to her, coughing and gagging.

Rosie stood up and made her way to and up the trees.

Natasha followed, only a few seconds behind.

Rosie watched the lion claw at the trunks and jump, attempting to climb one, but whenever her body would land heavily on a branch, it would break, or, if her claws grasped the tree, the bark would shed.

Natasha paced at the base of the trees, looking upward to find Rosie, but she was completely concealed.

"Alright, Connors, you are supposed to use your environment to fight, not hide!" Professor Manger called. "Class, this is exactly what I don't want you to do. If you hide, you will inevitably lose, because your enemy will snuff you out eventually—"

Justin cheered as Rosie, with a spear-like branch in hand, dove from the treetops directly on top of Natasha's back. Both rolled on each other for a moment, but Rosie pinned Natasha, so she was belly up and straddled her, holding the sharp point of the branch against Natasha's throat.

One of Natasha's paws tapped her lightly twice on the arm, which Rosie took as a surrender.

With pride filling her, Rosie stood and helped Natasha, as much as she could, to her four feet, and she stared into Professor Manger's sickly face before her vision faded, and everything went dark.

* * *

Rosie thought it was worth passing out from the surge of adrenaline from her brawl with Natasha for the respect she gained from her classmates. No longer was she seen as a mere defenseless human but someone who could stand her ground. Not even the exhausting amount of work Rosie had to do for school, in the library, for the Valtic Illumination team—June still made sure her, Justin, and Garrett were keeping up with practice training even though they weren't there—and having to treat the claw marks on her back with a stinging ointment could put her in a bad mood. Rather, it was just another challenge to her, and it made her first week at King's Preparatory fly by. It wasn't until Friday that she realized just how fast it actually went when she found herself knocking on Doctor Witam's door.

"Come in, Rosie." Rising from behind his desk, he gestured for her to sit on the couch and handed her a glass of water. "Well, Rosie, the next forty-five minutes are yours. Tell me how your first week here has been. I know you had a rough start, but I hope it has gotten better."

"I think it has. I've decided to continue helping Ms. Pamfet in the library part-time now my punishment is up, and other than being forced into battle, I think I am doing well in my classes."

"Well, I can't speak for the other teachers, but you are in my class. And I'm sure Professor Manger is just pushing you to be your best. I hope you understand and realize how important it is for you, an intellect, to be well trained for someone or something, supernatural or not, that may harm you."

"I suppose I understand."

"Also, before I forget, Professor Shay asked me to collect your history paper that was a part of your punishment. Do you have it ready?"

"Yes, I do." Rosie retrieved it from her bag.

Doctor Witam read the title on her cover page out loud, "*The Only Immortal? By Rose Connors.* Interesting. Why the question mark, if I may ask?"

"Well, how do we know James Kingsley truly is the only immortal being in the world, and, if so, how was it that he is the only one with this particular makeup? I understand everyone has their own set of DNA that makes them unique, but, if you were to look at immortality as a disease or variant, you would think more people, even if it was only one other person, would have the same disorder."

"Very interesting. What makes you think being immortal resembles a disease or disorder?"

"Because James Kingsley claims that being immortal has something to do with his genetic makeup, but after looking at the data he has put out regarding his own DNA and that of his parents, I just don't understand how that could happen."

"Maybe it goes further back than his parents?"

"Possibly, but from what I have studied in the past and what is being laid out in front of me now, I just can't believe it."

"Well, Rosie, it sounds like you have a biology paper, not a history paper, and I don't think Professor Shay will be too pleased to read this."

"Wait, what? I know I took a side tangent to the book I originally read for this report, but James Kingsley is the foundation of this school and the community, so the basis of his being is history."

"Trust me. Professor Shay is an adamant supporter and follower of James Kingsley. This paper would only cause you trouble, and you would have to redo it anyway. At least with me telling you, you won't have to suffer further. I can tell Professor Shay that you need until Monday to finish the paper. Might I recommend the book, *Stone Power* by Jenet Dubs? It discusses how supernatural and natural beings have mined and used the Earth's resources for power over the years?"

"Yeah, okay." Rosie was defeated. She was sure her paper was valid, but she also knew Doctor Witam had a point. It wouldn't satisfy, not completely, as a history paper.

Doctor Witam noticed the disappointment on Rosie's face and grabbed a piece of paper from his desk. "Here are a few books that may give you some guidance on the various supernatural creatures and further provide insight on James Kingsley's immortality. I hope they help you as they have helped me. And, if you have any questions on the topic, best to come to me and ask before you talk to anyone else." He smiled and slid her the paper, and with a glimmer of hope of her understanding the topic more, she smiled back at Doctor Witam.

Chapter Ten

A warm wind continued to blow through the mountainside, even as September was ending. Rosie sat on a boulder, reading another book on the list Doctor Witam had given her, but, as she approached the end of the ninth and final book with still no answers she didn't already possess herself about James Kingsley, she slammed the cover shut and tossed it aside. Staring into the sunset at the sea of marigold, persimmon, plum, and indigo painting the sky, Rosie couldn't help wonder what knowledge she had to gain from these books. Was there some underlying message that Doctor Witam wanted her to find, or was this actually the information that helped him understand?

Rosie reached into her pocket and read the crumpled-up list. *Chasing Life: Ways Humans Have Survived; The Human Brain: An Intellect Mind; A Rising Power: How Witches Came to Be; Indestructible or Not?: Vampire Living; Sitting in the Sun: Harnessing the Fairy Light; The Turning: When Wolves Come Out to Kill; The Infinite Changes: A Shape Shifters Ability; Open Water: The Resurfacing of Mermaids;* and *Never Leave a Man Behind: A Protector's Guide.* What did all these books have in common that could give her the information she hoped to gain? She processed all the information she had absorbed and evaluated it.

"All the books have to do with supernatural beginnings and survival," she thought aloud. "And they refer to each supernatural creature in one way or another." Rosie grabbed the tossed-aside book and collected the others. "What else could these books give me? What else?" They have similar title structures and don't list an author. They were also all hard to find in the school's library, buried by other books and spread far and wide. One copy per book existed. She skimmed the pages of each. All were old and tattered and had stains from mildew and water. But Rosie spotted something. At first, it seemed like a normal wear and tear smudge, which was why Rosie hadn't noticed it before. In the bottom corner of the back cover in each book laid a discolored spot. What was this, she wondered? After gathering her things and jumping off the boulder, Rosie strode to campus.

In her secret study room in the Valtic library, she opened each book and laid them atop each other, so the smudges were lying in a column. They seemed similar, yet different. It was too hard to completely decipher them. Rosie sat upright. "Yes!" she yelled, remembering something she had learned in her cryptology class. "The smudge is only faded, not destroyed. I can see what it is if I ..." She took the book, and, as she blew slow, hot breaths on the smudge, one section of the secret marking darkened. She breathed harder and harder, but when she stopped to catch her breath, the smudge resumed its original state. Trying something a bit more dangerous, she held it above one of the candles, hoping not to set the room on fire. Inching the book closer to the flame, she held her breath and concentrated.

The emblem gradually revealed itself again. Rosie stepped forward, careful not to burn the mark before she uncovered it. It was a circle with a cone attached to the bottom. She thought it resembled a cone with an oversized scoop of ice cream. The marking darkened, and a letter *T* appeared centered in the circle. She reached for another book and held it up. This time, the cone had rotated ninety degrees to the right, and the letter *I* appeared within the circle. She continued to do this with each book until the last letter emerged from the last book. Sitting in only a circle with no cone attached was the letter *C*.

"T, I, O, I, S, H, N, R, C. An anagram? Shirt coin? Rhino tics? No, is it …" Realizing the variation of the logos and remembering what they resembled, she snatched a pen and paper and started with the *C* in the circle and moving to the letter in the circle with the cone hat. Continuing with each letter as it's cone moved clockwise, she read the revealed word and drew the emblem as if they were all laid on top of one another.

"C-H-R-I-S-T-I-O-N, Christion," she said, and the drawing of a compass rose next to it. *This had to be what Doctor Witam wanted me to find. He must not have been able to tell me outright what to look for because he would've gotten into trouble, but I figured it out, Doctor Witam. Don't you worry.* With triumph washing over her, she gathered her things and left the room back to the library to find what she could on the possible explorer Christion.

* * *

"I'm sorry, Rosie, but I am not familiar with any kind of

explorer or traveler named Christion in any of the books here in this library—or any supernatural library, as a matter of fact," Ms. Pamfet explained as Rosie sat behind the checkout desk.

Rosie had spent the week searching the Valtic library and the main library as she tried to search for answers on her own. Since learning the name Christion, Rosie had devoted all her free time to figuring out who the mysterious explorer was, but she'd had no luck. Nowhere in the entirety of the school could she find any information regarding the name Christion.

"Hey," a voice whispered behind her, with a hand on her shoulder.

Rosie jumped about a foot in the air, yelping a small scream.

"Whoa, whoa, Rosie, it's us!"

Rosie turned to see Justin, Eleanor, and Garrett staring at her, their faces covered in worry.

"Oh, I'm sorry, guys. I've been a little on edge lately."

"Uh, yeah," Garrett chimed in, and Eleanor elbowed him in the gut.

"What Garrett means," Eleanor recovered, "is you've seemed distracted. Is something going on?"

Rosie had yet to tell her friends about her extracurricular studies and what she had been trying to research. Worried they wouldn't understand what even she knew was a slight obsession, she carefully replied, "No, I've been swamped with school and studying for the Illumination Games and work and ..." Her sentence trailed off as all three eyed her skeptically. She could tell they thought she was lying, but, in all actuality, she wasn't. She barely could keep up this little side project while staying on top of all her other work. "You know, I didn't sleep that well last night." Which also wasn't a lie. "I think I'll go to my room and take a quick nap." She gave a slight grin to show them she was okay and left the library, wondering how she could learn more about Christion.

* * *

Traversing rows and rows of books, picking random ones and flipping the pages, unable to locate the name Christion anywhere, and walking deeper into another aisle, a shadow flashed by Rosie. Spinning and searching for the source, Rosie called out, "Hello?"

There was no answer, though.

She continued browsing, and another shadow whizzed by. "Who's there?"

Again, no response.

Rosie examined the room surrounded completely by books; then she couldn't see anything. As if the shadow had swallowed her, darkness consumed her ...

Rosie screamed, now sitting upright in bed. Breathing fast and deep and trying to regain control of her emotions, she whispered under her breath and giggled in excitement. "I know where to look."

* * *

Rosie entered the store where books surrounded her from every angle. Even though at the beginning of the year, she had promised to explore the Kingstown bookstore, this was the first time visiting the little town on her own and only after her late-night Illumination Team practice. And it still took her breath away. She had forgotten the greatness of books and how their designs and displays weren't tacky, like ones she had seen in a surplus shop or superstore. Rather, the books were displayed with elegance and grace to show the full beauty of the titles.

Forgetting why she was originally there, Rosie walked throughout the store, picking up different books and admiring them.

"May I help you?" a low, raspy voice came from above her.

She looked up to see a tall, pale figure hanging from the rafter. "Oh, hi, um, is the shop owner here? I don't think I ever learned his name, but I have a question about a particular book."

"Unfortunately, Jerry is away," the man continued with a mischievous smile and manner about him. "May I be of some assistance? I am Gyle. I am … Um, I am watching over the shop for Jerry. And you are?"

Chills and discomfort flooded Rosie in Gyle's presence. On edge and her heart racing, she squinted to get a better look at him. His eyes glowed red, and sharp teeth popped out, but she wouldn't let the creepy vampire deter her from her quest.

"Uh, Rosie Connors. Uh, Gyle, do you happen to know if any books here contain information on or are by a man named Christion?"

Gyle took an uneasy step backward, but he caught his shocked expression and smiled down upon Rosie, placing a hand on her upper back. "Why, yes. Such a book is located in this store, written by one Christion Flare."

Rosie's heart sped up. She had actually found a book by Christion. Before she could ask to see it though, Gyle continued.

"But I must say it is a cold, dark, evil book. Why would such a young, innocent girl be trying to locate such a thing?" He guided her near the back of the store and around the aisles.

"Uh, well, it's for a project I am researching at school, and I was told I could find more information here. My professor escorted me here and is waiting across the way for me." Rosie swallowed hard, as she could tell the vampire sensed her lie.

"Oh, but I can show you the book. It is just back here. Of course, if Jerry was with us, he would never allow such a thing. Such a delicate book could never be trusted with a child, but I think I can make special arrangements for you. Of course, it will cost you a little something."

"And what is that?" Rosie pushed on, now sensing the book near her. She could feel its presence and a faint whisper in her ear calling, *Rosie* … Was it Christion himself calling for her to find the book, she wondered? She planted her feet and summoned confidence. "Well, how much? I want that book."

"And I can show it to you … for a taste."

"A taste?"

"Yes. You smell exquisite, and I must say I haven't had a snack in quite a while." He flashed a sly smile and fixated on the quickened pulse in her neck.

She took a deep breath and stared him down. "Fine. But show me the book first." Rose felt a tug in the back of her mind. A small part of her said this was trouble and to leave, but that cast of fear was overcome with her desire to see what Christion Flare had for her to learn, especially about James Kingsley. Plus, she could use her necklace to call for help if trouble occurred.

Gyle used his vampire stealth and speed to lock the front door and change the open sign to closed. "Follow me."

Rosie entered the back office behind him, and Gyle closed the door. The room, like the rest of the shop, consisted of books and bricks supporting the roof as walls. Rosie sensed Gyle's presence close behind her and heard him distinctly sniff her hair. She stepped forward, attempting to move out of smelling distance, but from her studies had learned a vampire could smell human blood a mile away.

The vampires at school and in the community wore either their King's Preparatory stones or other enchanted talismans to not only allow them to walk in the sunlight but also to suppress their desire to feed. Rosie snuck a peek at Gyle's hands. He wasn't wearing a ring inlaid with a stone.

Gyle slid past her, eyes closed and wafting in another scent, and glided to the back wall. With no effort, he pushed aside the tall wooden cabinets and removed books from their places to rearrange them. He attempted to hide what books he was reshuffling, but Rosie kept inventory on each movement. After he had placed the final book in its new spot, the room rumbled, and dust fell.

Rosie thought an earthquake had started, but she realized that wasn't the case when the wall pushed itself backward at least fifty yards, turning the small office into an oversized hallway. Once the wall was set in its new position, doors revealed themselves, and candles ignited.

Gyle's cold hand pressed on Rosie's back, the chill of his undead body sending shivers through her, and he guided her down the hallway. As they walked, Rosie couldn't help but listen to the screams of anguish.

"Don't mind that. I am restoring a few older books, and they like their pain to be known. The process is not easy for them."

After continuing down the hallway farther, they finally reached the last door next to the shifted brick wall. Gyle produced a hidden leather strand necklace from underneath his shirt and placed a key in the lock.

Hearing a click, Rosie's thumping heart grew louder by the second. The door swung inward, and the first thing Rosie saw was the glass case containing a large, stitched-together, leather-bound book with the same emblem she had discovered and pieced together.

It called to her again, *Rosie …*

She stepped toward the front of the case and laid a hand on the glass, not removing her gaze from the book. "Can I see it?"

"You are looking at it now," Gyle replied, a hint of mischief in his voice.

"I meant, can you please remove it from the case so I can properly inspect it and purchase it?" Rosie faced him, annoyed.

"I said I would show it to you. I never said you could take it." His fangs protruded more as he advanced closer to her. "Now, it is your turn to honor our deal."

"Not yet. I want to read it, and then you can have your drink."

"Ha! This book is not for any mere being. And it is much too valuable to hand over to you, a simple human girl. Even its many masters could not hold on to it."

Rosie could hear the screams emanating from the hallway. "Those aren't books being restored, are they?"

"Let's just say Jerry got in my way. Now and on the day you first came in here—I couldn't resist your scent then either."

"You were the shadow following me, escaping into the

secret rooms."

"I can't figure out what you are. You are human, yes, but there is something else."

Rosie couldn't respond. That one small, fearful voice in her head now grew. Her adrenaline was pumping. She quickly clasped her necklace, but it didn't vibrate or emanate any kind of signal for help.

Gyle drew closer, inhaling even deeper breaths of her. "That stupid pendant won't work back here. It is just you and me." He was stronger, faster, and bloodthirsty.

There would be no escape, she thought, her hope diminishing. She tried to move around him but, suddenly, he wasn't in front of her anymore.

With his hand grasping around her waist and his other holding her shoulder, he pulled her backward. His strength had her pinned, and when she tried to free herself, he laughed and held tighter.

She thought he would dislocate her shoulder. A tremble went down Rosie as his cold body held her, and his nose pushed her hair out of the way to expose her neck. She wanted to shout but was in a state of shock that kept her from voicing anything until the pierce of his fangs broke the skin on her neck.

She screamed, but Gyle's hand left her shoulder and covered her mouth. Rosie felt the blood leaving her body and slowly entering his. It was like he was taking his time on purpose, she thought. Her eyes darkened, and now instead of the room, she saw a younger Gyle, handsome and happy. Children surrounded him, and a woman approached him to kiss his cheek. The vision whirled, and now Rosie saw those same individuals lying on the floor in a dark room, their eyes open and unmoving as Gyle regarded the family.

His teeth parted her skin, and blood dripped down her chest, and her eyes refocused to the room. "It's even better than I thought," he exclaimed. He bent his head to take another drink, causing Rosie to squeal in pain.

Her eyesight dimmed and was drawn into Gyle's memories and mind, but then she heard the book speak to her again, *Rosie, live…* At those words, light swelled inside her, and with a swift pop of her foot, she kicked her would-be killer with such a force, it even surprised herself.

Gyle, realizing a small girl had outmuscled him, showed his fangs with anger and tossed Rosie.

She flew through the air, and her forehead landed on the corner of the glass case. Blood covered her as it flowed from her head and neck and soaked her clothes.

Gyle, overcome with the strong scent of her blood, convulsed like shockwaves were flowing through him.

This would be her only opportunity to escape, she thought. She toppled the glass case so it shattered and grabbed the book along with a sharp piece of broken glass.

The crash had taken Gyle from his trance, and he stared her down with more fury than Rosie had ever seen before. He lunged forward, caught Rosie's arm and turned it so there was a loud crack.

Rosie screamed, knowing he had broken the bone. Dropping the book, she swung the piece of glass into his neck.

Blood erupted, and he screamed in agony.

Rosie yanked the leather necklace that had led them through the door off his chest and scooped up the book. She slammed the door behind her and locked it, trapping the vampire, but she knew as soon as he recovered and healed from the cut of the glass he would try to escape. She couldn't let that happen, not before telling someone and ensuring his arrest. She focused on the wall that led her down the hallway and switched the books to their original spots, and the floor quaked.

"No!" Gyle bellowed from behind the locked room, knowing his fate of being trapped.

The wall pushed Rosie forward and finally reset so she was once again in the tattered office. Not wasting another moment, she left the room. In the bookstore, things were as quiet as they had been when she had first arrived. Everything was in its place, and moonlight shone on a deserted town. Quickly understanding some sort of silencing spell must be on the back hallway, she sprinted from the store to the safety of King's Preparatory.

* * *

Rosie sat upright, surrounded by Doctor Geller, Nurse Chaplin, and Nurse Howard. Their faces looked too sweet for comfort. "Hello, Rosie. I'm happy you've woken up and are healing nicely," Doctor Geller said.

"Huh?" she managed to squeak out, but her throat screamed at her for making any noise.

"Don't worry about speaking. You had some damage to your neck, throat, and vocal cords, but rest assured, you should be better by the end of the week."

Rosie turned her neck to survey the room but felt faint again, and she fell on the pillow, seeing Riley running to her as she fell back to sleep.

* * *

"Jeez, is that all her blood?"

"Yeah, crazy, right?"

"Shh, you guys. I think she is waking up."

Rosie slowly opened her eyes.

Justin, Eleanor, and Garrett surrounded her bed with smiles on their faces and eagerness in their eyes. "Go slow, Rosie," Justin told her as she tried to lift herself, instinctively putting a hand on her back to help her, but the touch nauseated her, and she jumped away. "Oh sorry, I didn't mean to make you uncomfortable."

"No," she finally managed to say, her throat not too raw. "I'm sorry. The last guy to touch me there tried to kill me."

The three lost their smiles and regarded her with pity.

"Just a bad joke, guys. Trust me. I'm okay."

"What happened? No one has told us anything; only a vampire attacked you in town," Garrett said.

"Yeah. Last night, I went into town to go to the bookstore and—"

The three exchanged looks.

"What?"

"Rosie," Eleanor started, "you've been in and out of it for a week."

"A week? No, that can't be right. I missed a whole week of school?" She flung herself backward again, hitting her pillow.

"On the plus side, everyone thinks you're a total badass for escaping a vampire, and your arm healed right up while you were sleeping," Garrett tried to reassure her.

"And none of our teachers expect you to do the homework. You just have to do the readings," Justin added.

"What exactly do you remember, Rosie?" Eleanor reached to hold her hand.

Spying her bloodstained clothes folded on the table next to her bed, she recounted going to the bookstore to find a book from an emblem she had decoded and escaping the vampire. "I followed the road back and hiked up the mountain to the school. I remember reaching the banks of the lake and Professor Shay standing by the front entrance. I rushed to her and yelled out and then nothing. I guess that's when my body gave out on me."

The three hung on her every word.

Rosie conveniently omitted that she had found, stolen and hid the book by Christion Flare before approaching Professor Shay, then worry overcame her. "How's the shopkeeper? Jerry? Is he okay?"

"I wouldn't say he is okay, but he's alive. He's being treated at the Superior hospital," Justin said.

"Okay good. What about Gyle?"

"The vampire? Well …" Justin looked away.

"What?"

"He's being held here. At school. In some secure dungeon until he can be transported to his trial and then hopefully his grave." Detecting the worry on Rosie's face that her attacker was on the school grounds somewhere, Justin quickly changed the subject.

The four discussed other things that had occurred during the week until Doctor Geller finally asked her friends to leave her to rest.

Lying in the hospital bed, Rosie thought about the book and what answers it would finally bring her. Deciding to stop sitting around and thinking, she started to do. After quickly showering in her small hospital room and changing into some new clothes Eleanor had brought her, Rosie felt refreshed and ready to leave. But someone stopped her.

"Pst, Rosie," a voice called as she stepped into the hallway. "Rosie, over here."

She turned to look into the room next door and saw Riley. "Oh my gosh! Riley!" Rosie ran to the bed and sat, studying his black and blue face. "What happened?"

"Just got into a little scuffle in training, but I'm okay. Already healing. How are you? You were in and out of consciousness, and the staff put up a fight to let me see you."

Rosie chuckled. "I'm okay. All better. No crazed vampire can keep me down."

He reached for her hand. "I'm sorry for everything, Rosie. For being so distant and getting angry with you for no reason. I know I need to be a better friend."

"Riley, if being near death like I was a week ago has taught me anything"—she squeezed his hand—"it's to forgive."

"Okay, so you'll forgive me if I tell you this then. I moved your book."

"What?"

"The big leather stitched book. The one you hid before you passed out."

"Were you following me? Did you read it?"

"No, no, nothing like that. I was out for a run when I saw you. Covered in blood." He paused and moved his hand to graze her forehead where she had slammed her head into the glass case. "Anyway, I thought since you had gone through the trouble of hiding the book in the first place, you wanted it concealed. I made sure to hide it where no one else would find it."

He cupped her face, and she grabbed his hands. "Where is it, Riley?"

"I'll show you."

Chapter Eleven

Rosie kept a firm foot on the boulder, ensuring she wouldn't accidentally slip and hurt herself. "Riley, where on earth did you put it?"

"Hold on, just a little farther," he called back to her.

Rosie had estimated they had hiked about six miles from school. She had never ventured off this far.

"Okay, give me your hand." Riley extended his own and pulled Rosie to the top of the boulder, and Rosie gasped. Across from her was a tall waterfall hitting a small lake below. The water was a light aqua and smelled of wildflowers. "Okay, ready?"

"Ready for what?" she asked, but before he answered, he jumped off the boulder, taking Rosie with him. Her body landed in the refreshing lake below, and she swam to the surface. "Riley! I can't believe you did that!"

"Yes, you can." He laughed while swimming on his back. "Plus, I would never try to kill you."

Rosie's heart slowed, and she giggled. *What a remarkable place*, she thought. She watched Riley floating on his back, eyes closed. *Well, if he wants to play rough…* she thought and quietly submerged herself under the water.

"Rosie! Where are you? This isn't funny!"

Before he could call for her again, she shot from the water behind him and tackled him underneath. Both came up laughing, splashing and grabbing each other. Riley grabbed her around the waist, but instead of pulling her under, he pulled her close. The laughs stopped, but the smiles stayed as they stared at one other.

Rosie broke her eye contact first, pushing away a little. "So, um, where did you say you hid the book?"

"Oh, uh, yeah, come on." Riley swam to the waterfall and dove underneath.

Rosie followed, and when she came up, she found herself in a dark cave with only the light peeking through the waterfall for her to see.

"Here," Riley said, helping Rosie from the water and onto the cave floor.

"Riley, how did you find this place?"

"Well, when we weren't speaking, and I didn't want to talk to Gunner or Flynn, I would run, and I stumbled upon this place. Well, not really stumble. I was trying to find a place to hide. I disrupted a herd of snallygasters feeding—those small, weird dragon creatures. I fell into this undisturbed pool and decided it could be my own little escape."

"Well, it's amazing."

"Yeah, it is," Riley said, concentrating on her. "Anyway, here ya go." Riley reached into a small opening in the wall and retrieved the book, protected by a small black tarp. Riley laid it in Rosie's hands, and, as soon as it contacted her skin, Rosie felt a sense of belonging.

"How did you move it down here without getting it wet?"

"Well, if you follow me around here …" He stepped on a

ledge near the waterfall to reveal a path. "This will take us the back way out—or the coward's way I say, for those who don't want to take the leap like we did."

"We should go back. I have been wanting to check this out for a while now."

"I've been meaning to ask you about all of this, Rosie. What's so special about this book?"

Rosie pulled out her backpack—which, thanks to magic, was kept waterproof—and carefully placed the book inside. She hesitated. She didn't know how much, if anything, to reveal to Riley.

"Hey…" He grabbed her hand. "You can trust me."

"You're right, I can trust you."

* * *

Rosie had been surprised at how well Riley took the news of her suspicions of James Kingsley, her obsessive behavior on understanding supernaturals, and her quest for answers. He even offered his help where she needed it and told her he wouldn't tell a soul or step in the way unless she was in danger and needed help.

"Okay, I guess I'll see you tomorrow? Breakfast?" Riley asked, staring into her eyes in the dining room.

"Yeah, breakfast." Rosie reached up and hugged him.

He squeezed her back, and they separated to head into their own team libraries.

It was nine when they returned, and Rosie was hoping not a lot of people would be in the Valtic library—or, if there were, they wouldn't notice her. Entering the great room, she did not spy a soul. "Perfect," she muttered, climbing the steps to her secret study room.

"Hey, Rosie!" Justin called to her, entering the library. "Hey, did you finish the lab report for Chemistry? Want to work on it together?"

"Hi, Justin. Yeah, sorry, I already completed it." The book grew heavier in her bag. "I just need to grab a few books, and I'll be in the living room shortly."

"Awesome. I'll come with. I need to find a book myself."

"No! I mean, I have to find a few things that are personal and embarrassing, and I would rather you not see me in such a way. You know, acne remedies."

"Okay, well, I'll talk to you later." With disappointment in his voice, he stalked off.

Guilt overwhelmed her for lying to Justin, but the weight of her bag and the book it contained refocused her. Heading into her secret study room, she pulled the text from her bag and stared at the emblem on the cover. Each section of it had been sewed on with different material and embroidered on the material was the same design as the one decoded from the books Doctor Witam had given her to study. Her fingers grazed it, and a shiver went down her spine. The patches on the cover that comprised the emblem were not cowhide. She pulled the book closer and clearly understood that it was wicked. The fabric that bound the cover was made of skin— human skin, mermaid scales, rough werewolf fur, and so on. Her hand grazed the material, and she opened the book, *Being* by Christion Flare.

Her mind absorbed everything her gaze landed on—the diagrams, the pictures, the words. Christion Flare was a genius, Rosie thought. Surely an intellect. He could map out and dive into facts she hadn't yet learned regarding all nine beings—supernatural and not. The book must have been close to a thousand pages, and Rosie finished half of it in a mere two days and the other half the following two.

Her mind whirled with knowledge, knowledge of how to collect fairy dust by trapping one, how to control a vampire rather than have it control you, how to become the alpha of a werewolf pack even when you aren't a werewolf, how to force a shapeshifter to shift on command, how to make a mermaid drown herself or anyone you please, how to steal magic from witches and wizards and use it as you wish, how to control the minds of protectors and humans so they act like mindless zombies, and finally, how to properly brainwash an intellect so they act of freewill but want to do your bidding. The book outlined the weakness of each being and how to use the body of each for potions and spells. Gyle was right, Rosie thought. This book was evil. Curious about why Doctor Witam had pointed her in this book's direction to learn more about James Kingsley, she went back through it, trying to understand his mind.

"How does this connect to James Kingsley's immortality? Where is the answer?" Flipping through the pages to try to solve the problem at hand, she found herself restudying all the beings and how they were connected and how they vary.

"The book states all creatures are connected in some way. A small group of humans became intellects. Those intellects studied magic, and those who possessed the proper will and heredity became witches and wizards. A few witches and wizards studied necromancy and black magic and created vampires to out-best death. But the vampires became bloodthirsty, and their ravenous hunger led them to lose their humanity, especially when their lives became so prolonged, and they themselves witnessed too much death.

The still-human witches and wizards created fairies to shed light on the vampires and werewolves to defeat the worst of them and guard them at night. A few werewolves evolved and became shapeshifters. A few shapeshifters further evolved into mermaids. Finally, once humans saw how many supernatural beings had been created by their hands, they designated protectors to defend themselves from supernatural evil.

This is different from what Professor Shay taught in class. Professor Shay said through genetics and behavioral analysis, we can determine that becoming a supernatural creature is caused by a hereditary trait—that witches did have a small hand in creating and implementing this gene change in other supernatural beings, but it was due to being born with magic and having a predisposition to harness magic. This book is thousands of years old. Why would she lie about the creation? Does she not know the real way? Is this even the real way?"

Questions spun messy webs inside Rosie's head. Tangled and bunched, she tried to sort them, but the only thing that made sense was to do something very stupid and very dangerous. She needed to speak to the person who knew more than her about the book. She needed to talk to Gyle.

* * *

"Are you crazy? You want to go find that lunatic?" Riley stared at Rosie with such shock and amazement that he spilled half a spoonful of soup on himself. "Oh, man! Now look what you made me do!"

Rosie couldn't help but giggle at his mishap. Since getting

attacked and their hike to the waterfall, Rosie and Riley had gotten back to how things had been before being accepted to King's Preparatory. She handed him a napkin and, in a shallow voice, whispered, "I'm going with or without you. I wanted to see if you would join me or not."

"Well, of course, I'm coming. I'm not going to let you—"

"Hey, guys!" Rosie said, abruptly cutting off Riley.

Justin, Eleanor, and Garrett sat next to the two. The rekindling of Riley and Rosie's friendship thankfully didn't affect her other ones. Rather, all three Valtic students welcomed Riley into their group with very little disruption—except for Garrett, but Eleanor explained it was just his inner werewolf aggression that had an issue. Rosie was fascinated to learn that when a werewolf starts a fight, he must finish it or else it will gnaw at him. Riley obliged this phenomenon and allowed Garrett to land one hard, swift punch to the jaw.

"What are we planning? Is it an adventure? Uh, I am desperate to leave campus," Eleanor whined.

"We can't go on an adventure. Not until after midterms."

"Justin, you are such a party pooper."

"We will have some fun this month, guys, don't worry," Garrett said, grabbing Eleanor's hand. "We have our first Illumination Game next week, and the homecoming dance is the same night as Halloween. Nothing is better than that!"

Justin turned toward Rosie and Riley. "Yeah, are you ready, Rosie? Have you done the studying and exercises June assigned?"

"Yep. I was just reviewing a few things with Riley—"

"You what?" Justin and Garrett both yelled in unison, and Justin further elaborated. "Rosie, he is on the Surgent team—no offense, Riley—but you can't trust him with our secrets and attack plans."

"Come on, guys. I wouldn't tell anyone. It's not like I'm on the Surgent Illumination team," Riley said.

"That's exactly what a spy would say." Garrett eyed him skeptically.

"Okay, okay." Rosie raised her arms like a criminal and said with a laugh, "No more trading secrets with the enemy. I understand." She saluted the two boys. "Anyway, I have to go to the library. Ms. Pamfet has a lot for me to do today."

Riley knew the truth, and Rosie could sense his disapproval. Rosie wasn't going to the library to work. She was going to find a map of the school, a map that would lead her to Gyle.

***

Sorting and searching for hours through the old, dusty documents and torn papers related to the school's architecture, Rosie finally surmised Gyle was imprisoned in a chamber connected to Professor Shay's office.

"I'm going, tonight," Rosie whispered to Riley as they sat eating dinner.

"Okay, me too."

"No, I thought about it, and I think this is something I need to do myself. I don't think Gyle will talk to me if you come along."

"Then he won't talk to you because I'm not letting you go alone."

"Fine. Let's meet at two tonight—" Rosie realized Justin was watching her, focusing on her mouth, but once he noticed she was looking at him, he grinned and waved. "Weird," she muttered but waved back and refocused on Riley to finalize their plans.

* * *

The school seemed chillier than normal that night. The stone that covered the walls and the clouds that hid the moon made it as though no one could watch over Rosie. Was this an idiotic plan, Rosie debated with herself? *Of course, it is, but, if it works and I obtain the information I need, it will be worth it.* It was midnight. Rosie had led Riley to believe they would be doing this together, but it needed to be done by her and her alone.

Rosie traveled the corridors and staircases, knowing the general area of her destination but unsure of exactly how to find it. Professor Shay's school office was on the administrative floor and by the lobby, so she could speak with parents freely and not have them interrupt school functions, but her teaching office—the secret one where she can perform her duties, school-related and not—was attached to her living quarters, and that was where she could access a hidden door and enter the secure prison that held Gyle.

Rosie took the old yellow blueprint from her pocket, unfolded it and studied it, turning it and analyzing where she was and where she needed to be. She traversed the school, climbed the staircase and paused at one of the suits of armor. "The blueprint says a room should be right here, but how?"

After slipping her head past the armor and getting a closer look at the wall, she spotted a slightly protruding brick. Reaching around to grab it and unveil the passage she needed, her shoulder bumped the armor. Clanging and clattering echoed through the hallway as the metal armor broke apart and scattered down the steps, taking other metal men down with it.

Rosie bounded up the steps. Someone was sure to come to investigate the noise, she thought.

A black body of movement shifted a few flights down, and Rosie stopped and hid behind another suit of armor, attempting to maneuver up to the lobby level.

More disturbances came behind her.

"Hey, who is that?" Professor Manger's voice called as he shuffled his feet.

More than one pair of feet sounded. Rosie couldn't let them catch her. She was sure if they did, she would be expelled for attempting to break into the headmistress's private living quarters so she could meet with an attempted murderer and learn more about James Kingsley's immortality.

Rosie hopped through the door leading to the waiting room and ran into the lobby. She searched for cover, but wherever she hid, they would definitely find her. She caught the eyes of James Kingsley staring at her, and a glimmer crossed them. Was the portrait a passageway? She had no more time to question it. She heard the trapdoor open. Rosie climbed onto the lobby front desk, but she was too short to walk through the portrait even if it was opened.

She stretched as far as she could and placed her palm on the painting, attempting to push it open, but the top half of her body fell through the veil, revealing the portrait not as the covering to a passage but a hologram. She held her breath and pulled the rest of herself up and through the entrance just as the lights of the lobby flicked on. Able to look through the portrait like it was a thin curtain over an opening, she watched Professor Manger and Shay circle the room, inspecting every corner.

"There's no one," Professor Shay said. "It must have been a rat or something."

"I swear, a body came up here."

"The shadows must have been toying with you tonight."

The two left the room, and Rosie aired a breath of relief. She turned to see she was in an office. On the desk facing the veil was a golden nameplate, and written in an artful font was the name, James Kingsley.

"Interesting," Rosie muttered, approaching the desk. Looking at the thin layer of dust that covered the top, Rosie estimated no one had been in the office for a few months—most likely not since the day they had accepted her into the school. Circling the room, she surveyed the cluttered papers covering the desk and floor and the pictures on the walls.

A low hollering noise erupted throughout the room. Rosie had read about enchantments that could be placed upon houses and rooms to scare off intruders, but this sounded different than what she had read. No scary voice was telling her to leave. Rather, it sounded like someone was trapped and trying to reach out for help. Another scream echoed—Gyle.

"Of course. If James Kingsley, the leader of all supernaturals, had a hidden office inside the school, there must be an entrance to Gyle's holding cell."

She paced around the room, frantically trying to find an entrance. But moving around books, opening desk drawers, and trying to open paintings and portraits brought no luck. Another scream erupted, but this time, she discovered where the noise was coming from.

She moved to the back of the desk, removed the chair that sat in her way, and closer inspected the ground underneath.

Another trapdoor was hidden. Climbing under the desk and lifting the almost-invisible latch, she discovered a long, steep tunnel, dark and cold, leading into blackness and the tortured screams. Rosie held her breath, knowing there was only one way down.

With the wind rushing through her hair and clogging her ears, she fell down the opening and landed on the stone pavement hard and rough. She stood and felt her ankle throb. She moaned in pain, but another scream refocused her.

The dark hallway before her had no end in sight, but she headed down it with only glimmers of the dim moon shining in. Bars lined the way, and they produced their own kind of moans as the wind blew through them. Rosie turned around and didn't recognize where she had started down the path. She worried she would not find Gyle down here but something worse. *What if I am in the wrong dungeon? But how many dungeons could this school have?* As she started to lose hope and began to turn to walk back, a hand emerged from between two bars and caught Rosie's shoulder. Rosie screamed loudly and stepped backward to the other bars across the way.

Emerging from the darkness, Gyle's face appeared. "Ah, Ms. Connors. You seemed to have been drawn back to me. I knew you couldn't resist." His voice rasped and creaked. It was not the same voice Rosie had heard before in the bookstore. Creepy, yes, but it was also polite.

Moving, so his face came between the same bars he had grabbed her from, Rosie saw he had become a decaying body. With no blood source, he was deteriorating at a slow pace, and Rosie was unsure of how stable he would be. "Hello, Gyle. I have a few questions for you."

"Of course, you do, but may I first ask for a drink? It has been a while since I have had anything to eat, and I believe I am too exhausted and lack too much energy to be of any help."

"You're fine. I know vampires will go into a coma if they don't have access to food, and that usually takes months, so you will answer my questions."

"Maybe for a vampire who hasn't been drained of their blood and left to rot. I am already beginning to fall into a sleep by just talking to you." He fell further into the bars, trying to support himself. "Just one drop will do."

"And how do you suppose you will receive this drop? I'm not coming near you."

Gyle pointed to a small glass next to Rosie.

"Fine, but I am giving you only one drop. If you answer my questions, I will give you more."

"Yes, yes." He waved his hand as if not to care about one drop, but a red glow emerged in his eyes.

She grabbed a jagged piece of chipped stone flooring, pricked her finger and let one drop of blood fall into the glass. As the drop slipped down, another roar came—loud and piercing Rosie's ears. Rosie screamed, dropping the glass, and pressed her ears tight against her head. When the pounding wail ceased, Rosie slowly removed her hands and picked up the cup, thankfully still intact. "What was that?"

"My dungeon mate. A banshee. The annoying fairy is sensing death is close, either to herself or someone near. Probably for me. Ha."

Rosie placed a new drop into the glass and set it on the ground within finger-grasping distance of Gyle. Rosie surveilled him, ensuring he wouldn't try to attack her. And, to her surprise, he didn't. After she backed away, he reached for the glass.

The blood drop slipped into his mouth, and his eyes closed. Immense pleasure covered his face, and part of the decay withdrew. "Thank you. Now, what would you like to know?"

"I read the book I took from you. It has some pretty interesting information, but I am still trying to understand how it connects to what I want to know."

"And what do you want to know?"

"If James Kingsley was born into immortality or—" Stopping, she didn't know if what she was about to say would be considered treason or illegal in this world.

"Or … what?"

"Or if he made himself immortal."

A thin smile slid over Gyle's face. "That is a very dangerous question, Rosie. I suppose I could tell you everything I know, but it will cost you."

"Why should it cost me? All I have to do is leave, and the Superiority will take you away. They will most likely execute you, so what do you have to lose?"

Anger engulfed Gyle. "You think I don't know that, you silly girl! I know I have nothing to lose, but I want to live! I seek revenge!"

"Who do you seek revenge against?"

"Feed me. Give me my strength."

"No. You'll hurt or kill someone."

"I promise I won't." His tone and eyes softened. "Please, I just need enough to escape. I will tell you all I know if you assist me." Desperation dripped over every word. He wouldn't kill anyone. For some inexplicable reason, she just knew this, but she still refused to release him.

"You tried to kill me. Trap me and drain me."

"I know. A lack of control, but that is fixed now." Gyle lifted a long chain attached to a stone. "I didn't used to be so evil. I can tell you what you want to know, but I need help."

"Tell."

"I assume we have a deal? Alright. Well, you probably don't realize how old I actually am. I have been living in this world for more than one hundred and eighty years, and I settled here in eighteen sixty. I had a nice home, a loving wife, and three beautiful children. We lived happily for a few years when, suddenly, a string of disappearances and killings began. Thinking we would never be targeted—or, if we were, we would be safe due to our supernatural abilities—we didn't fear any attack. I was so wrong.

I went out one evening with a search party of other settlers. I figured I could help the town with the disappearances while getting something to eat. The group couldn't find any trace of where the missing persons went. When I finally returned home, I found my house in utter chaos."

"The memories?"

"Yes. When a vampire feeds, they can transfer their thoughts and emotions and even memories. It can be controlled, but, as you experienced, I had no control of my bloodlust."

"Someone murdered your family?"

"I ran to the bedroom and found my loving family on the floor, unmoving, their mouths full of blood, as someone had forcibly removed their fangs and teeth. I held my wife in my arms, vowing to avenge her death and the death of my children. It has taken me many years to discover the information I know and to find the prized book by Christion

Flare. I stumbled along the way, of course, occasionally detouring into a blood-crazed frenzy, but when I read that book, I learned why the fangs of those I loved had been taken."

"They are the most magical part of a vampire."

"Yes. They were used in some sort of ritual—a ritual, I believe, the one and only, great Premier James Kingsley had performed."

"Why do you think that?"

"Because, over the years, I learned about the lives of the other missing people who I assumed had been killed. As the book covered all sorts of beings, supernatural and not, so did the killings. Sure, there were a few discrepancies here and there I had to filter out, learning they were tragic but not connected to the killings that interested me. The ones that did interest me though were of people from each type of creature—a human, an intellect, a protector, a witch, a werewolf, a fairy, a mermaid, a shifter, and, finally, my family. Why did he kill my entire family? I'm not sure. I can only guess it was to prevent witnesses. But to also take their fangs?" Gyle paused and lowered his head.

Rosie could hear sniffling and a stifled cry. "Why did you suspect Kingsley? And how did you learn about all the other killings? Surely mermaids were not settling in Arizona back then."

"Premier Kingsley moved to the area a few months after my family had. He was an up and rising wizard in our small supernatural community, and he didn't let anyone know about his immortality, as he says now. He spoke about coming together and forming a supernatural society unknown to the natural world."

"That doesn't sound devious."

"I wasn't finished. He spoke about having a supernatural society unknown to the natural world but using humans at our disposal, whether to subdue our hunger or test experimental spells."

"But that goes against what the Superiority teaches and governs."

"Once Premier Kingsley didn't receive the support he had expected, he disappeared, and when he reemerged after my family had already been slain, he used the supernatural killings as a platform and refocused on becoming a hidden society—safe from humans. He said he would fight for the community and always stand before them, unable to be killed, and he showed us just how immortal he was.

Through my still-fresh sorrow, I narrowed my vengeance on the Premier and his previously unspoken abilities. He spoke about how he had always been immortal through his genetics but never spoke of it earlier because he thought it would make him vulnerable. I suspected dark magic, so I uncovered where he had been during his time away.

I learned of his past, the places he previously lived, and where he was planning to go. I drove myself mad with obsession, and, as I said earlier, it possessed me, causing me to spiral. I would always find my way back, though, and pick up his tracks, and I always knew he would remain here. He soon established the Superiority and gave himself the title premier. He would stay here as long as he wanted to rule and have power, especially in the place where I believe he became immortal."

"Why do you think he became immortal here?"

"Because I remember one night when a forceful monsoon rolled in over the small town. Rain poured down, causing floods and mudslides, and hundreds of thousands of lightning strikes killed multiple people. I remember the electricity coursed in the air. When the lightning ceased, and the sun rose, a magical pulse came alive. I can still feel it now. This place has an immense magical pull. It draws in all supernatural creatures."

Rosie thought to herself, giving Gyle a moment to mourn his loss. She had felt that pulse when she had first arrived, that belief of belonging and purpose. James Kingsley had taken the most magical part of each supernatural being and had made himself immortal, creating that magical sensation. He hadn't been born into it but took the lives of others. He must have had possession of the book at some point. But *Being* had only given information on the creatures. An immortal spell wasn't listed anywhere. At least that she had discerned.

She retrieved the same rock and sliced her forearm. She held the cut over the glass and let her blood drip into it. "I'm sorry about your family. That doesn't excuse you for what you did to me and Jerry or anyone else who you have hurt, but a deal is a deal, and you have held up your end. I have one more question, though. How do you think James Kingsley figured out the spell and ritual? It isn't listed in the book anywhere." She handed him the glass.

"I know. I have searched through the book myself with no luck, but I believe he either read between the lines or composed the ritual himself."

Rosie took the glass and poured more of her blood into it and handed it back. "Thank you, Gyle." She walked away, needing to further process what she had learned and whether she would tell anyone about it.

She creaked through the dungeon until finally finding an

exit that led to outside. Rosie walked in the darkness, her thoughts fighting. *Should I tell Riley—or Justin maybe? Should I go straight to Professor Shay with this information? No, she loves and follows James Kingsley so loyally she would sure think it was a hoax. What if James Kingsley found out what I've learned? Would he try to kill me?* Her mind was circling and tangling, and she didn't even notice the arm that grabbed hers and pulled her behind a tree.

A scream began to leave her mouth, but a hand covered it, tightly. Relief flooded Rosie when she saw who was holding her—Justin.

"Shh, Rosie, you can't let them hear you." He removed his hand from her mouth.

"Justin, what are you doing?"

"I was looking for you. Eleanor texted me and said you were gone, and when I saw Professor Manger stalking and scoping the grounds, I knew I had to find you fast. He was heading back this way, and I didn't want you to get caught. You would definitely not be competing in the Illumination Games if he did."

"Thanks." She noticed he stood a lot closer than normal.

He gently tucked a piece of her hair from her face to behind her ear. "What are you doing out here anyway?"

"Oh, I needed some fresh air and to clear my head."

"I've been meaning to talk to you about that." The two came from behind the tree and started to walk. "You've been acting different lately. Is anything going on? You can talk to me if you need to."

"Yeah, I know, Justin. Thank you for saying that. I've been figuring out some personal stuff, you know? Internal struggles and all." Rosie stopped walking and turned, notating her surroundings. "Where are we going exactly?"

"Have you never used the front exit from our dorm?"

"No. I thought the front doors were for show."

"Well, they aren't. Here, follow me." Justin led the way through the boulders and trees, stepping around bunches of cacti and tripping over rocks, and, finally, approached the beginning of a hump on the mountain. "Here we are."

"Where are we?"

Justin lifted a skinny shard on a rock, the ground rose, and an opening into the human dorm lobby appeared.

"Rosie!" Eleanor ran to the entry and hugged her. "Where the hell were you? I woke up, and your bed was empty, and I thought you were in the bathroom, but you weren't there or here or in the Valtic common room or library, so I panicked, and…"

Riley stepped out next to Eleanor, his face scrunched and glowering.

"I'm okay. Thanks for being so worried about me." She gave her arm a little squeeze.

"Well, I thought, since you have been so weird the last few weeks, you had done something drastic, but I knew you could never do that. You're the most levelheaded person I know."

Riley raised his eyebrows at Eleanor's comment while still glaring at Rosie.

"Oh, good! You found her! Rosie, it's dangerous to be walking around out here at night," Garrett called, walking up behind Justin.

"Hey, I thought you weren't supposed to know where our dorm is," Rosie said to him.

"You can't be me without knowing where everything is on this campus."

Rosie decided she could trust her friends and even use their help. Her friends had gone out to search for her in the middle of the night and had wanted to ensure she was okay even though they could've gotten into serious trouble themselves. She focused on Garrett and said, "Well, can you tell me where the secret dungeon is where they keep dangerous threats? Like the vampire who attacked me?"

"Uh, no," Garrett answered with confusion, as did Eleanor and Justin, but not Riley. His eyes begged her to tell him it wasn't true, that she hadn't gone alone to talk to Gyle.

But she spoke, strong and confident. "Well, I do. And I must tell you what I have been doing the past few weeks that has kept me so closed off." And her story unraveled, and she told them everything.

"That is so ridiculous! We spent an entire month learning about how Premier Kingsley's immortality gene kicked on and how he is the only one due to his specific genetic makeup. There is no way he killed a bunch of people and is now running the Superiority. No one would ever let that happen," Garrett said.

"They would if they believed whatever comes out of his mouth. Think about it. Has anyone ever questioned James Kingsley or opposed him?"

The four considered it and stared at each other. Finally, Justin broke the silence. "Rosie, you've met the man. You had a long interview with him. Do you think he could honestly be capable of murder in such a magnitude?"

Rosie was dumbfounded. Her friends didn't believe her. They thought she was crazy and that all she had said was a conspiracy. She turned to Riley, who was also staring at her with pity. For the first time, she really doubted herself. *Are they right? Have I become so involved in this that my hobby has turned into an obsession? Have I alienated myself, like Gyle has?* Her shoulders dropped, and the tension that held her left. "But it doesn't make sense."

"Rosie. It does, though." Justin cupped her hand. "How about we talk to Doctor Witam tomorrow about it?"

"Doctor Witam! Yes! He was the one who put me on this track. He told me to find this book."

"But you said you found the book by decoding an emblem."

"Yes, but it was Doctor Witam who recommended the books to me."

"You don't think he was just trying to enlighten you?"

Rosie paused. Was he only trying to teach her? Somehow finding *Being* could've been one big coincidence, but was it? Her mind revisited her conversation with Gyle. He believed her. But her friends didn't. A crazed vampire who had tried to kill her believed her.

Did I create this obsession based on book smears? Her mind swirled and stopped on only one thought. *Am I going crazy? Had the supernatural environment heightened and elevated my emotions and obsessive perfectionist behavior, like it was heightening others' emotions and personalities? The dreams and the consuming of supernatural knowledge, had it really taken over my mind and life? How?*

"I have done it before too, Rosie." Justin wrapped an arm around her, and the others followed, comforting her and helping her inside the dorm. "I've let a topic drill into my mind where I needed to know more, yearned for more. You're not alone. Try to sleep, and we will all feel better in the morning. Plus, we need to focus before we play Astive in the games on Friday."

"Yeah, okay," Rosie muttered and stalked to her bedroom. When she and Eleanor reached their door, she turned to her. "Hey, I actually need to grab something from the Valtic library. I'll be back in a second." Before Eleanor could ask to go with her, Rosie was bounding up the steps and through the portraits until she was in her secret study room.

She cleared the desk and laid out the books Doctor Witam had recommended earlier in the year. She turned toward the emblems she had uncovered, trying to understand if it was all a coincidence. She flipped through the pages again for some answer or clue. She spotted a diagram. She had never really taken note of the diagrams before because she had been determined to read about immortality, not random information about each being.

The chart was in *The Turning: When Wolves Come Out to Kill*. She flipped through another book, *Indestructible or Not?: Vampire Living*, and found a similar diagram. Then another in *The Infinite Changes: A Shape Shifters Ability* and *Open Water: The Resurfacing of Mermaids*. Soon, Rosie noticed specific diagrams in each book. She grabbed her notebook and scribbled down the diagrams and found a piece of paper she had used on her first day of classes, for her first cryptology class. She laid the papers side by side and stared at the almost identical symbols she found in the books compared to the symbols from the cipher Professor Walker had given her and Justin.

Forgetting the dilemma regarding Doctor Witam and if he had tried to inform her or put her on a long, dangerous scavenger hunt, Rosie attempted to solve the puzzle at hand. The cipher wasn't read left to right, but by going down columns, she discovered.

The first column showed a moon setting and a sun rising. Next to it was the symbol for Pluto. The next grouping was the sun. From the *Sitting in the Sun: Harnessing the Fairy Light* and *A Rising Power: How Witches Came to be* books, Rosie found a picture depicting sunrays being taken and used for harm. The next two columns Rosie discovered were of lunar and solar eclipses, and the fourth column in the grouping was of the symbol Uranus. In *Never Leave a Man Behind: A Protector's Guide*, Rosie discovered Uranus meant unpredictable changes—something there and then gone. Finally, the last grouping, the only symbol in it was found in *The Human Brain: An Intellect Mind* and *Chasing Life: Ways Humans Have Survived*. It was the symbol for Mercury.

Rosie studied the diagrams in the book, and what they indirectly represented, what they showed rather than told. The first group represented rebirth, transformation, returning. The next group expressed something missing, stolen. Finally, the sign of Mercury symbolized intelligence and knowledge. Each symbol wasn't a letter but an overall idea, something she and Justin had failed to recognize before. Rosie read through the possible meanings and what the message could be, finally uttering, "Return the stolen knowledge. Return the stolen book."

Chapter Twelve

Rosie had hardly gotten any sleep the last couple of nights. She would wake in sweat and terror from the horrid dreams that taunted her. She thought about the cipher and if the knowledge and book it spoke of was the *Being* book she had taken. But she had gotten the cipher before she had even read *Being*. Maybe it was referring to something else?

On top of her trying to decide if she should tell Professor Walker if she uncovered the cipher or not, her classes with Doctor Witam weren't going smoothly either. Rosie was happy though that Justin didn't make her talk to Doctor Witam for an emergency session so she could confess all her thoughts and feelings to him. Because the more she thought about it, the more it embarrassed her.

She believed he would patronize her, the misinformed human girl. What was worse was she didn't know if she could trust him anymore, the person who was supposed to be helping her adjust to this new world. Thankfully, she had Justin, who understood her theories and debated them with her, making excellent arguments on how actually unsound they were, helping her finally let the gnawing thoughts about James Kingsley go and allowing her to focus more clearly on her schoolwork and the Illumination Games.

"Alright! Listen up, everyone!" June was commanding the Valtic team in an isolated corner in their library.

All eyes turned to her, and silence spread across the group.

"I got the clues for tomorrow's games. We'll really have to put all our effort and brains into solving them if we want to win tomorrow. I'm sure the Astive team will realize what the clues are during the challenges, so, Rosie, Justin, I need you two to assist with this."

Both Rosie and Justin were elated. They were happy to help and perked up to find out what they could potentially be facing tomorrow.

Rosie's team were also focusing on June as she removed the clues from a small box. With the variety and makeup of the team, she thought they would have an amazing shot at winning. Rosie ran through everyone, notating their special skills and how they could understand the clues and assist in solving them—June, the captain and senior werewolf; Garrett, a sophomore werewolf; Pine, a junior fairy; Aquamarine, a sophomore mermaid; Francis, a senior vampire; Penelope, a senior witch; Reese, the freshman cardinal shifter; Madeline, a junior wildcat shifter; and, finally, Justin and Rosie, two normal humans with high IQs. Rosie could tell June was nervous at first about the team since half of it was composed of lower classmen, but she gained confidence in her choice after practices started.

"Rosie!" June's voice roared. "Are you even paying attention? The team needs you to pay attention too. You and Justin have to solve these."

"I thought the whole team had to solve them?" Garrett asked sarcastically, winking at Rosie.

"Take note of these and help." June picked up the box again and started from the beginning. "The first clue is some sort of circular ring. It can be clasped and unclasped. The next clue is a pack of gum. Finally, the last clue is a note." June unraveled the tiny scroll and read, *"Follow the lighting."*

"Hey, I know that!" Rosie shouted out.

"Know what?"

"That saying. It was told to me when I first got dropped off here. The driver told me to follow the lightning, and when I did, I found the school."

"Do you think it will be the same type of deal? Will they have lightning striking the campus and we have to go to it?" Justin asked Rosie.

"I don't know, but I think we should watch out for it."

"What about the other clues?" Pine asked Rosie, taking the box from June and giving it to her to inspect.

"The gum, I'm not sure about. But this ring isn't just any kind of ring. I've seen them before. It's a nose ring for a cow or steer or—"

"Or a bull," Justin chimed in.

Talking erupted from the group as they deduced the clues even further. Rosie and Justin set off into their own discussion about each, and June finally called off the meeting at midnight.

"Okay, I think we have discussed enough and have solved as much as we can. Go rest and meet tomorrow here an hour before the games, and we can head to the start."

"Do we know where the start will be?" Justin asked.

"No. We never know until a professor guides us there. I am just hoping it is Professor Walker and not that goon Manger." June tossed the box and its contents into the wastebin as everyone left.

"Hey, won't we need those?" Rosie asked her.

"No. At least I have never needed a clue during the games. They only serve to help us solve the challenge, not use them during." She turned and walked away.

"We better take them anyway." Justin retrieved the box from inside the garbage can. "Even if they won't be useful, I could still go for some gum."

"I couldn't agree more," Rosie said, joking, and the two left for a good night's rest before their first Illumination Games.

* * *

The morning seemed it would have gone on forever. Rosie's Friday classes droned, and her session with Doctor Witam was even worse.

"Are you excited for your first Illumination Games tonight?"

"Yeah, they should be fun. Hopefully, I don't slow down the team though, since I don't have any super skills or powers."

"Your mind is your superpower, Rosie. I'm sure you'll use it in an effective manner and come out succeeding."

"I hope you're right."

"Do you wish to discuss anything, Rosie? The last few times I've seen you, you have been distant."

Her cheeks flushed. She knew this question would come, but she still hadn't devised an answer for it. Rosie didn't know if she should flat out ask why he had sent her on a wild goose chase or if he honestly didn't know the path she would take.

"I'm full of nerves. But I'm excited too. I want us to win tonight." *Coward,* she thought to herself.

"Okay, well, if you have nothing else to discuss, I have some other things to finish up so I can watch you and the rest of the Valtic team succeed."

"Alright, sounds good." She stood, opened the door then turned to scrutinize Doctor Witam for even an ounce of sinister in him, but none showed.

"Are you okay, Rosie?"

"Yeah."

"Okay, you can talk to me about anything. You can always trust me."

Rosie gave him a smile and a nod then left the office.

"Hey, Rosie..." Justin came running up to her in the hallway.

"Hey yourself. What are you doing here? Didn't you have your session yesterday?"

"Yeah, but I had a few more things to review with Doctor Witam for class. Are you done already? Isn't your session another twenty minutes?"

"We didn't have much to discuss today, so he's all yours."

"Thanks. I'll see you tonight." He pushed himself into the office and closed the door, and Rosie heard a faint click as it locked behind her.

* * *

"Alright, how is everyone doing? Good? Aqua, you're looking more blue than normal. Everything will be fine, guys. We must keep our cool. We can win this."

June's attempt to give the team a pep talk before the games was sweet, Rosie thought, but it was hard to accept her encouraging messages when she too was shaking.

"Okay everyone, here comes our escort. Now, don't peek at where they take us or else the other team gets a twenty-second head start."

"Good evening, everyone," Professor Shay said. "Hope you all are ready for tonight's events. Please put on these blindfolds and chain up so I can guide you to your destination."

The team complied and grabbed hands.

"Alright, a few steps forward. Go to the side. Okay, now down."

Rosie's body moved without her control. When she thought they should be in the dining room, a breeze tickled her nose, and cheers and screams from a crowd pounded her ears.

"You may remove your blindfolds."

When she lifted hers off, Rosie saw she was in Kingstown. Her classmates lined the streets, barricaded from them to make a clear path down the road.

"Were we just transported?" Rosie asked, leaning over to Justin.

"Uh, yes, we were."

The two stared in awe.

"Hey! Focus up, everyone." June grabbed Rosie's arm and forced her into the huddle. "Okay, guys. We got this. Let's crush Astive and win these games!"

The huddle separated as Professor Shay quieted the onlookers. "Good evening! Let the first Illumination Games of the year commence!"

More roars and cheers sounded in every direction.

Rosie was confused. Had the first challenge started? Were they supposed to wait for Professor Shay to yell, *Go*? What was she supposed to do? She turned to Justin, but he also had the expression.

"Everyone, I feel the first task. Run!" June yelled, and the team followed her.

"Why are we running?" Rosie yelled.

"That's why!" June pointed behind the group.

A herd of bulls rounded the corner of town and charged fast toward them.

"Holy crap!" Garrett screamed and half transformed so he could move faster.

"Everyone, if you can transform to run faster, do so! If you can't, find someone who can to carry you!"

Before Rosie could even look for someone to grab her, June threw her over her shoulder as the team sped up. Using the time on June's back, Rosie evaluated the Astive team as they followed close behind. The bulls inched closer, and Rosie realized June had no idea where they were supposed to run. For all she knew, it was just *reach the end of the road and they were safe*, but they got there, and the bulls still came.

"Now what?" Pine yelled.

Confused and worried, June had no idea where to go next.

"That way, June!" Rosie yelled.

"Why?"

Rosie opened her mouth to answer as a streak of ruby lightning hit the mountaintop. "Go!"

They ran up the mountainside, neck and neck with the Astive team, who was chasing a sapphire lighting strike.

They finally made it, and June threw off Rosie to catch her breath. "Okay, genius, now what—"

Another strike flashed from the sky and hit the ground right in the middle of the group.

Rosie closed her eyes. The brightness stung, and when she rubbed away the spots that clouded her vision, she saw the group was no longer on the mountaintop.

"Where are we now?" Madeline yelled.

"Penelope, can you give us some light?" June asked.

Penelope whispered a spell while clasping her necklace. The stone beamed like a flashlight.

Rosie surveyed her new surroundings. They were inside, but walls were up around them, directing them where to go. "We're in a maze. We have to find the end before Astive does. Pine, Reese, can you two fly above the walls and determine a path?"

"The walls go all the way to the ceiling," Justin said, pointing.

"No, they don't." Rosie grabbed the light from Penelope and pointed it up to show a slight opening.

"Pine, go lead us," June ordered. "Good job, Rosie."

The team followed Pine's faint voice through the maze. They had to have covered at least a mile before finally finding a door that Rosie assumed was the end.

"Yes! Good job, Pine!" June yelled.

Pine transformed to his human self.

"Okay, team, I don't know what the next task is, but I am proud of you all." She opened the door to a small landing and an up-staircase.

"We are so close, guys," Garrett said, jumping the short staircase to the door. His hand landed on the handle, and he started to twist it open.

"No! Garrett! Stop!" Rosie yelled, spotting the water leaking under the door, but it was too late.

Water pushed Garrett backward into the group, and it quickly filled the staircase.

Aquamarine shifted and indicated for everyone to hold hands. She forced herself through the shooting water and to the surface.

Rosie spewed out water and coughed. "We're in the lake!"

The students who had been in the town now surrounded the body of water, cheering and roaring, with a few boos from the Astive students. The Astive team was nowhere in sight.

"We have to swim to the other end." Rosie pointed to the finish sign on the sandy bank. Rosie, for a second, thought they were about to win the games, but bodies rose to the surface on her left—the Astive team. "We have to hurry!" She started swimming but stopped. With her head submerged underwater, she looked around. *Where is that singing coming from?*

Mermaids from Astive were singing, trying to put her into a trance, trying to lead her away from the finish.

The mermaids had already enthralled her teammates, the long, scaly yet oddly mesmerizing tails had entrapped them. They even got Aquamarine.

No, I can't be swayed. I have to finish, but look at him. Rosie focused on one merman in particular. *He is so beautiful. He looks so strong, and his scales shine in the most alluring pattern. I need to meet him. I want him to hold me.* She glided her body through the water to him, listening to the melody he sang. She reached her hand to him, their fingers almost touching, but a hand forced her backward, and lips were suddenly on hers. The trance was broken. She quickly swam to the surface for air, realizing she had been underwater for too long.

"What happened? Why weren't you hypnotized?" she shouted at Justin.

"I knew we would need the gum! Chew some and put it in your ears. It will block the singing."

She did as instructed, and the two set off to the finish line. They were right next to one Astive team member, the others captured by the Valtic teams' few merpeople.

"Go!" Justin yelled to her as he swam toward the Astive member and tackled him, pulling him below the water.

Rosie reached the bank and ran to the finish. Growing close to the end, Rosie moved with all her might, but something wrapped around her legs and caused her to fall.

Sand eels popped out of the ground and started to pull her beneath the surface.

She turned back to the finish line, seeing it so close.

Some of her classmates cheered her to move, and others cheered because she was trapped.

She noticed Justin was losing his grip on the Astive member. *Quick, how will they release me?* Sand eels were blind and attacked based on vibrations in the ground. *Hold still, don't move.*

But the eels kept their grip tight.

Rosie searched around. What could help her, she thought. Then she remembered how she had evaded the snake while trying to get to the school back in August. She stretched out, still fighting the eels, and grabbed a rock. She threw it back, and with the creatures sensing the new vibration, they released her and tunneled to the rock and jumped out of the ground, seizing the object.

With her legs free, she moved fast to avoid being trapped again, and the Astive team member had reached the bank and ran up next to her. Neck and neck, the two ran, with the lifted sand creeping toward them, the sand eels on their heels. They burst from the ground and jumped toward the finish line.

Rosie landed as Valtic team members surrounded her, cheering and calling her name. She turned to see a large eel had trapped the Astive student on the ground just in front of the finish line.

"Our winners!" Professor Shay announced, setting off ruby fireworks.

Rosie heard the deafening cheers from her teammates, and Justin ran from the lake to her.

He grabbed her into a hug, swung her around, set her back down then kissed her for the second time that evening.

Rosie pulled away and stared at him.

He smiled. "You did it!"

"We did it!" she replied.

The rest of the Valtic Illumination team ran up to them, and the crowd surrounded the team.

Rosie searched for Riley, but he was nowhere. She turned again and spotted him stomping into the forest, punching a tree as he entered. *He saw the kiss. I have to talk to him.* As she moved to leave, Justin and Garrett threw her onto their shoulders and paraded through the crowd. Rosie looked back to where Riley was, but he was gone.

Chapter Thirteen

With the entire Valtic team packed into their living room, cheering and celebrating their win against Astive, Rosie gained a sense of purpose and belonging. She drank loose juice, chatted with team members she hadn't gotten to know yet and let Justin drape an arm around her. The celebration continued late into the night, and Rosie checked her phone when she finally reached her dorm room, showing it was one in the morning, and Riley had not responded to any of her messages.

Rosie's head hit the pillow hard, as it was too heavy for her to hold up any longer. Her body ached from the stress and work it had been put under during the games, and her fluffy bed felt like a cloud. Her eyes slipped closed.

"Rose," a soothing, tranquil voice whispered. "Rose. Come on. Not too much further, my dear."

Rosie opened her eyes, but the room was pitch black, and she couldn't discern anyone or anything that may have been in the room. As she stood and walked to the door, Rosie was ready to meet any person who may wait behind it, but when she opened the door, she was hit hard and fast and found herself being swallowed up by water like she had during the games. She swam fast to the surface, and once above the body of water, she gasped for air. Warm water splashed over her, impairing her vision. Finally, as she cleared her stinging eyes, she searched for help, and, as she tried to swim to the bank of the lake, she saw two figures dancing in the rain.

The first was leading, and the body was too difficult to decipher; the darkness and water did not allow Rosie to see properly. She did recognize the second person though—it was the woman in the white dress. "Help!" she gurgled out, but the water continued to consume her presence. "Help!" she screamed again, unable to voice her immediate danger. The pouring rain and the thrashing waves masked any sound she made.

The two people were gone, and Rosie had to swim out before she drowned. She dove under the surface and forced her body forward, swimming toward the shallows. But when she surfaced for a quick breath, the lake had somehow transformed. No longer was she swimming in warm freshwater, but rather, she was swimming in a hot, red, thick substance. Spitting out what she had accidentally swallowed, she tasted something metallic. Her mind whirled as the waves of blood forced her under the surface. As she sank into the dense liquid, her mouth filled again as she tried to scream.

Rosie sat upright in bed, her screaming stopped, but another sound was coming from her.

"What's happening?" Eleanor shouted, standing up fast and rushing to Rosie's bed.

But Rosie couldn't respond. She was choking on something.

"Rosie!" As Eleanor prepared to give her the Heimlich, Rosie finally coughed up what was stuck.

A thick, red, gooey substance with the same metal flavor

she'd tasted in her dream landed on her comforter.

"Oh my gosh! What is that?"

Catching her breath and staring at the goo, Rosie shook her head, unable to explain how something from her dream had manifested itself into something real.

The two girls sat in their room in silence. Eleanor helped Rosie clean up and finally words formed. "Rosie, do you know what that thing was?"

"I think so."

"Are you okay?"

"I had a dream. I was drowning in blood, and then I coughed up a substantial amount. No, I'm not okay."

"Sorry to ask."

She shouldn't have responded to Eleanor so poorly, she thought. "No, I'm sorry. I have been having nightmares lately, and I don't know why and, huh, I'm sorry I reacted like that. I'll be okay."

"Okay. Want to think about something else?"

"More than anything."

"Okay good, because I have a lot planned for us today."

"What do you mean? I was going to do some homework and rest."

"That is no way to redirect your brain. Instead, we are going to do our makeup, put on pretty dresses, and go to the dance."

"The dance? I wasn't planning on going. Eleanor let's just—"

"You're going. You have to be my date. No one has asked me yet, and I know you don't have a date, so I thought we could go together. Please, Rosie, please."

Rosie surveyed Eleanor and interpreted how badly she

wanted to go. Her eyes tore and pleaded with her. "Fine, but I don't have anything to wear."

"We can go to town. That's even more of a reason to get out of bed. Now march!"

Rosie laughed and rolled out of bed, and once ready, they meandered to the dining hall. "You have to promise nothing too ruffly or froofy for me, Eleanor."

"You're no fun. I will say though, if I find an amazing dress for you, you will wear it."

They found a seat by themselves to eat as Riley sat by Rosie.

"Hey, Riley. I wasn't sure you'd be here."

"Yeah, I had to clear my head after the games, which, by the way, you did great."

"I wouldn't say great. I almost got lured away by one of the Astive mermen and devoured by a sand eel."

"But you didn't, and you crossed the finish line, winning it all for your team, so you deserve a pat on the back." He placed his hand on her shoulder.

Goosebumps rose on her skin, and tingles swarmed all over.

"Anyway, I was curious. The dance is tonight, and I wasn't going to go, but my mom sent me some clothes, and I thought, why not? You know? So, would you want to—"

The entrance from the Valtic library flung open, commanding the attention of all sitting in the dining room. Sparks and bangs filled Rosie's ears. Plumes of smoke rose around the room, and mini fireworks exploded near the ceiling. Exiting the Valtic room were Garrett and Justin, holding mini crystal balls with fireworks detonating inside, as if what was occurring in the ball was happening in the dining hall. As they approached Rosie and Eleanor, the two boys threw the crystal balls onto the floor.

The two girls turned their backs to avoid glass hitting them, but none did. Instead, sparkler lights flew into the air and formed the word, *Homecoming?*

It took a second for Rosie to understand what was happening, but, as soon as Eleanor shrieked, "Yes!" she realized Garrett and Justin were formally asking them to the dance. Rosie turned to look at Riley, but he had left her side and had disappeared. Why would he leave? Didn't he want to ask her? She was annoyed at his behavior and noticed Justin now sat next to her.

"So, Rosie? What do you say?"

Rosie scanned the room again for Riley before finally saying, "Yes, let's go."

* * *

The town was full of students finalizing their last-minute preparations for the dance. Girls were buying gowns, boys were buying suits, and employees were trying to oversell everyone on the so-called latest trends and arrivals.

"Here, girls, look at this new corsage with the ever-rare filia plant. It will catch any guy's attention with its irresistible scent."

"No, girls, this way! Try to wear our organic makeup. Sure to make your eyelashes ten times longer and thicker."

"This way, ladies! We have the largest selection of vintage dresses, dating all the way back to the early nineteen hundreds."

That last one caught Eleanor's attention. She pulled Rosie's hand to guide her into the near-empty building and browsed the displays, grabbing the most luxurious dresses she could find.

"Eleanor. You might want to check the price tag before trying on anything," Rosie called to her, but Eleanor was already in a dressing room.

Garments flew behind the door, and she couldn't help but giggle at Eleanor's love for clothes. Even in a world full of supernatural creatures, clothing still was more amusing to her.

Slow and quiet, Rosie walked through the store, gazing and admiring many of the beautiful pieces. The jewels that draped along the long gowns and the tulle that bounced right into the aisle was a sight to see. Rosie slid her hand along the different materials and textures and stopped at a simple black gown. It had a fitted, straight across, strapless top and a flowing bottom half starting at the waist. She read the price and was surprised she could afford it with the school's monthly stipend, along with what she had made working in the library. "The only thing left is to try it on," she said, talking to the dress.

She slipped it on, and, while it was half an inch too big, she couldn't find anything else to her liking in the store that she could afford. Eleanor was still trying on clothes, and Rosie took her gown to the checkout, ensuring the cashier placed the dress in a garment bag and removed the tags with care.

Eleanor exited her changing room and strutted to the checkout. "Okay, I think I finally found one."

"Perfect," Rosie said, admiring Eleanor's taste. The dress was a deep red and had a thigh-high slit that reached the ground on one side. Thin straps held up the straight-across top, and Rosie thought Eleanor's frame would fill out the dress nicely. "Is it weird we are buying gowns instead of costumes for the dance? I mean, it's Halloween."

"No. Garrett said the dance isn't a costume party and that witches and wizards take offense to anyone dressing up."

"Then why was he so excited about the dance falling on Halloween?"

"I guess the curtain separating the living from the dead is almost nonexistent tonight. Not only because it is Halloween, but it is also a blue moon, you know, a second full moon in the month. Garrett thinks the dance will be populated with spirits and ghosts."

A cold air hit Rosie's neck, and she shivered at the thought of seeing the dead. Wanting to move past the subject, she asked Eleanor, "Is there anywhere else we need to go?"

Checking the time, Eleanor gasped. "We need to get ready now."

"What are you talking about? We don't have to meet the boys until six."

"Rosie, we have to do hair, nails, makeup, find shoes, and there is so much more to be done! Come on!"

The entire process was overwhelming, but Rosie was grateful she had Eleanor to help her, spend time with her, and guide her. Back home, Glenda Zimmers would normally be the one assisting Rosie. As Eleanor was applying Rosie's makeup, she remembered how Glenda would give Rosie one of her old charity ballgowns for her middle school dances and do her hair and makeup. She became a princess, something her own mother could never make her. If she was back home, she thought, Glenda would most likely be helping her again, convincing her to take off work and spend time as a normal teenager would.

"Okay, take a look." Eleanor pivoted Rosie to look at her

transformation.

"Oh my gosh, Eleanor. I'm…" Rosie stared at herself, lightly touching her face and the dangling curl on her cheek.

"You're gorgeous. I know! I am a beautification genius. Now, come on. We need to dress and meet the boys."

The two slid into their gowns, and Eleanor rolled up her arm-long ivory satin gloves, making her look more glamorous than she already was. They sashayed into the crisp air, using the dorm's front exit rather than going through the portrait hole. It was a beautiful night, and the light breeze that swept over the mountainside brought the scent of fresh flowers and pine. Rosie was elated and happy. As the two continued, Rosie felt a hard tug at the train of her dress and a harsh tear.

"Oops," Olive said with a firm heel dug into the dress, grinning a sinister smile. "I guess I really should watch where I walk." She turned to strut off.

"Maybe I should be careful where I put my fist!" Eleanor retorted.

"Eleanor, it's okay."

"No, it isn't! How dare she do that and act like she is so much better than us. She is such a little—"

"Witch?" The two burst out laughing, and once they finally caught their breath, Rosie spoke. "Go on ahead. I can't wear this to the dance. I need to change. Tell Justin I'll meet him there."

"Do you want me to come back with you?"

"No, I'm fine."

"Well, okay, but don't take too long. And go through my closet too. I know I have something in there."

Rosie ambled to the dorm, pondering what the night would bring and if she could actually enjoy herself. Deep in thought,

she rounded one of the tall boulders close to the dorm and—
"Oof!"

"Rosie, I'm sorry! Are you okay?" Riley extended his hand to help her up.

"Oh, hi. Yeah, I'm okay, just heading back to the dorm." Rosie got to her feet and stared at Riley, confused.

"Wow, Rosie, you look …"

"Ridiculous? Out of place?"

"No. Beautiful."

"Oh, well, my dress ripped, so I can't be that beautiful. Especially since I will probably be wearing one of my school uniforms to the dance."

"No, you won't. Come on." Riley, still holding her hand, led her to the dorm lobby. "Okay, wait here." He ran down the staircase and, a few minutes later, emerged with a giant black box.

Rosie couldn't help but be confused. "What is that?"

"Go to your room and open it. I'm sure with your brain you will figure out what to do next."

Rosie took the box from Riley, her hand gliding over his, and walked to her room. She gently lifted the lid and first read a note laying on gracefully folded gold tissue paper.

Rosie,

Riley told me that you had a dance coming up, and I couldn't help but send this dress to you. I wore it myself years ago and would love for you to have it. Please enjoy it and make memories in it.

Love you, Glenda Zimmers

Folding back the tissue paper, she spied a champagne-gold

beaded gown, as well as gold strappy heels. Rosie's hand glided over the beads, and she gently removed the dress and held it up, looking in the mirror. She removed her own torn dress and slipped on this one, caressing her body and appreciating this was what she was supposed to wear to the dance. The sweetheart neckline, mermaid fit and flare, and design detail made Rosie feel royal. The final thing she did was wrap her Valtic necklace around her wrist like a bracelet to show off the gorgeous neckline.

She ascended the steps to the lobby, and Riley donned a starstruck expression and displayed the same goofy side smile he would always wear when they were together, and Rosie couldn't help but giggle—not from embarrassment of the attention but at how much the two had endured, and that at that moment, things were like they had been back home.

"Well, Ms. Connors ..." Riley dipped a gentlemanly bow. "May I escort you to the dance?"

"Why, yes, Mr. Zimmers," she replied, curtsying back. "You may."

"Wait. There's one more thing." Riley pulled a smaller black box from his pocket and opened it to Rosie.

Now she was the one wearing the starstruck expression.

"It looks expensive, but it's actually the diamond you caught on our first day. I got Paige to swipe it from your room. I told her what I was doing with it, and she thought it was cute and romantic. Then I had a Surgent wizard help me make the rest of it for a small fee."

Rosie was shocked. In the box was a gold diamond necklace with the two-carat diamond centered in the middle and gold earrings, both perfectly matching the dress.

Riley guided the necklace around her neck, clasped it and

adjusted it. "There we are. Now we can go."

Rosie wrapped her arm around his, and they swaggered through the mountainside. He even carried her over some rough parts to not damage the dress or tear it like the last one. Finally, deep in conversation, the two climbed the small hill, surveying the grassy field where the dance was taking place, and their entrance made all heads turn toward them. As they were about to descend to the dance, one of Rosie's heels got wedged between two rocks. Pulling her foot as hard as she could, she got free but lost her balance, propelling herself forward.

Riley quickly grabbed her hand and pulled her close.

Rosie's yelp had gotten the attention of almost every student below.

Heads stared up at the two, and whispers flew across the crowd as Rosie spotted Justin, looking dashing and handsome, while he started up the side to her.

"Rosie, wow, you look amazing."

"Thanks, Justin."

His hand extended to her, and, for a split second, she had forgotten she was supposed to be at the dance with him and not Riley.

She grabbed it and turned to Riley. "Thank you for escorting me, Riley. And please, if you talk to your mom, thank her for me." But she felt it wasn't enough, so she released Justin's hand and gave Riley a hug and kiss on the cheek, then retook her place next to Justin to enter the crowd of staring faces—some happy and some envious.

"Care to dance?" Justin asked with a hopeful expression.

"Sure, that would be great."

The song was upbeat, and Rosie and Justin strode to Eleanor

and Garrett who seemed to be having a blast.

"Rosie, where did you get that dress?" Eleanor asked, screaming over the music.

"Riley's mom sent it to me. I forgot about it until my dress ripped." Rosie didn't want to lie, but she also didn't want to tell everyone how Riley had presented the dress to her, or the jewels he draped on her.

"I would never forget getting a dress like that."

Rosie smiled and continued to dance with her friends. She didn't expect to have as much fun as she was having, but everything else seemed to fade away—her schoolwork, her strange theories and hunting for answers, and her new emotions forming for her best friend. It was like the dance made her mind go into a euphoric place. She was in such a state until she saw Riley from the corner of her eye sitting at a table alone, watching her. Her gaze kept catching him and how he declined dancing with a few girls who asked him.

Justin grabbed Rosie's hand, completely catching her off guard, and twirled her, bringing her in close to him after.

Letting out an awkward giggle, she peered up at Justin.

"Hey, do you guys want something to drink and eat?"

"Oh, yes please," Garrett responded. "I'm starving."

Rosie turned to Justin, and his grip loosened around her waist. "Yeah, sure. Let's go."

He started off without her, and she walked next to Eleanor, guilt filling her stomach.

"Hey, Riley!" Eleanor yelled and went to sit at the same table. "Mind if we join you? Looks like everywhere else is full."

"Definitely. I think Gunner and Flynn are coming too. Maybe we can finally join forces rather than be enemies?"

"I highly doubt that," Garrett said, chuckling and bringing Eleanor a drink and a small plate of appetizers.

"Come on, guys," Justin said, returning with Rosie's drink and plate, "I'm sure they feel the same way about us. We can at least try." His hand moved to Rosie's back as he placed down her food.

Strange, she wondered. It was like his mood did a complete one-eighty.

"Anyway, I suppose they can also join us, granted they are cool enough."

Confused at what Garrett had said, Rosie replied, "Join us? Where are we going?"

"There's always an after party. It's a little way out into the desert, but it is so worth it. Last year a bunch of upperclassmen chose an underclassman as prey, and they all shifted and tried to catch him. It was hilarious!"

"Garrett!" Eleanor swatted his arm. "That's not funny at all."

"Relax. I was the underclassman, and I volunteered. And I won. No one caught me, and I forever have *cool guy* branded on my reputation."

"It sounds like fun," Riley said.

"Yeah, but aren't you worried about the roaming spirits?" Rosie asked.

"No, most are just visiting and don't want to cause real harm."

As Garrett answered, Rosie spied the crowd for any faces she didn't recognize—a face of a ghost—and spotted a white cotton dress. The woman in white, she immediately thought, but, as fast as she saw the figure, it was gone.

"Hey, you okay?" Riley whispered into her ear.

"Yes, I'm fine," she replied, refocusing on her friends.

They hung out for a little longer until Gunner and Flynn joined, and Rosie was surprised at how well the two melted into their group. Gone were the days of fighting in the dining hall. Rather, the three Surgents found they had a lot in common with the four Valtics, especially as she witnessed Gunner mature since becoming Riley's friend.

"Are you guys ready? Better to leave now while a lot of people are still here rather than go near the end, and all the supervisors can spot where we're headed."

"Yeah, let's party!" Gunner yelled, and the group laughed.

They hiked through the rocky mountainside, the boys assisting the girls whose footwear did not help the journey. Finally, venturing farther into the desert, Rosie spotted where all the other students had gone. A treehouse, the size of an actual house, supported by tall saguaros and thick trees stood in the middle of the mountain. Students were on the ground as well as spread across multiple levels on landings and crossings, and Rosie was amazed she hadn't seen this before while out exploring.

"I had no idea this was here," she said to Garrett.

"Yeah, neither do the professors. Some seniors awhile back put an enchantment on it so only those under the age of eighteen could find it."

"Smart," Justin said, looking around in awe at the construction.

The group walked up a ramp to another level of the party with a dancefloor. Everyone proceeded to it, all except Rosie and Riley.

"Want some air and to go for a walk?"

"That would be great. This is all a little much to take in. But

I better go tell Justin. I don't want him to worry."

"I don't think he will." Riley pointed to the dancefloor where Justin was happily dancing with a Surgent girl, laughing and showing off to her.

Relieved to see he was having fun, Rosie turned, and the two started back down to the ground.

"So, did you have fun tonight?" Riley asked as the noise from the party grew farther behind them.

"Yeah, I did. It was nice to go and not have to worry about anything for once—no crazed vampire killers, no hunting for clues, nothing. What about you? Did you have fun?"

"Yes, I did. It was nice to watch you let loose a little. I don't think I've seen you like that since… actually, I've never seen you let loose."

She bumped her shoulder into his. "That's not true."

He paused and faced her. The two stopped walking, and the moment stood still. They stared at each other. Going on a journey together like this was only possible in storybooks, yet there they were, she thought.

Riley's warm hand slipped into hers, and the weight of him drifted closer. "Rosie, I—"

"Riley, I know." And with her free hand, she touched his cheek and leaned into him, and their lips touched gently. She pulled back, her eyes still closed, enjoying the moment. She opened them to look into his eyes, but horror was spread across his face. "What? Was it that bad?" she asked, but then felt something warm hitting and dripping down her cheek. Whipping her head upward, she jumped back in terror.

High in the trees was a student dangling from her ankles with arms extended like an upside-down cross. Huge gashes laid on her back where her shoulder blades were—where her fairy wings would be if they hadn't been sliced out.

Chapter Fourteen

"Rosie, go find help!" Riley yelled as he was already halfway up the tree to recover the attacked girl.

For some reason, though, Rosie couldn't move. She gaped up at the dangling girl, shocked but also in amazement.

"Rosie! Go!" Riley ordered again, snapping her from her trance.

Rosie turned to go find help and spotted an envelope. As she listened to Riley struggle to cut down the girl, Rosie opened the envelope and removed a thick card like the invitation she had received to test into the school. On the card, strange symbols and characters looked back at her. Some she recognized, but before she could inspect them further, Riley called at her again.

"Rosie! Go!"

She spotted his desperate face and sprinted to find someone, dropping the card where she had found it. She sped through the mountainside, trying to find anyone who could help, but she was alone. She halted, trying to figure out where she was. "Help!" She turned in a circle again, and behind a saguaro, the flow from a white dress flittered out, and Rosie stopped. She spied the woman in white running from her, and Rosie knew she had to follow.

Sprinting as fast as she could in her dress, Rosie tried to catch the woman, but when she turned around a hill, Rosie lost her. She continued forward, hoping to find her again, but instead, she spotted Professors Shay and Manger talking in the woods.

"Professor Shay! Help!" Rosie ran toward them as they turned to look at her, stunned—embarrassed even—but their expressions quickly turned to confusion.

"Ms. Connors, what's going on? What's all over your face?"

"Please, Professor Shay, you have to come with me." Rosie turned back to run to Riley, but he was already heading her way, the girl in his arms.

"Mr. Zimmers, what is this?"

"She's alive, Professor, but please, she needs help!"

"Oh my. Jon, please take this girl to the hospital. Doctor Geller needs to examine her immediately."

Professor Manger scooped the girl from Riley's arms and bolted toward the school. Professor Shay, Riley, and Rosie followed not too far behind.

* * *

Rosie and Riley stood, waiting to learn the girl's condition at the hospital. They watched Professor Shay as she spoke with Doctor Geller and Professor Manger. The three hurried behind a curtain where the girl laid. Shadows were the only thing Rosie and Riley could see. Hands were over the girl's body, and hushed whispers filled the area.

Professor Shay pushed the others out of the way and placed her hands over the gashes. A faint shadowy whirl of wind went over the girl's back, and the girl sighed with relief, and silence presented itself over the room.

Professor Shay and Professor Manger stepped out behind the curtain and clopped to the two students.

"What happened? What did you two do?" Professor Manger asked, his accusations startling Rosie.

"What? We didn't do anything!" Riley stated.

"We found her. In the woods, strung up."

"Humph. Likely story. I told you, Charlene. We should've stopped letting in humans ages ago."

Rosie and Riley remained silent, their gazes on Professor Shay, hoping she would conclude they were telling the truth.

"What were you two doing in the woods so far away from school and the dance?" she asked them.

"We, um…" Sputtering, Rosie knew she had to tell the truth but didn't want any of her friends in trouble.

"We left the dance and went for a walk. We haven't had time to be alone and catch up," Riley stated. "We have been best friends all of our lives, and since coming here, we haven't had the same quality time as we used to."

Rosie listened to Riley in awe as he took charge of the conversation, and when he finished, she refocused on the two teachers and nodded in agreement.

"Fine. But, if I find out you two are lying, you will be seriously reprimanded. Jon, go wake the other staff members. We need to conduct a search of the school and a headcount of each student in their dorm. Whoever performed this heinous act might still be on campus."

Professor Manger nodded at Professor Shay, and before leaving, he let out a low growl to the two freshmen and ran off.

"Now, you two will have to answer some questions. Go to your dorm rooms and await further instructions. And, if I hear so much as a peep that you didn't follow directions, you will both be on the first flight home."

Nodding, the two left, solemn and worried. As soon as they were far enough away from Professor Shay and any other listening ears, Rosie turned to Riley. "Someone has to tell the partygoers that they are searching the campus."

"I know. But, if we go and are caught, we will definitely be expelled."

"True, but what if there was a way we could get there with no one seeing?"

"How?"

"Remember when I went to find Gyle? Remember the blueprints?"

"Of course."

Rosie grabbed his hand, and they hurried to the secret passage through James Kingsley's portrait to return to the dungeons. "Come on. I think there's an exit near the treehouse here." Rosie lifted one of the stone tiles to reveal a dark cobwebbed-filled shaft.

Riley jumped in first, and, as Rosie was about to enter it herself, a light brightened the hallway. As fast as she could move, Rosie maneuvered into the shaft and replaced the tile on top to not arouse suspicion and stayed near the top to hear who was there.

"Quiet down here. I don't think we have anything to worry about," Professor Manger stated.

"I agree. But wait, isn't the vampire supposed to be down here?" Doctor Witam asked.

"You're right. He is normally moaning and begging for

blood." Professor Manger's heavy footsteps sounded above her.

She prayed he wouldn't break through the stone, exposing her and Riley, but her mind shifted gears when she realized he was right. She didn't notice Gyle when they had passed his cell. Rosie heard a gasp, and Professor Manger let out an angered grunt.

"He's escaped!" The two men ran down the dungeon hallway, and the door slammed behind them.

"Riley, we have to move fast. Everyone is in danger."

The pair shimmied down the shaft, and Riley kicked out a stone, filling the small area with fresh air and moonlight. They sprinted to the party and were relieved no one was injured or hurt and were still dancing and laughing.

"Everyone! Back to the dorms!" Riley yelled. "Hurry! They are doing searches!"

Rosie had never seen all the students and teams work together so well. Shifters and wolves carried slower students. Vampires ran with humans on their backs, and witches and wizards cloaked the treehouse, covering any trace it had ever been there. Stampeding through the desert, Rosie worried someone would hear them but was shocked and pleased Olive had cast a spell over everyone to mute any noise that would escape the group.

Garrett swiftly let Eleanor and Justin off his back and joined the other wolves to their dorm.

"Come on," Rosie said, grabbing Eleanor's wrist, and dragged her down the staircase to their room. The safety of being behind a locked door sent waves of relief through Rosie. She couldn't believe they had helped everyone to their dorms without anyone getting into trouble. The relief, however, faded as fast as it arrived. Guilt consumed her next. Then worry.

Eleanor asked, "Rosie, are you okay? What happened? What's on your face, and how did you know they would be doing searches?"

But Rosie couldn't answer. She ran to the bathroom and locked the door. She rushed to the toilet, and she tasted everything she had consumed that day a second time. She crawled into the shower and let the cold water wash over her, hiding the tears that slid down her face.

It was her fault the vampire had attacked the girl, and it was her fault such extreme danger existed on campus. She was the one who had set Gyle free. She was the one who had set a killer free.

* * *

Rosie woke the next morning, unsure how she had gotten to where she was. She was in her pajamas in bed. She shot upright, surprised. In her room sat Professor Shay, Professor Walker, and another lady Rosie didn't recognize.

"About time, Ms. Connors," Professor Shay said.

"Good morning, Rosie," Professor Walker said as she handed Rosie a hot mug. "Here, drink this."

The vile liquid made Rosie's face contort, but, as to not offend Professor Walker, she flashed a weak smile.

"Don't worry. It isn't supposed to taste good, but to help you relax."

"Ms. Connors," Professor Shay started again, "this is Agent Hurwell. She has a few questions for you and Mr. Zimmers. If you will please meet us in my office in ten minutes. I have made the mirror, here, an entry point."

Professor Shay and Agent Hurwell left the room.

Professor Walker put her hand on Rosie's and whispered, "Drink up. You'll need it," and followed the other two through the swirling mirror.

What happened last night, Rosie wondered as the scenes of the evening played through her mind? Her stomach knotted, and tears refilled in her eyes. She chugged the tea for some hope of forgetting, but she didn't. Her memories were not gone, but her mind did ease, and her stomach untangled, and she could blink away her tears. Rosie finally stood, the pressure and tightness held in her muscles releasing and no longer aching. The tea was working, and Rosie finished getting dressed and walked through her full-length mirror.

Light filled the spacious office as the morning sun shone through a great window. Rosie spotted Riley sitting in one of the high-backed chairs in front of Professor Shay's desk, and Professor Shay sat behind it. Professor Walker, Professor Manger, Doctor Witam, and Agent Hurwell were also present. Rosie, knees weak and wobbly, made her best attempt to the chair next to Riley but failed, and Doctor Witam came up next to her and assisted her over.

Professor Shay spoke to the two before Rosie had plopped into the chair. "I want to know every detail from last night. I want to know where you found Ms. Lightstrom, how you found her, and if you noticed anything out of the ordinary."

"You mean anything else besides a student strung up in a tree? No, I think that was the only *out-of-the-ordinary* thing we saw last night," Riley retorted.

Rosie stared at him, shocked at how he had responded, and Professor Shay glared at him. "Mr. Zimmers, I don't think you understand how much trouble you are in."

"Trouble?" Rosie asked, confusion and anger coursing through her.

"Yes, trouble for—"

"You should be awarding Riley a medal. We found that girl in a tree, hung upside down, with her arms sprawled out. Riley climbed up there and cut her down while I ran for help. He carried her to you and made sure she was still breathing when you two"—Rosie glared at Professor Manger—"were in the woods, doing who knows what. So, I could be telling you the same thing. You, Professor Shay, should be the one in trouble because we students were the ones saving each other—not a teacher, not the police, not even the headmistress." Her face flushed and fists balled. She had squeezed them so hard her nails had broken the skin on her palms. Rosie expected to be lectured or even yelled at, but all was calm.

"Do you know who *that girl* you saved was?" Agent Hurwell asked, her voice not fluctuating once.

"I know she was a Haply girl. A fairy," Rosie responded, now looking at the agent.

"Yes. Her name is Sunnie Lightstrom, and she's part of a family line dating back thousands of years. She is a part of one of the oldest families known to the fairy community, meaning she is from one of the most powerful, if not *the* most powerful, fairy families known to us. Do you know what happened to her?"

Riley answered no, but she did know what happened because she had studied it before. Christion Flare had depicted it, taught her. Rosie didn't answer and looked at her hands in her lap.

"Her wings were clipped. She was mutilated. She is a fairy

no more," Agent Hurwell said.

The silence and tension in the room thickened. Eyes bored through her, and she didn't know what to say or confess.

"Now, I believe the two of you are telling the truth."

Rosie and Riley glanced at Agent Hurwell, her face stern but her eyes holding a glimmer of warmth.

"Are you kidding me, Agent?" Professor Manger spat. "These two are trouble and—"

Agent Hurwell raised her hand to silence his complaints. "Please, can either of you shed any light on who may have done this? Unfortunately, Ms. Lightstrom could not identify her attacker."

"I'm sorry, Agent Hurwell, but we didn't see anything," Riley replied.

"There was a card," Rosie said, eyeing Professor Walker.

"What did the card say?" Agent Hurwell asked, indicating they didn't find a card.

"It was strange symbols. A code I think," Rosie continued, still staring at Professor Walker.

"Okay, you two are free to go about your Sunday. Please keep this interview to yourselves, as this is an open and ongoing investigation, and a colleague or I may need to speak with you again." She turned to Professor Shay. "We need to go back out and locate this card. Can you put together a team for me?"

"I'll go," Professor Walker said.

"We all will," Professor Manger added.

Professor Shay nodded in gratitude and addressed the students. "Off to breakfast, and you are still required to finish all lessons and homework as planned. Doctor Witam will also be available, should you require his services."

He nodded and smiled at her. The students stood, stronger than before, and left the heated and bothered conversations in the office.

"Come on, let's eat," Riley said, but she had no appetite, and she pulled away from him. "Hey, will you be okay?"

"I think I need to go for a run. Clear my head."

"Okay. Do you want me to come with you?"

"No. I need some time to myself." Knowing he would be offended and hurt, she turned and hurried up the steps to the lobby and out to the lake.

She was happy no one was roaming the grounds outside. They probably were too afraid to leave or weren't allowed to leave due to the attacks, but Rosie couldn't sit inside and eat breakfast as if nothing had happened.

As she ran around the lake, up the mountainside, and over boulders, Rosie felt something inside her loosen. She ran faster and harder, barreling to one of the peaks and turning every few minutes to ensure no one was following, ensuring she was actually alone—even from the woman in white.

She bounded and leapt, and the slight chill in the air kept her cool. Rosie slowed to a stop, realizing where her body had unknowingly brought her. The vast valley of stacked boulders sat below her—the one she had seen in her dreams, the one where danger constantly happened in her mind. Her brain was telling her she shouldn't go into it, but her heart wanted her to continue. Before she could consider going through the maze or not, her feet moved like they had decided for her.

She descended into the valley, rocks and boulders towering over her. She knew where to go even though she had never been there in person. Walking through the maze, she examined every rock and noted it, ensuring she could find her way out even if each rock seemed the same. Then she saw the strange rock structure from her dreams, the one that always had some sort of glow emitting from behind it. She drew closer, it pulling her forward.

As her fingertips were about to touch the boulder, a distinctive snap of a branch echoed through the rocks. She tossed around her head. Was it an animal? Or the wind? She contemplated the different possibilities—the rational and logical possibilities. But a dimmed flash caught her peripheral vision. Not far behind her, the sun had cast a shadow of a person. Her feet guided her through the maze as she sprinted and cut through different paths, trying to find an exit, but a force pushed her backward. The back of her head smacked against the hard ground.

When she opened her eyes, the spots from the fall cleared to reveal the attacker standing over her. Gyle.

Chapter Fifteen

Rosie's lips slammed shut as Gyle's hands firmly pressed her open mouth closed.

"Shh, please, I'm not going to hurt you," Gyle told her in a soft, calm manner.

Rosie stopped wriggling her arms.

"Okay, good. Now, I am going to remove my hand. Please don't scream. I only want to talk."

Rosie knew she should scream as soon as he lifted his hand, but her heart rate slowed, and her eyes landed on his. As he pulled his hand away, her mouth remained closed.

Gyle, sighing a breath of relief, extended his hand to her. "I'm sorry about pushing you down. I didn't think I would hit you that hard, but, as soon as I recognized you, I had to talk to you."

"Did you hurt that girl?" Rosie asked, anger welling inside.

"No, I swear I didn't. I only learned about it this morning. I know the Superiority thinks I did, but please, I promise it wasn't me."

"Why should I believe you? You know the secrets of the book. You know what removing Sunnie's wings would do to her and the power they could hold."

"If that is the only evidence you have, I could accuse you of the same thing. You have also read the book and know the knowledge and power it contains. Listen. I know my word isn't much, but you have to listen to my story. I am asking you to believe me. I didn't do this. If I had, I wouldn't stick around for anyone to find me."

"Why *did* you stick around?"

"To make sure someone heard my side of the story before I left for good, and I am happy it's you I can tell it to."

"What happened last night? Why did you decide to leave then? You have had my blood in your system for a few days. Why didn't you go when I first gave it to you?"

"I learned about the dance and figured there would be a lack of security around my cell. More staff would supervise the students, so my best chance at escape was to leave last night. That's why the attack was so strange. An abundance of teachers and staff members must have been at the dance and on the mountainside. Why would I go all the way across campus, through the dance to attack someone? I could have easily done that after I got far enough away from campus. I think someone knew I was planning on escaping. They had to have seen my decaying stopped. They must have realized I had fed."

Rosie considered his pleading. He was right. It logically didn't make sense for him to put himself in that much danger. A professor would have caught him. "Are you saying you think someone was aware you would be escaping the night of the dance and framed you?"

"Yes."

"But who would've seen that you were stronger? I thought no one was paying attention to you until the Superiority came to take you to your formal trial."

"A few checks occurred here and there with a few different people, but only a handful of them got a good look at my face. I'm sure they could tell the color had returned to it—a witch and Headmistress Shay. And a doctor who had checked on me when I first arrived, and that giant man. Manager, I think?"

"Manger."

"Yeah. Him. Before the dance, Shay and Manger tugged on my shackles and cell bars."

"Maybe they were checking if the chains were weak enough for you to break them?"

"Maybe. They walked away from my cell, yelling, mad and rapid. I heard them say they would have to be extra careful."

Rosie sat, digesting every part of Gyle's story. Could Professor Shay and Professor Manger be behind the attack? No, that was ridiculous, she thought. She refocused on Gyle, and his icy hand grabbed hers. Her muscles loosened more. He hadn't attacked Sunnie Lightstrom. "Gyle, you need to leave. I will relay your story to the right people at the right time, but you must leave. I know what the Superiority will do to you if they find you." She squeezed his warming hand.

"Thank you, Rose Connors." He looked at her one more time, and, like a bolt of lightning, he was gone.

As Rosie ran through the maze of boulders and rock-climbed out at top speed, her mind swirled with suspects and reasons. She was delving into the background of Professor Manger when she stopped at hearing his voice.

"Charlene, we need more time. We can't let this happen until he knows."

"Premier Kingsley will know soon enough. But first, we

have to make sure the Lightstrom family is set up and Sunnie is welcomed back."

"Welcomed back? She is now a plain ole human. Her magic is gone. She should have been killed."

"Don't say that, Jon! Wait … Do you hear something?"

The two looked to where she was hiding.

Rosie ducked behind a ridge and moved swiftly around the sea of saguaros to escape the two arguing professors. Her suspect list suddenly was shortened to two.

As she found her way to the human dorm, she had the intense urge to tell Riley her theories, but Rosie halted at the sight of Professor Walker and Doctor Witam searching around the dorm's entrance. Professor Walker would definitely lecture her, and Doctor Witam would want to have a session. She turned back on the path but halted. Poking out of the top of Professor Walker's skirt was a piece of paper—a card scribbled with strange characters. Was she hiding it, Rosie thought?

With her legs moving quickly, she devised a new plan to use the entrance by the field. As she adjusted her weight to run uphill, Rosie's feet slipped out from under her, and someone tugged on her arm.

"Well, what do we have here?" Professor Manger said as Rosie tried to touch her toes to the ground.

Was he waiting for me? Of course. He must have heard me or picked up my scent.

"Well?"

"I was just out for a run."

"And did you see anything on this run that sent you in such a hurry to come back?"

"No. I was just doing my training. Like you taught me."

"Get inside. I wouldn't want you getting hurt. Yet it looks like you already have." He nodded to her bloody, matted hair.

She paused, remembering how she had gotten the cut. "Clumsy me. I tripped on a rock and barrel-rolled to save myself. But I ended up hitting my head on another rock. Ha," and without another word, Rosie awkwardly sidestepped to the building and made her way with as much discretion as possible to her room.

Rosie managed to slip past students in the dining hall, study room, and common room, and when she reached her dorm, Eleanor was nowhere to be seen. Breathing a sigh of relief, Rosie relaxed and got ready for the rest of her day.

She planned on how she should prioritize her homework and her investigation into the attack. There would be more to come.

Rosie washed the blood from her hair, and after getting dressed, she gathered her belongings and retreated to her hiding place to lay out all the work she needed to do. Luckily, the schoolwork was easy. All she had to do was finish her chemistry lab report, write a paper on sociopathy versus psychopathy for Doctor Witam's class, research and find facts regarding the Great War of Lights, which was caused by vampires tempting multiple fairy clans, diagram each sasquatch subtype and list their complete, proper anatomy, and finally, develop a code for cryptology. Rosie finished all this in a mere three hours. Being able to remember everything she read only once granted her an advantage over the other students, but only when her mind acted as a storage facility and not as a bowl of spaghetti.

She stowed her schoolwork and retrieved what she wanted to study from the beginning—*Being* by Christion Flare. Rosie ran her fingers over the monogram on the front, over the circle and the rays, noting how she now depicted the emblem as a sun and not a compass rose. With her notebook and pen ready to write, she opened the book, but horror ran over her. She flipped through the pages and saw nothing. The book no longer held the text she desired to see. It was blank, the pages empty and bare.

"What happened?" she muttered aloud, grazing the pages and bringing the book closer to her. She whispered to it, "Christion," but she got no response. The text no longer called to her. Slamming the book shut and knowing she couldn't do anything else to resurrect the writing, Rosie placed the notebook in front of her. She would have to pull everything from memory.

First, Rosie drew the symbols from the card she had found under Sunnie. Only two symbols were familiar to Rosie from the cipher she had solved for Cryptology. Everything else was foreign to her. She set the new cipher aside and mapped the events that had occurred on campus, her suspects, and a timeline. She formulated an idea about what was happening.

"The book outlined various details about each being, natural and supernatural. It also described the most magical parts of each being. The light, fluttering wings were the most magical part of a fairy. They had to have been taken for power. But is that crazy? It was mentioned that the Lightstroms were one of the strongest fairy clans, surviving the longest. Could this have been an isolated attack regarding power within the fairy community?" Rosie's head swam as she contemplated this troubling thought. Theories generated and died as fast as they came to her. When she finally checked the time, she was shocked. She had been alone with herself the entire day, missing lunch and dinner. She didn't want to stop her research but had to. Her head throbbed with pain. Most likely a small concussion, she thought, rubbing the spot she had hit earlier in the morning.

Rosie left her things, as she would return to the room in the morning, hid the book in an unseen hole in the wall and slipped out of the room. Her mind told her no one would be in the library this late with her, but she was wrong. Descending the steps toward the portrait leading to the common room was Garrett, staring directly at her.

"Hey, Garrett."

"Hey, Rosie. Can we talk for a sec?"

"Definitely. Is everything okay?"

"Well, this is awkward, because I'm not typically this kind of guy, and I know you have been dealing with a lot lately, but you have to talk to Justin."

What, she thought? This was what he wanted to talk to her about?

"He's worried about you, and he likes you. Can you just tell him if you like him or not? Because the guy is driving me crazy with all his pining and whining."

She knew she would eventually have to have this conversation with Justin, but with all the other urgent events, talking to Justin wasn't high on her list of to-dos. It wasn't that she didn't like him, but too much was transpiring. "Yeah, I will talk with him first thing tomorrow."

Garrett's shoulders relaxed, and his overall stance became less rigid.

"Thank you, Rosie." He gave her a grateful hug. "On another note, what do you think June will make us do in practice tomorrow? I mean, we won Friday, so I would hope we could have a relaxing week, but knowing June, we will be doing something excruciating."

She smiled at Garrett. "I have to agree with you on that. I don't think she will lighten up until we win the entire season."

The two laughed and headed to the common room then separated for their own dorms. Reflecting on everything that had happened over the last few nights, Rosie was grateful for running into Garrett. He always got her to snap out of her depressing thoughts and make her smile. Eleanor was lucky, she thought as she admired her sleeping roommate in bed and closed her own eyes.

* * *

The next morning was bustling with students finding spots to eat, finishing last-minute assignments, and running to their first class. It seemed the weekend events didn't only distract Rosie but everyone else as well, and Rosie was disappointed she couldn't break away from Eleanor and visit her secret room to investigate *Being* further.

Leaving their dorm room, late to breakfast, Eleanor discussed whether the attack was random. Rosie wasn't paying much attention though and grabbed a slice of toast to eat on the way to class, but before leaving the dining hall, she spotted a group of girls and boys surrounding a table. Curious about what the commotion was, she headed over.

The group of students were in a close-knit circle. There was no way to see what was in the middle, so she turned to head to the exit as someone called her name. It was muffled, but, as she turned around, Riley emerged from the middle of the group. He was the source of the commotion.

"Alright, guys, later."

Groans came from the group, wanting to hear more from him and his heroic actions from the weekend. Rosie noted they were especially loud from the girls who wanted to be more friendly with him.

"What's all this about?" Rosie asked with a smile and pointing at the disbursing students, already knowing the answer.

"Just some people who wanted to hear about the big rescue."

"The what?"

"That's what some people are calling it. You know? Us finding Sunnie and what not. Haven't you been getting questions about it? I am constantly getting hounded."

"No. No one has asked me about it, but I prefer it that way."

"Yeah, I'm not too into it either," he said, but his face said otherwise. "Anyway, have you found out anything else? About the attack, I mean? I assume you have some sort of theory."

The hallway to class was full, and she could sense eyes on them. "Yes, I do, but let's talk about it later. There are too many eyes and ears on us."

"Okay, wanna go for a swim, maybe?" He winked at her, which threw her off.

"Um, no, let's meet in the library. I have work, but it shouldn't be too crazy, since midterms were last month."

"Okay, sounds good," Riley said, dissatisfied as if he was expecting her to disregard her responsibilities to hang around him like the other girls were.

The two entered their new history class with the rest of the other freshmen. All of them had passed Professor Shay's class with success, and now Professor Stodge would be teaching them.

Rosie sat in the front of the class next to Justin and retrieved her notebook, ready to learn, but, as Professor Stodge was still writing, she turned to Justin, who was buried in his book. "Hey, Justin."

"Hey, Rosie." He lowered the book and smiled at her.

Rosie couldn't believe what a wonderful friend he was.

"How are you doing? Been getting too much attention, like Riley?"

"Thankfully, no. But I did want to talk to you about something."

"What's up?"

"I just wanted to say thank you for asking me to the dance on Saturday and that I had a great time with you."

His cheeks flushed, and a hand shuffled through his hair as he broke his gaze and grinned. "I'm happy you had fun." His eyes raised back to hers. "I only wish I was with you when you found Sunnie. I'm sorry you had to witness that."

Rosie gazed into his eyes. How could she break his sweet heart? "Justin, you are so kind and are such a great friend."

He sighed and muttered, "Here it comes," his mood shifting.

"Yeah, I know you might want something stronger than friendship with me, and I would be lying if I said I didn't have some of those feelings myself, but I can't be involved right now. I have too much going on in my head, and I don't want to disappoint you."

"I understand, Rosie. It is perfectly understandable. We will always be friends." Justin grabbed her hand, smiles spreading on both faces.

"Alright, everyone," Professor Stodge said, facing the class. "Let's open our textbooks to page two fifty-four..."

As his droning continued, Rosie's mind went elsewhere.

She already had read ahead and didn't have to pay close attention to the day's lecture, so she didn't. Instead, she spent the period and every other class thinking about the attack and her suspects and their motives.

* * *

With *Being* still filled with empty pages, her mind wandered every day, attempting to remember every detail it contained, and when she wasn't brooding about the book, she recounted the bloody scene she had witnessed that led to her intensifying nightmares during the brisk November nights.

The dreams remained mostly the same. She would be in the maze of boulders, running and fighting or searching for the mysterious woman in white, but her fate was always the same. She would either be hurt, attacked, or killed before reaching the mysterious glow behind the misshapen boulder.

Sitting upright in bed, her hair matted on her forehead, dripping sweat, and her heart thumping, Rosie took in her surroundings, ensuring she was actually in her room and not waking up in the cold desert valley.

"Rosie, are you okay? Have another nightmare?" Eleanor muttered from her bed, still half asleep.

"Yes, I'm okay. Go back to sleep."

Eleanor grunted as heavy breaths came from her again.

Rosie slipped from bed and grabbed her phone. Five in the morning. Knowing she wouldn't be able to slip back into a slumber, Rosie got dressed and welcomed the crisp air into her lungs right outside the human dorm. Her runs had become a refuge that helped her mind clear and organize itself.

The campus was still, but not just because of the time. It was Thanksgiving break, and most of the students had departed campus for family festivities and rituals. Only a handful of students had stayed behind—Eleanor, Justin, Garrett, and Riley included.

Running and jumping over rocks, leaping over fallen cacti, and bounding up the mountainside, Rosie unwound not only her mind but also her body. She heard the owls hoot, hunting wakening mice, the coyotes howl, making one last kill, and the snakes rattle, warning her to stay on the path. She enjoyed the sounds the desert brought her. Her feet turned, and she decided on a new course. A fresh start. She would run up the side of the mountain and down to one of the water deposits from the lake—a more secluded part to just sit and think, watch the sunrise and rest without anyone finding her. She had been to the pond before and loved how the sun hit and warmed the water.

When she got up the mountainside, and over the ledge, her feet stumbled and got caught. Her forceful stop made her fall forward and spy on what waited at the bottom—a mermaid singing and playing in the water. Rosie smiled, seeing she wasn't the only one enjoying the morning. She turned back and ran to the lake and the school's front entrance.

Entering the dark lobby, Rosie stared at James Kingsley's eyes boring into her. She focused on the portrait, wondering if answers resided in the premier's office. She rounded the front desk and stepped up. She inspected it closer, and, as she reached to test if the veil was still there, a hand grabbed hers.

She shrieked, stumbled backward and landed on the ground.

James Kingsley exited the portrait with a smile. "I'm sorry

to have scared you, but I just couldn't resist." He floated down and helped Rosie to her feet. "May I ask what you were doing?"

"I-I wanted to have a better look at you. I have only ever seen you a few times, and I was curious."

"Mm, I have been told I am a mystery. So, Ms. Connors, correct?"

"Yes."

"I'm aware you found Ms. Lightstrom's body after the Homecoming dance. I'm interested in hearing your tale of the events."

"Oh, uh, well, I thought Agent Hurwell reported everything to the Superiority?"

"She did. A great agent she is, but I would like to know what happened in your own words."

"Okay, um, I was going for a walk with my friend Riley, when—"

The lobby entrance burst open as Justin shouted, "Premier Kingsley! I need help! She needs help!" Justin was carrying a mermaid, still in fish form, her tail bloody and most of her scales missing.

"Bring her here." Kingsley removed pillows from a couch.

Rosie bent over the girl on the couch and grabbed one of her hands. "Shh, it's okay. You're safe."

The girl moaned in immense pain, and Rosie realized she was the mermaid she had spotted swimming and playing carefree. She wondered if she had stayed and swum in the pool—alone or with the girl—if she too would have been brutally attacked.

"Justin, did you see who did this? Who attacked her?"

He didn't answer. Pale-faced and in shock, Justin stared at

the flopping, naked tail.

Rosie watched Premier Kingsley's every move.

Over the mermaid's screams of agony, he remained focused and analyzed her body, her tail specifically. "Ms. Connors, if you could please hold down her tail."

Rosie moved to the other end of the couch and seized the tail. The mermaid was strong and thrashed in pain, but Rosie held tight, positioning it for Kingsley.

Once the tail was secure, he hovered his hands above it and chanted, letting the magic flow into the mermaid, healing her. Her legs formed first, showing gashes throughout them. Then the wounds closed, and the bleeding halted. It wasn't perfect. Tiny scars covered her legs, but it was better than bleeding out, Rosie thought.

James Kingsley ordered Rosie, "Go find Doctor Geller. He should be in his office by now."

Rosie rushed to the hospital wing and, sure enough, he was there.

"Rosie? Why are you here? What's happened?"

But all Rosie could say was, "Follow me," and turned to run back to the poor victim with Doctor Geller close on her heels. When Rosie returned to the lobby, the girl was sitting upright and crying but talking to James Kingsley.

Doctor Geller rushed to his patient but stopped when he realized who his patient was talking to.

"Doctor Geller, please escort Kai to the hospital wing and locate Doctor Witam to talk to her. She has been through a lot."

Doctor Geller assisted Kai from the room.

Rosie looked at the elusive man, who had intrigued her since the day she arrived, but remembered Justin. She ran to his still frozen side. "Justin, what happened? Are you okay?"

"I-I'm f-fine."

"Mr. Fent, do you mind if I peek into your mind and see what happened?"

Justin collapsed onto the now unoccupied couch and nodded.

Kingsley sat next to him and grabbed his shoulder. His eyes turned blue, and he appeared as if he was no longer present.

Rosie sat next to Justin and grabbed his hand to comfort him, but, as soon as she touched him, her vision went, and she was transported to the edge of the pool. Rosie felt as if she was Justin herself and saw through his eyes. Where she had been when she had first admired the mermaid and her carefree attitude was where Justin was now, but rather than watching a happy, cheery girl, Justin was witnessing a horror scene.

A black figure glided from the crimson pool, holding a small pouch in one hand, then set an envelope onto a rock with the other. Before Justin was Kai, her front half-submerged in water and her tail flopping on the ground, dripping with blood. Justin sprinted down to her and pulled her from the water, breaking whatever spell that was keeping her submerged. Her screams filled the mountain range. The high pitch and volume shook the ground and sent waves through the water. Justin grabbed the girl and held her in her arms.

"It's okay. I'm here to help. It's okay," Justin reassured, but, as Rosie watched the memory, she knew the girl would never be okay again; almost every scale had been forcibly removed. Justin grabbed the girl's face. "What's your name?"

The girl, still shrieking in pain, managed to scream, "K-Kai!"

"Okay, Kai. Can you shift?"

"I-I d-don't-t th-think so!"

"Can you give me one good try, Kai?" Justin caressed her tail, as if encouraging it to turn into legs, but they hadn't, and her body stopped moving.

Silence befell the area, and Kai had lost consciousness.

Justin checked her neck for a pulse and found a faint thumping. He eased into the water and maneuvered Kai, so she was floating on his back. Justin held her while swimming to the main lake, moving as fast as he could through the chilled, dark water with a streak of red following behind. No one came as Justin yelled for help between breaths. He finally got Kai to the bank in front of the school entrance, scooped her into his arms and sprinted, careful not to fall or drop her. Justin bounded up the staircase and entered the dark lobby, and Rosie, through Justin's eyes, saw herself, then Rosie was looking back at Justin's hand.

"Thank you, Mr. Fent. That was very helpful."

Justin nodded, and Rosie brought him into a hug. She felt terrible he had to witness such a horror. As she was comforting her friend, a loud bang of a door opening reverberated through the vestibule.

Rosie wasn't surprised when Doctor Witam, Professor Shay, Professor Walker, Professor Manger, and Agent Hurwell strode toward the premier. Rosie tried to hear what they were saying to no avail.

After exchanging a few words with the premier, Professor Shay focused on Rosie. "Curious you found another attack victim. How do you explain it?"

"She didn't, Professor Shay. I did," Justin said, finally regaining his voice.

"I already took note of it, Charlene," Premier Kingsley said.

"The attacker left a card. Please retrieve it so we can read what other gibberish the attacker has left."

Professor Shay scanned Rosie and Justin for clues of deceit. She shifted to Agent Hurwell. "Agent, do what you need to." She huffed and stalked off.

Rosie, uncomfortable yet infuriated at Professor Shay's accusation, eyed Agent Hurwell.

"Why don't we talk somewhere more private?" she told the two students.

The three went to a small office Rosie presumed had been given to the Superiority special agent when she had arrived.

"Tea?" she gestured at the fresh pot on the desk.

Simply shaking her head, Rosie refused, as did Justin.

"What happened this morning?" the agent asked, but before Justin could answer, another person joined the three.

"Agent Hurwell," James Kingsley said, nodding at the agent.

"Premier Kingsley," Agent Hurwell responded and refocused on Justin.

Justin hesitated. "I woke up and went for a run."

"Is this your normal running route?"

"No, but I sometimes go the way I did when I want to watch the sunrise and take a swim."

"A little cold for a swim, though. Don't you agree?"

"Yes, but the sun warms that specific pond when it rises. I assume by magic."

Rosie could hear the attitude in his voice. This wasn't the way to prove his innocence, but she could tell his anger was overpowering.

"What did you see?"

Rosie watched James Kingsley while listening to Justin's answers, but he was studying the ground, clearly thinking about something else.

"I looked down at the pond and saw a dark figure over Kai's body. It was cutting out her scales and had some sort of spell over her that kept her top half underwater so no one could hear her. I froze. I didn't know what to do. He finished, and I finally got the courage to help. I didn't see the attacker. I'm sorry."

"How did the figure move?"

"What?"

"Did the figure move like a vampire or a shifter or run at a normal speed?"

"I guess they moved faster than a normal person but not as fast as a vampire—at least from what I have observed by being at the school for a few months."

"Okay, that's all for now."

Justin nodded, wearing a face of regret and guilt.

Agent Hurwell turned to Rosie. "What were you doing that made you witness this attack?"

"I didn't witness the attack. I was also out running then came to the lobby and met with Premier Kingsley, and we talked." Rosie was surprised; Agent Hurwell couldn't actually think she was involved, could she?

"Have you met the victim, Kai, before?"

"No, I mean, I haven't met her, but I did see her this morning. I also had the idea to swim in the pool, but Kai was there relaxing, so I didn't want to bug her. And I swear, when I left, she was perfectly fine."

"Okay."

"You don't have any other questions?"

"Do you have anything else to tell me that may help my investigation?"

Rosie sat straighter and thought. Should she tell the agent about her theory about who could be the attacker? Or that they are targeting the most magical parts of the different types of beings? She noticed James Kingsley had left his own thoughts and was now staring at her, most likely shocked that she had seen the victim just before the attack.

"No, nothing else." Rosie couldn't give her half-theories without evidence with the man she suspected being an attacker at one time in the room. She would probably be expelled or put in a similar prison Gyle was kept in for treason. Rosie and Justin left the room.

"Justin, do you want to go back to the dorm? Or have something to eat?"

"No, I think I need to talk to Doctor Witam." Without another word, he left her side and entered the doctor's office.

She was sorry for him and hoped Doctor Witam could ease his pain some way.

Heading to her dorm, her appetite nowhere to be found, Rosie thought about the attack, and, upon entering the dining room, she remembered the card the attacker had left at the scene. *I need to find it,* she thought and turned to leave, but someone grabbed her hand.

"Are you okay?" Riley asked, pulling her into a hug.

She noticed Garrett and Eleanor seated at a table, staring at her with shocked expressions.

Rosie, realizing she was still damp and had blood stains on her clothes, found Riley's face and shook her head.

The others stood and helped her to the table.

After sitting and a moment of them staring at her, she told them what happened.

"Did Justin or Kai see who it was?" Eleanor asked.

Rosie shook her head. "I don't think so. The person was well disguised."

"Are you okay, though? Are you hurt?" Riley placed a hand on her arm.

"No. I'm just tired and sore." She stood, and the others followed her movement. "I think I'll go lay down for a bit."

Eleanor gathered her things. "Do you want me to go with you?"

"I'm going to sleep and rest. You would be bored." Rosie left the dining hall toward her room, knowing Professor Shay had already retrieved the card. She could feel her friends' gazes still on the back of her head, all the way until the door to the dining hall closed.

* * *

The rest of the break was spent inside her dorm room. Rosie didn't want to see anyone, and she didn't want to be asked any more questions. Eleanor would bring her food and tell her all about the day and how everyone missed her and that she should walk outside for some fresh air, but Rosie's answer was always the same—"Thanks for the food"—and she would turn back over in bed. It wasn't until the first day back in class when Rosie had to face all her classmates and their own theories about her. And her predictions about the school day's events came true.

People were either steering clear of Rosie because they, like Professor Shay, thought she was the attacker, or they wanted to be her best friend to learn more about the attacks and the scene of events—basically, every detail. She was happy that Justin was taking things better, though. He went to Doctor

Witam for an extra session each week, and it was helping him heal.

Maybe I should talk to Doctor Witam more and open up to him, she thought as she entered the frigid month of December, still feeling closed off. Even the thought of her birthday didn't excite her. But, as she entered the dining room late that night on that special day, she saw her friends around a table with a beautiful cake.

"Surprise!" they all yelled together.

Feeling the love and comfort from her friends, Rosie ran toward them and hugged them. "Thank you, guys." She smiled, hoping they'd recognize her gratitude.

The group enjoyed cake and speaking to one another as they had before the attacks, and finally, when they were opening presents, Rosie knew how lucky she was to have friends like hers. Justin had given her a copper brooch inlaid with rubies. It was gorgeous, and Rosie couldn't believe the beauty of it.

"Wow, Justin! I want one of those for my birthday," Eleanor said.

Justin pinned it on Rosie and kissed her on the cheek.

"Thank you, Justin. It is stunning." She took the next present and opened it. Her heart jumped. "Riley? Where did you find this?" Rosie admired a tattered old photo in a crayon and macaroni frame.

"What is it?" Garrett asked.

"Just a picture," Riley said, still staring at Rosie, but it wasn't just a picture. It was a picture of them on the first day they had met in a frame they had made together. It depicted the start of their friendship—the best friendship Rosie had ever had.

She walked over to him and hugged him. "Thank you," she

whispered into his ear, her heart full of happiness. "Meet me outside of the dorms tonight. Around midnight."

He smiled and nodded.

Rosie knew the next conversation she had to have. With the party wrapping up and everyone in attendance leaving to their dorms for bed, Rosie turned to Justin. "Hey, can we talk?"

"Of course," he said, leading her from the others.

"I can't accept this gift. I know it is worth a lot, and I can't take it."

"Sure, you can. I got it for you. I want you to have it."

"I know, but I think you wanted it to be for your girlfriend, and I can't be that for you. I'm so sorry, Justin."

His shoulders fell, but his response surprised her. "I completely understand, Rosie. I know you like Riley, and I would hate to be the person to stand between you two." He hugged her. "I promise I will still be your friend. Plus, who would you come to for help in Chemistry when your microscope is wonky?" He laughed and clapped her shoulder.

"Thank you, Justin."

They left together for the dorm.

* * *

Rosie checked her phone—11:55. Riley would be out soon, and she couldn't wait to talk to him, to kiss him. Butterflies fluttered around her stomach, and her heartbeat rose. It was funny, she thought, how she could keep her composure in hand-to-hand combat with a transformed mountain lion but seeing the boy she loved made her disorganized and nervous.

The wind whirled, tossing up her hair and making a low

whining sound. But another noise hid in the wind—a low growl. Was a shifter out, messing with her? Or was some sort of wildcat prowling the grounds?

Rosie walked from the dorms, following the sound. Another growl, but this time it was closer. She continued toward it, curious as to the animal making it. Louder than before, snarls broke out and leaves crumpled. Finally, a scream erupted. Rosie sprinted toward it. *Another attack*, she thought as her legs drew her near the fight.

She found the brawling creatures. The same figure as before—the black-cloaked figure—was cornering and fighting a mountain lion with a hunting knife. No, it was fighting with Natasha. Rosie ran directly into the body and tackled it to the ground. Finally, a surprise the attacker had not foreseen, Rosie thought, but it wasn't without hurting Natasha.

The tackle had sent Natasha backward, her head hitting a rock. Unable to check her classmate, Rosie turned to the attacker. She held down the figure but was no match for the strength of whoever hid under the cloak.

The knife in its hand flew up and cut across her cheek.

Falling slightly, not completely off the body, she faltered to regain her stance, but the attacker made another movement, and this time the knife landed in her side. Rosie doubled over, clasping the deep wound, and warm liquid poured into her hands.

The attacker was free and not yet done with her or Natasha. It stalked to the unmoving shifter's body and took what it wanted: three fingers—half claw and half-human, appendages in half-shift. The figure returned to Rosie. Now peering down at her, its features remained hidden. It lowered itself, so its face was over hers, and Rosie closed her eyes as its covered hand softly grazed the cut on her cheek. Its other hand grabbed hers in a gentle manner.

She tried to pull away, needing to apply pressure to her gushing wound, but it wouldn't let her go. Finally, losing her strength, Rosie gave in, knowing her end was near. She felt the figure slide something into her pant pocket, and it leaned down to Rosie's face.

Air escaping its hidden mouth hit hers. She didn't know if it wanted to feed on her, kill her, or kiss her. She closed her eyes again, waiting for its next move. Cold air brushed her nose, and she opened her eyes, looking at the stars. It had vanished, and Rosie was unsure why, until pounding feet drew close to her, and, as her eyes were glazing over, the arms she had known all her life caressed her and carried her away.

Chapter Sixteen

Rosie peeled open her eyes, harsh light burning them. *Where am I? What happened?* Her mind soared with blurred visions—being attacked, looking at the desert's night sky, being held by Riley, being handed off to someone else. She sat upright, and a rush of blood surged to her head, and black spots blocked her vision. Blurs and snippets flooded her memory, and, as she remembered the horrifying events, a warm hand held hers.

Riley stared into her eyes and smiled, kissing her forehead.

"Hi," she said. Her throat was burning and scratchy.

"Hi." He pushed some of her hair behind her ear.

She winced at the pain in her side.

"Here let me help you." Riley helped her forward so she could be a bit more comfortable.

Rosie saw Natasha in the bed next to her, still asleep and her hand tightly bandaged. "Will she be okay?"

"Yes. She will live. Unfortunately, they couldn't regrow her fingers, but, if that is all that was taken from her, she's lucky. And so are you. What were you thinking? Running in like that?"

"Natasha screamed, and I ran to see what was going on, and

I realized I could catch the attacker off guard."

"What? With all hundred and twenty pounds of you? You honestly thought you could take down this person with your body while they were wielding a knife?" His tone changed. Anger now filled him.

While she was abrupt and brash about fighting back, deep down, she had done the right thing, she thought. "I couldn't just let the person kill Natasha."

Riley sighed. "I know. I just wish I could've been there sooner to help you and catch this guy."

A groan came from the other bed as Natasha stirred.

"Natasha?" Rosie asked, trying to find out any information from her.

"Yeah?" Natasha mumbled, rubbing her eyes and slowly opening them. "Ugh, where am I?"

"You're in the hospital. Listen. Do you remember anything from the attack? Did you recognize anything about the figure?"

Now fully awake and sitting upright in bed, Natasha unraveled the bandages covering her hand in a panic.

"Natasha, I don't think you should do that." Riley moved toward her bed, but she was becoming as undone as the bandage that fell to the floor.

Lifting her hand to her face, Natasha cried, now realizing what had been done to her wasn't a dream.

Riley grabbed her shoulders and refocused her. "Natasha, you will be all right." He embraced her, and Natasha hugged back and dug her face into him.

"Well, I am happy you're both awake." Doctor Geller entered their room to check Rosie's wounds and rewrap Natasha's bandage then excused himself.

Professor Shay, Agent Hurwell, and Doctor Witam entered the room. Professor Shay approached Natasha's bed and grabbed her hurt hand. "How are you doing, my dear?"

"I'm okay, I think. Just a bit shocked." She wiped tears from her red, puffy eyes.

"Of course, you are. Doctor Witam is here if you need to talk, but first, Agent Hurwell and I need to ask you a few questions. Would that be alright?"

Rosie was shocked. When she had helped the victims of the previous attacks, she was accused rather than checked on.

Natasha nodded in agreement, and Agent Hurwell stepped forward.

"Natasha," the agent said, "we have already gotten Mr. Zimmers accounts of the events after the attack, but can you tell me how this happened?"

"W-well, I was a bit restless and couldn't sleep. I decided to shift and go for a run. I had made it around the bend when I felt a surge flow through my body. I fell to the ground and transformed back. This dark figure charged toward me. I instinctively stood to fight, but his knife swung at me."

"The person who attacked you was a man?"

"Honestly, I don't know. I just said *him* because it seemed like a guy. I transformed back. I thought, as a mountain lion, the man wouldn't stand a chance, but in mid-transformation, Rosie tackled him. I don't remember anything else. I fell back and must have passed out."

"You hit your head," Rosie said. "Sorry, I didn't know you would be thrown backward."

Natasha gave a small smile to her.

"Well, Natasha, you are very lucky that Rose was nearby," Professor Shay said, looking into Rosie's eyes. "Why were you out at that hour, Ms. Connors? I wouldn't expect you to have restless shifting urges?"

"She was there because of me," Riley answered. "I asked Rosie to meet me, and I ran a few minutes behind. That's how I found them. I heard the fight and ran to help. I think I scared away the attacker."

"He did," Rosie confirmed. "I was waiting outside the human dorms when growls and screams erupted. I went to inspect the noises, and the dark figure was attacking Natasha, and I believe it was the same figure who attacked Kai. I made a split-second judgment call and rushed the attacker. I had to help Natasha. I got whoever it was pinned, but they swiped at me and stabbed me."

"Did anything else happen thereafter?"

She hesitated for a moment while eyeing her folded pants on a near table. "No."

"Well, Ms. Connors, it seems we need to be rewarding you, not berating you," Doctor Witam said. "Ladies, I do think we should give these two a chance to rest. I will return later to talk unless you want to do it now?"

The two girls shook their heads.

"Alright. Mr. Zimmers, may I recommend you return to your own classes. Your friends will still be here afterward."

Riley hugged Rosie tight. He would be back, and when he did return, she would have to decide whether to tell him about the brief moment with the hooded figure.

* * *

The healing powers of supernatural creatures and the remedies they had continued to amaze Rosie, even after spending as much time as she did in the hospital with Doctor Gellar and his staff. Rosie was able to leave, recovered, the following morning and return to her classes. The downside now though was that while she no longer was treated like a suspect, she was treated like a magnet for attacks. Students avoided her like the plague, and she felt like Hester Prynne more now than ever. Thankfully, she still had her friends, who continued to stick up for her and tell others they were acting like idiots.

With the campus almost near empty again for the holiday break, Rosie thought about her first semester at King's Preparatory.

"All *A*'s!" Justin yelled at the bulletin board posted in the dining hall.

They had the pleasure of seeing their scores in person rather than through the school's website, allowing them the opportunity to object their grades if need be, but none of them had to.

"Best Christmas gift ever!" Like Thanksgiving, Rosie would be spending the holidays on campus with her best friends, but now she hoped there wouldn't be any more attacks to interrupt her fun, and she would have the opportunity and time to investigate more.

After being released from the hospital, Rosie stowed the note the attacker had placed in her pocket in the secret room. The same symbols she had seen at the other attacks were present on a small card—another cipher. Rosie had snuck away, trying to solve it, but without any indication of what the key might be, it was unsolvable.

Justin ran to the table. "What about you guys? Achieve the grades you wanted?"

Riley, Eleanor, and Garrett grumbled, but Justin was only

looking at Rosie to learn her scores.

"Yeah," Rosie replied. "All *A*'s."

"Well, of course, you two were going to receive all *A*'s," Eleanor blurted. "You're the two smartest people in the school. Including the teachers."

"Ha, I wouldn't say that. Doctor Witam is a genius, and Professor Walker is also pretty sharp. Too bad neither of us figured out her extra credit assignment from the beginning of the semester, but at least we didn't need it," Justin said, now picking over his breakfast.

"Oh, yeah," Rosie said, wanting to change the subject and hoping to make Eleanor smile. "I wouldn't say we're the best. All of you got higher *A*'s in combat training than me."

"I guess that's true." Eleanor sat a little straighter, proud of her accomplishment.

"Anyway, what's the plan for tonight? We need to make Christmas Eve fun. Even if it's only us," Riley said.

"Well, I'm hoping it'll snow, even if it's only a little bit. We can go sledding and mess around outside," Garrett said, looking at the lake ceiling.

"Yes, a white Christmas!" Eleanor agreed, snuggling into him.

"Snow in Arizona?" Riley asked the two lovebirds.

"Yeah! It has happened before."

"Will there be a dinner of some sort?"

"There should be, but it won't be crazy. They will put up some decorations, and the food will obviously be delicious, but there won't be a party or anything. I expect it will be only us and the few staff who decided or were forced to stick around because we're here."

"Since it is Christmas Eve, I think we should throw our

own little party of sorts," Riley said, smiling at Rosie.

"Oh, yes!" Eleanor agreed. "And we should try to incorporate our different family traditions. I will make homemade eggnog for everyone."

"I'll find a Christmas tree for us to decorate," Garrett said.

"We can exchange small gifts and go into town for supplies," Justin suggested.

"Definitely, and we can invite the teachers to the gathering and share the cheer," Riley said.

"Rosie, do you have any fun traditions or anything to include?" Eleanor asked.

"Mine are the same as Riley's. I don't remember what I used to do with my mom all that much. Just tell me how to help, and I will."

* * *

After running out for the things they needed and setting up in the dining room, Rosie was impressed with what she and her friends had accomplished; the dining hall looked like a winter wonderland. They set up a tall tree in the middle of the room that they had cut down and transported to campus. In town, they had found lights, and Rosie and Eleanor made ornaments to hang. Holly covered the walls, and even the staff helped once they caught the students' spirits. Professor Walker supplied nutcrackers, and Doctor Witam hung lights around the room, and even Professor Shay and Manger joined. The group played music and danced and feasted. Everyone enjoyed the night and forgot the terrible events that had taken place on campus during the first semester.

The next day was no different; as they emerged from their

rooms and met for Christmas Day breakfast in the dining hall, the students were shocked to see a stack of presents underneath the tree for each of them, shipped in from their parents. Even Rosie had a few gifts. They tore into them, and Rosie had been given a little something from each of her friends—a new makeup kit from Eleanor, a complete index of Intellects and how they shaped the world from Justin, a new notebook from Garrett, and a locket from Riley.

"It won't open," she said, looking at him.

"It will at the right time."

"Guys we have to go outside!" Garrett yelled.

"Why?" Justin replied, playing with a quiz ball Rosie had gotten him in town.

"What if it snowed? It got below freezing last night."

"I don't think it would here, Garrett. I think it was too dry and not cold enough," Rosie said, feeling sorry for the poor wolf who wanted to run and play.

"I wouldn't be so sure about that Rosie," Doctor Witam said, standing with Professor Walker. "I think you should all go check. What do you say?"

Rosie knew Doctor Witam and Professor Walker must have done something to the weather to bring snowfall to their school. The group ran through the front entrance. Sure enough, the lake had frozen, and white piles surrounded them.

"Come on. Let's change and meet back here in ten!" Riley yelled, but Garrett was already diving headfirst into a snow pile.

The group laughed and rushed to change. Rosie didn't have anything that would be warm enough, but she didn't care. If she were running and playing with her friends, she would be kept warm. The group reconvened and immediately threw snowballs as a battle ensued.

Eleanor and Rosie retreated up a tree to ambush their enemies below. Spotting them, Rosie and Eleanor waited for the perfect moment to strike, and once in their territory below them, Rosie yelled, "Now!" and she and Eleanor unleashed more than three dozen snowballs on the boys. They climbed down the tree and retreated to the school entrance, but Riley had caught Rosie. They both tumbled down a snowy hill.

The two friends laughed and giggled and grew close together. Rosie tilted her head to see a purposely placed plant with leathery leaves and waxy red berries hanging from a branch above them. Riley stared at Rosie and, without any hesitation, leaned in.

Their kiss was more magical than the appearance of the snow, the frozen lake, the charmed gifts they had received, or the mythical creatures that also came out to play, Rosie thought. She slowly separated from Riley and smiled. Time standing still. A pop came from her locket as it opened, and a picture of that moment developed on one side.

* * *

As the snow melted and Christmas break ended, Rosie remembered her enchanted break with Riley. With school restarting and students returning to campus, it was difficult to meet him. One student, the Valtic team captain, June, made it close to impossible for the two to meet. June had an entirely new training plan for the second semester.

"Alright, everyone. I hope you had a good break, but now is the time to refocus. We are playing Surgent this Friday, and we have only had two weeks to practice. I am not very confident at our chances of winning, especially since the Surgent team captain, Rawly, keeps hinting that they have some sort of secret weapon. We must be prepared for anything. Do you understand?"

The group responded in agreement, but Rosie still had a difficult time focusing with her new class load, her job in the library, and secret investigation she was still conducting when she could. It wasn't until Friday at lunch when Rosie could have an actual conversation with Riley rather than just exchange pleasantries.

"Hi, I'm sorry I'm late. I had my session with Doctor Witam, and he wants me to drop a class or stop working at the library. So, now I need to tell Ms. Pamfet I quit, which will be tough in itself, but I can't be at three places at once. Or can I?" Rosie stopped as Riley stared at her. "What's wrong?"

"Rosie, I have to tell you something. I've kept it from you, but—"

"Hey, Riley! Can we talk to you for a second?" Gunner and Flynn approached Riley and put a hand on each of his shoulders.

"Hold on, guys. I need to talk to Rosie."

"It can't wait, bud. We really need to talk to you."

"But—"

"No," Rosie said, gathering her things. "I have to go anyway. I'll catch up with you after the games?"

"Uh, yeah," he said before Gunner and Flynn ushered him off.

Rosie thought it was weird, but she had to focus and help with the clues for the tournament. Rosie opened her notebook and read the list of clues she had noted from meeting with the Valtic team the previous day. Clue one was a parachute, clue two was a flag with the Surgent crest and colors, and clue three was a small scroll with a drawing of a muscular arm and a pair of glasses. After the first Illumination Games against Astive, Justin was in charge of holding each clue and bringing them to the games.

Rosie wanted to meet with him and take another look in case she had missed something, but she had a good idea what two of them meant. The first, she believed, was related to getting down from a high area, maybe having to maneuver the ropes course without using the ropes. The second, she thought, was related to the game capture the flag. They were in charge of hiding the Surgent team's flag and would have to find theirs. She figured the Surgent team got a flag with the Valtic crest and colors. The last one was more confusing. Brawn and brains, maybe? That clue would have to be worked out during the games when she had more context.

Rosie closed her notebook and gathered with the team in the Valtic library and relayed her thoughts to them.

"That sounds like what I got," Justin said, confirming her theories.

"Okay, so let's bring the chute and flag and listen for my command. We can take these guys down!" June cheered.

* * *

Like the first game, the team was blindfolded and taken through teleportation to their first task. A breeze passed through Rosie's hair, and again, they were starting outdoors. Removing her blindfold, Rosie viewed her surroundings and noted they weren't in town or at the ropes course. The team was on a flat roof of one of the buildings that actually protruded out of the mountain rather than be hidden within it. Rosie scanned their surroundings, but the Surgent team was nowhere in sight.

"Okay, we have to climb down somehow," June yelled at everyone.

The team searched for an entry point that would lead them indoors, but there was no way to access the inside of the building.

"We'll have to jump," Rosie called out over the blistering wind to the group as she stood on the side of the building, looking at a giant X on the ground below.

"Are you crazy? We have to be ten stories up, Rosie," Madeline, the wildcat shifter, said.

"Yeah, there has to be another way," Penelope added.

"I don't think so. The X is there for a reason; it's a landing zone. Reese, can you shift and check it out?"

"Definitely." In a flash, Reese's clothes fell, and a bright red cardinal flew from a sleeve. He fluttered by Rosie, who gave him further instructions.

"Okay, Reese, I want you to freefall down. Aim for the X, and, if you are too close to the ground for your comfort, zoom upward. Got it?"

He chirped and did as Rosie said.

The team watched him fly over the edge and zoom down.

"I hope you're right about this, Rosie," June muttered to her, worried about the safety of her team, but Rosie knew he would be safe.

And what she had suspected was right; Reese had landed on something invisible a few feet above the ground. He chirped and flew up. After he had shifted back and gotten dressed, he told the team what he'd found. "Some sort of soft barrier is above the ground. It is safe to jump."

"Alright, well, who wants to go first?" June asked.

I have to, Rosie thought. It was her who told everyone to jump, so she had to be the one to show she would be safe on the bottom. "I will," she announced as she climbed onto the building's edge. Watching their shocked faces, Rosie fell backward. Her stomach leapt into her throat, and relief rushed over her when she landed on the soft, pillowy, invisible surface. Cheers came from above, and Rosie moved out of the way for the rest of the team to freefall.

Justin, who had to be persuaded and cheered on, was the last to jump, and when he joined the rest of the team, they moved into the forest, and Rosie spotted a card on the first tree they passed.

"Hey, over here!" Rosie yelled, and in a flash, her captain snatched the note and read it.

"*Plant the flag and find your own. Deliver it to those untold.*"

"Rosie, Justin, any ideas on this?" Pine asked.

"Yeah," Rosie said.

"We have to play capture the flag. We need to find a good place for the Surgent flag and find ours," Justin added.

"Exactly."

"And what about the last part?" Garrett turned to ask them.

"I think that is the clue on who we are supposed to give the flag to. The muscle arm is Professor Manger, and the glasses is Doctor Witam."

"Alright, Francis," June said, taking charge again. "Use your speed and strength to find the absolute best hiding spot for this, somewhere it would be difficult for the Surgent team to find and reach. And stick around to protect it. Hold off whoever comes near it so we have more time to find ours."

"But remember, June. The flag still must be visible. Those are the rules of capture the flag. You can't bury it or put it inside a tree. It has to be planted in the ground or hung high," Justin told her.

"Right, okay. Francis, got that?"

"Yeah." In the blink of an eye, the vampire had vanished with the flag.

"Okay, team. Let's split up and find our flag. We know who to deliver it to, so whoever finds it, take it to Manger or Witam. Justin, you will come with me. Pine, go with Madeline, Penelope with Aquamarine, Garrett, go with Rosie. And Reese, I want you to secure a bird's eye view of the area and look for where the Surgent team may have hidden our flag and find the closest person on the team. Okay, let's move fast and win this thing."

The group separated. Rosie ran with Garrett, and they went straight into the thickness of the woods. Professor Shay and some of the other staff had changed the school's environment for the games. Few cacti were seen, and Rosie didn't recognize any landmarks in this setting. Tall trees had sprouted, and the ground was softer, unlike the hard rocks and dirt she was used to hiking every day. It was more like the woods back home, and Rosie easily maneuvered through it, but when she looked up from stepping over a fallen tree, she had lost sight of Garrett.

"Garrett? Where are you?" She didn't think he would leave her behind without protection, but maybe he really wanted to prove himself to June and find the flag himself. "Garrett!" she called again. Still nothing.

As Rosie ran past trees and tried to see farther than ten feet in front of her, using the moonlight that barely lit the way, her fear grew. *Garrett wouldn't have left me unprotected,* she realized.

A loud howl of a wolf pierced the cold air and echoed throughout the trees; he had shifted, but why? She ran faster into the woods and tried to find where the howl came from. She heard a second one then a low whine. Moving rapidly through the trees, she finally found him emerging into a small clearing. Tufts of fur had been pulled out, and knife marks covered him. Rosie sprinted toward him, but she didn't arrive at him before Riley.

Riley, in a Surgent Illumination Uniform, was using his body as a shield, protecting Garrett. Rosie ran faster; she couldn't bear it if either of them got hurt. As she drew closer, she finally saw what the other two were looking at.

The dark figure who lurked through the woods drew closer to Garrett.

She had to reach them before the menace did. As she leapt over roots and pushed through branches, Rosie grew closer to Garrett, hope keeping her going. She entered the clearing, with Garrett in front of her, and Rosie sped up. "Garrett! Riley! Run!"

The two turned to Rosie, but the wolf attacked her, not realizing it was his friend. He jumped at her and took her to the ground. The wind was knocked out of her, and Garrett's shaking wolf form, seeing who he had just attacked, backed off. Whining and nudging her with his nose as an apology, he stood over her to protect her rather than run.

Riley ran to her side and helped her up.

When her breathing returned to normal, Rosie was scared and confused. "Riley, what are you doing here?"

"Helping." Riley turned back to Garrett and stood at his side, and Rosie went on the other side and placed a hand on Garrett's back.

"No, Garrett. Whoever this is wants you. They are going to slice open your throat. Go!"

But he didn't leave; he didn't even acknowledge Rosie. His golden eyes were transfixed on the dark body now entering the open field. The gloved hands moved and generated a wave of air.

"Garrett, move your eyes. Please! You have to be stronger than the spell!" Rosie pushed his head, trying to break the contact, but the big wolf was too heavy to move.

Riley also tried to move him, but still, no change came to the wolf's eyes. With the figure now only a few yards away, Riley positioned himself in front of Garrett, and she followed suit. She wouldn't let whoever was doing this hurt her friends.

The figure stopped and stared at the pair.

Rosie and Riley eyed one another, confused and neither knowing what would happen next, but they prepared themselves for anything. Well, almost anything.

Garrett's head viciously came between the two and pushed Rosie's clear across the field.

She watched from the ground as Garrett clamped onto Riley's shoulder and whipped his body to the other side.

With Riley's body out of the way, the figure again approached Garrett, controlling not only Garrett's gaze but his thoughts and movements.

Rosie looked back to Riley to see him on the ground, blood pooling from him, and she couldn't reach him, the wolf and dominant body blocking the way.

Garrett and the figure moved closer to each other, and

Rosie's eyes fell on the long, serrated knife in its hand.

"No!" she screamed painfully, as she was about to watch her friend die. She stood but wasn't fast enough.

The figure lifted the knife and slashed the object down.

Rosie stared in shock.

As the knife sliced through the air toward Garrett's throat, a gray blur barreled into the field and trampled the hooded figure. The tall, gray, emaciated human beast lay on top of the figure, biting into its flesh, revealing its once covered skin.

It was a wendigo.

Rosie gasped in awe at the decaying evil and at how something so skeletal could have so much force. Finally refocusing on Garrett, who was also still there but shaking, she yelled to him, "Run!"

Garrett didn't hesitate this time. He took off, howling for help.

Rosie turned back to the struggle, but now the figure was speeding away, and the wendigo was on the ground with a card tied to one of its gigantic antlers. Seeing the wendigo was no longer a threat, Rosie ran to Riley. Tears spilled from her faster than a faucet. "Riley? Riley?"

He stared at her, barely conscious.

"Help!" she screamed, praying someone would find them. "Help!"

"Oh my gosh! Rosie!" Justin bounded into the clearing. "What happened?"

"We need help! He has to go to the hospital."

Without further explanation needed, Justin hoisted Riley over his shoulders and ran.

Rosie rushed after him but then remembered the card. She had to ensure she read it before anyone else. She moved to the beast and leaned carefully down to the body. She lifted the card and read the note, memorizing the cipher. When she finished, she leaned down to put the card back, but something was different.

The wendigo's eyes were now open. It rushed up and using her training, Rosie reached her hands through its decayed rib cage and ripped out its heart. The wendigo fell backward.

Rosie knew it was terribly wounded but not dead. She took the opportunity to run and followed the trail of Riley's blood through the woods.

"Professor Manger!" she heard Justin call.

She hopped over a ridge, and he was moving fast toward the large body standing in the woods.

"Took you long enough to find your flag! What's this?"

"He's been attacked!" Rosie yelled as she ran. "He needs medical assistance now!" Rosie was still running to Riley, to hold him and to comfort him, but Professor Manger had already grabbed him from Justin and left for the hospital wing. Rosie collapsed to the ground, sobbing. How could this have happened?

"Hey, he'll be okay. Doctor Gellar will make sure he is. Okay?" Justin leaned over her, hugging her and consoling her. "Rosie, we have to go to Professor Shay. We have to tell her what happened. Can you do that?"

Rosie nodded her hung head.

"Okay, come on. Here you go." Justin helped her stand, and the two walked to the edge of the woods.

At the edge was a crowd patiently standing by, waiting for someone to return as the winner. As soon as Rosie and Justin emerged into the desert scenery, cheers roared from the Valtic students. But, as the two drew closer, the crowd saw Justin holding up Rosie, both covered in blood, and stopped.

Professor Walker and Agent Hurwell ran to them.

"What's going on? Did you fall in the woods?"

Rosie shook her head no, not looking up at the questioning eyes.

"Riley was attacked. By a wendigo. Professor Manger is taking him to the hospital now."

"Attacked by a wendigo?"

"The wendigo didn't attack him. Garrett bit him. The attacker forced him to bite Riley," Rosie spoke, regaining her voice. "The figure was out there. He put Garrett under a spell. The wendigo tackled and injured the attacker and brought Garrett from its trance. I told him to run. When I looked back, the wendigo was on the ground, and the attacker had vanished, and I-I called for help, for Riley, and…" The thought of Riley dead took away her voice. Her hands opened, and the heart of the wendigo slipped out and made a thudding sound as it hit the dirt.

"Okay, Professor Walker, I think it is best if we end the games now. I'll take Ms. Connors to her dorm; she doesn't need to be here any longer. I suggest you make finding the werewolf boy your top priority. If whoever did this is still out there and can control minds and still wants this boy, you need to get him to safety." Agent Hurwell leaned down to the heart and, with a silver blade from her belt, pierced it.

A loud, painful screech sounded in the distance as the wendigo perished.

The noise quieted the crowd from their speculating whispers and stares, and Professor Walker amplified her voice so everyone in the area could hear. "Students, return to your dorms. Move quickly and in pairs. Staff, rejoin at the edge of the endzone."

Rosie's knees trembled as her classmates dispersed around her, except for one.

Eleanor ran up to her. "Rosie, are you okay? What happened? Where's the rest of the team? Where's Garrett?"

Rosie couldn't answer her. She couldn't tell her roommate and closest girlfriend that her boyfriend had attacked her. She couldn't tell her that he was almost killed. She couldn't tell her that he could be killed if he isn't found soon. Rosie focused on the ground and walked with Agent Hurwell at her side, listening to Justin explain to Eleanor what was happening—at least what he thought had happened.

Once she learned of Garrett's attack, Eleanor fell to the ground and sobbed.

Agent Hurwell led Rosie to her dorm. "Rosie, I know this is difficult, but can you tell me anything else that happened tonight?"

Rosie shook her head. She had told the agent everything she wanted her to know, and still, the person behind it hadn't been caught. She asked the same questions after each attack and still got nowhere. Anger grew inside Rosie, but she controlled it and ensured it didn't show.

The two approached the exterior of the dorm, and Agent Hurwell left Rosie to join the other faculty to search for Garrett.

Rosie entered the lobby, but instead of going to her dorm room, she went to her secret space. In there, Rosie screamed as loud as she could. She grabbed the Christion Flare book and threw it across the room and grabbed a wall-hanging plate and smashed on the ground. A shard shot up and cut her hand, causing her to become angrier. "You stupid book!

You have only brought trouble and pain!"

She ran over and grabbed the book with her shaking hands. She opened it and tore out the pages. The pages wouldn't rip, though. Instead, her bloodied palms smeared the paper she grabbed. She tugged harder but still couldn't rip the book into shreds. She finally resisted, breathing hard and staring at what brought her misery. The smeared pages were laughing at her, she thought. She threw it across the room, so it hit the wall and slammed shut on the ground.

Rosie turned away, trying to organize her thoughts, as a creak echoed in the room. She turned to the closed book, but it was no longer shut. Opened and on display, the blood that had covered the pages moved and took shape. She snatched it from the ground and inspected what was occurring. Words formed, diagrams returned, and the book beckoned her. She wiped her eyes, peering at the book spelled out in blood.

She flipped through the pages; everything had reappeared, plus more. Symbols emerged on the pages that weren't there before—symbols she had seen on the cards the attacker had left, the key she needed to break the code. Turning to the last page, which had once been blank, Rosie admired pictures, diagrams, and a spell that emerged. Not even a complicated spell, she noted. It was only two words in Latin. She closed the book and stared at the wall, making a silent vow—a vow to find and punish the figure hurting her friends, for hurting Riley.

Chapter Seventeen

The wind that swept through the boulders sent shivers up and down Rosie's spine. Maneuvering between the rocks, Rosie followed the soft glow. Rain fell, making it more difficult for her to find the light, but she was close because warm started to engulf her. *Will I finally find what is behind the strange rock?* She moved around another boulder and saw the large, crooked rock blocking the light.

Its roughness caught her skin, and gliding around the heavy, tall boulder with wonder and awe, she saw an exposed opening to a cave, and the dim light grew stronger. She moved inward, out of the pelting water. Once inside, the tranquil pitter-patter of rain hitting the ground eased her nerves. She moved farther into the cave, looking for the light, and found a small fire flickering behind a curve. She warmed as she stepped closer but lost her footing on a ledge and fell forward.

The ground was damp and sticky, and when she peered at the fire again from the ground, it illuminated a puddle behind the edge—a bloody puddle. In the middle of it lay a woman's body—the woman in white.

Her body was ridged with fear, her white dress was stained crimson, her eyes set to a glowing blue, and her chest, carved open to show an empty vessel.

Rosie backed away, and a scream she didn't recognize left her throat as she peered at the face on the cold, damp ground. It was her face.

Hunched over *Being*, sweat dripping down her forehead and her heart pounding, Rosie jerked her head around, ensuring she was no longer in the cave. No, she was safe and secure in her secret room. Why would she have such a horrible dream, she thought, still trying to calm her heart. "Was that a precognition? Did *Being* implant visions in my mind? Did I somehow have a vision of my own future? But, if that was my future, this wouldn't happen for a few years. The girl in my dream was older."

Rosie rehashed the terrifying dream again, the room getting a few degrees colder as she did so. The dream was dark and cold, and Rosie didn't know what to do with the information it told her. She eyed *Being*. She did know, however, that she needed to figure out who was committing the attacks and why—especially now that the encounters were escalating and becoming more dangerous and deadly.

Playing through the night's events again, Rosie snatched a small, scribbled piece of paper and sprinted from the room. She needed to see Riley and to find out if they had located Garrett.

The school was strangely quiet as Rosie ran to the hospital wing, devoid of a single soul on the way. An eerie air floated about, and Rosie didn't know what to expect when she saw Riley. Would he be asleep in a hospital bed, or would he be on a cold slab of steel, a sheet covering his dead body? She entered the hospital and immediately saw him. Her eyes stung from the hot water filling them, and her body shook.

He's alive, she thought.

"Ah, Rosie. How are you doing?" Doctor Gellar approached her.

Still, in her bloodied Valtic Illumination uniform, dark circles under her eyes and a paled face, Rosie managed to muster, "I'm fine. Can I see Riley?"

"Of course. There is a chair over there."

She gave him a small nod as she approached her best friend.

"Hey," his cracked, drugged voice said as Rosie sat next to him.

"Riley, how are you feeling?" Rosie grabbed his hand and leaned in closer.

"I feel like I just got bitten by a werewolf. Ha."

"I'm so sorry, Riley. I never wanted you to get hurt. I don't know why these attacks keep happening around me. I'm the reason you're hurt."

"Rosie, stop. That's not true. You're the reason I am alive. Come here." Riley scooted over in the bed, making room for Rosie to lay with him. "Do you know how Garrett is?"

"I haven't heard anything yet. I was going to go check a little later."

"No need to," the soft voice of their wolfy friend said.

"Garrett," Rosie said, sitting upright. With him were Eleanor and Justin.

"Hey, Riley. I didn't bite you too bad, did I?"

"Please, I'm ready for round two," Riley joked, smiling at him. "I'm not going to turn into a werewolf, am I?"

Garrett finally allowed a small smile to cross his face. "You wish, bud." He and the other visitors moved toward the bed. "Only on the full moon would that happen."

"Happy you're doing all right, Riley." Eleanor put a hand

on his while her other intertwined with Garrett's.

"Yeah, do you guys have any idea who or what could be doing this?" Justin asked the group.

Rosie studied her friends. Now was as good of a time as any. She stood and shut the door to Riley's room and turned to their puzzled faces. "I know what's going on, and I need you all to trust me and listen to me before asking any questions. I have been doing a lot of research on all of this for many months."

"Does this have to do with James Kingsley not being born immortal, because, again, Rosie, we've already talked about this," Justin said.

"No," she retorted. She wouldn't allow her doubt to overcome her conclusions again. "I mean, maybe. Maybe James Kingsley was born immortal, and maybe not. Either way, I think someone is trying to make something—a potion or collect specific ingredients for a spell."

"What kind of spell?" Eleanor asked.

"An immortality spell."

"But there isn't such a thing," Justin said.

"How do you know? Because I am pretty sure I found it, and I think someone, either a student or staff member, is trying to become immortal like Kingsley."

"You found the immortality spell? Where? How?"

"Yeah, how do you know this, Rosie?" Garrett asked.

"Remember that book I found? The one I thought Doctor Witam wanted me to find, but maybe it was my own willpower and mind leading me to it. Well, it's an ancient book filled with knowledge and spells and potions that I had never seen before in any other book—not in the library, Valtic study room, or bookstore. Last night, I unlocked the book further."

"What do you mean, *unlocked* it?" Justin asked.

"When I first got hold of the book, it called to me. Answered to me. Then one day, I found the pages were blank, and it was as if the book answered to another. But last night, the pages came back to me, this time with more information than before. A spell revealed itself. An immortality spell, I think."

"Wait, how did you find this book again?" Eleanor asked, disturbed.

"I stole it from Gyle when he attacked me in the bookstore."

"Yeah, and you went searching for him in the dungeons like a lunatic," Garrett added.

"Shh. Listen, Gyle isn't behind these attacks. He also gave me valuable information regarding James Kingsley and why I believe he wasn't born immortal, but that isn't the point right now. The point is I think someone else had seen this book before me, and before Gyle. And they are using what they learned from it to find the ingredients to perform a ritual to become completely immortal." Rosie surveyed her friends' reactions.

Garrett remained silent, angry; Justin was also silent and averted his eyes from Rosie, most likely mad she didn't share this book with him; Eleanor seemed to be in disbelief that she didn't recognize what was going on with her own roommate.

"What're the ingredients?" Riley asked. "What's the ritual?"

This returned everyone's attention to her.

"I'm unsure about the entire ritual part, but I am sure about the ingredients this person needs. They need the most magical parts from each supernatural and natural being."

"But natural beings don't have any magical parts."

"Sure, they do," Justin muttered.

"What?" Garrett asked, looking at him.

Justin's cheeks flushed red, and he kept his gaze down.

"What did you say, Justin?" Garrett repeated.

"During my studies for the Illumination Games, I had read that even normal human beings can possess some magic from what they feel."

"That's exactly right," Rosie said, turning back to the rest of the group. "I originally thought the only people who obtained some sort of magic were supernatural beings, but once I got my hand on this book, everything became clear. This spell needs a lot of power—"

"Ha, clearly," Garrett snorted.

"And, to possess this power you need access to each type of being. What better place to find your victims than at a school that houses every single type of being."

Eleanor squeezed Garrett's arm while looking at him. "How is this person choosing victims. Why go after Garrett? Or anyone else? And what do they want from them? What are the most magical parts?"

Rosie hesitated, unsure if her friends could handle the dark reality of it. "Well, if I'm right—and please correct me if I am wrong, Garrett—but Garrett is a descendant of the oldest werewolf pack in our history, the old-moon pack."

"Wait, really?" Eleanor questioned, looking at him.

"Yeah, and I am technically supposed to marry someone from my own pack, but let's not talk about that now," Garrett rushed and gestured for Rosie to continue.

Eleanor sat stunned and silent.

"The attacker would want Garrett since he possesses some serious werewolf strength and ability."

"What did the figure want again?" Riley asked her.

"The most magical part of a werewolf is the vocal cords that give them the ability to howl and send out a message miles away."

"So, you're saying that if you and Riley weren't there to save me, I would be dead right now?"

"Yes. Your throat would have been slit and the cords removed."

Silence fell over the room for a few seconds before Garrett regained his posture. "Why attack me then and there?"

"Whoever it is must have known we would have been secluded in the woods, searching for the flag. It was their best opportunity of getting you alone to do the deed. As for the others, Sunnie Lightstrom hails from one of the oldest fairy communities, and they stripped her of her wings, and, I believe, Kai was attacked based on the opportunity; it was Thanksgiving break, and, from my understanding, she was the only mermaid on campus. With no one to watch her tail, she was an easy target."

"But her tail wasn't taken. Just her scales."

"Yeah, she is lucky. The book states the mermaid's tail is the strongest."

"No, it isn't," Justin muttered and sighed. "The scales are what control the transformation. They can change color for camouflage; they shimmer for distraction; they are the root of mermaid magic."

Rosie stared at him, amazed. "You're right. They do. How did you learn that?"

"Um, well, I-I talked with a few mermaids at the party after homecoming. They explained their control to me since I was curious after the Illumination Games against Astive."

"I thought their voices were what drew us in?" Garrett

asked. "That's why the gum worked on you and kept you out of their control. You couldn't hear them."

"Yes, it was partially their singing. Remember folklore about sirens? But the shine their tails gave off in the water, the swirls and shimmers, it's hypnotic. You'll also remember how we were more focused on their tails than faces."

"What about Natasha?" Eleanor asked Rosie.

"While shifters know how to control their transformation, they still are on edge and have a desire to shift and be in their animal state. Natasha wanted to change and run, and I suspect whoever the attacker is, understood shifter anatomy and urges, giving them the opportunity of attacking one. They were familiar with where the dorm was located and waited for someone to show up. Natasha happened to be the unlucky victim. They took three of her fingers—half of them normal human and the other half mountain lion. The most magical part is a half-human, half shifter body part."

"Why take three fingers and not only one?" Eleanor asked.

"Extra, just in case? I'm not sure. All I know is they definitely have three of the items they need, assuming they don't have any other parts from earlier attacks or unknown attacks, which means there's more to come."

"Well, there shouldn't be any more at school, right?" Justin asked nervously. "Since they are sure to step up security."

"I wouldn't bet on that, but before I jump to that point, let's talk about suspects. The attacker has to be a student or teacher, and they have to have extensive knowledge of the campus."

"Do you have anyone in mind?" Justin asked.

"I do, and it is a little crazy, but I think Professor Shay and Professor Manger might be behind them."

"What?" Riley asked.

"Are you crazy?" Eleanor added.

"There is no possible way!" Garrett announced.

"Shh, keep it down. Think about it. They have the means and motive to do so. I have overheard conversations they've had on two occasions now that were suspicious, and who knows the school better than the headmistress? She also has the capability of holding off any more Superiority agents that may want to come and investigate with Agent Hurwell."

"Yeah, but Professor Shay was standing on the sideline during the Illumination Games last night."

"She wasn't there when Justin and I walked out of the woods. Agent Hurwell and Professor Walker met me. And Professor Manger was in the woods, waiting for one of us to give him the flag. What if he wasn't waiting at all but hunting instead? Hunting Garrett."

"Whoever attacked me was a witch or wizard," Garrett said. "They had me under a trance, remember? And Professor Manger is a shifter."

"Are you sure he is? I have never seen him shift before. I can't recall a time where his eyes glowed like a shifter's either. Do you even know what he is supposed to shift into? Maybe he's lying and isn't a shifter at all."

Garrett was silent; Rosie had made her point. He could be a wizard in disguise and lying about his true powers.

"Why would they want to become immortal?" Justin asked.

"Power, obviously. Manger always has to be the most prominent and well-known person in the room, and Professor Shay adores James Kingsley and would do anything for him. She emulates him. What a better way of flattery than to become like him?"

"Alright, so what do we do next?" Justin questioned. "We can't just go to the head of the school and tell her everything, especially since she is a suspect."

"We do our own investigation. At each assault, the attacker left a cipher. It may contain a clue to identify them, and I think I discovered the key." Rosie pulled the scribbled, crumpled piece of paper from her pocket and gave it to Riley.

"What's, egilvidarruud?"

"I'm not sure yet." She took back the piece of paper and read it. "A plant or spell or different language? It was part of one of the ciphers the attacker left. I think we should meet up nightly to discuss our findings and take on different people to investigate, follow, and protect. Once we have enough evidence, we take it to Agent Hurwell."

"What about a teacher or someone we can trust? We should tell someone just in case, right?" Justin asked.

Rosie pondered his suggestion. "Yes, I suppose we should. But who?"

"Doctor Witam. We can trust him, and I will tell him during our session, so he has to keep it confidential."

Rosie nodded. "Okay, but I think I should be the one to talk to him."

"What? Why?" Justin stammered.

"Because I know the most about this, and I know how much is too much to reveal. Now, we need a focused plan. Eleanor, concentrate on the human students, the other protectors, and the Valtic team members. Garrett, you talk to any supernatural students, especially those in Haply. It shouldn't be too hard, since everyone wants to hear your story about the attack. Justin, talk to the professors and college students in our classes and the Astive students. I know you are friends with quite a few people, so you should be able to cover that group. I'll work on the ciphers and try to uncover what else lies in the book that could help us. Finally, Riley, talk to the Surgent team members. You are the big man on campus after saving me and surviving a werewolf bite—no offense, Garrett."

"None taken," he said, giving one of his award-winning smirks.

"And apparently, you're now on the Surgent Illumination Team, which we will have to discuss you not telling me later."

"I was trying to tell you, but—"

"I know," Rosie said, grabbing his hand. "But, for the sake of the investigation and only the investigation, talk to any girls who want to know more. When do you think you will be out of here?"

"Later today."

"Perfect." She smiled and faced the rest of the group. "I know I have my suspects, but that is all they are. Someone else could be orchestrating these attacks, and we must be a hundred percent sure who it is before we talk to Hurwell. Everyone knows the plan?"

"Yes," they all replied.

"Okay, let's start and meet up again tonight. I have the perfect spot."

* * *

In the Valtic library, the group stood on the third level behind many shelves and cases, hidden from any other eyes.

"I thought only Valtic members were allowed in our library?" Eleanor whispered to Rosie as she eyed Riley.

319

"Only if alone, but a Valtic member can escort someone from a different team. Most people don't recognize that rule, though, because they want their team spaces to be for only them."

"Okay, well, why are we up here and not in one of the study rooms?"

"Because I don't want anyone to catch wind of what we're talking about." She showed the group where she would hide herself away from the world.

"Wow," Justin said, looking around. "So, this is where you have been coming when none of us can find you?"

"Mm-hm," Rosie said, closing the door.

"Is this where the book is?"

"Yeah." Rosie pulled *Being* from her bag, placed it on the table and rested her arms on it. "What did you guys find out?"

Everyone was quiet, not knowing what to say, staring at the thick novel's sewn pieces of skin and supernatural body parts.

"Well, I talked to June," Garrett started, finally raising his gaze to meet Rosie. "You know, to find out if she felt any strange werewolf transforming signs during the games, but she didn't, so I know the attacker was targeting me. I don't know if that means whoever this figure is will attack me again or go for someone new, but I thought it was interesting."

"I talked to some other spectators who had been standing near me at the games," Eleanor added. "They told me Professor Shay had snuck off for a while. She told Hurwell she was running to the bathroom since she didn't know when the winner would be revealed."

"Before they let me out of the hospital, I saw Professor Shay and Manger talking. I tried to read their lips, but they turned their backs to me. Professor Manger came in a few minutes later to help me to my dorm."

"Interesting," Rosie said and turned to Justin.

"I talked to Doctor Witam."

"What? I was going to!"

"I know, but I asked him for an emergency session and told him our theory. This couldn't wait any longer."

"What did he say?" Rosie crossed her arms and tapped a foot.

"He thought it was creative and would think about it more but doesn't think there is much substance behind it. You're right, Rosie. We have to gather more evidence before we present this to anyone else. Can I see the book? Is that wolf hide?" He reached to touch the cover, but Rosie slowly pulled away the book.

"I think so, and okay," Rosie said, disappointment in her voice. "Well, we should start to identify any other potential victims."

"We would have to protect the entire school, Rosie," Eleanor said in disbelief.

"I know. It is a huge task, and I know we can't watch everyone all the time, but we can try."

"What should we do?" Riley asked, encouraging her to continue.

"A werewolf, vampire, witch, protector, intellect, and human haven't been killed or attacked on or near campus since Garrett was targeted, at least that we know of. Again, maybe the attacker already has what he needs from elsewhere, but we must be safe and assume those are the targets. We can't protect every human in the surrounding towns, but I remembered from a conversation I had with Katherine that a few have been trusted with the secret and come to campus to allow vampires to feed on them. Some of their memories are wiped, but they are still drawn here once a month to feed. Those are the humans we should focus on protecting."

"What does the attacker exactly need from each being?" Eleanor asked.

"Does the book list it out? Can we read it?" Justin added.

Of course, he wants to study the book more, he is an intellect, Rosie thought. "The book does list it, but it is dark, and it changes you. I feel different from reading it, so I don't think it is safe for anyone else to do so."

Justin gave a look of disappointment, but he nodded.

"We know the wings of a fairy, the scales of a mermaid, a half-turned part of a shifter, and the vocal cords of a wolf. From the other beings, they need the fangs of a vampire, the tongue of a witch or wizard, the muscle from a protector, the brain of an intellect, and a human's innocent heart that is in love."

"Why so specific of a human?" Garrett asked.

"Because natural beings can possess magic if they themselves possess powerful emotions. An innocent human is pure of heart, and love fills the heart, so, if the potion calls for a human ingredient, it better be something potent in magic."

"And what about you and Justin?" Riley's concerning voice broke.

This concern was bound to come up. She and Justin were the only intellect students on campus. They were easy targets and had to watch their backs, but the same could be said for Riley and Eleanor. "Justin and Eleanor will always be close to Garrett, and I will be with you. We will never venture off unattended, and we will all try to stay in a public area or place surrounded by students so we can't be caught alone with the attacker. For now, let's keep digging and tracking Professor Shay's and Manger's whereabouts when possible. We have to find out who is doing this, and I have a hunch I will be around them when they attack again."

The group murmured and agreed and conversed with one another, leaving Rosie to contemplate the next attack and if it would be her under the attacker's knife as she had been before.

Chapter Eighteen

The chilliness of January and February came and went without new attacks or information to assist with the group's investigation. The friends met every night in their secret study room, but after a few weeks of no updates, their gatherings turned into homework and study parties rather than crime report status meetings. Hoping the last attack was the one that had really scared the attacker or attackers, Rosie let her reigns loose a little, even going for a run one early morning. Not wanting to be caught in a deadly situation though, she ensured to carry a small knife, just in case.

Inhaling fresh air and her feet hitting the path without having to worry if someone was right in front of her, she glided through the mountainside at the pace she wanted. The air warmed, and her run took her to the waterfall she and Riley would visit to break away from the craziness of schoolwork and Illumination practice. Alone but not scared, Rosie felt the solitude she craved.

She grew closer to the cliff overlooking the small lake, but the screaming that came from the water made her throw her body to the ground. Moving low and on her stomach, inching closer to the edge, she peered down. In the water beneath the waterfall, was Professor Shay and Manger, swimming together and laughing. Rosie tried to hear what they were discussing, but the roar of the falling water disguised all conversation other than squeals of laughter. Rosie had to hear what they were talking about. Carefully moving around the cliff, she found the staircase that would lead to under the waterfall and stood behind the two suspects, the rapids hiding her.

"Charlene, I don't know about the dance," Rosie heard her hefty teacher say.

"It will be the perfect opportunity, Jon. Come on. Premier Kingsley will think it is an honorable dedication to him."

"Okay, but we should also consider the Illumination Games the night before too. The whole school will be there as well."

"Fine. I will think about it, but, for now, let's enjoy ourselves a bit more." Through the streaming water, Professor Shay wrapped herself around her colleague.

Oh my gosh, Rosie thought, they are working together because they *are* together. Rosie slipped up the staircase and sprinted to campus. She had to tell the group. The dance and games were only a month away, and, if they were going to catch the attackers in action, they would have to develop a plan.

* * *

"Ew, so you actually witnessed Shay and Manger making out?" Eleanor said shuttering. "Your poor eyes."

Ignoring the comment, Rosie continued, "Don't you see? They are planning something big one of those nights."

"I agree, but how can we stop it?" Riley asked.

"We can join the dance committee," Justin suggested. "They control the dance location, theme, everything. If we join, we can control what happens."

"That's great, Justin," Garrett said, "but what if they do something during the games the night before instead?"

"You, Justin, and I will be in the games, while Riley and Eleanor are watching," Rosie said. "They can keep an eye on them on the sideline."

"But what if they are in the games, like last time?" Garrett said.

"We will have to ignore the games and find and follow them if that happens."

The group nodded in agreement.

"Okay, yeah," Riley said. "So, when does the dance committee meet?"

* * *

The dance committee met twice a week for the entirety of March. With the group comprising most of the committee, they could control every detail of the dance.

With her homework, practice for the upcoming games, and planning the dance that would catch the attackers, Rosie was exhausted.

"You look tired, Rosie. Is everything all right?"

Her Friday sessions with Doctor Witam went smoothly after they got over the awkward hump of him mentioning her investigation that Justin had spilled to him. She explained she was just trying to help, but she would stop investigating and leave it to the professionals, like Agent Hurwell. A lie, but she felt it was necessary after hearing his response from

Justin.

"Yes, I'm okay. I have a lot on my plate."

"Well, now that it is April, we should plan a separate meeting to review how your first year with us went. I can give you feedback about how you did as a student, and you can give us feedback on the school."

"Wow, that seems like a lot of feedback."

"Yes, well, we like to improve our school, as you should accept feedback to improve yourself."

"I guess that's understandable. But first, Doctor Witam, can I talk to you about something that has been bugging me for a while now?"

"Sure, go ahead."

"Okay, so I didn't talk to you about this earlier, because I was embarrassed and confused, but why did you tell me to read those specific books? The book list you gave me near the beginning of the year, the ones about supernatural beings."

"I simply thought you wanted to know more about the lineage of each creature and understand the genetics so you could gain a better understanding and more insight into James Kingsley's genetics."

"Okay, so you weren't trying to tell me anything else?"

"What do you think I was trying to tell you, Rosie?" He regarded her in wonderment and curiosity.

"I thought you were giving me some secret code." Rosie laughed. Just saying it out loud to Doctor Witam seemed ridiculous.

"That would be extraordinary if you found such a code." He paused to assess her reaction. "I would have hoped you'd have told me if you did so. Anyway, like I said when I first gave you those books, they helped me understand the different beings and how James Kingsley's immortality genes could be related to different genetic codes in each species."

"Well, in some way, it did help, so thank you."

"You should really be thanking Professor Walker. She's the one who recommended the books to me in the first place."

"Professor Walker did?" Rosie recounted Professor Walker's behavior throughout the entire school year. She remembered the first day of classes and the cipher she had given Rosie and Justin, and she thought about how the professor, in some way, had been around each attack when they happened.

"Yes, now it looks like our time is up. Good luck tonight. I will be cheering you on."

Rosie left the office, confused more now than ever. Was it Professor Walker who knew something about Christion Flare? Had she seen *Being* before? She continued her thoughts as she walked to her next class, Cryptology. *I need to talk to Professor Walker.*

"Rosie!" a voice called from behind her.

"Hey, what's going on, June?"

"I got all the Valtic Illumination Team members out of their classes for the rest of the day. We need to work on these clues, and since they called our last matchup against Surgent a tie, we have to win tonight. Come on."

June led Rosie to the Valtic library where the rest of the team was waiting for them. "Okay, does anyone have any ideas on the clues?"

Penelope spoke up, but Rosie couldn't see her behind the giant clay pot sitting on the table. "The pot could mean we are replanting something."

"Okay, good. What about this flower? Does anyone know

what kind of flower this is?"

"I believe it is a Cirsium Arvense," Pine said.

"Speak English," Garrett said.

"I can't remember what it means exactly."

"I think it translates to Canada thistle," Justin said.

"Okay, so maybe we will be transported to find this flower?" June reasoned.

"Or whoever concocted these games planted it in the desert for us to find and bring back?" Garrett said, eyeing Rosie.

"Rosie, any thoughts? You normally have some by now," June said, the entire team turning to her.

"What was the last clue?" she asked.

"Here." June tossed a mattock at her.

Her arms fell as she caught it. "I think you all are on the right track. I bet we have to find the flower in the picture and use the mattock to dig it out and replant it in the pot."

"But where do we bring the pot afterward?"

"There are similar pots in the library. Maybe we have to bring it there. Yes, I'm sure of it," Rosie said. "I remember Ms. Pamfet talking to me about expanding the green room and adding more flowers to the collection. Pine, what is the Canada thistle used for?"

"The weed actually has a detrimental effect. It clears out other plants and creeps its roots down deep, stealing whatever nutrients it can find. It may be possible that we are free labor for the school to remove the pesky weeds to allow other things to grow. Is there a reason Ms. Pamfet would want these weeds in the library?"

"It could control some of the other wild plants that grow and eat the books," Rosie said.

"Okay," June announced. "Let's be prepared to be transported anywhere and have a plan for getting to the library. Our best bet will be the greenhouse entrance. Rosie, you know the library better than anyone. You will know the spot where the pot will be placed."

"How will I know?"

"You worked there. If something is out of place or gone, you will know."

Rosie nodded, and, as she did so, Doctor Witam entered the room. "Alright, everyone. Blindfolds on."

"But the games don't start for another two hours," June said, looking at him in shock.

"They do this time. Professor Shay wanted to throw you a curveball. You should know anything can happen in the games better than anyone, June. Alright, up we go."

Rosie's heart thumped against her chest cavity. She grabbed Justin's and Garrett's shoulders. She was shaking, and whatever would happen couldn't be good. Suddenly, she was on an uneven, rocky terrain and removed her blindfold with one swift movement. Riley and Eleanor didn't know they had left or that the games had even started, and, as she looked around, she grew even more uneasy, seeing they were still in their normal, rocky habitat and hadn't been transported somewhere far from the attacker.

"Everyone!" June announced, calling for the team to gather. "Let's split into pairs again and look for this flower. Once you have found it, call for us to come and help you dig it up so we can replant it. Same pairs as last time but, Reese, you scout and, Francis, you will come with me and Justin. And, Rosie, don't let your partner wander off again to be attacked, huh?"

The group separated, and Rosie kept her eyes on Garrett and their surroundings. She wasn't looking for the flower but rather looking for an attacker.

"Do you think Professor Shay or Manger will show up?" Garrett asked, helping her over a boulder blocking their path.

"I'm not sure, but they said it would either be tonight or tomorrow." An hour had passed with no luck finding anything. That was until a loud scream echoed through the mountain—Justin's scream.

"Garrett! It's Justin!" The two ran toward the echoing yelps and found Justin running toward them, followed by June and Francis.

"Run!" Justin yelled at the two.

"Run? What do you mean, run? We have to catch the attacker!" Rosie called at him.

"Not an attacker but—"

Rosie couldn't hear what Justin said next as short and stout, bearded men covered in dirt with pink flowers sprouting off their heads ran at the group. "Dwarfs?" she questioned but noted the weapons they were running with—axes, swords, and mattocks. She turned to run, catching up with Justin. "So, when did you realize those weren't Cirsium Arvense but Cirsium Acaule?" She stifled a laugh as she ran.

"What are they?" Garrett yelled on her other side.

"The flowers aren't Canada thistle. They're dwarf thistle!"

"Dwarfs? I thought they lived in the mountains. Mining."

"Not these ones! These ones protect land rich in minerals."

"How do we stop them?"

"We have to replant them. We have to grab one, fill the pot with the same rich soil that you found them in and take him with us."

"How do you expect us to do that? A whole hoard is chasing us!"

"We have to lead them to their holes and trap them under the soil while we take one. Come on, we have to loop back around!"

The rest of the team was now running behind Rosie, with June giving her directions to where they had found the plants. Francis carried the heavy pot, and Garrett wielded the mattock, knocking back any dwarfs who got too close to the group.

"It's directly below that ridge!" June pointed to the top of the hill.

"Okay, let's move up there," Rosie directed.

"And wait for our deaths?" Penelope questioned.

"As soon as they are close enough, we will move and have them run over the edge, back into their holes. But, Garrett, grab the last one before he runs over. Francis set down the pot, and everyone start filling it with the soil and dirt. We need it to plant. Go! They are getting closer!"

With the team moving and rushing, getting covered in dirt and mud, they filled the pot substantially.

"Okay, here they come!"

The dirty dwarfs shouted and swung their blades, ready to strike anyone who disturbed their land.

"When I command, jump out of the way and let them fall. Okay, wait. Wait. Wait. *Now!*"

Everyone on the team moved and watched the small men dive into the ground and snuggle into it.

"A little help, please!" Garrett asked, wrestling a small dwarf and trying to lift its squirming body into the pot.

The team rushed over and, finally, succeeded getting the dwarf to settle. Rosie thought it was curious, seeing this rugged man nuzzling into the dirt. The dwarf's beard disappeared, and the only thing above ground were the pink flowers poking from the top of the pot.

Laughter burst from the group. Dirt and grime covering them, they traipsed to campus, the red cardinal guiding the way.

"Okay, Rosie, where does the pot go?" June asked as they entered the greenhouse part of the library.

She scanned the room and found an empty area where a pot of Anthyllis Vulneraria had previously been. "There," she said, pointing to it.

As Francis put the pot in its place, the team waited.

Rosie thought they would've been teleported, but nothing happened.

"Are you sure that is the right spot, Rosie?" Justin asked.

Rosie noted the room, seeing no other openings or spots. "Yeah, I'm sure. Come on, let's go to the dining room. Maybe everyone's there."

The team walked through the dark stone hallway. Rosie was unsettled, her stomach knotting and nausea turning her green. They entered the dining hall, and, sure enough, the entire school was gathered there.

Quiet tears streaked a few faces.

Rosie found Riley and Eleanor and started to rush toward them, but Professor Walker got to the group first. "I need all of you to please go into the Valtic library and wait for me there."

"What's going on, Professor Walker?" June asked, stepping forward.

"Not now, June. Just go."

The team walked across the room, most faces staring at Rosie.

The Valtic library door closed to reveal Agent Hurwell standing at a table. "I am sure you are all curious what's going on. During the Illumination Games, when all of you were off doing your tasks, there was another attack. Now, I have to know if any of you saw anything that could help in finding out who did this."

"How could we help?" Garrett said. "We weren't on campus during the attack."

"The attack didn't happen on campus. Like the last one, it happened during the games. A girl on the Haply team was the victim. Now I need to know, did anyone see anything?" Hurwell's gaze landed on Rosie.

"Agent Hurwell, I promise you, no one on my team saw anything. We didn't even cross paths with the Haply team. They must have been in a different area."

"There was only one place where the dwarf thistle was growing. According to Professor Walker, she took the Haply team to their designated starting point and returned to the school. If you finished the task and never ran into them, that means the attack took place early on, before they could find the meadow. You may join the others now."

The team re-entered the dining hall, and after taking their seats, Professor Shay stood and addressed the group. "Students, I know as a campus, and as a family, these horrendous attacks have shaken us, but I promise we will find this fiend and try them to the highest standard of the law. I know what has happened to Ms. Ancer is truly horrific, and Doctor Gellar is doing everything in his power to heal her and make her better." Rosie turned to Riley.

He mouthed, *Witch*; the girl's tongue had been removed.

"We've contacted your parents to make them aware of the

situation. That being said, you will remain at school, since it is still the safest place for you."

Murmurs spread across the room.

"What?" Rosie said aloud, heads turning to her.

"We will be bringing in more security and more help from the Superiority. They will chaperone the dance tomorrow night, and we will enforce a strict curfew. The dance will end at ten o'clock. No student is to wander off the grounds, no afterparties are to be thrown, and no one is to go anywhere alone."

"Why are we still having the dance?" a student yelled, others shouting in agreement.

Professor Shay tapped her stone and increased her volume, silencing the room. "Because we are a strong institution, and we will not be bullied by some crazed person hiding behind a robe and attacking children. We will stop this person, and we will come out as a stronger institution by doing so."

"That, and she has the opportunity to attack more people," Garrett whispered to Rosie.

"Alright, students, off to bed, and I look forward to seeing everyone tomorrow." Professor Shay walked off, and the students surrounding Rosie stood.

"What are we going to do?" Rosie asked Riley, who had walked up to her.

"For now, we will meet at the dorm and continue making plans." She smiled at him.

Tomorrow would be the night they would take down Professor Shay and Manger, and the school would once again be a place of freedom and assurance.

* * *

The next day was long and tiresome, even more so than fighting off the tribe of ground dwarfs. Rosie and her friends set up the dance and ensured they had their positions known and places ready for when it started.

Rosie and Eleanor went to their dorm to get ready for a night to remember. Their plan to infiltrate the dance committee and make all the necessary arrangements to catch the attackers had worked. The dance was taking place inside the dining hall rather than in the field where the attacker could easily target students. With the help of a few witches and wizards, they had made floating platforms that were scattered throughout the room for students to dance on, ensuring one platform was close to the glass ceiling and only available to the group of friends who had given themselves the duty to watch over everyone. Finally, they planned out where each of them would be stationed, so they were readily available to move fast and thwart an attack.

"Do you think we'll catch Professor Shay and Manger tonight, Rosie?" Eleanor asked.

"I don't know, but we'll try our best."

"What if there is another attack?"

"We can't think that. We can only try to stop it and put an end to all this craziness."

"Yeah, I guess you're right. Let's go through the plan again."

"You and Garrett will be positioned on one side of the dining hall next to the Astive and Haply portrait entrances. Justin will be by the Valtic and Surgent entrances—"

"What about Justin's date?"

"She will most likely be there but hopefully will be oblivious to our plan."

"I don't know. She is a vampire in Astive, so she not only

has heightened physical abilities, but her mind is also sharp."

"True, but Justin knows how to multitask. I'm sure he can entertain her while keeping a watchful eye on everyone else. Riley and I will be on the top platform, able to keep a bird's-eye view on everyone below, Shay and Manger included."

* * *

Standing on the platform in a gorgeous white lace gown, Rosie peered at the crowded room of students, all dancing and laughing, having forgotten what had happened the night before.

"Rosie," Riley said, looking at her, forgetting his duties, "you look stunning."

Smiling, she eyed him. "You look rather handsome yourself."

"Yeah? I couldn't get an opinion from Gunner. He took off yesterday. I found a note saying he had to get home for a funeral. Poor guy."

"Better to be there than here, even under the circumstances. Come on, we must keep watch. Shay and Manger want us to be distracted so they can implement their next attack." Rosie refocused on searching the room for the two professors.

They were sitting and watching the students dance from the head table. Every few minutes, one would lean in and whisper something to the other.

"Something has to happen. I know they were planning it," Rosie mumbled to herself, Riley unable to hear her over the blaring music.

Bodies wrapped in long black hoods exited from each team's portrait entrances and entered from the main stairwell toward the dancefloor to dance in sequence.

Some sort of performance, Rosie thought. "Riley! Look!" She pointed to the sea of black.

"What's happening?"

"I don't know, but Shay and Manger are gone. This was the distraction they had planned." She scanned the room for the two, but they had disappeared.

The students had become entranced with the dancing and were joining.

"Rosie, stay here. I'll go down and find them. Lower the platform if you need to." Before Rosie could protest, he had already hopped to a lower platform and jumped from one to another until he was far below her.

Panic and fear overcame her, and the worst thoughts filled her mind. *What if they have already taken someone and are torturing them now? What if we can't reach the victim in time to help? What if someone dies?*

"Rosie, are you okay?" Justin now stood on the platform next to her.

"Justin? How did you get up here?"

"I had a witch help levitate me up."

"Okay, but you should be at your post."

"I know, but after all of those bodies came onto the dance floor, Professor Shay and Manger threw on the same robes and danced through the room. I am pretty sure they left the dining hall and went into the stairwell."

"Did they have anyone with them?"

"I think they followed someone."

"We have to move down there, Justin. Can you help me lower this so we can find them?"

"Sure." Justin took his King's Preparatory stone ring and

held it directly in the center of the platform.

They got closer to the ground, and before they touched down, Rosie grabbed Justin's hand and hopped off. Still holding on to it, she weaved through the crowd to the staircase.

"Which way do you think they went?" Rosie asked, looking up and down the stairs.

"I think down here." Justin descended toward the high school and college classrooms.

They entered the hallway, able to view the contents of every classroom through the clear walls.

"Justin, I don't think they came down here."

"Wait, Rosie. Look!"

She turned to watch, in Doctor Witam's classroom, a dark moving creature emerge from the ominous cave. She moved closer, but the weight of a heavy object on the back of her head knocked her down. And she stayed down, unconscious and with one of the attackers.

Chapter Nineteen

Rosie's head bobbed up and down. Dim light streamed into her barely open eyes, and her head throbbed with every step her attacker made as it shifted her body.

How long was I asleep. Where am I? She opened her eyes farther, evaluating her surroundings. *A cave? How? I was just at school? Ow.* She reached for her head; blood matted her hair. She searched for Justin. Did they take him too? Was he hurt? Then a familiar voice spoke. It was distorted. Different. Evil.

"Hurry. Set her down here," the hoarse voice demanded.

She closed her eyes, pretending to be still passed out. Her attacker's arms gently laid her on the floor. Taking a risk, Rosie opened her eyes to obtain a better idea of where she was.

The two cloaked figures' backs faced her, their identities hidden. One of the attackers glided toward the other.

Maybe I can make a run for it. She rolled over to not make a single sound to alarm her kidnappers and eventual murderers. She pushed herself upright, starting to regain the entirety of her vision, but it was gone again as her grip on the rocky cave ground slipped, and she fell, hitting her chin on the cold stone floor. The sound that came from her mouth as pain filled her jaw let her attackers know she was well awake. She looked at her hands. They were dripping blood, and she found the feet of a lifeless form lying in the dark behind a curved edge. The scene reminded her of her nightmares.

"Justin," she muttered, tears in her eyes.

"It looks like our intellect is awake and with us."

Rosie was still in shock; she couldn't believe Justin was dead, that he was just another victim to the spell and evil force she had worked so hard to uncover.

"Oh, Rosie, don't worry. His life went to something much greater, but please tell me how you are really feeling?"

She turned to the man she had thought she could trust—the man who had originally guided her to mad theories and to hunt for information.

Doctor Witam gawked at her, a nefarious smile spreading across his face. "What? Surprised I'm not grumpy, big Professor Manger? Or silly, pathetic Kingsley-loving Professor Shay? Or maybe human-adoring Professor Walker? No, they don't have the brains or the courage to do what I have done, to accomplish the most incredible task—the task of becoming immortal."

Rosie sat, staring at the lunatic man who she thought was her most trusted advisor and teacher. "The book list you gave me wasn't random or from Professor Walker. You wanted me to find the Christion Flare book."

"Of course, I did. I couldn't step foot in that bookstore without revealing my true intentions. I needed someone else to retrieve the book for me."

"The blank pages," Rosie said to herself.

"Yes, yes, stolen. I've always known James Kingsley wasn't

born immortal since he came out saying he was back in the eighteen hundreds. He had conjured and played with dark magic. I discovered the book of *Being* before he did. I was reading it, but he stole it from me before I could finish—before I could understand and reveal all the secrets hidden within—only discovering a few pieces of secret knowledge."

"James Kingsley stole the book from you?"

"Of course, he did! And he achieved my plan. He discovered the spell, as you had, hidden in the pages before I could reveal them all. I figured out the ingredients, but I didn't know the spell. Kingsley was able to conduct the full immortality ritual. Which, of course, you were more concerned with uncovering rather than becoming immortal yourself. I really wanted you to be on my side, Rosie. Your brain is unlike any other. Thankfully, another came to take your place. A trusted apprentice, I must say so myself." Witam's hand was on the shoulder of his accomplice, who still didn't face Rosie.

"But why not reveal Kingsley? Why let him rule the supernatural world?"

"Because it was genius, and I planned to steal his place, come out that I had the immortality gene as well, but he hid the works of Christion Flare. I remembered bits and pieces from the *Being* book but not everything. I searched for the book and finally realized Kingsley had left the book under another's protection. It was actually brilliant. Kingsley donated hundreds of books to the bookstore owner. It wouldn't have been prudent for the great premier to own such a book. If it was discovered to have been in his possession, the public would have defeated him. After all, you've seen the true history and past of the supernatural world. So, he kept the book where he could continue to read it but not have it be known to others.

Those ciphers, the symbols I remembered, were intended for Kingsley. He would know the key, and he would learn I was rising and that I would be unstoppable, that I would end him and show him the man he stole from." Doctor Witam turned around and clasped at the wall. He hunched over, grabbing his side and moaning due to the uncomfortable state he was in. He turned back to Rosie, revealing his actual face. "My true identity, Ms. Connors. I am not Doctor Witam. I am not human, and I am not a weak person. I am Egil Vidar Ruud, and I will rule!"

Rosie stared at the disgusting figure that stood before her. Gone were the glasses, sweet face, and concerning looks of her mentor. Standing there was the real Witam, the man who referred to himself as Egil. Egilvidarruud, Rosie thought. It wasn't a spell or plant the attacker wrote in the cipher but a person. He had left his real name in the ciphers to be discovered, to be realized by James Kingsley.

Egil Vidar Ruud stood in front of her, a tall, scary thin man with a pale face, hollowed cheeks, red lips, and a wide mouth full of spiked teeth, ready to rip off Rosie's head. His eyes gleamed blue, and his hands found Rosie's throat, his long, yellowed fingernails grazing her puncture scars where Gyle had fed on her before. He stared into her eyes. "Come, my child." He moved back to his accomplice. "Now that I have revealed myself to our guest, it is time for you to do the same… before we use her to complete our work."

The other cloaked figure turned while lifting the cloak's hood.

Rosie once again felt her head grow woozy, her vision double, and her stomach lurch.

The sweet, innocent eyes looking back at her told her this couldn't be true.

"Go on, grab her," Egil said, and the strength of the second attacker overcame her as she was still shocked at who it was.

Justin held her down, his eyes peering into hers.

Rosie glanced at the stone-cold body on the floor. "But I thought you were dead!"

"You mean you didn't realize who our dear friend here was?" Egil sneered. "Well, far be it from me to not allow you to grieve." Egil lifted the body into the light. It was Gyle. His mouth bloodied, fangs missing, and his eyes set open, vacantly staring.

Rosie was sure Gyle had made his escape. Her eyes stung, and she turned back to Justin. "Justin? Why?"

"Why?" Egil yelled. "While you were the more suitable candidate to be my apprentice, Justin understood what you couldn't. He found the brilliant strength of the *Being* book and how it would change the lives of all."

"I want to hear him speak!" Rosie spat, glaring at him.

Justin turned his head from her eyes.

"Justin, tell me how. Tell me why."

"I-I followed you."

"He's been following you, Rosie. He was a good foot soldier for me."

Rosie didn't look at Egil as he spoke such damaging words.

"Ever since you first started acting peculiar, back in October. I guess my curiosity overcame me because I wanted to know what was bugging you."

"Did you see when I got attacked at the bookstore? Did you try to help?"

"I didn't know what happened in the bookstore. I saw you

running, bloody, and spied the book you took. I wanted to know what it was, but I lost you, and I didn't know what you did with it. You got help, and I went searching. I told Egil about it, though, before I called him that name. He told me I had nothing to be ashamed of. I was curious, intrigued." Justin eyed his mentor, who was nodding and encouraging him to continue. "I told him I wanted to, no, *needed* to study the book. He suggested I find it and bring it to him. But I couldn't locate it until you told me your theory on James Kingsley. The first time you brought it up, I told Egil about it, and he knew you had it, so he told me about the book and its marvels and insight."

Rosie interrogated her former teacher. "That's why you never mentioned the subject or your book list or my theories again. You had already found an apprentice, someone who wouldn't fight you or stop you but rather help you." She turned back to Justin. "Justin, he has you brainwashed. The book explains it. Intellects can be manipulated if done by the right person."

"I know, Rosie!" he burst out, anger suddenly overcoming him. "I read the book! The book was answering to me before you called it back!"

"I thought Egil called it?"

"I conjured a spell to help my friend here." Egil placed his sickly palm on Justin's shoulder. "He needed to be enlightened further, and I was happy to help."

"I knew you were hiding the book somewhere in the Valtic library. You were always disappearing in there and randomly turning up. I just didn't know exactly where it was, but that was all Egil needed to know to pull the words from it and put them into a different source."

"Justin, he isn't your friend!"

"No, Rosie, he is! And he can be yours too." Justin loosened his grip from her arms and brought his delicate hands to her face. "You don't have to be the intellect sacrifice. You can join us; you can help us. We can find another to take your place, and you can also become immortal." Cupping her face, he leaned in and kissed her, but with her arms free, she pushed him away.

"Get off me! You're the one who attacked Natasha! You're the one who attacked me!"

"Now, now, Rosie, don't be too tough with this gallant, young man. He needed to prove himself, and prove himself he did." Egil helped Justin to his feet, and they cornered Rosie. "Now, Rosie, please indulge us. I believe you could do great things with your mind. We could rule the world. We would be unstoppable."

"You're crazy. Plus, you haven't finished the potion yet. You still need—"

"Werewolf's vocal cords? Muscle from a protector? The heart of a human in love? Please, we finished securing those. See, Rosie, it's funny. Yes, I am a wizard, but can you guess what I was before that?"

"What do you mean? You can't be anything else, unless—"

"That's right. I was an intellect. Why do you think it was so easy to convince young Gunner into my office after the games last night? Where I could chop off a chunk of his leg and dump him in a cell where no one could find him?"

Rosie gasped, and her eyes welled with tears. Guilt filled her; she couldn't protect him.

With no sympathy in Egil's eyes, he continued, "In the very beginning when I realized my potential and learned about the supernatural world, I taught myself magic and gained the supernatural forces needed to evolve further, and after many years studying, I became something else.

"A wizard," she hissed under her breath.

"As the book of *Being* teaches. This made me capable of winding magic around those who could be controlled, like your friend Garrett. But he escaped. Who could have foreseen a wendigo in the woods that night? Tsk tsk tsk, bad luck, but I continued my quest, knowing I would have to use my ultimate power, the power I have possessed for longer than you could have ever guessed—something that would help me stay in this state and keep my magic but that I don't use or show people since it is primitive and ignorant. But I think I can make an exception here and show you how I trapped and killed a lone werewolf. How I convinced a stupid human, Massie Touble, to relinquish her heart to me and how I overcame your attacker-turned-friend Gyle and gain his fangs."

He glided up to her, his face close to hers, and the tug of his hand pulled her hair so her head would fall back and her neck would be exposed. His glowing blue eyes first turned purple then changed completely to blood red, and his fangs pierce her skin.

Rosie screamed as her blood pulsated out.

Egil released her and stood, staring down at her. "I am not only one supernatural being, but I possess the power of three."

Justin ran to kneel beside Rosie. "Are you okay?" He tied a scarf around the bite, attempting to control the gushing blood.

"Don't come near me," she said to Justin, trying to stand.

"Justin, now is the time. Hold her arms back. We need to

finish the potion."

Rosie knew what would come next unless she kept talking. "You don't know the words that have to be spoken to complete the spell!"

"The words will be revealed as your brain hits the potion, and then I will speak them."

"Tell me where we are? Are we in the cave in the valley of boulders?"

"Yes, we are, as a matter of fact," the deranged figure answered as he prepared a tray in front of him.

"How did we get here unseen?"

"Haven't you ever wondered what the cave in the mountain, the one behind my classroom wall, led to?"

"The caves are a network of tunnels, aren't they?"

"Very good, Rosie. Your brain will be especially potent in this little recipe. I suspect it will make me be the most powerful creature to walk the earth."

He turned to her, his tray in one hand and a scalpel in the other. "My apprentice, make sure you have a strong hold on her."

Her blood ran hot as he approached. She had to think up something fast if she wanted to live.

A flashing wave of bright light behind Egil formed. It was disorienting but began to take form. It was the older version of herself, the one from her dreams. She nodded at her, trying to communicate something, something Rosie could use to escape, then the light entered her.

Egil grew closer, set down the tray and grabbed her chin with one hand. "Rosie, thank you for your offering. It is the best we have gained yet." The cold, sharp knife scraped her forehead.

She closed her eyes, and searing pain shot through her as the knife went deeper. As she muffled a scream, something else grew within her. Unable to control the pain any longer, she screeched, and when she opened her eyes, both Egil and Justin were on the other side of the cave, groaning and disoriented.

"No," Egil moaned. "It isn't possible. She's too young." He advanced toward her, Justin following.

Rosie raised her hands and pushed on the two bodies who came to grab her. She screamed again and saw what had propelled them backward the first time. Streaks of light flew from her palms and sent waves into the men.

Justin hit the cave wall so hard he fell, limp and unconscious.

Rosie studied her palms shocked and, momentarily distracted, didn't see Egil's next move coming.

Using the power he possessed, he knocked her backward, grabbed her throat and held her against the cave wall.

She tried to breathe, but his hand blocked her airway, and the scalpel pressed against her head again. Rosie grabbed his hand, forcing the scalpel to fall.

Angered, he used his strength to pull her off the wall and slam her back into it. He released her neck, and she coughed harshly and gasped for air. She couldn't just stand there, waiting for him to return and kill her. She kicked him in the gut, and, as he tried to pull himself off the ground, she ran to where the potion had been brewing and swiftly knocked it over, spilling all of the contents onto the rocky earth.

"No!" Egil screamed, causing the entire cave to shake.

Rosie knew this could be the end as he sprinted at her with death gleaming in his eyes. With his potion gone, he couldn't use Rosie's brain, but he could still kill her for ruining his plan. Charging her—disheveled, angry, and crazed—he tackled her, and his hand with the scalpel came down on her shoulder.

The scalpel was no longer in his hand but protruding from her skin. With both hands free, he wrapped his hands around her shoulders and jerked her up, his mouth once again next to her pulsing neck. "Gyle did have one thing right; your taste is incredible, and now I know why. You aren't just an intellect; you're like me. You could still join me, Rosie. You could join me, and we could rule the world together."

With disgust in her voice, she whispered back, "I am nothing like you, and I will never stand by you."

"Death it is." His razor-sharp teeth dug deep into her.

She tried to keep her eyes open, but the blood loss and the exhaustion from fighting overwhelmed her. She closed her eyes, and rather than be absorbed by Egil's memories and thoughts, she envisioned the older Rosie from her dreams. The vision took over, and she saw the bloodied body of her older self on the cave floor and a blurred figure above the body—a lot like how Egil was above her. The figure defined itself and became clearer. Before she could decipher the face holding the heart of the lifeless body on the floor, it turned away. Was this someone from her past, or was this her future? She didn't know, but the dead Rosie turned her head to her, life in her eyes again. "Fight, Rosie. You have to fight." The light faded.

Blinking her own eyes open, she saw Egil still on her, drinking her dry. She couldn't let it happen; she couldn't let him continue his killings. With a newfound charging sensation in her and the will to fight back, as the vision told, she pushed her hands to his chest, and he leaned back.

"Rosie, you're still with me? Don't worry, it won't be much longer now." He bent his head back in, but she wouldn't let him.

"No!" she screamed, and a bright light—bigger than any of the previous ones she had conjured—surged out of her.

Egil flew back, his body making a bone-chilling crack as it hit the ceiling and bounced to the ground.

Rosie got ready for him to retaliate, but he stared at her, open-eyed and still. She found Justin, who was also unmoving on the ground. She thought it was over, but, as she turned to rest a moment, snaps and cracks of Egil's bones popping into place echoed throughout the cave. Without further hesitation, she ran from the tunnel and into the field of boulders. Her feet moved, but it was like a dream; she was moving at a sluggish pace, the blood loss slowing her. She tried to scream for help, but nothing left her mouth.

"H-Help ..." No one could hear her unless they were within a few feet of her. "Help!" Still nothing. Clumps of dirt filled her hands as she began to crawl, and once more she called out, hoping someone would hear now, as she was on the mountainside. "Help!" Her voice boomed as Professor Shay did when addressing the entire school.

"Over here! Quick!" someone called as Rosie clawed to the group of figures running toward her. "Rosie! Rosie! You're okay! We're here!" Riley ran and picked her up, Eleanor, Garrett, Professor Shay, Manger, and Walker following.

"J-Justin. W-Witam."

Riley turned to Professor Shay. "She is saying Justin and Witam. They must also be under attack."

"We have to find them," Professor Shay said, but Rosie grabbed her arm before she turned to search. "No. Justin. Witam. Dangerous. They are dangerous."

"What is she saying?" Manger blurted.

"Justin and Doctor Witam. They are the attackers," Rosie said.

Professor Shay went stone cold. "Professor Walker, take Eleanor and Garrett back with you and go call the Superiority and have Agent Hurwell come here. Professor Manger, stay focused. We don't know what could be lurking out here. Rosie, are you sure it was Doctor Witam who attacked you? And Justin? He is only a student. A human student."

"Yes, and his name isn't Doctor Witam." Rosie spoke clearer now. "It's Egil Vidar Ruud. And yes, Justin. Egil brainwashed him."

"Show me where this happened. Can you walk?"

"I think so."

Leading the way to the cave with ample reinforcements and Riley to help her, Rosie could face Egil. The fire in the cave had dimmed, and Professor Shay illuminated it so they could see.

Rosie turned to see Justin moaning on the floor, rubbing his head.

Manger grabbed his arm and looked around.

"Where's Egil, Justin?" Rosie yelled, rushing to him. "Where's Witam?"

"I don't know, I swear. I just woke up from your blast."

"Blast? What's he talking about, Rosie?" Riley asked, but she was running around the cave, searching for Egil.

There was no use; he was gone.

Chapter Twenty

A week had passed, and Egil Vidar Ruud still had not been found, and Justin gave no indication where he may have gone. With the school emptying as the semester ended early due to all the disturbances on campus, Rosie was ready for a break.

"I can't believe Justin could do something like this," Eleanor kept saying, still in shock about how all were completely clueless to his involvement.

"It wasn't him. Egil had strategically brainwashed and manipulated him," Rosie replied and finished her smoothie.

"And it's still weird that you are calling Doctor Witam *Egil.*"

"Rosie, explain to me again how he was brainwashed but was also acting with his own free will," Riley said, still trying to understand the complexities of the supernatural mind.

"Okay, remember how Egil had put Garrett into a trance? How he had complete control over him and could make Garrett do anything he wanted?"

"I sure remember," Garrett grunted.

"Well, it is almost impossible to perform that type of magic on an intellect. Our minds can overpower it and realize we aren't acting how we wish, and we actually do have our free will to act as we want. But a powerful mind, more powerful than any other intellect, can manage your thoughts, your wishes, and your desires if they please. That's what Egil did to Justin. He found his weaknesses and what he craved and told him how he could achieve it all. It also didn't help that Justin wanted to please his favorite teacher and confidant. That power imbalance is what really helped Egil gain Justin's trust and allegiance."

"That's insane, though. I mean, I don't think I would ever do such heinous acts," Eleanor said.

"Sure, you would. You already have," Riley said, absorbing everything Rosie had said. "Think back to Protector Training when Manger had us compete and fight against each other. We wanted to fight each other and did it willingly to prove our worth to him, to show him we deserved to be at the school. It definitely isn't on the same scale as what Justin did, but we have been manipulated before and didn't realize it until later."

"Exactly," Rosie said. "Justin most likely didn't even know Egil was controlling him." Rosie had told her friends and teachers almost everything Egil had revealed to her but kept details about James Kingsley to herself, still not knowing the whole truth.

"Hm, well you would think Professor Shay and Manger would have kept a better eye on the staff and students, especially during all the attacks, rather than plan some stupid tribute to Premier Kingsley," Eleanor said, annoyed.

"Yeah, they definitely need to reevaluate their priorities," Garrett said with a laugh. "I mean, who plans a dance performance when students are being offed all around them?"

"Someone obsessed with pleasing James Kingsley." Rosie nodded at Professor Shay and Manger, who had entered the dining hall with the famous founder. She kept an eye on the group as they shook hands and parted.

James Kingsley turned and walked straight to the group of students. "Hello, everyone. I was wondering if I could steal Rose for a minute?"

Rosie stood, concerned and confused, but ready to talk to the man and ask him questions she had been curious about all year. She followed the founder of the school, government, town, and anything remotely organized involving the supernatural community.

Kingsley led her from the dining room and into the lobby.

Standing under his giant portrait, Rosie felt herself lift and enter the painting. Now in his office, the place she had been once before to hide, Rosie glanced around. It hadn't changed much.

"Rose, please have a seat. I wanted to talk to you further about the attacks and understand how you came to the conclusion about Egil Vidar Ruud and Justin Fent."

"I didn't conclude anything. I happened to find out it was them when they attacked me in the school."

"Right, but from my conversations with Justin—"

"You've spoken to Justin?"

"Of course, I have. I need to understand the damage that has been done to his brain so he can receive the proper help needed."

"What help? What did you tell his parents?"

"I explained that he would benefit further from staying in town so we can help him with his involuntary involvement in some attacks that happened around the school and that we can make sure he returns to the happy son they know and love."

"And they agreed to let you take care of him?"

"Of course. They understand the best chance Justin has of getting better is to remain here and be, as one would say, deprogrammed."

Shocked someone would allow this to happen to their child, Rosie grimaced, but she remembered her own mother would do this to her. Maybe she didn't know Justin or what his life was like at home after all.

"Rose, I would like you to tell me more about your findings and what exactly you remember about the spell Egil was trying to perform. And how you could stop him from killing you."

His bluntness caught her off guard. She wanted to be the one who had control of the conversation, to let him know she suspected he was hiding something. "Justin didn't tell you anything?"

"Some but not enough."

"Well, Egil was performing a ritual. He was trying to perform some spell you had performed in the eighteen hundreds from a book you stole from him, a spell that would allow him to be completely immortal. Of course, this is what he had told me. That can't be true, though, since your immortality comes from your genetics, right?" Rosie studied his facial expressions and movements for any reaction to her statement that he was lying about who he was and the powers he possessed.

But he just stared at her and smiled. "Egil wouldn't be the first individual to try to disprove my lineage and superior genetics. I do believe you are right, though. Egil was attempting this dark ritual with the hopes of manipulating his DNA to match my own. Do you know where the book Egil used for this dark magic ritual is? I would like to have it so it can be destroyed in the proper manner and so no one else can try to replicate his awful doings."

Rosie stared at Kingsley, still suspicious of him and wary of telling him where the book was. Why would Egil lie to her and tell her James Kingsley stole the book if he was going to kill her? But he was the premier. Maybe she had him all wrong from the beginning. Then Rosie listened to the cool soothing voice of the book whispering to her. *"Rosie."*

"I have no idea where the book could be."

A smile spread over his face after looking at her with curiosity. "Oh well. We will have to hope Egil doesn't try any of this again and that he is in a weakened state from your battle. Speaking of which, how did you manage to escape and fight off a very old and very powerful vampire, witch, intellect amalgam?"

"Amalgam?"

"Yes. It's what we refer to as someone who possesses multiple supernatural powers or is a hybrid of supernatural creatures."

Again, she was hesitant to tell him the truth, but Professor Shay and Walker already knew, so she suspected he was aware of her newfound ability as well and was attempting to give her an opportunity to confide in him. "Well, I had a burst of energy and forced him away. I believe I have witchlike powers, but I am still unsure if it was me or if it was …" She didn't want to tell him about her vision, but she had already started to speak about it.

"Was what, Rosie?"

She sighed. "There was something, someone, a spirit. She kind of looked like me, and she told me to fight. I don't know if it was my inner strength telling me to not die or if it was something else."

"Very interesting. Well, Rosie, thank you for sharing these remarks with me. I won't be on campus for much longer, but I believe you will be. Professor Walker will talk with you further about it. Actually, I think she is waiting for you in the lobby. And, Rosie, please, if you ever need to talk or have anything else to tell me, don't hesitate to let yourself in here. Even when I'm not around, I can contact you."

Rosie turned to leave but not before taking a large gulp and realizing he was aware she had been in his office earlier in the year when she had gone searching for Gyle. Rosie quickly jumped from the portrait hole and found Professor Walker, who was waiting to speak with her.

"Hello, Rosie. Let's go talk."

She followed Professor Walker like she had when she first arrived at the school—following the clicking of her heels and the graceful sway of her walk. Descending the staircase and navigating to the edge of the lake, Rosie didn't know what to expect from their conversation.

"Rosie, can you try to perform what you did to Egil in the cave? Can you recreate that burst of energy?"

"I can try." Rosie stood concentrating and raised the palm of her hand, but nothing happened. She closed her eyes and willed herself to try harder, to focus on the energy inside and create something. Heat grew in her hand, and she opened her eyes; sitting in her palm was a small flame. It flickered and shone brightly. Rosie stared at the flame, forgetting Professor Walker was in her presence.

"Rosie?"

Rosie broke her concentration and looked at Professor Walker, causing the flame to extinguish and her hand to return to its normal temperature.

"Rosie, do you realize what you are?"

"A witch?"

"Yes. Do you recognize why that, to most people, seems impossible?"

"No? I thought intellects had the ability to become witches and wizards with practice and study."

"Have you practiced and studied to become a witch, though?"

Rosie was dumbfounded; of course, she hadn't. All she wanted was to earn good grades, read about the supernatural world, and find a place to fit into it. "No. I guess I haven't."

Professor Walker started to walk, and Rosie followed by her side. "Rosie, I believe you were born a witch, but your powers didn't manifest themselves until recently."

"What? But every supernatural creature has powers from an early age. There haven't been any recorded findings of late-bloomers in the supernatural world."

"There are no recordings of it, but that doesn't mean that they don't exist. Tell me, do you remember either one of your parents having some sort of ability? Did they ever do anything strange that seemed impossible?"

"Other than being good at leaving me behind? No, I can't say that they did anything as extraordinary as magic."

"Mm, well, a grandparent or other relative?"

"I've never met anyone else in my family, but..." Should she tell her about her vision? She had told James Kingsley, and she trusted Professor Walker more than him, so she decided to continue. "But I have been having dreams and visions throughout the school year. I always thought the woman in them was an older version of myself. She looked like me but was a few years older. I thought the school was enlightening me with prediction and psychic powers, but I suppose it makes more sense that an ancestor was helping me? Giving me clues?"

Professor Walker smiled at her. "I do believe that's what was happening. Even in death, magic still looms and is passed down from witch to witch and wizard to wizard. This ancestor was trying to reveal your powers."

Rosie stared at her hands and her body. A tingle surge throughout her, like someone was telling her it was true.

"Rosie, I would like you to stay here this summer. I would like to train you and teach you about your powers and have you catch up with the other wizards and witches in your grade. Do you think you could do that?"

"Absolutely. There isn't anywhere I would rather be this summer." But Riley's face popped into her mind.

"Okay, good. You will still have to move out of your dorm, however. You will be moved to the witches and wizards' dorm for the remainder of your years here. It's too dangerous to have your untapped magical gifts around humans and those who don't know how to defend themselves from your magic. You understand?"

She nodded. She was disappointed, of course. Eleanor was an amazing roommate, and she was living in the same building as Riley, but she wanted to tame this power and learn how to conduct magic.

"Okay, good. We will start first thing Monday after everyone has left campus. I look forward to training you." Professor Walker began to leave.

"Wait, Professor Walker."

"Yes?"

"Why did you give us that cipher at the beginning of the year?"

"It was the cipher left at the first attack. Mrs. Massie Touble. I didn't know what it said or meant. I was trying to think outside the box on how to solve it, give it to two intellects to solve. I should have never burdened you with that. I'm sorry." Guilt spread across Professor Walker's face as she turned and walked away.

Rosie wondered if she should call out and tell her what the message had said, but it seemed pointless now. Instead, she stayed outside, enjoying the scenery, the fresh warm air, and the noises the birds and wildlife made in the distance.

"Hey, care for a walk?" Riley said, walking up to her side and wrapping his hand around hers.

They sauntered along the bank of the lake, and Rosie slipped off her shoes and waded to the edge of the water.

"Still beautiful, isn't it?"

"Yeah. It is," Rosie said, staring at the clear blue sky.

"But it will be nice this summer. We can relax and spend time with each other. We can go to the country club and swim at my house, and we can—"

"Riley, I'm staying."

"What? What do you mean, you're staying? For the entire summer?"

"Yeah. Professor Walker wants to teach me, to help me gain control of whatever power I have surging inside."

"Oh." Riley wore an expression of clear disappointment, but his head jerked up with excitement again. "I'll stay too. I can help you, and you clearly need a full-time protector around, so I will call my parents and let them know—"

Rosie pulled his face to hers and kissed him. She pulled

back, looking into his eyes. "No. I have to do this alone."

"Okay."

Rosie loved Riley. She loved that he understood she had to do this training on her own, that she needed time to find herself, that she needed time to learn her history, her powers, and whatever else she could about her guardian angel ancestor.

"I think Eleanor and Garrett want to say goodbye before they leave," Riley said, staring into her eyes.

"Okay, but let's just sit for a while. I want to remember this moment, here with you."

The two best friends sat on the bank and watched the sun glisten on the water, and Rosie was happy, warm, and secure, knowing she wouldn't want to be anywhere in the entire world other than King's Preparatory.

Epilogue

The dark, thick woods concealed Egil Vidar Ruud's mangled body as he moved from tree to tree with a swiftness unseen by any normal human. His body, damaged; his plan, foiled. All by a little girl. His anger overpowered him, and revenge had to be sought.

Still moving up the side of the tall mountain, Egil searched for the thing he needed, the thing that would eradicate Rose Connors, James Kingsley, and anyone else who would dare stand in his way, the thing that would give him eventual immortality and the strength to not only rule the supernatural world but every being alive.

Searching for the powerful object would come at a price, this Egil knew, but his desire for it overcame any challenge he would have to face to obtain it.

Reaching the peak of the mountain, Egil found the place he had longed for, the place that held the great mystical power of the unknown black magic he practiced—the magic that would give him everything. The cave on the other side of the hill resembled a black hole. Its opening swirled, and Egil grew closer to it.

Standing right before it, admiring the opening, something

happened he wasn't expecting. Rather than entering the cave on his own accord, hundreds of arms jolted out grabbing his hair, arms, legs, and clothing, and pulled him into the dark hole, suffocating his screams of terror as his body was carried across the threshold.

About the Author

For S.A. Alba, writing a novel had always been a dream and making that dream a reality with her first book, King's Preparatory and the Book of Being, has been a thrilling adventure. S.A. Alba looks to inspire and entertain readers far and wide and hopes others will delve into her other writings as they become available. For more information on the author and upcoming books, please visit bysaalba.com.

To learn more about the magical King's Preparatory world, please visit kingspreparatory.com.